ON THE VERGE

By Karen Lenfestey

She cringed thinking of how she would enforce such strict rules. Not that she had any better ideas.

Val folded the drawing and the test scores and tucked them in her purse. "I have to get going."

When Mrs. Bean reached out to shake Val's hand, she had a smudge of red ink on her index finger. "I hope we can work together as a team."

"Sure." Whatever. Chip was with Mrs. Bean seven hours a day. The woman had a degree in elementary education and yet she couldn't get Chip to read. What could Val do?

Out in the quiet hallway, Val faced Nathan. "Thanks for coming. I'll go get Chip from after-care and take him to the bookstore. Maybe if he gets to pick out some books, he'll be more motivated to read."

Nathan squeezed the back of his neck as if he found the meeting as stressful as she had. "Instead of buying books, why not stop by the library?"

As usual, she appreciated Nathan's sound advice.

# # #

Darkness crept through the slats of Chip's blinds that evening as Val sat next to him on his blue sheets. She opened the "Go, Dog. Go!" book and held it between them. "How about I read a sentence and then you read a sentence?"

He fumbled with the top button of his racecar pajamas. "No. You read. I like it when you read."

Her shoulders tightened. "But Mrs. Bean said you need to read. This is important. Please try."

Chip shook his head. "You read. I can't."

So she read to him, pointing to each word as she went, just as the teacher had suggested. She read about dogs on skates, dogs on bikes and dogs driving convertibles. But Chip wasn't following along. He looked at his Matchbox car collection sitting on his shelf. The display shelf Nathan had built just a few weeks after they'd started dating. The man had even donated a few of his own toy cars from when he was a boy.

Chip squinted at the shelf. "I lost my yellow Mustang. Have you seen it?"

Her head ached and she wished it were her bedtime, too. The wedding weekend had been exhausting and today's meeting with Mrs. Bean still weighed on her mind. Tonight after dinner, Nathan had done the dishes while Val helped Chip study the week's spelling words and do two math worksheets. The homework seemed a bit excessive for a seven-year-old. But she didn't want her son to fail, either. "Chip, pay attention."

"Do you need me to come in there?" Nathan called from down the hall, sounding foreboding.

"No." She and Chip answered in unison. She could

use some help, but didn't want this to turn into a battle of wills. She could be too easy on her son, she knew, but Nathan could sometimes be too demanding. "Chip, it will work better if you look at the word while I'm reading."

"Hey, Mom. Where's my red shirt? Tomorrow the first graders are supposed to wear red shirts."

Sighing, she shook her head. "I don't know. Maybe it's in the dirty clothes hamper." Her eyelids lowered and she fought to keep them open.

Chip jumped down off his bed and ran to his closet. "But I have to wear red. Mrs. Bean said we could get extra credit if we wore red."

She slapped the book shut. Enough for tonight. She walked over to his dresser and opened a drawer, searching. No red. Why did they come up with these silly things? All the first graders wear red shirts. What did any of this have to do with reading? Because reading was all that really mattered, apparently.

She peeked into Chip's closet, where he was tearing clothes off the hangers and throwing them on the floor. "Chip, stop making a mess. It doesn't matter if you wear red tomorrow. If you don't start participating in class, Mrs. Bean isn't going to let you go on to second grade." As soon as she said the words, she hated herself. Her child didn't need the added stress of worrying about flunking.

He froze and his mouth formed a tiny "O." "What does that mean? I won't be with my friends?"

"No." She fumbled for the right words. "I'm sure she's just bluffing."

"What does bluffing mean?"

She rolled her tired eyes. "Never mind."

"I need a red shirt. Mrs. Bean said so. She won't pass me if I'm not wearing red."

Chip was so extreme. Val kept searching even though her patience had shriveled up and died. "How about this?" She held up a blue shirt with horizontal red stripes.

"No. Red. All red. I know I have a red shirt. My dad gave it to me."

Val knew which shirt he meant. It was a red T-shirt her ex had won in a bar trivia contest. It was actually too big for Chip, but he wore it every chance he got.

"I don't see it, honey. It must be dirty."

"Wash it then." Boy, he was bossy.

The laundry room was in the basement and she just didn't feel up to it. "No, Chip. I'm not doing laundry tonight. I have work to do." She needed to sketch out some ideas for a new client's living room.

"Pleeeeease, Mom?"

Guilt stabbed between her ribs. How could she say no to her son? Deep down he was such a sweet kid. He was struggling to accept that he had a stepdad. And what kid wouldn't have a hard time with that? "Well, okay."

He let out a cheer.

She patted his head and tucked him in. With a hug and a kiss on the forehead, she remembered when he'd been small enough to fit into her arms. "Who's my favorite little boy in the whole world?"

He grinned, showing off his missing two front teeth. "I am."

"That's right." She turned off the lights and closed the door behind her. Then she sighed. She needed to wash his silly red shirt. It was so important to him.

She walked into the bedroom where Nathan sat on the bed reading *Parenting with Love and Logic*. "I'm worried about Chip. He shows absolutely no interest in reading."

He put down the book and looked at her. "What can I do to help?"

"We could each read him a story. The more exposure to reading, the better." She picked up a laundry basket of clean clothes that hadn't been folded and dumped it onto the bed.

"What are you doing?"

"Chip is supposed to wear a red shirt to school tomorrow. So, I thought I'd do a quick load."

Perhaps Nathan could see the exhaustion in her eyes. "You haven't sat down all evening. Let me do it."

She hesitated. As a single mom, she wasn't used to having anyone else pick up the slack. "Maybe if you twist my arm." She reached out her hand and he pretended to turn it. They both laughed and he let go. Handing him the empty basket, she told him to grab Chip's red shirt out of the hamper in the hall closet. Then she flipped the channel to HGTV before she started folding the wrinkled laundry. She listened as Nathan's footsteps moved down the hall and the closet door squeaked open.

It was so nice to have someone help her. God, motherhood was tiring. She hadn't had a day off in seven years. Even when she'd been married to Chip's dad, she'd felt the weight of the world on her shoulders. Things were different with Nathan. He seemed anxious to ease her burden. And she desperately needed him to.

A few moments later, she heard slow steps descending the stairs. When she felt confident he was half-way down, she flipped the channel to a show about ghost hunters.

A loud thud interrupted the sound of Nathan's steps. Then silence.

She sprang to her feet and rushed to the stairwell. Nathan lay sprawled, face down at the bottom of the stairs. Not moving.

Her palm pressed against her chest. "Oh my God!" The laundry basket had toppled over and red clothes spilled around him, matching the blood gushing from his forehead.

Val stood there like a zombie.

Chip ran out of his room, rubbing his eyes. "What's wrong, Mommy?"

Unable to answer, she stared at Nathan's body. And the yellow toy car near his foot.

CHAPTER TWO

Three Days Earlier

Val took a sip of pop--her fifth one of the day--then studied her unhappy fiancé as he drove them toward the church. "I don't want to argue the day before our wedding, but. . . ." She couldn't cave this time, either.

She placed her drink in the cup holder and toyed with her solitaire engagement ring, watching it sparkle in the rare sunlight. Over the last few weeks, Michigan's winter and spring had been tangoing, with cloudy, blustery days taking the lead most often. Fortunately, the sun had made an appearance for the weekend of her wedding. She took it as a sign.

Nathan ran his hand through his thick brown hair. "What was wrong with the last house we toured?"

"Everything. The purple shag carpet, the paneling in the basement."

"But you're an interior decorator. You could fix all of that."

"You don't understand. That house isn't worth

fixing." She didn't mention the negative energy that nearly suffocated her when she walked through the front door. He wouldn't understand.

He pursed his lips before speaking. "Okay. But the mortgage payment on that place is so low, we could start saving for Chip's college. Doesn't that sound good?"

Her skin tingled. She loved the way he took on her son as if he were blood. She studied Nathan's adorable face, wondering how she'd gotten so lucky. His eyebrows tilted up toward each other like two slopes of a mountain. Beneath them, his eyes alternated between kiwi and olive depending on the light. He had a cleft in his chin and strong, capable hands.

Nathan continued speaking. "Did you see that oak in the backyard? I figured Chip and I could build a tree house in it. Maybe we could even get a dog."

On the way to another sip, she jerked the bottle away from her lips. The brown liquid sloshed against the plastic sides. "I didn't know you wanted a dog."

"Since my dad was in the army, we moved around all the time and my parents never let me have one. But if I were to imagine the perfect childhood, it would include a dog."

So sweet. She kissed him on the cheek. "Maybe when Chip gets a little older and can help take care of it, we could talk about a dog. For now, let's live in my duplex a while longer. That way you can buy into Rod's Garage and we can save money for our dream house."

The car lurched as traffic stopped in front of them. Her head bobbed. Her palm braced against the dashboard.

Red and blue lights flashed from several blocks away. The car in front of them crept forward. Val rolled down her window and tried to see what had happened. No luck. She checked the dashboard clock and her heart beat faster. She looked for an escape route. "You can turn right past that bush."

Nathan craned his neck toward her. "Is that a road or another driveway?"

"I think it's an alley between the houses."

He paused, no doubt considering his options. "But if it's just a long driveway, we'll be stuck for sure."

"Take a chance."

He turned down the narrow gravel road and she crossed her fingers that this would lead them to the next street and not to an old garage behind one of these houses. In this part of town, many of the large homes had been converted into apartments with parking in the back. As their car bumped along the single lane, Val caught sight of houses she'd never seen. She sighed with relief. They'd made it to the next street over.

After checking traffic, Nathan eased his Honda back onto a paved road. Val watched with awe as they passed Tudor-style mansions and other once-majestic homes. "Oh my gosh. Did you just see that house?"

"No." He kept driving.

She turned around trying to catch a glimpse of it. "Back there. It's a house for sale. A beautiful house. Let's stop and take a look."

"Val, we're going to be late for the rehearsal. We can check it out another time."

She shook her head. "No, they're having an open house right now. Kind of strange to have one on a Friday, but can't we please take a look?"

He studied his watch. He slowed down a bit. Finally, he parked his car against the curb.

Val couldn't wait any longer. She sprang from the car and headed toward the amazing house. The sirens from the next block grew louder. The wind chilled the back of her neck while tossing her long, black bangs into her eyes.

Past the OPEN HOUSE sign, she paused near the orange and blue tiled fountain to wait for Nathan. When he caught up to her, she dipped her fingers into the water and splashed him. He laughed and wetted his fingers. Promising revenge, he chased her onto the front step where he flicked water droplets at her cotton dress.

A two-story hacienda accented with wrought iron balconies and an arched entry towered over them. She stood there a moment admiring the craftsmanship of the carved front door until someone pulled it open from inside.

A forty-something woman in a silk blouse and a navy pencil skirt greeted them. Foundation had settled into her wrinkles and her peach lipstick had faded, but she offered them an enthusiastic handshake. "Good to see you. Come in, come in." She handed Val a flier with a photograph of the hacienda on the front.

Val didn't take the time to read the details, except to notice the price was over their maximum budget. Not by as much as she would've expected, though. Maybe they could negotiate if the place needed some work. Lots and lots of work!

Drawn to the terra cotta foyer and the white pillars to her left, she couldn't wait to see the place for herself. She turned toward the grand living room where a few other couples milled around. Inhaling, she realized the air smelled like fresh-baked apple pie. She figured the realtor had lit a scented candle somewhere, though she didn't see it. Even so, the trick worked because she felt welcome.

Sailing toward the fireplace, she touched the marble mantel. Dust caked onto her index finger. She sensed that the home had been built with love, but its current owners didn't appreciate it.

The real estate agent shadowed them. "It has six bedrooms, two and a half baths. Constructed in 1925. It's registered, you know."

Goose bumps popped on Val's arms. A registered landmark. She could live in a home with historical significance.

The agent's tired eyes seemed to come to life. "You appreciate the beauty of old world design, don't you?"

Val nodded, anxious to move through the house yet wanting to linger over the details. The living room must've been twenty-five feet long, lined with floor-to-ceiling arched windows whose frames flaked with old paint. A black piano with a carved music stand and cabriole legs fit in the corner. The matted carpet beneath her feet needed to be replaced.

Arched French doors opened out back onto a covered patio. In spite of the cobwebs netting the rusted lawn chairs' legs, she pictured men in button-down shirts and women in sundresses laughing and sipping wine. If she ever opened her own design studio, she could entertain clients here.

Why hadn't she tried harder to save money, like Nathan had? Sure, she had Chip to take care of and student loans to pay off, but she'd been guilty of buying herself paintings or sculptures whenever she found an artist she admired. That was the problem with decorating for rich people. She was always falling in love with something that she couldn't afford.

The real estate agent recited her well-rehearsed speech. "The architect is A.M. Strauss. Down the hall you'll see a large kitchen, breakfast nook and dining room."

Nathan cleared his throat. "Val, we really must go. People are waiting."

Val sighed with frustration. Why did everything happen at once? She looked at the paper clutched in her hands. Even though they couldn't afford the place, she'd love to see the upstairs. They simply didn't make houses like this anymore. "I'm afraid we don't have time to see the whole place now. Could we come back?"

The woman checked her watch. "The open house ends in half an hour."

Val thought of the rehearsal and the rehearsal dinner afterward. Her parents, who had flown in just for the wedding, would give her hell if she rushed off. "We won't be able to make it back today."

"I might be able to get you in tomorrow afternoon."

Val shook her head. This wasn't meant to be. "We're getting married tomorrow and leaving on our honeymoon right away."

The agent lightly touched Val's arm. "Oh, congratulations! This house would be perfect for newlyweds. It's so romantic with fireplaces in almost every room."

Nathan shifted his weight. "It's quite impressive, but it also needs some work. How much are they asking?"

Val told him and they exchanged disappointed looks. "I know. It's just not within our reach." Licking her lips, she looked toward the scrolled iron railing that led to the second floor.

The agent shook each of their hands. "My name and number are on the flyer if you change your mind. But I must warn you, I've had several interested couples here today. This diamond in the rough won't be on the market for long."

Val winced. It *was* a diamond in the rough. But they had other priorities right now. Swallowing, she thought of her friends and family waiting at the church. "We've got to take off. Thank you." She felt a little guilty, hoping the place didn't sell.

Once outside, they could still hear the sirens blaring.

CHAPTER THREE

Val rushed into the chapel where the sun streamed through mosaic stained glass windows. All of the bridal party appeared present except for Chip. Had he decided to boycott his role as ring bearer? He certainly wasn't thrilled with the idea of a stepfather who would back up Val on discipline issues. He preferred the odds now.

Her friend and co-worker, Joely, walked toward her. "Your parents took Chip and Anna in the choir room for a snack. Our kids were getting a little restless." She leaned down toward Val's ear and lowered her voice. "Everything okay?"

Val hated that Joely interpreted her tardiness as something worse than it was. "We took a little detour is all." She addressed the room. "Sorry we're late. It's my fault." People waved their hands dismissively and mumbled kind platitudes.

The minister clapped his hands like a football coach rallying the team. "Let's get started. Everyone gather around so we can run through this."

She noticed the minister matching up the groomsmen with the bridesmaids by height, just as she had planned. Free-spirited artists with piercings in their noses and up and down their ears would be escorted by an odd combination of men: Nathan's boss in a polo shirt, his brother, who always dressed to impress with a thick, gold chain around his neck and one of his co-workers in a gray T-shirt advertising Rod's Garage.

Joely, who looked a little like Cindy Crawford with the mole above her lip, pulled Val near. "This will be a big adjustment for all of you. If you ever need anything, I'll be here."

"Thanks. I'm sure we'll be fine."

Her friend reached toward Val's hair and brushed the ebony strands out of her eyes. "How are you going to wear your hair tomorrow? Cool, artsy Val or conservative, trying to impress the old folks Val?"

Val felt Joely's fingers creating a part on the opposite side of her head. She knew this revealed a streak of pink usually kept hidden during the day when she interacted with her clients. "I think I'll do my mother a favor and not embarrass her at this wedding."

A frown formed across Joely's face. "I'm worried you're stifling the real you."

In her teens and early twenties, Val had been wild

and spontaneous. She'd jumped off a jagged cliff into a quarry filled with rainwater. She'd hitchhiked across the country to hear a new alternative band, The Electric Butterfly, and gotten a tattoo as a memento. In fact, she'd never even worn a watch or considered getting an associate degree--until she had Chip. Motherhood had forced her to keep track of things, to think about tomorrow, to worry. "Now that I have Nathan, maybe I can relax a little."

Joely hugged Val with one arm. "I just want you to be happy."

She caught sight of Chip entering the chapel and joy surged through her. "I am happy. I'm marrying a man who loves me and my son. Wait 'til I tell you about the house we saw."

# # #

On the table in front of Val, the unity candle flickered. Above that, an earth-toned tapestry of Jesus with his arms open wide offered solace. Two contradictory signs. Val decided she would not worry about such things today. Today was about celebrating.

The minister closed his Bible with a soft thump. "I now pronounce you man and wife."

Nathan lifted Val's veil. He kissed her left cheek, then her right before brushing his warm lips against hers. It was their signature kiss. Today's kiss ended quickly-- probably because public displays of affection embarrassed him. He never gave her more than a hug when her son was in the room. Now everyone they knew watched.

Together the couple turned and faced the packed church. Her cheeks hurt from grinning, but she couldn't stop herself. This was going to be everything her first marriage wasn't. Arm in arm, they walked back down the aisle. Some of her friends spilled from the pews on her side of the church over to his. How fun it was to see everyone she cared about in one room!

They took their places in the hallway to greet guests as they exited. Nathan squeezed her hand. "I have a surprise for you."

The house. Had he bought her the Spanish hacienda? Her chest lightened as if filled with helium. She knew he had some money in savings, but she didn't know how much. Was it enough to buy into the business *and* get a house? Anticipation zipped across her nerve endings.

Before she could respond, a non-stop stream of people hugged her as they went past. Nathan made introductions to the people she didn't know and she returned the favor. Once the line finished, she looked at her husband. Somehow she managed to grin even bigger than she already was. Husband. She hadn't expected the giddiness that bubbled inside of her.

He swung her hand nervously. "Ready?"

She nodded. Off they went, dashing down the church steps, her bouquet of pink and white orchids blocking the tiny bits of birdseed tossed at them. Faces blurred as they made their way to the car. In a split second, Nathan stumbled and started falling head first toward the sidewalk. Her stomach leapt into her throat. She clutched his arm, digging her fingernails into his sleeve.

Her heart thumped like mad. Somehow she'd steadied him. "Are you all right?"

He nodded. "Me and my two left feet. Just wait 'til we're on the dance floor at the reception." They smiled at each other and kept going.

Now at the bottom of the stairs, she searched for Nathan's Honda. But it wasn't there. Instead some kind of dark green, antique automobile waited for them. It had an open top, big round headlights and she guessed it'd been made in the nineteen-twenties or thirties.

Nathan walked her around to the passenger's side and opened the door, which hinged in back instead of the front. She gave him her best quizzical expression and climbed in. The well-worn leather seats gave way beneath her.

He took his place in the driver's seat and put the stick shift in neutral. He reached for the wooden dash-board to turn the key and pull some kind of lever. The car started and the engine grew loud. He adjusted the lever again, calming the motor, then drove away.

She looked around. "No seatbelts? That doesn't seem like you."

"We're not driving far."

That was true. Flanagan's Restaurant, with the large banquet room in the basement, stood just a few blocks away. She propped her arm against the open window and enjoyed the contrast between the sun and wind against her face. "Cute car. Whose is it?"

"I borrowed it from my brother. It's a 1934 MG. I thought it'd make a nice surprise."

She smiled. This was even cooler than a limo.

Nathan raised his voice to be heard over the wind. "His credit cards are maxed out and he asked our widowed mother to help make his last mortgage payment, but he has an antique car collection." He shook his head.

She knew Nathan disapproved of his brother's don't-fret-about-tomorrow attitude, but she also detected a hint of jealousy in Nathan's voice. "Would you like to own a car like this?"

"Sure. Especially this one. It belonged to our grandfather." His expression loosened as if his mind were far away. "My grandfather taught me how to change the oil on this car. Then we'd get cleaned up and he'd take me to town for ice cream."

She could tell that he felt the same fondness for his grandfather as she did for her grandmother. Except instead of ice cream they'd indulged in Dr Pepper. Too bad her grandmother wasn't alive to see her marry the right man. "Wait. Is this the surprise?"

He turned and smiled. "Yep."

Her spirits dropped. A borrowed car was the surprise?

An image of the Spanish hacienda with the fountain splashing out front formed in her mind. She'd tried to forget about it, but when he'd mentioned a surprise, that historic home immediately popped into her head.

She longed to live in that house. Desperately craved it. And when she saw something she really wanted, she ran toward it.

For better or for worse.

CHAPTER FOUR

"Please don't go, Mom," Chip pleaded. Her son's mood had alternated between grumpiness and happiness throughout the reception. When he knew his mom was watching, out came the lower lip and slumped shoulders. When other boys in the room suggested they steal the lace bags of mints at each place setting, he grinned and snuck around like a little spy. Too busy chatting with friends, Val had pretended not to notice.

Still in her ivory gown, she approached her son who had long ago removed his bow tie and jacket. "May I have this dance?" She held out her hand.

He shook his head and sat down. Too short to reach the floor, his legs swung forward and back. The black patent shoes shone under the fluorescent lights.

"Come on. I'll teach you." She looked toward the small clearing where couples danced to "Butterfly Kisses" on the parquet floor. Behind them, sheets of pink tulle cascaded down the walls. She took a step, but her son wouldn't budge.

"I promise I'll be good. I'll eat my vegetables. I'll clean my room. Pleeeease? It's not any fun at Joely's house."

"But you'll have someone to play with." She'd always felt bad that Chip was an only child. At least Joely had a daughter Chip's age.

He crossed his arms. "Anna's a girl. All she wants to do is girlie things."

Val understood. Almost from the start, boys and girls deviated in what they did for fun. Her brother had not once helped decorate Malibu Barbie's beach house with her. If she'd wanted a companion, she'd been forced to play war or cops and robbers or whatever her older brother had wanted. But it was better than being alone. "Well, maybe you can take turns doing what the other one likes."

He wrestled with his fuchsia cummerbund. "Can't I go with you?"

"On my honeymoon?" She laughed a little, buzzed from the champagne. The next moment, guilt tightened around her like a corset. She'd never left her son for an entire week before.

But what would Nathan think? Maybe she could bring it up. Her eyes scanned the crowd to catch a glimpse of the man she'd just married. She spotted him across the room, dancing with his mother.

"What do you say?" Chip asked. "I promise I won't ask for anything ever again." Her son was nothing if not persistent.

"Let me think about it."

"Aww. That means no." Once again, his lower lip thrust forward.

She hated to see him so miserable. But could they even get him a last minute plane ticket? Would the hotel have a bigger room available? "Why don't you get some cake and visit with your grandfather? You don't get to see him very often."

He pouted for a moment longer. Permission to overload on sugar eventually won out. He jumped up and darted toward the tower of cake. "Yippee!"

She hadn't had much time to savor the strawberry cake herself, but she liked how it matched the bridesmaids' dresses and the orchid centerpieces.

Just then her mother approached her. "You look beautiful." She'd developed a hint of a Southern drawl since she and Dad had retired to Georgia a few years back. "It's so nice that you incorporated First Corinthians 13:4 in the ceremony: 'Love is patient. Love is kind.'"

Val smiled and waited.

Her mother smoothed her gray locks. She didn't believe women should color their hair. "I'm surprised you chose to hold the reception here, though. I'd think someone who earns a living making places attractive, would've chosen a location with a view, not the basement of a restaurant."

Val counted silently to three and reminded herself not to take it personally. She and her mom had a way of pushing each other's buttons. The truth was, she and Nathan had decided not to splurge by renting the Harrison Mansion. She'd enjoyed the challenge of decorating this place and was proud of the way it had turned out. "This fit our budget."

Her mom picked a piece of microscopic lint off of Val's shoulder. "Dear, all you had to do was ask. We could've chipped in to make our only daughter's day special."

Val swallowed. "Thanks, Mom. This is fine." She'd never ask for her parents' help. She knew better.

Nathan headed toward Rod who sat at a table twirling a gold coin to entertain his three kids. Nathan recognized it as his boss' good luck charm that he took everywhere. It must work, too, because Rod had it all: a happy family, his own business and if times ever got tough, he could sell the coin for $1,000.

Rod tucked the gold piece into his pocket and rose to offer Nathan a firm handshake. "From bachelor to family man in one day. How are you feeling?"

Rod's son and two daughters took off to go play elsewhere. Nathan glanced around the room to see if Val was within earshot. A minute ago she was squatting in front of Chip, trying to cheer the boy up. Now she was talking to her mother. Far enough away for Nathan to be honest. "Nervous. All through high school I had a crush on Val, but we ran in different circles. She was Homecoming Queen and I was in shop class." Unlike the other popular girls, she'd smile at him when they passed in the hallway. "I never had the nerve to ask her out. Then all of these years later, we bump into each other again. Who would've thought stopping to help a woman broken down on the highway could lead to this?" From across the room, he admired her as she adjusted her veil. His eyes traveled to her son. "I have to admit, I'm afraid I don't know how to be a father."

Rod patted Nathan's back. "No one's ever really prepared for parenthood. You learn as you go along."

"I've been reading all of these how-to books, but they contradict one another."

Rod laughed. "Books? Boy, you sure are taking this stepfather thing seriously."

"Of course I am. I feel sorry for the kid. Since Chip was two, it's just been him and his mom." Nathan's father had been gone a lot, but at least he'd had his grandfather's guidance and attention. "Chip's father doesn't even care enough to pay child support." Nathan had discovered that fact while balancing Val's checkbook--something she never bothered to do.

Across the room, Chip shoved another piece of cake into his mouth, dropping icing onto his shirt. Nathan looked Rod in the eye. "He told me he wants to come on our honeymoon with us."

Rod sighed. "You're between a rock and a hard place. Whatever you do, don't make that woman choose between you and her son."

What could he do? Didn't a man deserve at least one night alone with his wife? Of course he did. But what did Chip deserve? His father to give a shit, that's what. If the boy's father had offered to watch Chip during the honeymoon, the boy would've been overjoyed. But having a kid around didn't fit into the bum's lifestyle. Floating from one dead-end job to another, drinking, smoking pot, and who knows what else wasn't fun with a kid tagging along.

Nathan knew he shouldn't judge. He'd wasted a couple of years inside the bottle, too, but he'd made a conscious decision to pull himself together. Since then, he'd been working for Rod, learning the business, rising from mechanic to service department manager in record time. He'd also been saving every last nickel and dime. "Maybe after Val and I decide where we're going to live, you and I can hammer out the details about becoming business partners."

Rod nodded. "I'd like that."

The photographer approached Nathan and asked if he could get a few more poses. "The bride is hoping for a picture of the new family."

Nathan allowed the photographer to herd the threesome together. He glanced at Chip's chestnut hair and wondered if that was Val's natural color. Somehow brown seemed way too ordinary for Val. She had a spark in her that he admired.

Click after click. Nathan tried to be patient, but clearly Chip had no intention of smiling. And the photographer didn't want to give up.

Nathan heard the cell phone in his coat pocket go off. He pulled it out, but it wasn't ringing. He fished in his pocket again and selected Val's phone. She'd asked him to hold it for her just in case Chip's father changed his mind. He handed the phone to his bride. He grinned at the thought. His bride.

Val held the phone against her ear, pushing her jet black hair out of her eye. She was so beautiful--like a sexy Snow White. She was a fun combination of artist and business woman. Someday she hoped to run her own interior design studio, just as he dreamed of co-owning the auto repair shop.

Val finished the phone conversation with a dark expression. "Chip, that was Mrs. Bean. She said that she wanted to confirm our parent-teacher conference on Monday. Why didn't you tell me she wanted to see me?"

Chip shrugged and looked sheepish. He smiled, too. The damn kid smiled.

CHAPTER FIVE

On the ride home from the reception, Joely lifted the hem of her floral dress and rubbed her swollen knees. She'd taken something for the pain and waited for it to kick in. While Jake drove, she tried to distract herself by chatting about how lovely Val had looked and how orchids were an unusual choice for the bouquet. "Do you think I should've tried harder to tell Val my concerns?"

Jake glanced at their six-year-old daughter, Anna, in the backseat as if this conversation were not child appropriate. "There's no rationalizing with someone when they're in love." He flashed her his killer grin as if to say, "I know because I'm in love myself." He paused. "Besides, Nathan seems like a good guy."

"I think he's nice, but I'm worried Val rushed into this. She's the first person I'd invite if I threw a party and he's the kind who'd rather sit on the couch and watch TV."

"Maybe Val is past the party stage in her life and she wants to settle down."

She thought about Val hoping once she married Nathan, she could relax a little. "You're probably right."

He parked in front of her apartment. His long fingers lingered on the keys in the ignition. "Do you need me to come in? Is your kitchen sink still leaking?"

"No. The landlord fixed it." She laughed. "As if you'd know how to fix anything."

"I may have been born with a silver spoon in my mouth, but I've decided a tool belt is more practical." He stared at the welcome plaque she'd painted with sunflowers and mounted on her front door.

She looked at his striking profile—the perfect triangle of a nose and the tiny U-shaped scar under his right eye, caused by a childhood fishing hook gone astray. Warmth surged through her. They knew each other so well. Yet they'd never managed to make it down the aisle.

They'd almost married in college, but it hadn't worked out. She wasn't proud of it, but seven years ago they'd reconnected and had an affair, which resulted in Anna's birth.

Fighting the urge to ask him to spend the night, she gave him a peck on the cheek. She didn't want Anna to know that they were sleeping together. "Thanks for the ride."

Anna unbuckled herself and stuck her chin over the front seat. "Daddy, you can't leave. I want to show you something."

He turned his dark blond head so he could see his daughter's face. "What is it?"

"Um." She bit her lower lip. "It's a surprise. Just wait here for a minute."

Joely couldn't help but shrug and climb out of Jake's BMW sedan. After Joely unlocked the front door, Anna pushed past her and told her to wait outside. The door closed in Joely's face. She stood there, fiddling with the brown curls resting on her shoulder for a moment before growing tired. She returned to the passenger's seat. After about ten minutes, Anna opened the apartment door and waved her parents inside.

One of Anna's navy sheets with white stars on it served as a tablecloth for the kitchen table. On top were two place settings of Joely's Fiestaware. Instead of using plates and cups all in the same color, Anna had used a rainbow assortment. Joely couldn't help but smile at her daughter's creativity. "What's all this?"

Anna pulled out a chair and gestured for her mom to sit. "Miss Val only dated Nathan eight months and they're already married." She ran around the table and pulled out a chair for Jake. "You two have known each other for *years* and you're not even engaged! Well, I can't wait any more. I want my mommy and daddy married."

Joely and Jake laughed nervously and made eye contact. Lifting Anna's piggy bank which served as a center piece, Joely rattled the coins inside. "And why is your bank on the table?"

Anna put her hands on her hips as if it were obvious. "That's money for your honeymoon." Again, the adults chuckled. Anna picked up a toy ring with a pink stone and handed it to Jake. "I couldn't exactly afford a diamond, but what matters is you have a ring. Now give it to Mommy."

At this, Joely's cheeks flushed with heat. "This is all very sweet, Anna, but you--"

Jake raised his hand in protest. "I think we should hear our daughter out."

Anna ran to the front window and peeked out. "I ordered pizza, but it isn't here yet."

"How did you know how to do that?" Joely asked.

"Papa's Pizza is on speed dial. Anyway, I'm going to stay in my room all night. You won't hear a peep out of me." Offering a grin that showed off a mixture of baby teeth and permanent ones, Anna bowed. "Enjoy!" She skipped down the hall and closed her bedroom door.

Joely poured herself a glass of water from the orange Fiestaware pitcher. After she took a sip, she dared to look at Jake. "Sorry about this."

"She's right, you know." He studied the pink ring,

twirling it between his fingers. "We should be married."

A calming breath. "I don't know why you'd want to chain yourself to me when I'm sure there are plenty of attractive associates at your accounting firm who'd like to date you."

He rolled his eyes. "We've been through this before. There may be other women interested in me, but I'm not interested in them. I don't want to date anymore. I want to live under the same roof as my daughter. I want to come home every night to my wife. I want us to be a normal family."

"Nobody's normal these days." She'd hoped to make him laugh, but it didn't work.

Fear screamed inside her head: He'll get tired of being married to someone who's sick. He'll resent me for not having the energy to cook dinner and clean the house. In the end, he'll leave me for someone else.

She pictured herself confined to a wheelchair, just as her mother had been near the end. Her father had been a devoted caretaker and husband, but he was a rare breed. At her support group, she'd heard about too many boyfriends and husbands that called it quits. "I'm not sure you're up for this."

"I am. I've read books about lupus and I'm ready." He placed the toy ring on the starry tablecloth. "Whenever something happens at work--good or bad--I think 'I can't wait to tell Joely about this.' Whenever it's your weekend with Anna and I have to hang out in my apartment alone, I wonder what you guys are doing. Whenever I see a family walking through the park holding hands, I want to be them." His right hand reached into his pants pocket and pulled out a velvet box.

Her pulse throbbed. She'd seen this box before and she'd barely been strong enough to turn it down then. "Jake. . . ."

He knelt on one knee beside her. Up flipped the gold-trimmed lid. Inside sat a square-cut diamond, flanked on each side with blue gems. Jake was good at remembering things like that--the fact that sapphire was her birthstone. Jake was good at a lot of things. . . .

She gnawed on her lip, trying to deny her destiny. Deep down she'd always felt as if he were The One. He hadn't offered to make an honest woman out of her, though, until a year ago when he lost his entire family in a house fire. Needless to say, that delay left her a bit leery of him.

Now she had Anna to think about. If Jake eventually decided that being with Joely wasn't worth the effort, he'd break their little girl's heart. At least now, both of Anna's parents were on speaking terms, gladly trading visitation weekends and parenting tips as necessary.

Thank God the doorbell interrupted them. Joely rose from her chair to answer it. After she'd paid and tipped the teenager, she placed the pizza box on the table. "Let's eat."

Jake had already returned to his commanding six-foot-two-inches and she hoped he wasn't too embarrassed. He'd proposed to her a few months ago and she'd told him she needed more time to be sure. A man with his charisma probably didn't have much experience with rejection.

Stalling, she opened the cardboard box. Her stomach was still full from the reception. "Mushrooms or pepperoni?" Even though she already knew the answer.

"Real men don't eat fungus." He didn't laugh. Instead of taking his seat, he crossed the room. He picked up a picture of Anna on her bicycle from a stack on the coffee table. "Pretty soon she won't need training wheels any more."

"I know. We practiced on the sidewalk in front of the apartment. Anna scraped her knees a couple of times, but kept getting back up and trying again. She gets her confidence from you."

He turned to face her. "She deserves to live in a house with a long driveway where she can ride her bike. She deserves to have both of her parents there applauding her the first time she can balance a two-wheeler on her own."

Tears stung Joely's eyes. She nodded. "I want that for her."

He came nearer. "Then what's the problem? I love you and you love me. That's the recipe for a happy marriage."

She lifted one shoulder halfheartedly. "I'm afraid that someday you'll wish you had built a life with someone healthier."

"I know I've made some mistakes in the past. I'm older and wiser now. And I choose you."

"But--"

He placed his index finger on her lips. "I choose you. And I will always choose you." His finger moved away and his warm lips slipped against hers.

As usual, her spirit skyrocketed at his touch. She inhaled his musky cedar cologne and her knees wobbled. She wrapped her arms around him for support.

Who would've thought a woman in her thirties could still feel this kind of rush? When their bodies eased apart, she smiled at him. She could hardly catch her breath. "Okay."

"Okay?" His sky blue eyes grew wide.

She nodded. "Yes. I will marry you."

Anna burst from her bedroom clapping and jumping up and down. "Hooray!"

Jake picked up the toy ring from the table and slid it onto Anna's finger. "When I marry your mom, I'm making a commitment to you, too." He picked his daughter up and twirled her around in circles. "Here's to my two favorite girls." He put Anna down and leaned in to kiss Joely.

His eyes studied her, as if making a silent promise: *I choose you. Forever.*

CHAPTER SIX

Joely was so excited she dialed her older sister's number without thinking of the consequences. After all, Kate had banned Jake from ever setting foot in her house. What were the chances she would welcome him into their tiny family? "Hi, Kate! Guess what!"

Her sister whispered, "Shhh. I hope the phone didn't wake the baby."

Joely glanced at her watch. Nine p.m. "I'm sorry. I never know when is a good time to call."

"That's because it's never a good time. Brianna hasn't slept for more than twenty minutes at a time all week. I don't even know why I shhhed you. I'm so tired I could cry."

Joely chuckled. Her sister had thought motherhood looked so easy from the outside.

"I'm serious. I could burst into tears right now." Kate's voice quivered. "I don't know what's wrong with her."

Anna's infancy flashed through Joely's mind.

Sometimes her daughter didn't sleep because she wanted to stay awake and explore, but other times, she'd screamed bloody murder for no apparent reason. With babies it was so hard to tell. "Does she have a fever?"

"No. I keep checking every morning and throughout the day. I think I'm going to call the pediatrician tomorrow."

"That might give you peace of mind. Does she seem sick?"

"She cries off and on. But other times, she smiles and tries to roll over. God, there should be a twenty-four hour hotline for new moms."

"That's what sisters are for. Call me when you need to talk."

"That's nice of you to say, but I don't want to wake you. You already have such a hard time getting a good night's rest."

Joely nodded to herself. "Lately it hasn't been so bad." An idea came to her. If pain kept her awake, maybe that was Brianna's problem. "Could Brianna be cutting a tooth?"

"How should I know?" Kate sounded exasperated.

"Does she put her hand in her mouth a lot?"

"Of course. That's what babies do."

Joely took a breath, trying not to let Kate's mood

rub off on her. "You could give her a cold washcloth to suck on. Why don't you leave Brianna at home with Mitch and come visit me?"

"I'm so tired, I don't know if it's safe for me to drive." The baby started crying in the background. "Oh, no. I can't take much more of this."

Empathy surged through Joely. She remembered how a few nights without rest could make you crazy. Feeling helpless to soothe your own baby ratcheted up the pressure even more. Anna had been a handful, always moving at breakneck speed through the milestones: crawling, walking, talking. Kate had been a lifesaver and Joely wanted to return the favor. "Kate, ask Mitch to take over tonight so you can get some sleep."

"But I'm her mother. I should be able to comfort her."

Apparently, emotions had already replaced rational thinking for Kate. "Put Mitch on the phone." She wanted to ask on her sister's behalf for help, but Brianna's wails intensified.

The high-pitch crying demanded immediate attention. Kate snipped, "Gotta go" and hung up.

Disappointment filled the gaps where joy once lived. After all, Joely hadn't cheered her sister and she hadn't had the chance to share her own news either.

# # #

Monday morning Val groaned when her alarm clock buzzed. She hit the snooze button and rolled over. Then she remembered. She was Mrs. Nathan Sullivan. One eye opened to peek at the man lying beside her. Only he was sitting on the edge of the bed, stretching his arms over his head. The muscles in his back seemed to be putting on a show especially for her.

"Morning, hubby." A small pain pushed inside her skull. Spending all day yesterday with her difficult mother had spurred quite a headache. Tossing aside the covers, she forced herself to sit up. Because if she slept in, Chip would miss the bus.

Nathan pulled on a white T-shirt and crawled across the haphazard comforter to kiss her neck. "Stay in bed a while longer."

"I can't. Chip--"

"Tell me your routine and I'll take care of Chip."

Turning her head, she looked at him with disbelief. "Really?" Already her mind swirled with possibilities and doubts. Chip moved like a sleepy bear in the mornings and she sometimes had to help him pull on his socks or spoon-feed him breakfast or risk his being tardy. She'd been so looking forward to a few days focused on being a bride rather than a mom. Those plans had been put on hold because Chip's teacher insisted they needed to talk face-to-face this afternoon. Val's shoulders slumped just thinking about it.

Nathan climbed out of bed, cinched the belt of his navy robe and inserted his feet into his sheepskin slippers. "I know Chip eats Lucky Charms for breakfast, but maybe next time we're at the grocery, we should pick something healthier."

She shrugged. It was hard to make her son eat nuts and twigs when she liked her shredded wheat frosted. "Maybe. As far as getting ready for school, he needs to dress first, eat cereal and drink some oj, careful not to spill any on his clothes. Then brush his teeth and make sure his library books are in his backpack. The bus comes at 7:30."

At this point, her mind ran through worst case scenarios, like Chip deciding that he wants to wear shorts even though it's only fifty-some degrees outside or her son deciding that he isn't hungry for breakfast. She was awake now and might as well get up.

Nathan put his hands on her shoulders and pushed her back into bed. "No, no. This is our first week as a married couple and I want to pamper you. Make sure you don't have any second thoughts about marrying a grease monkey."

She giggled and kissed the hand still on her shoulder. "No regrets. I hope after a morning alone with my son you don't start to wonder what you've gotten yourself into."

He shook his head. "Not a chance." Out the bedroom door he slipped and soon she heard him telling Chip it was time to get up. On cue, her son protested, and she pictured him pulling the pillow over his head. She felt the same way in the mornings.

She found herself eavesdropping on Nathan and Chip's interactions as she lay in bed with her eyes closed. How lucky was she to stay in bed past six thirty on a Monday morning? Even though she wasn't leaving town, she was still on vacation from work. Maybe she could take another look at that Spanish-style house with the fountain out front. Her eyes checked the clock. Suddenly she wished it was later so she could call the real estate agent. From the kitchen she heard Chip's young voice: "Today I don't want juice. I want what mommy drinks."

She cringed. Surely Nathan wouldn't allow that. Sugary cereal for a kid was one thing, caffeine was another. That was where she drew the line. Straining to hear Nathan's response, she heard a deep voice say, "Drink your oj or you won't get to bring your Matchbox car to school for show 'n' tell." Her son brought the same yellow Mustang every week. She smiled to herself. Nathan had successfully navigated his way through the irrational mind of a tired seven-year-old.

After she heard the loud engine and the squeak of the school bus brakes, she ran to the window to watch Chip climb aboard. She waved, hoping he would notice her, but he was busy chatting with the neighborhood kids. Spending the morning away from his mother hadn't scarred him in any way. In fact, he'd put up less of a fuss with Nathan giving the orders than when she did. Relief and defensiveness wrestled inside her. Having a man around would be good for Chip, but she didn't like the thought that someone else could handle her son better than she could.

She shook away the negative thoughts and listened to Nathan rattling around in the kitchen. Then she heard the glass door to the patio slide open. What was he doing outside?

Finally, she propped both pillows behind her back and flipped the remote control to the Home & Garden channel. Watching TV in bed seemed so indulgent. About twenty minutes later, she discovered another indulgence. Nathan walked into the room carrying a tray with an orchid from her bridal bouquet and French toast with funny black lines across it.

She sat up a little straighter and turned off the TV. "What's all this?"

"Breakfast in bed, of course. Surely you're familiar with the concept."

"Only in Hallmark Mother's Day commercials. Not in real life."

"Well, what's this tray for then?"

She shrugged. "Decoration." The truth was she'd bought a sterling silver tray for one of her clients and liked it so well, she'd purchased another for herself.

Her mouth started to water. She hadn't had a hot breakfast in a long time. Since she wasn't exactly a morning person, she never cooked this early. Chip wasn't old enough to use the stove and her ex hadn't bothered to do anything helpful around the duplex. "What were you doing outside?" Then it hit her. The black lines. "Did you grill this?"

He grinned. "Of course. I grill everything."

Curious, she cut into her grilled French toast. The first bite didn't disappoint. Crunchy on the outside and soft in the middle. A little squirt of syrup and it was perfect. Her lips turned upward with an "mmmm."

"You like it?"

Nodding, she took another taste. "Who would've thought you could make breakfast on a barbecue grill?"

"Give a man a stove and he'll order pizza. Give a man a grill and he'll cook." He cozied up next to her with his own plate—sans tray—and started cutting. "Oh, I almost forgot." He left her side and from the sound of his footsteps, he went back to the kitchen. When he returned, he held a coffee cup.

So, they didn't know each other that well yet. They had a lifetime to learn. That was the fun part. She offered the obligatory smile and took a sip. But it wasn't coffee in her cup. It was Dr Pepper. Now she gave him a real smile. "You're my knight in shining armor."

After breakfast, he kissed her on her left cheek, right cheek, and lips. Then he gave her something even more to smile about.

CHAPTER SEVEN

Pay backs are hell, they always say. Around ten a.m. Joely picked up the phone, but didn't dial. She put down the receiver and paced around her tiny office. Finally, she sat down, took a deep breath and called. "I have something to say and I need you to be happy for me."

Val's voice sounded gravelly, like she hadn't spoken much yet today. "Sure. What's up?"

Joely's knee bounced up and down. "Jake and I are getting married." She held her breath, waiting.

"You said yes this time? Congratulations!" Kindness laced through her voice.

Joely leaned back in her chair. "I'm glad you're happy for me. I don't know how I'm going to tell my sister. She's definitely not one of Jake's biggest fans."

"That's only because he hurt you in the past. But he's Anna's father and she should understand the need to make it work. I stayed with Chip's dad longer than he deserved, for Chip's sake. Two artists should never get married." She paused and Joely envisioned Val shaking her head. "Of course, we're not talking about me. Congratulations. Oh, I said that, didn't I?"

Her friend was trying to be supportive, which was more than Joely deserved. After all, Nathan had never cheated on his wife, never left Val heartbroken. Nathan was like a rock. A boring, brown rock. And Joely worried his dullness wasn't a good fit for someone who went skydiving on her twenty-first birthday. Perhaps Jake was right. Val wanted something different these days. "Hey, Val, best wishes to you and Nathan, too. I know that I see sides of Jake that you don't and it's probably the same with you and Nathan. I'm sorry if I rained on your parade."

"You didn't." Through the phone she heard a muffled male voice talking to Val, but she couldn't make out the words. Then Val uncovered the phone and continued their conversation. "So, are you excited?"

"Definitely. I was thinking I'd go look at wedding dresses. Are you planning on staying in bed with your hubby all day or would you want to come along?"

Val giggled and Joely suspected it had more to do with the guy sharing her bed than with her question. Another giggle. "Nathan is thinking about going into work, so I'll be free."

# # #

On her lunch hour, Joely waited for her friend on a bench outside of the "I Do Bridal Boutique." She watched Val park her tomato-red Accord.

Val paused for traffic to let up and crossed the street. "Are you sore today or can I give you a hug?"

She looked at her friend whose shirt matched the pink streak in her hair. "I could handle a gentle one." They embraced then squealed like schoolgirls who'd just been asked to go to the prom.

Val's face glowed. "It's been less than forty-eight hours, but I have to report that being married to the right man is better than sleeping alone." They both laughed. "I'm so excited. Now you and I can be newlyweds together. Maybe we'll get pregnant at the same time, too." As soon as the words slipped out of her mouth, her expression fell. "I'm sorry. Can you have more kids? I mean, perhaps you don't want any more. . . ."

Joely wasn't sure how to answer. "I would like more, but getting pregnant with Anna was a bit of a miracle. I'd have to go off all of my meds if I got pregnant again." And that would allow the lupus beast to gnaw at her joints nonstop. She could end up bedridden and in constant pain. She tried to leave those negative thoughts behind as she pulled open the glass door to the boutique. "Let's go shopping!"

They looked around a bit before a sales woman, dressed in a peach dress, approached them. She smelled of rose perfume. "Which one of you is the lucky bride?"

Even though she hadn't felt especially lucky for a while, Joely raised her hand. Something about chronic pain chipped away at her optimism and made it a challenge to stay her normal, bubbly self. What used to come naturally, now came from conscious effort.

The sales woman looked Joely up and down through her rectangular-shaped glasses. "I'm guessing you're a size--." She threw out a number.

Joely sucked in her breath. Several sizes larger than she expected. She corrected the sales woman.

The woman slid her glasses down her nose. "Are you sure? I'm usually spot on." She studied Joely's frame a moment longer. "What style do you like?"

"Do you have anything bohemian?"

Again, the woman's face scrunched together disapprovingly. "I have traditional and modern. White-white, candlelight or ivory."

Joely looked to Val for guidance. Her friend shrugged.

The saleswoman adjusted her glasses. "I tell you what. I don't think we have that many plus-size dresses, so I'll gather them all and you can try them on." She led them toward a dressing area with a long, white curtain instead of a door. Joely and Val sat on a big round ottoman while they waited for the woman to return. A few minutes later, she appeared with her arms full of billowy satin and lace.

Joely took the gown on top and went to change behind the curtain. She squeezed her hips into the mermaid-style dress. Unfortunately, it hurt her shoulders to reach around to the back zipper. Holding the bodice against her chest, she walked back into the waiting area where her friend sat. Thank goodness, the lady in the peach-colored dress had left to assist another customer. "Can you help me?" She turned and Val came over to zip.

As each tooth of the zipper connected, Joely crossed her fingers tighter. "I feel more like a mummy than a mermaid."

Val seemed to struggle with the zipper. "Can you suck in your breath?"

Joely complied.

"There." Val stepped away so they could both check out the front.

Waddling to the three-way mirror, Joely hated what she saw. Her skin spilled over the sides of the strapless dress. Her once hourglass figure looked as if all the sand had sunk to the bottom. "This is hideous." She shook her head, remembering how she'd been a size eight before spending years on prescription steroids.

"It's not that bad. If you like it, they'll order a bigger size and it will fit you perfectly."

With her head hung low, Joely grabbed the next dress and made her way to the tiny dressing room. This dress had lace sleeves that constrained her movements. She walked out so Val could see. "I don't know that this is any better."

Her friend offered a restrained smile. "Have you set the date?"

She shook her head. "I thought shopping for dresses would be so much fun, I decided to do it first."

"Well, if you knew the season, you'd know whether you could go sleeveless or not."

Joely nodded. Did she want to rush into this like Val had? "Was it difficult doing everything in six months?" She looked at Val, remembering how she'd looked so slender and perfect in her wedding gown. Envy poisoned her thoughts for a brief moment.

Val crossed her tiny legs. "It was a little challenging, but I've been married before so I was more relaxed this time. If you have a certain location in mind for the ceremony or reception, you're limited if it's already booked."

Joely shrugged. "I don't have any place picked out. The truth is, once I had Anna, I stopped dreaming about getting married. I just focused on being a good mother."

"Of course." She paused. "It wasn't ideal that our reception was in a basement, but it doesn't really matter now that the day is over. In exchange, we have more money for kids' clothes, family vacations, a house. Speaking of houses, I called the real estate agent today about that 1920's hacienda and the owners have already accepted an offer." Her posture slumped a little.

"I'm sorry."

Val shook her head. "I knew we couldn't afford it anyway." Her eyes stared off into the mid-distance for a moment. Then her focus returned to Joely. "As far as your wedding goes, figure out what you care about and don't sweat the other stuff."

"That's good advice. Thanks." Although she wasn't sure what mattered. She didn't belong to a church, so she couldn't envision where the ceremony would be held. She hadn't been raised to care about appearances like Jake had. Some place small and intimate would be nice. "I don't think I want a fancy wedding. Especially since I hardly have any family."

"But you have a lot of friends." Val grinned at her.

"Thanks." Forgetting her tight dress, Joely rushed over and gave Val a hug. When she lifted her arms, the lace ripped at the shoulder seam. "Oh shit." She gawked at the split.

Just then the saleswoman walked into the dressing area. Her fake friendly expression fell. "You're going to have to pay for that."

Joely changed back into her peasant skirt and blouse as quickly as possible. Before leaving, she allowed the clerk to scan her Visa for the repairs. Hopefully it wouldn't cost too much. Once outside of the store, she didn't stay to chat with Val on the sidewalk. Instead, she waved goodbye and went to buy some SlimFast.

CHAPTER EIGHT

Later that night, Val sat next to Chip, still in his race car pajamas, in the ER waiting room. Miserable-looking men, women and children held their bodies where they hurt--their stomachs, their heads, their elbows. She struggled to fill out the clipboard of paperwork the admissions desk had handed her. They wanted to know any and all medical conditions that Nathan had suffered from. Chicken pox, depression, headaches, polio, shingles, substance abuse, whooping cough, etc. What did she know? She didn't even know the address of his apartment, only how to get there. It was on Cherry Blossom Street. It was on the first floor. A one-bedroom that didn't have laundry facilities, which was why they'd been staying at her place. So Chip would have his own room until they could agree on a house.

Even though she checked the box "married" and put herself down as the emergency contact, she didn't really feel like Nathan's wife. She felt like they were in limbo. After all, they'd only been married for three days.

A tear threatened to drip onto the form she was trying to complete. She wiped it away with the back of her hand, scolding herself: *Pull yourself together for the sake of Chip.* A glance to her left revealed that Chip's attention was glued to the tiny TV screen bolted to the ceiling. It was playing a night-time police drama that she'd never let him watch on a normal day.

He hadn't a clue how serious things were. Was it possible she was about to be a widow? Her first marriage ended in divorce and now, her second husband might die on her. She shuddered then only stared at the remaining blank lines.

Her name was called and it wasn't until the nurse repeated it, that Val recognized it as her own. She stood, took Chip's hand and walked toward the reception desk. A nurse in blue scrubs furrowed her brow. "Mrs. Sullivan?"

She certainly wasn't used to being called that. "Yes?"

"The doctor wants to talk to you. Go through that door and down the corridor."

Val nodded. Everything around her seemed surreal. A woman hobbling on crutches passed by as she and Chip walked the hall. Standing in an open doorway, a man in a white coat approached her.

The doctor looked about thirty and didn't smile.

"There's a hemorrhage in your husband's brain. It's very serious. If we don't operate, he could die."

OhGod-OhGod-OhGod. Breath lodged in her throat. Her trembling hand took his pen and signed the unread consent forms. It didn't even look like her writing. "Is he going to be all right?"

"He hasn't regained consciousness. Right now we need to take care of the swelling before it's too late." Taking the forms from her, he hurried out of the room.

# # #

The elastic of Joely's sweat pants dug into her waist as she stepped onto the treadmill at the health club. Disgusted with herself, she ran her thumb along the red line etched into her gut. "I have a lot of work to do."

On the machine next to her, Kate pushed the buttons to select her workout. "I feel out of shape too. Between the office and Brianna, I don't have time to exercise."

That may be true, but her sister still had the same petite frame she'd always had. Due to their height differences, plus Kate's ivory skin and cobalt blue eyes, they had always been teased that one of them must've been the milkman's baby. Ever since brown-eyed Joely had been diagnosed with lupus, she'd been especially thankful for their contrasting DNA. She prayed every day that Kate stayed healthy forever. "I'm glad you decided to take me up on my offer. Even moms need a night off once in a while."

Dressed in matching turquoise shorts and shirt, Kate started walking. "When we finish here, I want to call and check on Brianna. This is the first time I've left her overnight since we brought her home from the hospital."

"You shouldn't worry." Joely's brother-in-law was one of those guys you could depend on. He probably knew the baby's eating and napping schedule just as well as Kate did. In fact, he'd been more than accommodating when Joely called and suggested that her sister needed a get-away. "Mitch can handle things."

Her sister nodded. "I know. I just hope Brianna doesn't wake up in the middle of the night crying."

"You need to get some rest, too." Only half-listening as her sister went on a mommy guilt trip, Joely read the questions on the screen. Type of work-out: fat burner. Age: thirty-seven. Weight: ? She'd passed by the scale as they'd entered the fitness center, but had been afraid to look. After all, this body didn't seem as if it belonged to her. She tried to skip the weight question, but when it wouldn't let her, she typed in her best guess. Then she started speed walking.

She took in her surroundings. In front of her, muscular men and skinny women filled elliptical machines and stair climbers. Above them, a row of TVs, each set to different prime time shows with closed captioning activated. Through the stereo speakers in the ceiling came pounding hip-hop music she didn't recognize. Somehow this place made her feel old and out-of-it. Didn't anyone pudgy come here to workout?

Pushing the "up" arrow button, Kate transitioned into a jog, her honey blond hair bouncing against her shoulders. "So you're thinking of joining this gym?"

"Yep." They were using a one-day free trial pass that had come in the mail. "I want to lose weight before the wedding." She glanced over to see Kate's reaction. This wasn't how she planned on dropping the bomb, but no matter when she said it, her sister wouldn't be happy. The treadmill speed increased and Joely struggled to breathe.

"What?"

"Jake asked me--". Two quick breaths. "--and I said yes." She grinned at her sister's shocked face.

Kate closed her mouth and focused on her jogging for a moment. "I thought you told him to wait at least six months before proposing again."

Joely's knees screamed in protest with every step. Hard to believe she used to find running a pleasant experience. She grabbed onto the side rails to see if that made it any easier. "I did." She huffed and puffed. "But

Anna really wants us together. In fact, she's the one who arranged this engagement."

Kate lowered her eyebrows. "I'm supposed to believe that? Did she buy you the diamond ring, too?" She glanced at Joely's left hand. She hadn't missed it. Joely had slipped off the engagement ring before her sister arrived, so she could break the news on her own schedule.

"No, Jake supplied the ring. He had it in his pocket when Anna informed us that it was time we make a commitment." Joely smiled at her daughter's gumption.

"He just happened to have the ring with him? Are you sure he didn't put Anna up to it?"

Joely shook her head and gripped the sides even tighter. She didn't want to lose her balance or trip. "It was Anna's idea. She wants her parents together and who can blame her?"

Kate continued running, barely panting. "I don't know what you want me to say."

"Say that you'll be my matron of honor."

Kate pushed the emergency stop button on her machine. She turned and wiped the tiny beads of sweat on her brow. "I worry about you. You need someone who will take care of you when you have a flare. I'm not sure Jake has the right personality to be married to someone with a chronic illness."

Joely's heartbeats pounded on top of one another.

She slapped the red stop button in front of her. Bending down, she tried to catch her breath. Exercise and arguing didn't go together.

"Are you all right?" Concern wove into Kate's voice.

Joely nodded. She didn't like for anyone to fuss over her. "I know Jake has been selfish in the past, but he's stuck with me for a long time now." She straightened her spine. "One weekend he even took Anna when it was my turn because my lupus was acting up."

"One time." Kate rolled her eyes.

"The fact is, I do have a chronic illness and maybe it would be nice to have a partner in this." She shook her head and clasped the side rails. "That's not why I want to marry Jake. I want to marry him because I've always loved him. Long before I got sick, I wanted to be with him." That was the truth.

"Is he pressuring you to lose weight? Because if he is--"

"No. This is my decision. I hate my body. It's enormous."

Kate shook her head and placed her hand on top of Joely's. "Don't hate your body. You're beautiful. A few extra pounds can't change that."

Joely despised the way her heart raced as if she'd

overtaxed it by jogging. She squeezed her eyes tight. "It's more than a few extra pounds." She looked at her sister's dainty figure. "I want to look pretty on my wedding day." The dress shopping fiasco played over in her mind. "I'm so fat, they don't have any gowns in my size."

Kate glanced at a thirty-something man in a tank top who lingered near them, as if he wanted to use the treadmill. She lowered her voice. "Hey, let's get out of here. I want to call home."

The clock read eight thirty. They hadn't even been there for fifteen minutes. Joely sighed and stepped off the exercise equipment. She limped her way toward the child care room to pick up Anna. "How am I ever going to lose weight if my joints hurt?" She offered a pleading look to Kate.

Kate placed her hand around her sister's waist, trying to help her walk. "I don't know. Maybe do something low impact. Swimming perhaps."

Joely grimaced. Kate knew darn good and well that she didn't know how to swim. Neither of them did. Theirs had not been a childhood filled with swim lessons or ballet or horseback riding.

After picking up Anna, the three of them walked through the dark parking lot to Joely's car. When Joely opened the door, her cell phone beeped. She checked her voicemail and heard her friend's voice. "Nathan's in the hospital. . .I-I don't know what to do. . . Call me."

Outside, rain drizzled from the morning sky, forming puddles in the hospital parking lot. Funny how the weather sometimes matched one's mood.

Val looked at Nathan lying in the bed. He'd made it through the surgery and now had a white wire, called an ICP monitor, attached to his skull to check for more swelling. A ventilator helped him breathe. His eyes remained closed and she had no idea how long that would last.

Alone in the room, she took a deep breath, the scent of disinfectant permeating her nostrils. The odor made her gag and she felt a little dizzy. After all, the last time she'd seen her grandmother alive was in a hospital that smelled like this. And she knew the longer a patient stayed, the more likely they'd never leave.

Nathan's mom, looking frail and older than her fifty-some years, burst into the room with her arms outstretched. Last night Joely had helped Val track down her mother-in-law's number to tell her the horrific news. Now Val walked toward her and they embraced. They barely knew each other, but because of this tragedy, the hug felt natural.

Her mother-in-law eventually released her grasp

and looked into Val's eyes. "I know you told me this on the phone. . ." Her voice quivered with each word. "But tell me again how he fell."

"Nathan was going to do laundry and he somehow lost his footing on the stairs. Maybe he couldn't grab the rail because he was holding a basket." Maybe he tripped on one of Chip's toys, but she would never admit that. "Next thing I knew, he was unconscious." She winced, remembering the crimson blood gushing, remembering how he'd hurt himself while doing her a favor.

"It doesn't seem possible. How can my son be in a coma? That's something in soap operas, not in real life."

Val nodded. "I know."

Nathan's mom--they'd never discussed if she should call her Lydia, Mrs. Sullivan or what—wrung her hands. "What can we do?"

Val shook her head. "Right now Nathan's in a drug-induced coma and the doctor said it's best to let him rest."

"I can't sit here and do nothing."

The doing nothing part was already driving Val crazy. Except for meeting Joely in the lobby and asking her to take Chip, Val hadn't left Nathan's room all night. Fear and loneliness ached in her bones, so on some level, she appreciated the company. She'd called her own parents and when they'd asked if she wanted them to fly in, she'd found herself saying it wasn't necessary. They'd had a terrible trip home from the wedding, with delays and missing a connecting flight. Deep down, she'd hoped they would somehow know that she really did need them. But they didn't.

Lydia remained standing, rubbing her hands. "I'll go see if I can find some newspapers. Nathan always starts his morning by reading current events."

Val waited in the room, watching her sweetheart's face. When Lydia came back, she read out loud from the *Lansing State Journal*, but her voice kept breaking.

A nurse stepped into the room. "You shouldn't read to the patient. His body and mind need quiet." She dimmed the lights as if to emphasize her point.

Lydia didn't say a word. Once the nurse left, Lydia found a tissue in her purse and wiped her eyes. She stared at Nathan for a long time. Eventually she opened a quilted Vera Bradley bag to retrieve a knitting project. It looked like yellow baby booties.

Val didn't think Nathan's brother's wife was pregnant. "Who are those for?"

Looking mischievous, she shrugged. "You never know."

Then Val understood. She and Nathan had discussed having kids right away. Her soul actually hurt.

The future father of her children lay motionless, practically lifeless--her dreams of a happy family destroyed.

For an hour, the only sounds in the room were the rain and the clicking of knitting needles. Eventually the clicking stopped and the widow looked up. "I'm going to get myself a cup of decaf. Would you like something?" She rose and turned, placing her project on her chair. "I'd prefer the real stuff, but I have enough trouble sleeping these days as it is."

Val hadn't slept, either. "You wouldn't happen to have a cigarette, would you?"

Facing Val, her mother-in-law cocked her head. "I didn't know you smoked."

"Used to. I quit when I got pregnant with Chip." God, she could use a smoke right now. Lydia had knitting to soothe her nerves, but Val needed something stronger. "Funny how I haven't craved one in years. . . . They say nicotine is just as addictive as heroin."

Covering her mouth with her bony hand, Nathan's mom looked horrified at the mention of illegal drugs.

"No thanks. Just get yourself some coffee." Once she was alone with Nathan, she reached for his hand and squeezed it. "Wake up so we can go home." His hand remained limp. Her throat started to close. She swallowed. The fact that she'd been awake for twenty-four hours caught up with her—intensifying her dread. Her mouth opened and sobs came out.

The emotion surprised her. She'd done her best to keep the tears bottled up, out of Chip's and then Lydia's view. Val wasn't one to cry normally, but now she didn't stop. Couldn't stop.

Nathan was comatose. He could die.

Eventually, her body didn't have the energy to cry any more. Somehow she felt even worse. Completely drained.

Tasting her salty tears, she leaned forward and kissed Nathan's scratchy cheek. "I need you. Chip and I need you."

CHAPTER NINE

When the doctor weaned Nathan off the meds that kept him in a coma, Val held Lydia's frail hand. Through their vigil, they'd hugged and held each other's hands more than they had in the previous eight months.

This was it. The moment they'd been anticipating. Sweat pooled between their palms. They expected something to happen. . .but Nathan didn't wake up. The two of them stood over his bed for a long time, waiting.

Who knew how long they'd hovered there? Val swallowed, finally realizing that nothing was going to happen. "At least there's a chance that he could wake up now, right?" She needed someone to reassure her everything would work out. But her mother-in-law wouldn't fill that role. Neither would Dr. Chesney.

She started pacing the narrow room.

Lydia's face crumpled as if she were fighting back tears. They were both always on the brink.

Val kept walking back and forth, too wound up to sit. She had to do something different. When would this ever end?

A few hours later, Joely stuck her head in the hospital room. "Hello. How's he doing?"

Lydia stopped knitting and looked at her. "His temperature is up by one-tenth degree, but the nurse said it's nothing." She shook her head in frustration.

Val looked at the clock hanging above the door. "Is it noon already?"

Joely, who had been stopping by every day during her lunch break, nodded. She held a brown bag in her hand.

Lydia coughed as though she had phlegm stuck in her throat. She made her way to her feet. "I'll go see if I can find the doctor. Maybe he cares that Nathan's temperature is going up."

As Lydia left the room, Joely gave Val a hug. "How are you doing?" She pulled Lydia's chair next to Val's abandoned one.

What could she say? Val shrugged and sat for the first time all day. Her leg muscles ached, but she ignored them.

Opening the bag, Joely handed her a fountain drink and a sandwich wrapped in waxy Subway paper. "I brought these for you. I got a turkey on wheat for Nathan's mom, too."

Unable to see a reason to eat, Val set her sandwich on the window sill. She took a long sip from the straw. It tasted familiar. Her favorite. "You're a good friend."

"I printed something for you off the internet." Joely handed her a few papers. "Someone at my lupus support group told me about this thing called tapping therapy. It's supposed to help people with all kinds of medical issues from migraines to comas."

Val took the papers and started to read them. They said that trauma created blockages in a person's "meridians" or energies. Based on the Chinese principles of acupuncture, tapping helped to balance the meridians running throughout the body.

She'd heard that western medicine was finally beginning to acknowledge the healing powers of acupuncture. So, maybe this had some credibility.

While Val studied the printouts, Joely pulled a diet shake can out of her bag. "I read that a coma patient kept having seizures and the doctors didn't know what to do. A friend of the family asked if he could try tapping. The next time the patient started seizing, his friend went through the tapping sequence, and it calmed the patient down. The seizure stopped. At another facility a nurse tapped a bunch of patients and they woke up from their comas. It sounds amazing."

"I wonder if Dr. Chesney knows about this."

"Good question."

Val walked to the nurse's station to ask if it was safe for her to touch Nathan in this repetitive way. It was. She returned to the room, looked at the picture on the printouts and started tapping Nathan's feet with her fingertips. For a few minutes, the friends remained silent. Val kept referring to the instructions, moving from the side of Nathan's hand to under his arms. She skipped the taps on the head. "Thanks for this, Joely."

More silence. Val hated the silence. She'd had a week of almost non-stop silence. "What's going on with you?"

"You don't want to hear about me. My problems seem so trivial compared to. . . ." Joely's voice trailed off. She chewed on her lip.

"Please talk to me. I could use news of the outside world." Val grimaced.

Her friend hesitated before speaking. "Well, since it's tax season, Jake is busy at the accounting firm. Therefore, we haven't nailed down the wedding date or location yet. I'm mostly focusing on losing weight right now." She drank some of her shake and scrunched up her face as she swallowed. "I can't believe how hard it is. I'm hungry all of the time and when I workout, I pay for it."

"It's not your fault. Maybe you should go easy on yourself. Walk instead of run."

"But walking barely burns any calories."

"Tell me you're not going to postpone your wedding for something silly like a few pounds."

"You sound like my sister." Joely slurped the bottom of her can. She sighed and threw it into the trash can. "I want everything to be perfect."

"Of course you do. Why not set the date, pick a place and just accept yourself the way you are? After all, Jake does."

At that, a shadow of a smile formed on Joely's lips.

Val looked at Nathan's expressionless face and wondered if he'd ever smile again. She realized Joely was right. Her problems did seem trivial compared to this. How she longed for life to be trivial again.

# # #

Jake might accept Joely the way she was, but Mrs. Mahoney certainly did not. Jake's mom had insisted they meet at "the Club" on Saturday. The scent of fresh bread wafted from the country club's restaurant. Joely's legs wobbled like rubber bands as she walked into the large banquet room. She'd pushed herself so hard at the gym that she needed a cane to maintain her balance.

Mrs. Mahoney, dressed in a caramel-colored linen suit, wore pearls in each ear and a strand around her neck.

Suddenly Joely felt underdressed in her usual peasant skirt, blouse and Doc Martens sandals. Why hadn't she at least put on some tinted lip balm?

Jake's mom eyed Joely's cane with a crinkled nose. "I hope you're not going to walk down the aisle with that."

Well, nice to see you, too. Joely fiddled with the amethyst bracelet on her wrist. The stones promoted healing and happiness.

Jake dropped Joely's hand and leaned in to give his mother a peck on each cheek. Mrs. Mahoney had been raised out east and that was how she preferred to be greeted. Even though it felt odd to her, Joely followed suit.

After the hellos were over, Mrs. Mahoney straightened her back. "Where's my granddaughter?"

"Anna had a play date with a friend," Joely said. "Besides, looking at banquet halls wouldn't be much fun for a six-year-old." Warmth filled her as Jake clasped her hand again.

Mrs. Mahoney's face flashed disappointment. "I was hoping to see her. Besides, every little girl dreams of her wedding day. She might have enjoyed this."

Joely shrugged. *I'm not even enjoying this and it's my wedding.* "So this is where you think we should have the reception?" She tried to act interested. Jake had explained to her that weddings were big productions on the East Coast and his mother liked the tradition. Joely glanced out the large windows that overlooked the golf course. No doubt Jake's dad was out there on the green somewhere. The man preferred golf to family. "It's nice."

"Nice?" Mrs. Mahoney sniped. "This is where everyone wishes they could hold their reception. Not only is there a lovely view, but the chef trained at the Cordon Bleu. After delicious appetizers and the main meal, they fill this whole area with a dessert buffet." She gestured with her hand to a long beige wall. "They will have chocolate fondue, crepes made to order, pies and tarts. I'll have to pull some strings to get you guys in here."

Joely's knees throbbed. "I thought we'd just have wedding cake." Jolts of pain zapped her nerves like an electric fence. She looked for a place to sit down.

Worry lined Jake's forehead. He gripped her hand tighter. "Are you all right?"

She shook her head. "I need a chair."

He crossed the room and carried a padded dining room chair to her. He grasped her elbow, helping her to sit.

Joely waved him away. "I'm fine. Thanks."

Mrs. Mahoney rolled her eyes and crossed her arms over her designer suit. "Is this what it's going to be like? You won't even be able to dance with my son at his wedding? Are you in need of a full-time nursemaid?

Because my Jake is bound for greater things."

Jake's head shot up. "Mother!"

Rubbing her knee, Joely hated that her body had failed her just now. She didn't need Mrs. Mahoney making her feel worse. Thank goodness Jake had been raised more by his nanny than by this woman. "Lupus is unpredictable. With any luck, I'll be able to walk without a cane on my wedding day."

"Are you sure you're really in that much pain? A woman in my bridge club has lupus and she seems perfectly fine to me."

Joely took a deep breath. So many people didn't understand how the disease could torture you one week and be manageable the next. "Does she come to every meeting?"

Mrs. Mahoney touched her white-blond hair. "Well, no."

Even though Jake whispered for Joely not to bother, she continued. "That's because when her lupus flares, she probably stays home. She doesn't want you to see her at her worst. Or she's in so much pain, she can't even drive herself there."

Mrs. Mahoney's mouth opened slightly, but she didn't speak. She appeared to be thinking.

Jake placed his hand on Joely's shoulder and

rubbed it gently. "Mom, you need to accept that I am marrying Joely and that she really is sick. She isn't faking it for the attention. She fights it every day, trying to live a normal life."

His mom took a step closer and looked him in the eye. Her voice lowered. "Why would you want to marry someone who's crippled?"

Joely flinched. She hated the word "cripple."

Jake's fingers froze. "Because I love her. I love her even more for the way she handles her lupus. The last thing she wants is for anyone to feel sorry for her. But I also love her because she's creative, she's smart, she's a great mother, and she doesn't care about stuff like this." His free arm opened wide. "She doesn't care about country clubs and money and appearances. She's the most genuinely, sweet person I've ever met."

Mrs. Mahoney's face remained tight. "Well, then." She brushed her hands together as if brushing off Jake's speech. Pointing out the window, she squinted. "Just down the road, you can almost see it from here, is the cathedral. Isn't that convenient?"

Joely didn't know what to say. They hadn't agreed on a church. He'd been raised Catholic and she'd stayed home on Sunday mornings playing with her sister.

Mrs. Mahoney checked her diamond-studded watch. "It's time to go. I scheduled for you to meet with the priest in ten minutes."

Jake's hand clenched Joely's shoulder. "Mom, I told you we aren't sure we want to get married in the church."

She gasped and reached for her chest. "Are you trying to give me a heart attack? Of course you'll get married in the church. Don't tell me you'd rather go to city hall."

He cracked his knuckles. "Not really, but. . . ."

Gripping her cane, Joely forced herself up. She looked Jake's mom in her cold, dark eyes. "If *Jake* wants to talk to the priest, I'm willing to do that."

Studying Joely's face, Jake's features softened. "Really?"

Joely fiddled again with her bracelet. Health and happiness—that's what she longed for. Therefore, she'd do her part to make the relationship with her in-laws a pleasant one. "It can't hurt to talk."

Mrs. Mahoney tracked down the manager and spoke in hushed tones as Joely limped out. Ten minutes later, the three of them got in their vehicles and drove to the limestone Cathedral. Once inside, colorful stained glass windows greeted them. Worn-smooth oak pews lined the sanctuary ready for a few hundred parishioners to show up for Mass. Joely couldn't help but whisper, "Wow" as she admired the beautiful details.

Looking at her, Jake lowered his eyebrows. "Do you like it?"

"It's a work of art."

His mom clapped her hands. "Excellent. Now follow me and I'll introduce you to Father Paul." She led them to an office where she made the introductions.

Father Paul had thinning hair, a husky frame and kind eyes. He shook everyone's hand and told them to take a seat. But only two chairs sat across from his desk. Jake's mom looked around for her spot.

Jake cleared his throat and looked at her. "Mother, you can go. This is between Joely and me."

Mrs. Mahoney didn't leave.

Father Paul told her they needed a volunteer to chair the homeless shelter food drive. He told her to get the details from the secretary in the next office. At this, she made her exit.

Jake closed the door behind her then sat next to Joely. He reached over to hold her hand. "I'm not sure what we're here for. My mom scheduled this without telling us."

Father Paul leaned across his desk and folded his hands. "I hear you two are getting married. Congratulations."

They both nodded and smiled.

"I understand there is a child already?"

Joely squirmed in her seat. Nothing like setting foot in a church to make her feel like a sinner. "Yes. Anna. She's six."

He narrowed his eyes. "I assume she has been christened, brought up as a Catholic?"

Crossing her legs, Joely decided to let Jake field the rest of the questions. She gave him a look to indicate this was his problem.

Jake took a deep breath. "Father, it's complicated. Joely isn't Catholic."

Father Paul furrowed his brow at her. "Why do you want to be married here if you do not believe?"

"I'm not sure that I do want to be married here. I mean, it's beautiful and all, but this is more for Jake's family."

The man scratched his thinning hair. "The only way I'll perform the ceremony is if you agree to raise your child and future children in the church."

Her hand squeezed Jake's. Future children. She wasn't sure she could give Jake any more kids. Somehow, she felt even less worthy to marry him.

Father Paul continued, probably unaware of the turmoil he was causing. "If you do not commit your children to the church, they cannot be accepted into the Kingdom of Heaven."

She uncrossed her legs. She didn't really want to get into a theological debate with a priest. "Perhaps we should go."

Jake gave her a conflicted look--one that she didn't quite know how to interpret. A moment later, he stood and they left.

CHAPTER TEN

The ventilator hissed with artificial breath in Nathan's room. Lydia's incessant knitting was starting to get on Val's nerves. Not to mention the way she rumbled the phlegm in her throat every five minutes.

As if on cue, Lydia hacked like she had a hairball. "Maybe we should read the newspapers again."

Val shook her head. She was tired of reading aloud. Tired of making small talk with her mother-in-law. Tired of having to put on a brave face. She wanted to be alone with her husband. "Why don't you go to Nathan's apartment? Take a shower, check his mailbox, give yourself a little break?"

Lydia didn't miss a purl. "No. I want to be here when he wakes up." She'd finished the baby booties the second day and now seemed to be knitting the world's longest scarf. "Maybe you should do tapping again."

At least three times a day, when the healthier patients were served their meals, Val did tapping. It couldn't hurt to do it again. She lifted the covers and pulled off Nathan's socks. She held her four fingers tight together and tapped them against the soles of his feet. He had long, calloused feet. Feet that usually wore work boots. Now they seemed so exposed. So raw. So useless.

Lydia made that nasty sound in her throat again. Val paused, her shoulders tight. A moment later she moved up his body. It felt good to have something specific to do. Feet, hands, collar bone.

Each place on the body served a different purpose from healing to boosting immunity. It didn't matter that she didn't remember which location did what. It also didn't matter that Dr. Chesney thought she was crazy when she mentioned it to him. There were lots of things science couldn't explain.

Which meant no one had any idea how long Nathan would remain like this. Thank goodness her boss had given her some time off of work and Chip had school all day. She couldn't imagine being anywhere but here by Nathan's side. Talking, tapping, reading, and hoping. Surely he could feel her presence. Sense her longing for him to wake up.

One of the papers she'd signed had asked if Nathan had a living will. They'd never discussed such morbid things. Would he want her to pull the plug after so much time? How long would that be? Weeks? Months?

Years? No, she would not allow herself to think like that. He'd only fallen down the stairs. People fell all the time. This shouldn't be a big deal. Even though it clearly was.

In her mind's eye, the unity candle flickered. Had that been a warning about this? She shook her head. "Come on, Nathan. I'm waiting for you to open your eyes. Come back to me."

Lydia paused from her knitting. "Yes, Nathan. We all miss you."

His face was flat. Expressionless. After Val had tapped him from bottom to top, she started over again. She expected him to respond when she touched his flesh since he was extremely ticklish. But he never flinched.

She stopped tapping to touch what was left of his thick hair around the shaved surgical area. His brown hair had started graying at the temples (when his father died two years ago, he'd told her), but he still had a young face. In fact, he could pass for someone in his twenties, even though he was in his early thirties. She used to tease him about his baby face. Remind him to bring his i.d. when they went out for dinner. Not that he ever ordered a drink.

A young, curly-haired nurse came into the room pushing a cart with two bowls full of water. "Hello!" She was a little too cheerful, as if she were new. "It's time for Mr. Sullivan's sponge bath." She wrung out a washcloth and loosened the top of Nathan's gown.

For some reason, Lydia dropped her knitting and rose. "I'll do that." She reached for the cloth in the nurse's hand.

The bright-eyed nurse pulled away. "No, I'm trained to do this. It's no big deal."

Lydia rolled the cart toward the foot of the bed and out of the other woman's reach. "I'm his mother. If anyone should wash him, it should be me."

"Wait a minute," Val said. "I'm his wife." She stood. "I think Nathan would prefer if I were the one washing him."

The nurse tilted her head in confusion. Perhaps this was the first time people had argued with her over a sponge bath. "Really, it's my job. I'll do it." She tried to move around Lydia to reach the soapy water.

Lydia grabbed at the cloth again. "Let me do it. He'd be mortified to have some stranger see him."

"Ma'am. Ma'am!" The nurse wrestled away the rag and hid it behind her back. "If you won't allow me to do my job, I'll have to ask you to leave."

A crazed look crossed Lydia's wrinkled face. This wasn't like her. Val clutched her mother-in-law's shoulders and tried to calm her down. Lydia flung her arms up in the air, breaking free. "This is my son. My oldest son. My firstborn." Her head dropped and she started sobbing. "It's my job to take care of him." Suddenly all of the fight in her dissipated.

Tears filled Val's eyes. She bit her lip and escorted Nathan's mom out into the hallway. "Let the nurse do her job."

They made their way to a bench in the waiting area. Lydia buried her face in her hands and cried. Val was tired of crying. Tired of not knowing.

The doctor said that these first few days were critical. The swelling had gone down and now they just had to wait. If Nathan remained in a coma for too long, Dr. Chesney said they'd have to insert an endotracheal tube. Something to do with preventing pneumonia. He already had tubes in his stomach, his mouth and his skull. All she knew was she didn't want any more tubes in her husband's body.

She hadn't prayed in years, but found it only natural now. She pressed her eyelids together. God, please make Nathan wake up. Please. I'll be the perfect wife if you bring him back to me.

Children weren't allowed in the rooms past visiting hours, but the nurse on the night shift made an exception for Chip, saying she had a soft spot for single mothers. That same nurse said she thought she saw

Nathan's big toe twitching last night. Just a centimeter or so. But Val hadn't seen any movement from him all day. Her hopes had been deflated by hours and hours of inertia.

Somehow Val convinced Nathan's mom to leave the hospital. The nurses had begged them both to go home, claiming they weren't helping. Too tired to knit, Lydia finally conceded around six p.m. Since she lived an hour away, she went to Nathan's apartment. Val would have to leave soon, too, to put Chip to bed.

As the sun disappeared from view, Val's son sat on her lap and looked into her eyes. "Mom, do you think I left one of my Matchbox cars on the stairs and that's why Nathan fell?"

Even though it was possible Nathan had tripped on the toy Mustang, she didn't want her son to bear that burden. After all, Nathan had tripped on his own feet after their wedding. "It's not your fault, Chipmunk." She'd nicknamed him that as a toddler because of the way he nibbled at his Cheerios. He'd had a tuft of brown hair, little brown eyes and two buck teeth, which furthered the resemblance. He'd been cute as a chipmunk. Still was. "We don't know why Nathan fell."

"Are you sure? You're always reminding me to pick up my stuff so someone doesn't trip."

"This wasn't anyone's fault. Accidents happen." Glancing at her son's face, she squeezed him tight. His hugs were the only thing that made her feel slightly better. She returned her gaze to her husband's limp body. It didn't make sense. Why had she married Nathan if only to lose him? Her son didn't need to lose another father figure.

"Mom, can I watch TV?"

"No. Let's read one of the books Mrs. Bean loaned us." It was hard to find the energy to keep fighting this battle with Chip, but she had to.

"Aww, can't we skip a day? Let me do tapping first."

Every muscle in her body ached, so she allowed him this delay tactic. He went to the end of the bed, removed the covers and tapped on Nathan's feet. Exhausted, she leaned back to rest her eyes for a few seconds. Seconds turned into minutes.

"Mom, look!" Chip's voice startled her awake. "His eyelids are moving." Chip pointed toward Nathan's face.

The breath caught in her throat. Nathan's eyes fluttered as if he were dreaming. She sprung to her feet. "Nathan? Nathan! Wake up!"

His eyes squeezed shut and seemed to be moving beneath the lids--side to side, up down. But never open.

She reached for his hand and stroked it. "Nathan. It's me, Val. Open your eyes, honey. Open them." Chip's body pressed against her side. "Chip and I are right here."

Nathan's Adam's apple moved downward and back up. The hand she'd been holding jerked a little.

Then Nathan's eyelids ever so slowly cracked open. His sea green eyes fixated on the ceiling.

She gripped his hand tighter. "Nathan. Thank God." She leaned forward and kissed his cheek. His whiskers pricked her bottom lip. Instead of looking at her, he remained focused on the ceiling. He moaned.

Beside her, Chip was jumping up and down. "He's awake! He's awake!"

She grabbed her son and pulled him up off the ground into a bear hug. Tears streamed down her face, but she didn't care. "You did it. The tapping worked." So much adrenaline pumped through her that it caused her arms to quiver.

Then it hit her. The doctor. She needed to tell the doctor. She put Chip down, looked for the "call" button and pushed it. There was no way she was leaving Nathan's side. The medical staff would have to come to them.

First, a nurse arrived and checked his vital signs. Nathan coughed. She smiled as if she were a personal friend of his. "I'll alert the doctor."

Nathan kept coughing. It seemed like forever before the neurosurgeon made it to their room. He wore a white lab jacket over a khaki shirt and a striped tie.

"Welcome back, Mr. Sullivan. I'm Dr. Chesney." He spoke to Nathan while shining a penlight into his eyes. Nathan did not respond.

The doctor examined Nathan from top to bottom and Val desperately tried to interpret the expression on the doctor's face. But he was good at disguising his emotions.

"Can you take him off the ventilator so he can talk?" she asked.

The doctor pinched Nathan's arm. No response. Uh-oh.

Dr. Chesney asked Nathan to squeeze his hand, but Nathan didn't move. "Let's not rush things. It's not like you see on TV when someone wakes up from a coma and starts talking."

Val searched Nathan's face to see if he understood what was going on. He remained still, only his eyelids were open instead of closed. He wasn't quite the same.

# # #

Later Nathan started grabbing at the tube in his throat. Val told him to stop, but he didn't seem to hear her. Scared he'd hurt himself, she wrestled with him and called out for a nurse. Soon several staff members came and tied his hands down.

Watching her husband struggle against the straps was almost as terrible as watching his listless body.

The next day Nathan's eyes started tracking, which the doctor told her was a good sign. Apparently, it wasn't easy to start breathing again on your own and it took three days to wean him off the ventilator. He still didn't talk.

Once the ventilator was removed, Dr. Chesney unbound Nathan's wrists. "Good afternoon. I'm going to examine you." He slipped his palm into Nathan's. "Can you squeeze my hand?"

Nothing.

"Mr. Sullivan, I need you to squeeze my hand." His voice a little firmer.

Val sat on the edge of her chair, watching. Nathan's fingers curled.

That's the last thing she remembered. Apparently, she blacked out.

When she came to, she learned that she hadn't missed a thing. That was it. Fingers curling. For another week. Another week of Lydia knitting and Val reading the newspaper aloud to the shell of her husband. Only now the nurses seemed worried about Val, too. They kept encouraging her to eat, bringing her snacks from their private stashes.

Finally, one afternoon Nathan moved his hand toward his head. He let it drop halfway there. "Damn."

Val sprung to her feet, dropping the Sylvia

Browne book she'd been silently reading. "Nathan? You can talk!" Lydia rushed to his bedside.

Nathan blinked. "My head . . .."

Val burst into laughter. "I bet it hurts. You hit it pretty hard." She heard her breath exhaling. "Thank God, you're alright."

Nathan's slanted eyebrows made him look permanently surprised. He studied her. "Where . . .am . . . ?" He seemed to give up on finding the word. His gaze landed on Lydia. "Mom?"

The fifty-year-old woman with dark circles under her eyes leaned in and hugged him. "My baby." She started to sob.

A minute later Nathan's focus landed on his left hand. He touched the shiny gold band on his finger. "I'm . . . married?"

Val's heart hammered beneath her ribs. "Yes. We got married a few weeks ago. Remember?" She laughed nervously.

Her husband stayed fixated on his wedding ring. "No."

The room seemed to wobble. Val grasped the bedrail to steady herself. She would not faint again. But how could he not remember their wedding?

She made her way to a chair and sat down. After a few deep breaths, she pressed the "call" button.

As he entered the room, Dr. Chesney tugged on the stethoscope around his neck. "Hello, Mr. Sullivan." He listened to Val's and Lydia's summary of events before speaking. "It's normal for patients to have short-term memory lapses. He might also have trouble finding words and multitasking." He focused on Nathan while running him through a series of simple requests such as squeezing each hand and moving each foot. "Hopefully it will get better in time."

Val didn't get up. She hadn't eaten breakfast and still felt a little fuzzy. "How soon before he can come home?"

Dr. Chesney tucked his hands into the pockets of his lab coat. He looked at Nathan and then back at Val. "There can be physical repercussions such as headaches, weakness on one side, seizures, difficulty walking, and sometimes the loss of senses--vision, hearing, smell."

Why hadn't he answered her? She figured they'd probably keep Nathan for a few days for liability's sake, give him some prescription pain pills and discharge him.

The doctor continued looking at Nathan. "Therapy can help. But some things aren't so easy to fix." He gestured toward Val. "You should be aware of the emotional repercussions. Patients with injuries to the frontal lobe can be more irritable, depressed, angry."

Her dizziness passed. She rose so she could stroke Nathan's hair. "I don't think Nathan could possibly act like that. He's so even-tempered."

Lydia cleared her throat. "My Nathan was always mild-mannered."

Dr. Chesney looked at Lydia then turned his attention on Val. "Your husband is luckier than most of the patients I see, but you need to be prepared for these possibilities. The CAT scan does show damage has been done."

"You mean . . . brain damage?" Nathan asked, speaking slower than normal.

The doctor nodded. "No two head injuries are the same. But I want you and your family to be aware that this can have long-term ramifications."

"Will I be . . . able to . . . work?" Nathan asked.

Dr. Chesney asked what Nathan's job was. He paused after Nathan said he was the service manager at Rod's Garage. "It's hard to say. You'll have to be patient and see how it goes."

Val pushed her black bangs out of her eye. "When will he remember me?"

"Again, it's hard to say. We'll start speech and physical therapy right away. In time, he might be able to recall more."

Val squeezed Nathan's hand, feeling tears welling in her eyes. "So he can come home soon?"

Dr. Chesney seemed non-committal. "Hopefully he can transition to outpatient therapy after a few weeks. We'll have to wait and see."

CHAPTER ELEVEN

Joely's arms trembled as she struggled to maintain the downward dog pose in her first yoga class. She thought slow yoga would be easier than regular yoga, but apparently it entailed holding the poses for longer time periods. How was she ever going to survive sixty minutes of this?

"If you ever need a break, remember you can always return to child's pose," the instructor cooed.

Too bad Joely didn't remember what child's pose was.

The rail-thin yoga teacher, also in downward dog, looked around at the people with their butts in the air. "Now walk forward and stand." Her body moved as if she had liquid joints.

Following everyone else's lead, Joely rose and flattened her hands in front of her chest in prayer-like fashion. "Namaste." She had to admit she liked the soothing, plunking music and the calmness of the teacher's voice. Her mind kept struggling to focus on the here and now, however. She wondered if everybody was right about Jake. That he was the kind of guy who should marry an heiress whose only goal would be to birth him some perfect, blue-blooded babies and raise them in the Catholic Church. To be honest, Joely didn't have much to offer the man.

The next time the class moved into child's pose, she made a mental note. They curled up like an egg with their arms stretched out. It was amazingly comforting. If only they could stay here for a while.

But it didn't last long. Soon they spread their legs wide apart, one foot forward and one foot back. Their spines twisted, elbows on opposite knees and Joely fell over. Embarrassed, she glanced around, but no one seemed to be staring. She returned to the child's position and spent most of her time there. When class was finally over, she was surprised that she needed to wipe sweat off her face.

She rolled up her mat and put it by the instructor. "Thanks."

The woman whose hip bones jutted out beneath her black leotard, smiled. "You did well for your first time."

"Was it that obvious?"

"It's harder than it looks, isn't it?"

Joely nodded. "I'm trying to get in shape for my

wedding." She didn't want to whine to this stranger about her physical challenges. So far she'd tried and failed at running, aerobics, spinning and now this.

"Well, yoga should help you relax if nothing else. Planning a wedding and trying to make everyone happy can be very stressful, as I recall."

"Exactly." Was Jake happy that they weren't getting married in his church? She shook away the concern. "Does yoga burn a lot of calories?"

The woman touched her protruding collar bone. "Yoga isn't about trying to change our bodies. It's about embracing their untapped strength."

Joely watched as the other students cleared out of the room. They were all thin like the teacher. Hopefully yoga had something to do with that. She waved good-bye and the instructor said, "Namaste."

When she got home, she maintained an unusual sense of calm as she prepared dinner and Anna did her math homework at the kitchen table. In a stroke of genius, Joely placed the peas on one-fourth of the plate, the salmon fillet on one-fourth, applesauce and bread on the other half. Then she quizzed Anna on the fractions. For dessert, Joely got six Oreos out of the cupboard and asked Anna to divide them in half, then into thirds. Like most things, her daughter easily understood the concept.

Staring at the cookies, Joely started to salivate. She'd been starving herself for weeks. She deserved a cookie. Just one.

She shoved it into her mouth so fast she didn't have time to taste it. Then she reached for another. After Anna went to bed, Joely compulsively snuck a few more Oreos.

Sitting on the couch, feeling fat and guilty, she dialed Kate. "I'm weak. I've just undone my diet. I don't know why Jake wants to marry me."

"Hey, stop that. You're an awesome person, Joely. Maybe Jake isn't as superficial as he used to be. Maybe he sees that your personality is more important than your dress size."

"He said something like that to his mother." She studied her sapphire engagement ring. The blue stone not only represented loyalty, but could bring joy and peace to the wearer. She smiled at Jake's thoughtful choice. "Did I tell you Mrs. Mahoney wants us to get married in the Catholic Church?"

"Is that what you want?"

"Not really. But I'm starting to think that I should be willing to compromise a little. Jake is making all of the sacrifices in marrying me. With him I'm winning the grand prize and he's getting the booby prize."

"That's not true. You feel like he's getting the

short end of the stick because you're in love. I felt the same way when Mitch and I were engaged."

Joely paused, thinking things over. She didn't have strong feelings toward any one religion anyway. "I'm going to do it. I'll promise to raise our kids Catholic since that's important to Jake."

Kate let out some kind of disapproving grunt. "That's what I figured. You never could deny that man anything." Silence burned over the line. "What about Anna? Are you going to have her convert?"

Joely rubbed her sore shoulder. "I guess I'll have to."

"If you do this and your heart isn't in it, I'll lose respect for you. In fact, I don't know if I can be your matron of honor."

CHAPTER TWELVE

"Who are you again?" Nathan asked in the middle of breakfast.

Val's spoon of frosted shredded wheat froze in midair. Fear clutched at her heart.

He cracked a smile. "Just . . . kidding."

She pushed his shoulder playfully, spilling a bit of the milk from his spoon. "You're not getting rid of me that easily. You said your vows and I have plenty of witnesses."

Nathan was now home from the hospital. He'd gone from needing two people as support to walking on his own. When the speech therapist asked, "What does 'Don't count your chickens before they hatch' mean?" Nathan had said, "We're having omelets for dinner." He chuckled then gave the right answer. The doctor said he was impressed with Nathan's overall quick recovery and released him to outpatient therapy. His short-term memory, however, remained impaired.

Nathan continued eating his bran flakes. "I

remember you in high school. . . I thought you had such a friendly smile. . . but you dated football players." He shook his head. "I can't believe we're married. What kind of car was it that broke down? Something that started with an H?"

"A Hyundai." More than once she'd told him the story of how they'd reconnected last year during a thunderstorm. And how she'd had a bad cold and he'd given her a DVD of *Rear Window* he'd just bought to cheer her up. They'd enjoyed a spirited debate about which Hitchcock film was the best. He liked *Notorious* about an uptight American who falls for a party girl. She preferred *Rear Window* because it had been her grandmother's favorite.

He grinned at her. "Thank goodness for Hyundais."

Already done with his Lucky Charms, Chip drove one of his red Matchbox cars across the kitchen table, up Val's arm, across her back and down the other arm. "Mommy, look at me."

She glanced at her son and noticed his brown hair stuck up in the back. "Go check in the mirror and comb your hair."

"You do it, Mommy."

"Since when do you need me to help you brush your hair?"

He put his toy in his pants pocket and tugged on her wrist. "Mommy, come on. Help me."

She went with Chip to the bathroom and wetted down his flyaway hair. Then he asked her to go into his room and play with him. "Chip, we don't have time. You need to go outside and wait for the bus." He begged for her to at least pull some of his cars off the toy shelf. She checked her watch. "I'll get them down while you're at school and you can play with them later."

He stuck out his lower lip. "But I want you to play with me."

Nodding, she guided his shoulder toward the front door. "After school. If I have time."

"You always have time for Nathan, but not for me!" He shoved his arms into his windbreaker. He marched out the door and slammed it behind him.

She stood in the window, waving at him, but he did not look back. Finally, she went and sat next to Nathan. "Sorry about that. Looks like he's a little jealous. I'll have to make more of an effort to spend time with him."

"Sure." Nathan seemed to process that. "I think Dr. Chesney was . . . a little over the top, don't you? He said it would be hard for you. Said I'd have mood swings. Anger issues. I'm . . . good."

Val agreed. Nathan didn't seem much different to her. He talked a little slower and struggled to find the right word sometimes. But he'd been in a coma. He was doing great considering.

He glanced at the headline on the morning paper, but didn't unfold it like he usually did. He pushed it away. "I'm going to drive myself today."

"Are you sure?" Val asked. His mom had chauffeured him to his physical and speech therapy appointments yesterday. The rest of the time she'd hung around, hovering, just like in the hospital. Last night she seemed reluctant to leave. Probably because she was a lonely widow with two grown sons, who didn't visit often enough for her taste. Nathan only stopped by when Lydia needed her lawn mowed or something needed to be fixed around the house. His brother appeared less frequently, whenever he needed money.

Even though she'd like to drive Nathan to his appointments, Val had heard rumors that the hospital bills would be in the thousands of dollars. She needed to earn a paycheck after taking six weeks off.

Nathan stared at his orange juice. "I told Mom to go home. The doctor said I can drive. I want things . . . back."

Val's lips turned up a little. She wasn't sure what

that meant. Instead of scooping the bits of sugar floating in the milk at the bottom of her bowl, she stood up and dumped them into the sink. Time to figure out how to "get back."

###

Nathan lifted up the *Lansing State Journal* and looked under it. Nothing. He scanned the kitchen counter covered with dirty dishes. Apparently Val wasn't much for housekeeping. He started loading their three breakfast bowls into the dishwasher. Maybe if he cleaned up a bit, he'd find his car keys.

After scrubbing the pots and pans leftover from several nights' dinners, Nathan looked around the little kitchen. He smiled. He'd done something useful.

He noticed the rectangular numbers on the microwave. Shit! He was supposed to be at physical therapy right now. But he still hadn't found his car keys. He rushed into the bedroom and looked on the dresser where he kept his wallet. It seemed like he would put his keys there, too, but all he saw were bottles of Val's *Viva la Fleur* perfume and a framed photo of Chip at Chuck E. Cheese. He gritted his teeth.

He jerked open the dresser drawers, one after another, like a robber ransacking the place. When he reached the bottom, he saw them. The shiny jagged pieces of metal had fallen underneath the dresser. He grabbed them and headed for the door.

He jammed the keys into the ignition and pressed his foot on the gas. Stuck behind a car that didn't move when the light turned green, he pounded the steering wheel. Fiery anger threatened to explode like a volcano. "Let's go!"

Finally, the person talking on their cell phone accelerated.

He swerved around the jerk.

When he limped into the physical therapy building, it was twenty minutes past his appointment. He headed straight for the receptionist's window. "Sorry I'm late. I couldn't find my car keys."

The woman with the short red hair nodded and looked at her watch. "Hi, Nathan. I'll let her know you're here."

Nathan fidgeted with his wedding band. He wasn't used to wearing it yet. Several empty chairs lined the walls of the waiting room, but he couldn't sit down. This was the only thing he had to do all day and he couldn't manage to get himself here without his mom's help? How pathetic was he?

Just then the door opened and the familiar face of his physical therapist, Mia, smiled at him. "Nate, glad you could make it."

She was the only one who called him Nate, but he didn't bother to correct her. Instead he apologized again for being late.

Mia waved for him to follow her. "It happens to everyone. Don't worry about it. I'm so spacey, my boyfriend suggested I wear my keys around my neck like dog tags." They walked past some weight machines and an old man huffing and puffing as he lifted what looked like only twenty pounds.

They walked into a small room with a padded table against the wall. Nathan sat on it and waited for Mia's instructions. He noticed framed posters of skeletons and muscle groups hanging on the walls.

She told him to lie on his back and she used her hands to bend his right leg. Then his left.

He watched her work. She had dark brown hair and soft brown eyes. *Pretty like--what was that actress' name? The one that was in "My Cousin Vinnie"?* Mia reminded him of her. He'd always had a crush on her. Damn. How could he have forgotten her name?

Mia continued to move his limbs as if she were positioning a mannequin. Firm, yet gentle. She chatted easily about her day, her boyfriend, the litter of puppies her golden retriever just had. "You want one?"

He noticed that she'd stopped moving and her eyes seemed to implore him. "What?" he asked.

"Would you like a puppy?"

He laughed. "No thank you."

"You have a little boy, right? Every boy needs a dog."

Chip. He was so irresponsible, forgetting to brush his teeth, refusing to comb his hair, driving Val crazy. Maybe this was just what he needed.

Mia reached for Nathan's arm and raised it above his head. "I brought them with me today. After our session, you can have your pick of the litter."

Nathan slowly nodded. "I'll take a look." Their session went rather quickly since he'd been so late. Before he knew it, Mia gave him some handouts with exercises he should do at home. They walked to what must be the employees' break room. In the corner stood a white fridge and a water cooler. They walked past a round table and she opened the back door. Yelps immediately greeted them when they stepped out into the wind. Little blond puppies climbed on top of one another, poking their paws through the wires of a large cage.

Mia spoke in a singsong as she opened the latch on the top. "Hello, sweeties." The dogs tried to jump out, but couldn't quite manage. Nathan reached in and selected the most enthusiastic pup.

Mia stroked the dog's head. "Aren't they adorable? I wish I could keep them all."

"Yes." She didn't need to even give him a sales pitch. The pup licked Nathan's fingers as if he were covered in chocolate. He'd always wanted a dog. "How much do you want?"

"Oh, they're free. They aren't thoroughbreds because we don't know who the father is. Some dog in the neighborhood, I guess."

Nathan chuckled. "If I take one, do I still have to do my exercises at home this week?"

She smiled. "Of course. Plus walking the dog will be good for you. Help you regain your natural gait."

"So I can tell my wife the dog is part of my therapy?"

"Definitely. In fact, maybe that's what I'll tell all of my patients. I could be puppy-free by five o'clock." They both shared a laugh.

He petted the dog. His hand traveled from head to tail in the blink of an eye. So tiny. But so full of love and acceptance. He imagined coming home from a long day at the shop to find this dog waiting for him.

Mia's brown eyes sparkled. "What are you going to name him? It is a him, right?" She peeked at the dog's underbelly. "Yep. It's a boy."

"I don't know. How about Homer? Because he will always be there for me at home."

It would be nice to start making some memories instead of always trying to retrieve them.

Joely opened her apartment door and welcomed Jake inside. His musky cologne trailed him, ramping up her heartbeat.

He carried a stack of bridal magazines and spread them out on her coffee table. "Now if you tell anyone about this, I'll deny it." He held up a DVD. "I thought we'd watch 'Say Yes to the Dress' and search these magazines until we find you the gown of your dreams."

At the sound of Jake's voice, Anna left her bedroom and gave her father a hug. "Yea! Daddy's here!"

Joely's hand lightly touched her heart. It pleased her so much that Anna wanted this marriage as much as the bride and groom did. The three of them sat on the couch and each flipped through the glossy photos of models adorned in satin and lace. Anna kept announcing, "Oooh, I like this one. No, this one's better. When I grow up, this is going to be my wedding gown."

Toward the end of the show where the bride wanted to look sexy and her maid of honor wanted her to look demure, Jake's cell phone rang. He checked caller i.d. and made a face. "It's my mother." He answered it and gave her a bunch of one word answers.

Watching him, Joely tried to interpret their conversation, but couldn't. Jake stood and carried the phone down the hall for privacy. Joely and Anna dropped their jaws when they heard the gown someone had selected on TV cost $12,000.

"For one dress?" Anna asked, her eyes wide.

Joely shrugged. "Madness, isn't it?" She thought even one thousand dollars seemed expensive. It wasn't like the olden days when women would incorporate their wedding dresses into their everyday wardrobe. Of course, that was before white gowns came into fashion. Nowadays, a wedding gown was about conspicuous consumption, something Joely abhorred. Just like the country club reception that Mrs. Mahoney envisioned. Joely's shoulders tensed just thinking about it.

From the other room, Jake's voice grew louder. "I'm not going to discuss this with you any more. Good-bye, Mother." He quickly came into view, flipping his phone closed and clenching his jaw.

"What's wrong?" Joely asked.

He shook his head as if he didn't want to talk about it. When Joely persisted, he signaled toward Anna.

So, Joely told her to take a magazine into her bedroom and dog-ear the pages that she liked best.

Anna slouched. "Aww, Mom. Do I have to?"

"Yes." Joely handed her an especially thick

magazine and shooed her away. After the bedroom door clicked shut, Joely faced Jake. "What's going on?"

Heaving a sigh, Jake ran his hand through his dark blond hair. "Ever since we got engaged, my mother has been on a mission to talk me out of it."

Joely stiffened. "I knew she didn't like me, but she's still hassling you?" Her future mother-in-law's animosity mystified Joely. People always liked her. She had friends who were musicians and contractors, waitresses and accountants, working class and professionals. But for some reason, Mrs. Mahoney had been against Joely from the start. Maybe she was part of the reason why Jake broke up with Joely the first time around. "Is it because of our meeting with the priest?" Kate's threat to withdraw as matron-of-honor resonated in her head. A headache drilled into her skull. But making peace with Jake's family was important, too. Since Joely had been orphaned as a child, part of her had always hoped that her mother-in-law would fill a small bit of that void. "Because I just needed time to think about converting--"

"It's that. And yet it's not that. She wants me to marry someone from the same social circle." His hand made air quotes around the last two words as if he thought it was stupid.

She couldn't help that she wasn't a trust fund

baby, but she could still win Mrs. Mahoney over. "That cathedral was gorgeous. If you really want to get married there, I'd be willing to talk to the priest and do whatever he says."

Taking a seat next to her, he patted her hand. "That's sweet. But you don't know what you're agreeing to. Being Catholic isn't something you choose like a flavor of ice cream. I'm not even a good Catholic." Again with the air quotes.

"I never had much religious direction. It might be nice to have everything spelled out in black and white."

He shook his head. "It's not." He took a deep breath. "I don't care where we say our vows. All that matters to me is that we get married. Let's pick a date and stop worrying about my mom."

Heat sprang to her face. "A date? I don't know." She looked at her thunder thighs. She hadn't made much progress toward her weight loss goal. "How about in a year?"

He lowered his eyebrows. "A year? I can't wait that long." His arm reached around her shoulders and he planted a kiss on her lips.

"I don't want to wait that long, either. But I still need to find a dress and a location. Plus I'd like to drop a few pounds."

"Don't be ridiculous." He stroked her cheek with

his thumb and started singing Billy Joel's "Just the Way You Are."

She giggled. "Did I ever tell you that I was named after him?"

"Yep." Undeterred, he jumped to the chorus.

She covered his mouth with her hands so they could get back on track. "Thanks, but I hate how I look. I've declared war and I'm not giving up."

"Seriously, Joely. I love your curves. So let's talk about the venue. What do you envision when you close your eyes and think of our wedding?"

Instead of closing her eyes, she chewed on her thumbnail. "To be honest, since I don't have anyone to walk me down the aisle, I'm not excited about a traditional church wedding."

"So, maybe a destination wedding? Get married on a beach in Hawaii?"

"No. I don't want to ask my friends to spend a fortune on flights and hotels." Sometimes he forgot that not everyone had as much money as he had.

"In a garden here in the city?"

She shrugged. "I'll scout out some locations and see what's available. But an outdoor wedding depends on the weather. It could be wonderful or it could be a disaster."

Just like her past relationship with Jake.

CHAPTER THIRTEEN

"You've got to be kidding!" Val said that evening when Nathan told her that Homer belonged to them. She dropped her purse on the floor and left her coat on the sofa. She watched Chip holding a sock, trying to wrestle it away from the puppy's tiny teeth. Her son kept laughing and laughing, never getting bored.

Nathan gestured with his spatula. "Look how happy they are together." He opened the sliding glass door, going out to flip the burgers on the grill, still favoring his left leg a bit. A moment later, he lumbered back inside.

Val wagged her finger at him. "We can't have pets in this duplex. It's against the rules."

"Oh. I hadn't thought about that." Nathan scratched the side of his head. He'd told Val it itched as the hair grew back. "We'll move somewhere else. Some place with a big backyard."

Val nodded. "I'd like that. We can't agree on a house, though. Remember?"

For a moment Nathan looked clueless. "We've looked at a lot of houses?"

"Yes. You want something from the 1970s and I want a place with quality and character."

He re-read the recipe even though he'd never used one for burgers before. "We'll find something. Don't worry."

"Don't worry? Now that we have a dog, we have to find someplace fast."

"Perhaps we just needed something to push us into making a decision."

She sighed. "The last thing I need in my life is a push." She'd just found out she'd lost two clients since she'd been out of the office for so long. Kelly, the owner of the design firm, said she'd tried to explain the situation, but the clients wanted someone "right now." Plus since Nathan's accident, she hadn't been doing flash cards with Chip, like Mrs. Bean wanted.

Chip laughed and looked at Val. "Mom, come over here. You're going to love Homer. He already knows how to fetch. Watch!"

He threw the sock across the living room. Homer bounded over to it and started chewing on it. Then he carried it back to Chip. She hadn't seen her son so happy since--she didn't even know when. "Are you going to feed and water him every day?"

Chip nodded while still playing with the pup. Another toss and retrieval.

The dog was obviously smart. Maybe he would be quick to house train. Val watched in silence, putting her hand on her hip. "I guess we can keep him."

"Thank you, Mom!" Chip ran over, gave her a quick hug and returned to the puppy.

Pouring pop into a glass, Nathan smiled. "Yeah. Thanks, Mom."

"Ha, ha," she replied.

The phone rang and Val picked it up. It was their gruff neighbor with whom they shared a wall. "I keep hearing barking. Do you have a dog over there? Because if you do, I'm telling the landlord."

The next day, Val walked into the kitchen for her breakfast and noticed the ammonia scent in the air. Homer immediately came running as if to beg forgiveness.

"No way." She shook her head and went to the hall closet for the carpet cleaner spray. She hadn't needed it since Chip was a baby, when he spit up all the time.

Giving the dog the cold shoulder, she supervised Chip's morning routine--dress, complain while eating breakfast, brush teeth and head out for the bus. Except today he moved especially slowly because he kept stopping to pet the puppy. Focused on Chip, she ignored the rumbling in her own belly.

Finally, once he was gone, she opened the fridge. But it wasn't there. She went to the cabinet where she kept her extras. Empty. She was completely out of Dr Pepper. Nathan must've poured the last one without alerting her. Darn it! How would she ever make it through the day? She threw on her coat and said a curt good-bye to Nathan who still lay in bed.

She'd have to find a way to satisfy her craving elsewhere.

Nathan crossed his ankles on the coffee table in front of the TV. Still in the gray sweatpants and Rod's Garage T-shirt he'd worn to bed, he watched the morning news. His cell phone rang and he answered it, anxious for human interaction.

A female voice came over the line. "This is Tosh Physical Therapy. I'm afraid Mia is sick today and won't be able to make it in for your appointment."

Nathan slouched. "Will she be okay by tomorrow?"

"Hopefully. If not, I'll call you."

"Alright." He flipped the phone shut. Without physical therapy, he had no place to go today. He plopped back down on Val's striped couch--a bold design choice most people wouldn't be willing to try. That's one of the things he'd noticed about her. She wasn't like most women.

The news ended and talk shows began. He flipped through the channels searching for entertainment. Finally, he found "Die Hard" and put down the remote. John McCain was a real man. Despite walking on broken glass, getting beat-up and knowing he was outnumbered, he kept going. For the next hour or so, Nathan forgot about the time. Right when John McCain reached for the gun duct taped to his back, the screen turned black.

Nathan shook his head. "No! Come back." He picked up one of Val's green decorative pillows and threw it at the screen. That didn't help, of course. The cable had gone out. No, Val had a satellite dish.

He walked out on the tiny balcony without bothering to put on his coat. He craned his neck back to study the plastic semi-circle mounted on the roof. Nothing appeared to be blocking the receiver.

He returned inside to check the screen. Black.

He returned to the balcony and opened the storage area on the one side. Back behind Chip's old tricycle, Nathan found a ladder. Using his left hand, which was now stronger than his right, he pulled the ladder out. He opened the wooden frame and checked it for stability. In the past, he would've marched up those steps, but today he paused. If he fell, no one was around to find him. He looked up and counted the rungs. Twelve steps. His heart pounded. "Just do it, you big baby!"

Gripping the sides, he put his right foot on the first slat. The ladder settled under his weight. His foot faltered.

He stepped away from the ladder. Back inside, he checked the TV one more time. Still no picture. For once, Bruce Willis wouldn't save the day.

He returned to the balcony barely big enough for the open ladder. Forcing himself, he took one step. Deep breath. Another step. He kept looking up, growing closer to his goal. His hand clutching tighter to the wooden rails. Swallowing, he dared look down. Over the balcony railing, the ground looked distant and hard. The grass had long since died, snow melted, but no doubt the dirt was still solid. "Shit. Is it worth dying for TV?"

His racing heart said no. He glanced up. So close. If he didn't do this, who would? Left foot, then right. A strong wind kicked up and slammed the storage shed door. His body started to shake. "This is stupid."

He climbed back down, carefully, but quickly. Once on the concrete balcony, he dropped to his knees. Safe.

Homer scratched at the sliding glass door. Nathan abandoned the open ladder for the warmth of the duplex.

Ignoring the puppy, he checked the TV again. Disappointment filled his head. He peered behind the television at the spaghetti-like wires. Then he saw it. One of the cords had been chewed through. His fingernails dug into his palms. He shot Homer a stern look. The puppy practically kowtowed, looking remorseful.

Nathan noticed the pillow tossed on the floor and the wet spot where the dog had peed. "This place sucks." He kicked the pillow.

"Are you still mad?" a familiar male voice asked over the line.

Val hadn't expected Nathan to call her at work to apologize, but it pleased her. Cleaning dog pee certainly wasn't something she wanted to add to her morning routine. "I think 'stressed' is a better word."

"Well, you won't be in a minute. Because I bought us a house!"

"You what?" She stood up and squeezed the receiver in her hand. She pictured some ordinary, ranch house with shag carpeting. "Tell me you didn't sign anything."

"I made an offer. You're going to love it."

Val looked at her appointment schedule. She was booked up all afternoon. "I can't believe you did that without talking to me." She was starting to see a pattern. A very scary pattern.

"Don't you trust me?"

Val shook her head even though he couldn't see her. "Nathan, you need to call up the real estate agent and tell them you made a mistake. See if you can get out of it."

"No. I'll come by and pick you up. We can go see our new home together."

"I wish I could, but I'm very busy today."

"Too busy for me?"

She took a deep breath. "I'll talk to you later." As soon as she hung up, she went in search of Joely. She needed to vent. But Joely wasn't there and her office lights were out. Unfortunately, her boss, Kelly, was busy with a client.

Val fisted her hands. What had Nathan gotten them into?

By five o'clock, Val couldn't wait to leave the office. She waved goodbye to Kelly and didn't stay for their usual chitchat. She rushed out to the parking lot and was surprised to see Nathan standing next to her red Honda.

He tilted his head and gave her a pleading look. "Are you going to keep an open mind?"

She hoisted her purse strap a little higher on her shoulder. "It doesn't seem like you've given me much of a choice." She saw Chip and Homer in the grass on the far edge of the lot. Someone had wrapped a blue bandana she'd never seen before around the puppy's neck. "Chip, can I get a hug?" She reached out her arms and bent her knees.

He reluctantly walked toward her carrying the dog. Chip let her embrace him, but he kept both of his arms around the puppy. "Nathan took me to the pet store today and you should see all of the stuff we got for Homer."

She tried to hide her exasperation. "Let's get the dog in the car." She looked at Nathan. "I guess I'll follow you."

Nathan pulled the keys out of the front pocket of his jeans. "No. I want to see your reaction. Let's all go together."

She wondered if she'd be able to hide her disappointment. If he'd already signed papers, she didn't know what she'd do. Now that they had a dog, they couldn't stay at her place anymore, but that didn't mean she'd wanted him to pick something without consulting her first.

Nathan untied the bandana from around Homer's neck. Once it was loose, he faced her. "Come here."

"What are you doing?"

He held out the cotton square. "I'm going to blindfold you."

She laughed--his playfulness slowly luring her out of her funk. "This is silly. It doesn't make sense to leave my car here."

Chip scratched behind Homer's ears. "Come on, Mom. You never do anything fun."

The words of her youth echoed back to her. Her mom really hadn't been any fun. Making Val clean the kitchen every night, read the Bible an hour each day, and go to church twice a week. But Val had sworn she'd be a different kind of mother. "Oh, alright." She turned and allowed Nathan to secure the blindfold.

Just a slit of sunlight shined from below. Her arms reached in front of her, desperate to get her bearings. Nathan took her hand and guided her toward what must've been his Honda. The same model he'd convinced her to buy when her Hyundai wasn't worth salvaging.

She heard the door squeak open and felt Nathan's free hand on top of her head.

"Now sit," he said.

She complied, slowly as she searched to feel the seat. She recognized her son's laughter. "Yippee!" He clapped.

A few moments later their car moved down the

road. They'd taken a right turn out of the parking lot and eventually another right turn. In her mind she tried to visualize a map, but she quickly lost track of their location. All she could do was listen to the talk radio station. Today's topic included a new book about FDR, which apparently didn't reflect the former President in an entirely favorable light. The interviewer commented, "FDR would never be elected today simply because he was crippled. The American people still hold a bias toward a man who is permanently impaired."

Val shook her head. Unlike Nathan, she wasn't endlessly fascinated with politics. She wished she were in her car listening to her INXS greatest hits CD. The back-and-forth debating and bickering of radio hosts did nothing to ease her tension. She pictured the depressing 1970s ranch they'd last seen with the avocado refrigerator and the goldenrod stove. Nathan had terrible taste when it came to houses. "Are we almost there?"

"Be patient," Nathan's baritone voice answered. Homer started barking from the backseat.

She imagined Chip playing with the dog, getting it all wound up. A dog. Now they couldn't reschedule their honeymoon without getting a babysitter *and* making arrangements at a kennel. Her chest rose just before she let out a sigh.

Someone touched her knee. Presumably it was Nathan. "What's wrong?"

Oh, that sigh must've been too loud. "Nothing." First he gets a dog without talking to me and now he's put down money on a house. Maybe they could get out of it, though, considering he clearly wasn't himself. Dr. Chesney could write a note. "I don't like not seeing where we're going."

"Well, no worries." The car slowed and made a turn. "We're here."

"May I take off my blindfold now?" Her hands reached up.

"Wait," Nathan said. They drove down what she assumed was the driveway. The car came to a stop and Nathan turned off the ignition. "Now."

She pushed the blindfold up and off her head. The sunlight forced her to squint. She looked around and saw a two-car garage to her right and a two-story stucco house on her left. It didn't look that great.

"What do you think?" Nathan asked. Chip echoed his question.

She shrugged. "It's fine."

Nathan's forehead creased into three wavy lines. "You don't recognize it. This is the house. The one I thought you wanted." He unfolded a paper from his back pocket and held it toward her. It was the flyer from the open house and she'd drawn little hearts all around the margins.

Adrenaline pumped through her veins. Her chest filled with hope.

"I found this ad in your desk drawer and called the number." He gestured toward the two-story stucco wall in front of them. "This is the back side, which I guess isn't nearly as impressive as the front."

Her eyes scanned the plain façade and looked upward to see one wrought-iron balcony similar to the ironwork that graced the front. "Oh my God! Seriously?" She jerked open the car door so she could see it better. She stood and stared for a moment, then glanced at the yard. Off to the right she could barely see the covered patio that jutted off of that twenty-five foot living room. She made her way closer. Watering hoses, two grills and rusted patio furniture cluttered the space. It looked familiar.

She ran down the driveway to the front of the house, just to make sure. Yes! Her majestic hacienda with its rounded windows and carved front door stared back at her. Behind her, the fountain splashed. She noticed Nathan, Chip and Homer coming toward her.

Nathan's arms reached outward. "Well? What do you think of our new house?"

Her hands pushed against her heart, as if to calm

its rapid beating. "I love it!" She ran to Nathan and wrapped her arms around him. "You're the best!" He clutched her back, but did not pick her up and twirl her as he used to.

CHAPTER FOURTEEN

Unlocking the carved oak door to that 1920s Spanish hacienda opened a piece of Val's heart. Excitement crackled inside her like fireworks.

The first thing she did was run upstairs, the puppy nipping at her heels. She had to see what the bedrooms looked like. All six of them. How indulgent. The giant master bedroom held an antique four-poster bed sans canopy. Between two closets, the floor rose a step to create a nook with a floor-to-ceiling window.

She stepped onto the landing's worn, gray carpet to peer outside. Below her, a budding apple tree. Across from her, a view of her neighbor's Tudor style home.

Nathan entered the room. "How do you like it?"

"The architecture of this house is so unique. I could put a couple of chairs here for a reading area. After we replace the carpet, of course. Or maybe we can rip it up and refinish the hardwood floors underneath."

Downstairs she could hear Chip moving from room to room, opening and closing doors. "Cool," his young voice exclaimed.

She wondered what treasure had caught her son's eye. Unlike her, he usually preferred new things to old. New video games, new Matchbox cars, new friends.

Nathan came toward her, slightly limping. "Happy birthday, a little late or a little early depending on when it is."

How could he not remember? "My birthday is February fourteenth. You bought me a box of chocolates and wrote 'Happy Birthday' on my Valentine's card."

At the time she'd explained that her whole life, her friends had skipped her birthday celebration in order to go out with their boyfriends. The least he could do was try to make her feel special. Not try to slide by with a two-for-one deal.

He'd been contrite, but insisted that it was ridiculous to buy two separate cards. "A card is just a five dollar piece of paper that you end up throwing away after a few days," he'd said.

"Maybe if you wrote something personal on the inside, I'd save it." She'd gone home alone that night, refusing to give him the one thing every man wanted for Valentine's Day--or any other day for that matter. She'd expected him to try and make it up to her the next day with another gift, but no. He'd apologized and moved on. With the wedding fast approaching, she'd decided to let it go. Nathan was frugal and most of the time, she liked that about him.

Now she really forgave him. She twirled in a circle with her arms outstretched. "This is the best birthday gift ever!"

"Have you seen the other rooms?"

"Not all of them."

He took her hand and led her into the hall. Almost every room had not only a fireplace, as the real estate agent had promised, but also a mini balcony. There were so many bedrooms, Chip could pick one to sleep in and one for a playroom. The one in back with faded striped wallpaper would be perfect for her drafting table. That still left two bedrooms unspoken for.

She opened up a closet and caught a whiff of mustiness. The walls puffed out in little air bubbles. "The place needs some TLC."

Nathan grunted in agreement. "I can start fixing things around here until I'm ready to go back to work." He grinned, apparently glad to have projects to do.

"I'll be happy to help on the weekends. But I thought somebody else had made an offer on this place." After all, she'd called the real estate agent the Monday after their wedding.

He shrugged. "They must've backed out for some reason."

Homer, who had followed them from room to room, stuck his nose up in the air and froze. A moment later, he took off running down the hall at full speed, into the far bedroom and out of sight. Thunk! It sounded as if he'd run into the wall. Soon he came running toward them as if chasing an invisible cat. He practically tripped over his own paws until thunk! He bumped head-first into the wall.

Val looked at the bewildered puppy. "What are you doing, silly?"

Homer stood up and dashed down the hall again.

This time Val felt something brush against her arm. A touch that started off warm then turned frigid.

She jumped and looked over her shoulder to see who was there. No one.

# # #

Val didn't know where to start. She got a dust cloth and wiped the living room from top to bottom--the fireplace mantel, windowsills, end tables and the antique piano that the previous owners had left. Too bad none of them knew how to play it.

She'd never polished and obsessed over her own place like this. Sure, she'd wiped away dust and re-arranged vases in groupings of three for clients, but the sweat on her brow especially satisfied her because this house belonged to her. For once, she got to live in the home others couldn't help but admire. It would take some work to get it to that state, but she could easily see past the boxes stacked in the middle of the floor and the furniture that didn't seem logical. They had two mismatched couches--hers striped in pinks and reds and Nathan's in a boring brown.

She called to Nathan who was clanking the silverware as he unloaded boxes in the kitchen. "Let's get cleaned up and go buy new seating for the living room."

He carried his large grilling tongs into the room. "That sounds like fun."

She clapped her hands together--thrilled that for once, he didn't try to squash her spending spree. Up the stairs she bounded, to retrieve her shoes. She couldn't help noticing a stain on the landing carpet. "Why would anyone cover up hardwood floors with wall-to-wall carpet?"

"What?" he shouted from downstairs.

"Nothing." She spotted a fray near the baseboard. Without hesitation, she tugged on it. The carpet resisted. It needed to be cut. She searched through a couple of boxes in the back bedroom for an Exacto knife. Out the window she spotted Chip playing fetch with Homer. Her son finally had a backyard in which to play. She still wasn't pleased about the dog, but he seemed to make Chip happy, so she'd learn to live with it.

Once she found the knife, she returned to the hall. The blade sliced through the fibers inch by inch down the hall. Then she tugged, surprised at how heavy carpet could be. Her hand wiped more sweat from her brow and she rolled up the stained, worn-out carpet against one wall. The foam padding was a bit easier to wrangle and toss off to the side.

Nodding, she smiled at the oak floor planks. She'd remove the carpet in the bedrooms later. Before long, this place would look like a museum.

Nathan came up the stairs. "What happened here?"

"I thought I'd rip up the carpet and see what was underneath. Isn't it beautiful?"

He shook his head studying the faded, scratched wood. "Not exactly."

"Well, you have to imagine it polished. Maybe after we buy furniture, we can rent a floor sander." Even she could hear that she was talking too fast, tripping over her own words. But she couldn't help it. She wanted to fix every room at once.

Nathan pinched her behind, twisting it between his thumb and finger. "Race you to the shower."

"Ow!" She rubbed her sore skin. "That really hurt."

"Don't be such a baby." He moved past her into the bathroom.

Already the smarting faded beneath her palm. Maybe she had overreacted. More than anything, it had surprised her. Nathan had never been the kind of man to slap or pinch her butt.

Within seconds, she heard the pipes groan as Nathan turned on the bathwater. She and Nathan kept forgetting that this old house didn't have a shower, only a tub. Nathan's arm appeared out the doorframe holding his briefs. He waved them like he was doing the world's fastest strip tease.

She giggled and rushed after him.

CHAPTER FIFTEEN

After Nathan and Chip left for the hardware store the next morning, Val reached into her musty closet. She put on casual clothes--jeans and a tie-dye T-shirt--so she could work on the house. When she turned around, she noticed a light shining from one of the vacant bedrooms. Had Chip left it on? She could've sworn it was off a minute ago. She extinguished it and walked away. Homer ran past her into the empty room. Thud! She shook her head. He was chasing that invisible cat again.

The light behind her came on. Something seemed to lodge in her throat. She swallowed and returned to the back bedroom. She searched the four walls with its peeling, pinstriped wallpaper.

The delicate, sweet scent of baby powder tickled her nose. She inhaled deeply. This must have been a nursery at one time.

Sighing, she flipped off the light and went into the hall. A second later, she saw the silhouette of her shadow cast in front of her. Whipping around, she saw the room lit up again.

Her heart thumped in her throat. Was the house trying to communicate with her? She made her way back into the smallest of the six bedrooms.

A chill washed over her. She'd read about stuff like this happening when a spirit lingered with unfinished business. But what? "Who are you?" No answer.

Some papers stuck out of the abandoned bureau's top drawer. She went over and pulled at the wooden handles. Bills dated within the last five years and newspaper clippings in varying degrees of brown were shoved haphazardly in the drawer. She picked her way through them, searching for clues. Toward the bottom she suspected the papers belonged to the original owners and not the most recent ones. A sepia picture of an infant with its eyes closed caught her attention. Rose Elizabeth was scrawled in pencil at the bottom. Rose wore a long christening gown and her arms were straight by her sides. Something wasn't quite right. The baby wasn't sleeping.

Val looked up as if speaking to someone. "Did you lose a child?" The lights flickered. A sharp pain sliced through her heart. She knew the cruelty of a too-quick life and death cycle. "I'm sorry."

The room went dark. And stayed that way.
Spooked, she called her friend to see if she would come over.

Joely arrived twenty minutes later. First came the grand tour. Val loved listening to Joely behind her, oohing and aahing over the marble fireplace and carved pillars.

After they'd toured the entire first floor, Joely followed her up the stairs. "I can't believe you get to live here."

"I should probably ask you to pinch me, but I don't want to." Val laughed. She loved the opportunity to share her home with her friend.

She gestured toward the scratched floors and the carpet roll still resting in the hall. "Looks like you've been busy. How's Nathan feeling?"

"Pretty good."

They moved into the master bedroom with the four-poster bed. Joely walked to one of the arched windows and placed her hand on the pane. "There's so much light."

"That's because there are fifty windows in this house."

Joely gasped. "You're so lucky. Show me the other bedrooms."

They walked into the room with the flickering lights. Sweet talcum powder wafted into Val's nostrils.

"What's that scent?" Joely asked.

"You smell it, too?" Val grinned. She'd hoped

Joely would be sensitive to what this house had to say. She went to the bureau and pulled out the morbid photograph of the infant. "I think this was her room."

Joely lightly grasped the picture's yellowed corner. "Poor thing."

"This is the room I told you about. I think the woman who gave birth to this baby is still here."

"Why?"

"I'm not sure. Maybe she has some unfinished business."

"What do you know about her?" Joely asked.

Val went to the closet and pulled out the Chain of Title papers the real estate agent had given them. "All I have is this, but it's pretty legalistic. Lot #42 on this parcel of land with an apple orchard on it was sold to so-in-so in 1920."

Joely took it and flipped through the many pages. "Wow."

"The only interesting part is that the original owners almost divorced. That must've been quite a scandal back in the twenties."

"Does it say why?"

Val shook her head. "Not really. It just tells how they would've divided up their property--furniture,
 glassware, a typewriter--all sort of everyday items. But for some reason, the couple reconciled."

The lights extinguished. Val and Joely looked up at the chandelier then stared at each other with their mouths ajar.

Val moved to the switch and flipped it down, then back on. "See what I mean?"

Joely put the papers on the bureau. "Maybe the woman wants to communicate with you."

"How?"

"I don't know." Joely returned to the closet doors and gazed at the papers and trash. "If you sort through this stuff, you might find something helpful. Does this house have a safe? If these people were rich, it seems like they'd have a safe hidden somewhere."

The lights flickered as if in agreement. "We have the original blueprints. Do you think the safe might be shown on them?"

Val went into one of the other bedroom closets and pulled out the rolled blueprints. She flattened them out on the desk and searched. Finally, they noticed one of the drawn walls seemed unusually thick. They ran to the master bedroom and lifted a landscape painting off the wall. There it was. Just like in the movies.

Val gasped. "We don't know the combination, though." After twirling the dial several times and trying the latch, she gave up. She called a locksmith and even though Nathan would probably balk, she paid extra for him to come right away.

Once open, the mostly empty safe smelled of pipe smoke. It contained no money or jewels. Just a diary. Val shivered with excitement.

As she lifted the dusty leather binding, a photograph slipped out. It was a black and white portrait of a woman in a wedding gown sitting on a staircase. Val's staircase.

She looked at Joely, her heart beating with excitement. "I think I know what she's trying to tell us. You should get married here, in this house."

Joely's expression was hard to read. "That doesn't make sense. Why would the spirit care about me?"

Val shrugged and glanced at the photo again. "Maybe I'm wrong. But I still think it's a good idea. You want something small and intimate. We could hold the ceremony in the living room."

Joely's brown eyes opened wide. "Are you serious?"

She nodded.

Ever so slowly a smile spread across Joely's lips. "That would be wonderful."

CHAPTER SIXTEEN

Joely couldn't wait. From her car she called Jake, but he wasn't home. She tracked him down at his office and when he was as excited as she was, she dialed her sister. "Kate, good news!"

"You've decided to break up with Jake?"

Joely rolled her eyes. "I didn't have to. He said he's a lapsed Catholic for a reason. He doesn't want to get married in the church after all."

"What about your future mother-in-law?"

Joely looked out the car window at the historical neighborhood--grand homes surrounded by mature trees. She'd like to live in a small cottage herself, but this place would be perfect to host a wedding. "I don't think Mrs. Mahoney will ever like me, so I need to stop worrying about it. The question is, do I need to still worry about you as my matron of honor?"

"I'll be there. I couldn't skip my only sister's wedding. You have to understand, I was sleep-deprived and super cranky when we spoke." She paused. "I just don't want you to do whatever Jake tells you to. I want you to do what's best for you and Anna."

A cleansing breath. "That's exactly what I intend to do."

# # #

Saturday morning Val woke up next to Nathan in the antique four-poster bed that came with their new master bedroom. She looked over and saw that he was awake. He seemed happier now that he had something productive to do in-between therapy appointments. They'd hired movers to do all of the heavy lifting, but Nathan had done the tedious, time-consuming work of wrapping the dishes in newspaper and sorting through Val's old *House Beautiful* magazines. "Thanks for packing up all of my stuff."

"No problem. I'm glad to do it."

She leaned over and kissed him on the lips. The kiss lingered.

He looked toward the door. "Is Chip awake?"

She kissed down his neck to his chest. "He's probably watching cartoons downstairs." Pausing, she made her way to the door and confirmed that it was locked. She tiptoed back to her husband and started all over again.

When their lovemaking was over, she laid back and tried to catch her breath. The honeymoon may have been postponed, but the delay only seemed to increase their passion.

"You're amazing," he said.

Nodding, she felt her eyes moisten. "I'm so happy you're okay." To think she'd almost lost him scared her to death.

He stroked her hair. "You can't get rid of me that easily."

A chill skimmed her naked body. She pulled the cotton sheets up to her chest, but it didn't seem to help. "Do you feel a draft?"

"No. I'm pretty hot actually."

She saw the sweat glistening on his forehead. "I feel like a window's open or something." She wrapped her arms around herself and rubbed her hands against her goose bumps.

"It's an old house. Probably the windows need to be sealed."

Go out for breakfast. The thought entered her mind like a whisper. "Hey, let's go get some donuts."

"I don't know."

"Whatever. I just thought it'd be nice." *Go!* She searched the room for something, she wasn't sure what. Was the spirit speaking to her? "Did you hear that?"

Nathan propped himself up on his elbow and looked at her. "Hear what?"

Embarrassed, she shook her head. "Never mind." *Get out!* Val's heart raced. The spirit sounded angry. "I really want donuts right now."

Her husband and son obliged her. While the three of them sat at the nearby bakery, it started to rain. On the way home, she quizzed Chip on this week's spelling words. He refused to try and when he did, it seemed like he was purposely messing up.

Once home, Val told Chip to get the book he was supposed to read for school. She went into her bedroom to change her damp socks. She couldn't believe what she saw in the middle of her bed.

CHAPTER SEVENTEEN

The ceiling had fallen in. Literally. Hunks of plaster filled the center of their bed.

Val looked up to see the jagged hole in the ceiling. "Nathan!" She didn't know how to fix things. Her duplex might have been ho-hum, but it was new enough that nothing major had ever gone wrong.

Nathan came into their bedroom. "Shit."

"Good thing we went out to breakfast. Otherwise, we would've been hit." She wondered about that voice she'd heard. She'd thought it was a mean spirit that wanted them out, but now she thought it might be a protective spirit. Her eyes scanned the room, but she didn't feel it nearby.

"I'll get the phone book and see if anyone can come and re-plaster the ceiling today."

"Is that going to fix it, though? I wonder how old the roof is. Did the building inspector say anything about it needing a new roof?"

Nathan shook his head. "I don't remember."

Val stared at him. "How can you not remember something major like the place needing a new roof?"

He scowled. "I told you I don't remember!" On his way out of the room, he slammed his fist against the doorframe.

She jumped as bits of gray powder fell from the ceiling. Her heart rate quickened. She stared at the now empty doorway. Where did that come from? Nathan had never lost his temper in front of her.

She heard Chip bounding up the stairs before he came into her room. "What's--" He didn't finish his question because he froze when he saw the mess on the bed.

Out of instinct, she walked over and hugged her son. "No big deal. You have to expect that some things will wear out when you have an older home. Nathan's calling someone to fix it, though."

Chip walked closer and picked up a piece of plaster. "Cool!"

She laughed in spite of herself. Kids sure have a different way of looking at the world. "Let's go inspect the rest of the house for signs of water damage."

Their walk revealed cracks and bubbles in several different locations. When they were finished, they made their way downstairs. Nathan informed her that no one even answered their phone.

She shook her head. "It is the weekend. Can you call on Monday?"

Nathan closed the yellow pages with a thump. "Will do."

Monday evening Val entered the house through the back door. Ironic that she loved the carved wood of the front door, but never used it since their garage sat behind the house. The rear door brought her to the basement stairs, where the servants used to stay, and to the large kitchen with outdated appliances. She admired the black and white checkerboard floor which didn't really fit with the rest of the house. It reminded her of her grandmother's.

On childhood visits, she and her grandmother would sit at the kitchen table drinking Dr Pepper out of glass bottles, her grandmother's calico cat rubbing against her legs. Sometimes they'd take their pop into the living room and watch an Alfred Hitchcock movie on TV. Her own mother didn't allow her to consume pop or anything with sugar. Sugar was the devil, apparently. Sugar and TV and boys and art. . . .

Val shook away the memories and continued through the house. Once in the hallway, she spied Nathan sitting on the floor with one knee propped up and a butter knife in his hand.

He looked at her and grinned. "Look what I found today. Underneath all of the dirt on these tiles are little designs."

The foyer's tile had a jagged "before" and "after" line. Before, large and small brown squares formed a diagonal pattern. Now, curlicues and uniquely Mexican designs accented the small, orange squares. She crouched down to inspect what had been revealed beneath the layers of grime. "Wow! What made you think to do this?"

Shrugging, he scraped a little more with his butter knife. "I don't know. I just had a feeling."

She knew what he meant. "Do you believe in. . . ." Ghosts? She bit her tongue. Her own mother had laughed when she'd revealed her belief. Laughed, and taken her to see the minister for some one-on-one preaching. Since then she didn't like to share.

"What?" he asked. "Do I believe in what?"

"Never mind." Her fingertips grazed a tile that looked like an Aztec god. "See? This is what's so great about a house like this. Unexpected discoveries." She stood and started to go put away her coat when she turned back. "Did you call someone to fix the ceiling?"

Nathan paused from his scraping. "No. I forgot."

She looked at her watch. Six-thirty. No one would be around now. "How could you forget?"

"I started cleaning these tiles early this morning. Then the delivery guys came with our new furniture. I wasn't sure what you wanted done with the old couches, so I paid the guys extra to move them into the basement. Since then I've been working here all day." He gestured toward the floor.

She was anxious to see the cranberry couch and love seat they'd bought off of the display floor, but she didn't like the idea of sleeping on them. "I can see that. But the roof caving in is kind of a priority here. If you weren't going to do it, I could've called from work. I didn't, though, because I thought you were going to."

His grasp on the handle of the knife tightened. "Hey, I said I was sorry."

"No you didn't."

His eyebrows lowered and his jaw flinched. "Are you going to turn into a nag now that we're married?"

"I'm not nagging. I just need to know if I can count on you to do what you say."

"Screw you!" He hurled the knife upward. The blade bounced off the stucco wall and struck Val between her breasts.

"Ow!" Pressing her chest, she darted into the kitchen. Her pulse pounded in her ears. She grabbed her car keys and headed for the back door.

But Chip was home. She couldn't leave him.

Her hand rubbed the spot where she'd been hit. She dropped her keys. Bracing herself against the countertop, she watched her arm tremble. She struggled to catch her breath. As if she were drowning.

What the hell just happened? Was this the beginning? Would she someday regret not packing her bags and walking out at this minute?

She shook her head. No, this was crazy. This wasn't like Nathan. It was the head injury. The doctor said it could mess with Nathan's emotions.

Breathe. Just breathe.

A presence filled the doorframe. She looked up to see Nathan standing there. Fear spiked another adrenaline release. But she did not flee. Didn't do anything, but wait.

The floor creaked as he took a step toward her. His expression had changed. He looked remorseful, his eyebrows back in their slanted, two sides of a mountain position. It made him appear so innocent.

His Adam's apple bobbed as he reached out his palms, pleading. "I'm sorry, Val. I don't know why I did that."

She crossed her arms. "Don't *ever* throw anything again. You hear me? If you do, I. . . ." The words barricaded her throat.

His face turned red. "I won't. I promise." Closer he came. He reached his arms around her stiff body and hugged her. Within seconds, he collapsed into tears. "Sorry. . . I'm sorry. I love you so much. . . I'm sorry."

Her shoulders relaxed. In the eight months they'd been dating, she'd never seen him cry. *He must really feel bad.* He hadn't tried to hit her with the knife. It ricocheted.

Nevertheless, she wouldn't hug him back.

CHAPTER EIGHTEEN

Nathan stood beneath the contractor's ladder, shielding his eyes from the sun. Thank God it had stopped raining, but in the spring, the weather could change as quickly as a woman's mood. Like Val's, for instance. He couldn't stand the way she had glared at him this morning. She'd even recoiled when he tried to kiss her good-bye.

"I really need to get this fixed ASAP," he shouted up to the guy on the roof.

The man in faded blue jeans and a thick Carhartt jacket climbed down the ladder. He adjusted his sunglasses nervously. "You're not gonna like what I have to say."

Nathan braced himself. "What's the damage?"

"You have some serious problems." The man pointed toward locations that needed repairs. "Basically, the whole roof is ancient and needs to be replaced."

"Oh, man." Nathan shoved his hands in his pockets. The wind was vicious. "How much?"

"Here's the thing. Those shingles are called barrel tiles. They're handmade in Mexico. The men actually mold them over their thigh so they're bigger on one end and slide together."

Nathan groaned. He didn't like the sound of this. "Can you order them?"

"Sure. But you need to be prepared that it's gonna cost ya."

"How much?"

The contractor paused. What was this--a game show? Nathan didn't need the suspense.

"Thirty or forty grand."

Nathan choked on his own saliva. "Shit." Why did he feel as if he'd just been raped?

"It's not just the tiles. Some of your copper gutters have been stolen. The ones you have left need a lining in them to restore their integrity."

He shook his head. "My wife wants this done yesterday, you know what I mean?"

The guy nodded as if he understood about trying to keep a woman happy. "If you've got the money, I can order the tiles."

Nathan looked away from the man. He watched Homer digging in the sprouting grass as if he'd found buried treasure. "You order the tiles and I'll get you the money." Even though he didn't know how.

# # #

"I think maybe. . . you were right about Nathan." Val put down her ham sandwich and stared out the conference room window at the city skyline. She shook her head. "I rushed into marrying him."

Joely plunged her spoon into her non-fat Greek yogurt. "Don't tell me that. I don't want to be right."

"I can't believe I'm saying this either." She twisted the bottom of three studs in her ear. "He's not who I thought he was."

"Well, he hit his head pretty hard." Joely kept eating.

"But he doesn't even kiss like he used to." Fond memories of the peck on each cheek before their lips met warmed her insides. Now he went straight for her mouth like a teenaged boy. Not that she didn't like his new sexual intensity, but last night's anger flare freaked her out. Her pulse quickened. She touched the tender spot between her breasts where she'd been struck. A hidden bruise.

Her friend didn't offer any advice. In fact, she tilted her head and looked a little judgmental.

Val ran her hands through her hair. "You don't understand." After all, she didn't take marriage lightly. She'd chosen a man who would be the voice of reason to her sometimes impulsive choices. He was supposed to be the yang to her yin, not someone who lost control. "It's not just little things. He has a temper."

At this, Joely's eyelids stretched wider. "Did he hurt you?"

"No." She shook her head. "Well. . ." Even though she had started down this road, she realized she didn't want to tell Joely about the butter knife. She smoothed her hair again. "Last night we got in a fight. He had this look in his eye as if he wanted to come after me."

Finishing her yogurt, Joely wiped her lip just below her mole. "I don't know what to say." She paused. "Have you talked to his doctor?" She unwrapped a diet snack bar and bit into it.

"Not really. He recommended we get counseling once Nathan came home, but I didn't think we'd need it." She'd been so naïve to think things would return to the way they were before. Clearly, it would take some time for Nathan to recover both physically and emotionally.

Joely finished chewing and swallowed. "The only reason I didn't want you to marry him was because he was so dull."

"He's not dull anymore, that's for sure. The old Nathan would never have got a puppy without checking with me." And he never would've thrown a knife.

"He wouldn't have bought that house, either. It's like a Spanish castle."

"Or a drug lord's. Apparently, that's what the last

owners were mixed up in. That's why I felt they didn't love the place like they should. The neighbors told us one night there was a drive-by shooting, which left bullet holes in the stucco."

"Didn't you notice them when you looked at the house?"

"They're hidden behind some bushes in the front yard."

Joely seemed to process that for a minute. "Do you still feel that spirit in the house?"

Val nodded. "It told me to get out of bed the morning the ceiling caved in."

"That is so cool. I wish my place had a spirit." Joely took another bite of her snack bar.

A smile curved Val's lips. "It is cool, isn't it?" She loved her house, despite its leaky roof and worn out carpet. Her mind maintained a list of items that needed to be renovated, which grew faster than she could check them off. But she could envision the finished product. It would be spectacular.

Maybe she just needed to be as patient with Nathan as she was with the house.

# # #

Joely signed Anna in at the gym's child watch center. Her daughter gazed up at her. "Do I have to go here again?"

"I thought you liked it. You can color pictures or play with the other kids." In fact, the child watch center had been the deciding factor in signing the gym's year-long contract. The ladies who ran the place obviously adored children and some had taught preschool. Last time Anna had been here, the workers had led the kids on an Easter egg hunt. Anna had been thrilled with the little chocolates that had been hidden inside the plastic eggs.

Anna's blue eyes pleaded with her. "But we come here all the time. I just want to go home."

Mommy guilt flooded her veins. Was she being selfish dragging Anna to the gym several days a week? God knew Joely's body was growing weary. She had to pre-dose herself with pain pills before each workout. But now that they had a location, she and Jake would settle on a wedding date soon. She was running out of time in her battle of the bulge.

Joely gave her daughter a hug and promised she wouldn't be gone long. Anna made her way over to a little boy who was playing with a toy rocket and started telling him about Sally Ride. Joely's shoulders relaxed as she went back into the hall.

She passed by the scale, but made herself stop. It seemed as though she should be seeing some progress by now. Steeling herself, she stepped up on the scale. The number was hard to get used to, but it was half a pound lighter than last week. Hooray!

With almost a bounce in her step, she headed for the yoga class. Rather than slow flow yoga, she'd decided to try hot yoga. Maybe sweat away some pounds. She walked in the sauna-like room and unrolled a yoga mat. Around her, other students sat cross-legged and quiet. She followed their lead, but it hurt her knees. She straightened her legs in front of her.

"Excuse me," a female voice whispered.

Joely turned to see a woman about her age with chubby thighs sitting pretzel-style next to her. "Hi." Perspiration formed on Joely's face and she fanned herself with her hand.

The full-figured woman's ponytail bounced as she spoke. "I think I saw you in my zumba class."

Joely's cheeks flared. Another class that she'd had to quit before it was officially over. "Maybe. I liked the music, but I couldn't keep up."

The thirty-something woman nodded. "It's pretty intense."

"Exactly. All of that jumping is hard on the knees."

"If you liked the Latin music, you should try aqua zumba. It's much lower impact, but you'd be surprised what a workout it can be."

Joely smiled at the woman's suggestion. "Thanks. Maybe I'll check it out." Knowing all the while that she wouldn't. Not only couldn't she swim, but she hated to think what she'd look like in a swimsuit these days.

They stopped talking when the instructor entered the room and turned on the Middle Eastern music. The bony teacher wasted no time putting them in awkward poses with legs going one way and arms the other.

Oh my God, this room is hot! Joely swallowed and wiped her forehead. She thought about her conversation with Val. How could Val already regret marrying Nathan? Because he was a little moody? He'd suffered a head injury. If her good friend could feel that way about him, it seemed that Jake might turn against Joely sometime, too. After all, she'd be the first to admit that she could be quick tempered when she was in pain.

The class moved into downward dog. At least Nathan would probably get better with time, whereas she could only get worse.

Black spots. She blinked. She closed her eyes and tried to shake them away. Her stomach growled. Maybe she should've eaten a snack before class. The room started to spin.

Next thing she knew, her body was splayed on the mat and everyone was staring at her. The anorexic teacher held her hand. "Are you all right? You passed out."

CHAPTER NINETEEN

"Has anyone ever told you that you look like Marisa Tomei?" Nathan asked his physical therapist. The brown-eyed actress's name finally connected from one side of his brain to the other.

"Who's that?"

Boy, did he feel old. "She's an actress. Real pretty." Oops. Did he just say that?

Pink spread from her cheeks up to her ears. "You think so? If they ever make a movie of my life, I guess I'll request her." Mia worked her thumbs into his right shoulder.

He'd never had a massage, but suspected it felt something like this. "I want Bruce Willis to play me."

"You need someone younger."

He was glad he knew he never blushed. "Aren't you the smooth talker?" She giggled and it pleased him.

"Let me think." She put her finger on her chin. "Leonardo di Caprio maybe."

"I'm the king of the mountain," he tried quoting

Titanic.

"I think he says he's the king of the world."

"Oh." Embarrassment burned inside him. "I hate how my memory does that to me."

She continued pressing her thumbs into his shoulder. "No biggie. Everyone forgets things. You're too hard on yourself."

He nodded and thought more about the movie. If he were Leonardo, Mia could pose topless for him while he sketched her. Guilt surged through his veins. Why would he even think such a thing?

He shook away the image. Something about her gentle yet purposeful touch, her kind words. . .she'd become his daily confidant and coach.

An awkward silence lingered between them.

Finally, she cleared her throat. "How do you think your recovery is going?"

"I plan on returning to work soon." He swallowed. "I have to admit, I'm nervous."

"Why?"

"I don't want the guys to feel sorry for me. I still speak a little slower than I used to."

Her brown curls jostled as she shook her head. "I don't even notice it anymore."

He sighed. "But you didn't know me before."

"That's true. You've made a lot of progress in a short amount of time, though. Both here and in your speech."

"Thanks. I'm anxious to get back to work. That house Val wanted is such a money pit. As soon as I get one thing fixed, something else falls apart."

"That's right. You're married. I forgot."

Excitement zinged through his body. Such a thrill to think she considered him available. Then crushing guilt. What was this thing going on between him and Mia? Was it normal to develop crushes even though you were married? Was this all in his head or did Mia feel it too?

He concentrated on Mia's working hands. She was always professional. But something about being cared for by another woman and chatting about his day created this odd connection. He'd never seen a female doctor or dentist or even had his hair cut by anyone but his barber. Before PT, the only women he'd ever touched were girlfriends or one-night stands.

She tied a long green band on the doorknob. "Let's see if you're ready for the next level."

See? All business. She wasn't interested in him.

He stood and pulled the stretchy band with his right hand down to his side then back up again. Just like he practiced at home every morning and night.

"Good. Nice form."

He smiled. What a pain in the ass it was to have to work muscles that used to function perfectly fine on their own. It wasn't like lifting weights, where the end result was visible. This was trying to get back to normal. "Val doesn't realize how hard this is."

Mia untied the green ribbon and affixed a yellow one to the knob. "Head injuries really take their toll on families."

He rolled his eyes. "I'm the one stuck doing physical therapy and speech therapy. I'm fixing up the house and doing everything I can to make her life easier." Sure, he'd lost his temper once or twice, but he'd had good reason. His life had crashed and burned. He'd been screwed royally. Val had nothing to complain about. "She has a job she enjoys, a son who loves her and the house that she wanted."

A noncommittal "hmm" resonated from behind Mia's lips. Her full, moist lips.

# # #

Val walked into the empty house at six o'clock in the evening. "Hello? Nathan? Chip?" Nathan's car wasn't in the garage and she had no idea where they were.

She tossed her purse on the couch and wondered if she should cook dinner or if they'd all go out like they often did when she was tired. Up the stairs she went to change into jeans and her Lansing Community College shirt. The light was on again in the former nursery. She walked in and looked around, seeing only the desk and a bureau left by the previous owners. Of course, no one was there. Off went the switch. She shook her head, wishing she knew what the spirit was trying to communicate. So far the diary hadn't revealed anything.

Outside she heard the rumble of a car and it didn't sound like Nathan's. She peered out the back window to see Nathan and Chip riding in an antique automobile. It looked a lot like the one Nathan's brother had loaned them on their wedding day. Except this one was red.

She ran down the stairs to find out what was going on. Chip burst through the back door just as she'd made her way to the kitchen. He ran and gave her a hug. "Hi, Mom! Nathan and I had the best day!"

Nathan entered the house. "Want to go to dinner in our new car?"

"What? You bought a car?" Thoughts of unpaid medical bills and roof repairs bombarded her. "How much did it cost? And what happened to your other car?"

Nathan shrugged. "I traded it for this. Not exactly an even trade--I still owe them the balance. Isn't she a beauty? I always wanted a roadster."

"How much more do you owe? That thing doesn't even have seat belts, does it?" She noticed that Chip's face looked a little sunburned. "How long have you two been driving around anyway?"

Chip's eyes suddenly studied the checkerboard floor.

Nathan opened the refrigerator and pulled out two cans of Dr Pepper--one for him and one for her. "I took Chip out of school early."

"You what?" She set the pop on the counter without opening it.

Chip slunk out of the room.

Nathan, however, acted as if he'd done nothing wrong. He popped the silver tab on top and gulped his drink. "I told Chip if he got one-hundred percent on his spelling test, that I'd take him to the antique car show. Aren't you happy? He aced his test."

"I am happy, but you should've asked me first."

"I thought you wanted me to be more involved. Be his dad."

Val pushed on her temples. A piercing headache came out of nowhere. "I do. But I'm still his mother. You can't take him out of school--let alone risk his life--without checking with me."

Nathan's eyebrows lowered. He squeezed the can until brown liquid spilled over the sides and dripped onto the floor. "You're not the boss, you know. I can do whatever I want without checking with you first." He tossed the crumpled can into the sink causing a metallic rattle. He marched out the back door.

She watched through the window as he started the car and jerked it through a three-point turn. He sped down the driveway out toward the road.

One hand pressed against her forehead and the other against her pounding chest. Her legs gave way and she slumped down to sit on the tile floor.

CHAPTER TWENTY

After Joely drank some orange juice provided by the health club, the room stopped spinning. She hated the way everyone from yoga class stared at her. "I'm all right. I've been on this diet and with the heat. . . I feel better now." She started to stand.

The yoga teacher wouldn't let go of her arm. "Can I call someone to drive you home?"

Joely waved her hand. "No, no. I'm fine. The juice helped." Who would they call anyway? Val was busy with her own problems. Jake was working nonstop. And Kate lived two hours away.

It took at least fifteen more minutes to convince the instructor to let Joely go home by herself. Joely checked Anna out of the child watch center and left the gym, her face burning.

When they were near Joely's car, Anna tugged on her pants in a rather unlady-like way. "Look, Mom. I'm so fat."

Joely froze. She crouched down to look Anna in

the eyes. "You are not fat. You are a perfectly healthy little girl."

Anna's big, blue eyes stared at her mother. "But my pants don't fit. You always say that you're too fat when your clothes don't fit."

Hearing how harsh her own words sounded, Joely stopped breathing. Her hand stroked Anna's blond hair. "It's different when you're my age. I'm not still growing like you are." Even so, the word "fat" from now on, would be banned from her vocabulary. "It's important to eat healthy and take care of your body, sweetie. That's what I'm trying to do. But you simply need some new clothes. There's nothing wrong with you."

"I don't think there's anything wrong with you, either." Anna's lips turned downward, as if Joely's self-hatred reflected on her.

She reached out and gave her daughter a bear hug. "Thank you, sweetie. I appreciate that." If only it were true.

# # #

Val was desperate.

They'd cleaned the debris off the bed and placed a mop bucket under the leak. They'd been sleeping on the couches, but it was a hassle because all of their clothes were still in the master bedroom. It kind of felt like they were living out of a suitcase. The house was falling apart and she couldn't count on her husband to fix it. Instead he'd bought an antique car they probably couldn't afford.

She now sat on the edge of a leather couch twisting her wedding band. Joely had insinuated that Val wasn't trying hard enough to make her marriage work. So, here she was.

The marriage therapist appeared to be in her twenties, not old enough to be giving anyone advice. Her name was Barbara. She was fair-skinned and blond. "Nathan, tell me what first attracted you to Val."

He leaned back and crossed his ankle across his opposite knee. "First of all, I don't know why we're even here. And second of all, call me Nate."

Val's head turned to study him. "Since when do you prefer to be called Nate?"

Rolling his eyes, he released an annoyed sigh. "I want to be called Nate now. You don't have to make a federal case out of everything."

Barbara leaned forward, appearing to be interested in this exchange. "Okay, Nate. Tell me more about that. How Val makes everything a federal case."

Val stiffened. "Wait a minute. I do not make everything into a federal case."

Reaching out her palm to quiet Val, Barbara focused on Nathan. "Let's hear what Nate has to say."

Shifting in her seat, Val wished she'd put more effort into choosing a counselor. She'd asked Nathan to call Dr. Chesney for a referral, but of course, he hadn't. In a huff, she'd flipped open the yellow pages and called the first name listed under "Marriage and Family." Apparently that had been a mistake. Barbara was asking what made them fall in love in the first place as if they were a bored, old married couple. Val had no trouble remembering why they'd fallen in love. Her problem was those reasons no longer existed.

Nathan pulled a pack of gum out of his jean pocket, unwrapped a piece and stuck it in his mouth. "She comes home from work and starts in on me. 'Did you call the repairman?' 'Did you fix the shelf in the breakfast nook?' It's like she's my mother all of a sudden."

Val shook her head. "That's not true. Since he's home all day while I'm at work, I figure he can make phone calls and run errands."

"You're going to be in trouble when I go back to work next week then. You won't have anyone to boss around anymore." His breath smelled cinnamon-y.

Barbara interjected. "How do you feel about returning to work, Nate?"

"Awesome. Can't wait." He chomped on his gum without closing his mouth. Even that was out of character for him.

The therapist cocked her head in Val's direction. "How about you?"

"I'm happy for him. I think he's miserable being stuck at home. Plus we could use the money."

"You see?" Nathan swung his crossed leg down so his boot stomped the floor. "I bought her her dream house. And now all she can talk about is how poor we are."

"I love the house," Val said. "I'm glad you bought it. I'm starting to worry about finances is all." She'd never thought she'd be the one to fret. Nathan was supposed to be the responsible one.

The room grew silent. Barbara took this opportunity to scribble something in her notes. "Let's go back to the beginning. Val, tell me about when you fell in love with Nate."

Val hesitated to tell the story again. She hated that she was the only one who remembered it. "My car broke down and no one would stop to help. Of course, I'd forgotten my cell phone at home. I had a terrible cold and the only reason I went out was to go to the pharmacy. Anyway, I sat there for thirty minutes, waiting for the rain to let up when finally someone stopped. It was Nathan." She savored the moment. Her heart beat a little quicker. "He looked under the hood, declared the engine a disaster and called a tow truck. After a few minutes I recognized him from high school. He waited with me inside my car and we talked like we were old friends."

She glanced at Nathan. Did the memory warm him the way it did her? His expression remained neutral. Apparently not.

She continued. "When the truck arrived, he insisted on paying for the tow, then offered to drive me home. Once we got there, he handed me a *Rear Window* DVD. Told me to curl up on the couch and enjoy. I couldn't believe he liked Hitchcock, too."

Nathan smiled to himself. "*Rear Window*. That one's pretty good."

Shaking her head, Val glanced at Nathan. All he remembered was the movie. Although he looked the same, he wasn't the man she'd fallen in love with at all. Where was her knight in shining armor?

Barbara wrote on her notepad. "An old acquaintance turned into something more."

Val took a breath. "Here's the thing. I'm not big into this counseling stuff." Her mom had tried to make her talk to a counselor when she'd been a rebellious teen. "What I know is that my life is nonstop stress. My husband is injured, my son is failing the first grade, and our house is crumbling around us."

Nathan sat up straighter. "Chip's failing?"

Val nodded, trying to keep her emotions in check.

"If he doesn't start trying, the teacher is going to hold him back."

"Why didn't you tell me?"

"You were at the meeting with Mrs. Bean. I asked you to start reading to him at night. But that was right before. . . ."

He shook his head. "I don't remember. So you need me to read to him and that will help him pass?"

"Read to him and see if you can get him to read. The problem is he won't even try."

A glance at Barbara revealed a compassionate expression on her face. As if this was the kind of embarrassing, personal stuff she was hoping for. Val dug her fingernails into her palm. She would not give this chick the satisfaction.

CHAPTER TWENTY-ONE

While finishing up an oil change his fifth day back at work, Nathan overheard a man yelling at Rod. Irate customers were part of the car repair business, but Rod's Garage tended to have fewer than other shops.

Nathan wiped his greasy hands on a rag and reached for the vacuum. He'd noticed Cheerios and crumbs all over the backseat of this minivan. Women cared more about the pristine seat cushions and smudge-free windows than about what he did under the hood. But he took just as good care there, too, using the right oil when they said they didn't have a preference.

Rod's Garage was short-handed this week with three guys out sick, so Nathan had been performing all sorts of jobs he didn't usually do any more. The familiarity of it, though, brought him comfort.

In the middle of vacuuming, he heard someone

call his name. He flicked off the power button and looked over at Rod. The dissatisfied customer was still there, his face red and twisted. "This is a bait and switch!"

Rod signaled for Nathan to come near.

Nathan approached the man who was about his height--a little less than six feet tall--with a bit of a paunch pushing out his white shirt and tie. Nathan checked to make sure his own hand was relatively clean before he offered it to the man. "Hi there. I'm Nate."

The forty-ish man refused to shake. "You! You're the one who quoted me this price and now that the repairs are done, it's twice the estimate. What kind of crap are you trying to pull?"

Rod raised his eyebrows in Nathan's direction. "I told him we run an honest shop. That we respect our customers and want them to be satisfied."

Nathan nodded. "Let me see the paperwork." He took the lined form from the customer and recognized his own sloppy handwriting. Even worse than before the accident. He checked the numbers and the part prices seemed correct. He shook his head. "This looks right to me."

The man shifted his weight. "Well, then that's what I'm willing to pay."

Glancing at Rod, Nathan could see his boss wasn't

pleased. Despite that, Rod cleared out the computer and re-rung the car repair to match the estimate, losing a few hundred dollars in the process. Rod scribbled something on the original bill and thanked the man for his business.

Still a little miffed, the customer nodded tersely and left.

"Finish up what you're working on. Then I want to speak to you in my office," Rod said. After a quick wrap-up on the van, Nathan walked into the adjoining building. Rod sat behind a desk piled with papers and family photos. He handed Nathan a copy of the bill. "Take another look at your estimate. Don't you see what you forgot?"

Sweat formed in his armpits. Obviously, he'd made some sort of mistake. His eyes searched the page, desperate for his mind to work. "I don't."

Rod leaned back in his chair, crossing his ankles on top of his desk. "You forgot to add in the labor. You only calculated the cost of parts."

Nathan hit his forehead with the heel of his hand. "I can't believe it."

"Is it possible you've forgotten to add labor costs to every estimate you've given in the past week?"

Nathan shook his head. Surely not. That would cost Rod thousands. "I don't think so."

"I checked and you did."

"Shit."

Rod steepled his fingers. "I'm glad you're feeling better, but I'm not sure you're ready to come back to work yet."

Nathan's neck throbbed with blood. He was a failure. "No, Rod. I can do this. I'm sorry I messed up, but give me another chance."

"What if you forget to put back a distributor cap or tighten the lug nuts on a tire?" His boss shook his head. "Take some more time. Go home, Nathan."

He tried to stop his hands from trembling as he stood. Rod offered to shake. Nathan squeezed as tight as he could, hoping to convey strength, competence. He walked out without saying good-bye to the guys in the garage.

Driving away in his sports car, he knew one thing for sure. He did not want to go home. He headed toward downtown and let the wind pound in his ears. The thrill of driving his dream car helped only slightly to deaden the fear in his chest. The fear that he wasn't good enough. If a man couldn't work, he was worthless. What could he provide Val if not a steady paycheck?

Who knew how much time had passed before he found his way to his old hangout. He parked his car on the street so he could keep an eye on it through the front window. Even as he made the paces toward the door, he questioned whether he should go in. But he'd had a shitty day and he deserved this. He went in and took a seat at the bar.

"Nathan, my man. Haven't seen you in a while." Danny, the sixty-year-old owner with a gray crew cut, set a cocktail napkin down in front of Nathan. "The usual?"

Nathan shook his head. "Whatever's on tap." No need to hit the heavy stuff. He'd just mellow out a bit with a beer. He glanced to his right to check on his MG. He owned a red sports car. He'd married a beautiful woman. On the outside it must look like he had it all. His eyes settled on his own downtrodden reflection in the mirror behind the bar. As soon as Danny served him, he tossed back the glass without tasting its contents.

When he finished that mug, he ordered another. He studied the other customers in the room through the long mirror. In the booth behind him, a couple of businessmen joked and laughed a little too loudly. Probably in town for a convention of some sort at the nearby hotel. Worried that a co-worker might notice that they overindulged, they'd chosen this place rather than the hotel bar. Nathan understood, even though he'd never made it to their level of success. He knew about keeping secrets. Val had no idea how out-of-control he'd been after high school.

He sized up the other customers scattered throughout the room. Mostly men. The rest working class, like him. Although in the back corner, he saw the delicate wrist of a woman. He couldn't quite make out her face, though. She was drinking alone.

Gulping the last of the foam, he raised his finger to request another. His head felt a little lighter, but he didn't feel any better. Danny had tried to make chitchat, but Nathan had cut him off. He didn't want to discuss how he'd stopped drinking and supposedly pulled himself together. Shame snaked its way around his gut.

He watched in the mirror as Danny went over to the woman in the corner, probably to see if she wanted another. Danny might be old, but he couldn't help but fawn all over the pretty ladies. He'd retired from the marines and had spent many years bedding women. Married a few, too, if Nathan remembered correctly. Maybe three or four exes. Nathan shook his head. One was enough.

Lean forward, Nathan willed the woman in the corner. *Let me see your face.*

Sure enough, she did. Nathan nearly dropped his mug when he saw her. It was Mia, his physical therapist. *No. It couldn't be.* He stared as she spoke with Danny, smiled a little. When Danny walked away, she seemed to catch Nathan watching her. He averted his eyes.

Danny mixed peach schnapps and orange juice in a glass nearby. Nathan forced himself not to watch as the bartender carried the drink to Mia's table.

A moment later, Danny came back and leaned near Nathan's face. "I can't believe this. That pretty young thing said she knows you. She shot me down and then asked if I'd send you over."

Nathan's focus darted from Danny's weathered face to Mia's smiling reflection in the mirror. He stood and was surprised what a lightweight he'd become. A few beers and he felt a little tipsy. Forcing himself to stand straight, he made his way over to her table. "Hi. What are you doing here?"

She flitted her tiny hand at him in a wave. "Getting drunk. Isn't that what you're supposed to do when you get your heart broken?"

He offered her a short, conciliatory chuckle. "I guess that's kind of why I'm here, too."

Nathan and Mia spent the rest of the day swapping stories, but he let Mia do most of the talking. She hadn't shared much personal information during his sessions, he now realized. It turned out that she had a serious boyfriend and suspected he was about to propose. Imagine her surprise when she received a sentimental text message that he'd intended for his other girlfriend.

In his twenties, Nathan had played the "nice guy." Women cried on his shoulder when their bad boy lovers treated them like shit. Women hugged him and said he was a good friend. And sometimes they crossed the line from friendship to something more.

Mia ordered another fruity drink and somehow managed to get blitzed off of it. When it was gone, she looked at him with those big, brown eyes. "Want to do something stupid?" A little smile tugged at one corner of her mouth.

He chugged the last of his beer. "Hell, yeah."

# # #

Val strangled the telephone receiver in her hand. "My husband and I need to do some house repairs and we would like a home equity loan." She'd nearly choked when she saw the written estimate for the roof shoved in the kitchen junk drawer. When she asked Nathan if he had enough money in savings, he said he'd put most of it down on the house.

"Is your mortgage with us?" An uptight, I-went-to-Harvard, male voice came over the line. She wondered if she'd been transferred out-of-state. There weren't too many Ivy Leaguers who chose to live in the Midwest, after all.

"Yes. We just purchased it."

"What's the account number?"

She tapped her pen against the desk. "I don't know the account number." She told him her address and finally, he managed to pull up her information.

He hummed while he looked over the numbers. "I'm afraid you don't have enough equity in your house against which to borrow."

"What?"

"Like you said, you recently purchased your home. You haven't lived there long enough to have built up sufficient equity. I'm sorry."

"My husband said he put a bunch of money down."

"Well, the way we calculate it, you still don't qualify." His voice was devoid of emotion. This was just business as far as he was concerned.

"But our roof is leaking. What are we supposed to do?"

"See if you can work out a payment plan with the roofing company."

"Seriously? Your ads say you care about your customers, but obviously you don't." She pushed the disconnect button, missing the days when you could slam down a phone. Forty-thousand dollars. Where else but a bank could you get that kind of money? An idea popped into her head, but she extinguished it just as quickly.

# # #

In his wildest dreams, Nathan hadn't imagined that he and Mia would end up here. They'd stumbled out of the bar into the blinding sun. The dimly-lit bar had deceived him into thinking it was night. He'd pulled out his car keys, anxious to show off his recent purchase.

But Mia had insisted they were both too far gone to get behind the wheel. "Let's just walk and see where we end up."

They'd linked arms and helped each other down the cracked sidewalk. This alcohol-induced camaraderie warmed him with its familiarity. She giggled when he almost tripped on a ledge of uneven concrete and he loved it. Cars whizzed by them and before he knew it, she pulled him into a shop with a neon sign that said "Tattoos."

This almost sobered him and he stood a little straighter. The place smelled sweet like pot. "You want to get a tattoo? Have you ever had one before?"

She faced him, still laughing. "Yes and no. How about you?"

He shook his head. The image of a butterfly inked in pinks and purples near a jutting hip bone formed in his mind's eye. "My wife has one, though." He watched Mia's face for a reaction. It went blank for a moment and then the happy-go-lucky smile returned. What did that mean?

She walked closer to the wall to study samples that were posted there. "Then she'll understand if you get one. Probably think it's sexy. Now. . .what do I want?"

Val might think it was cool if he got a tattoo. She might be pissed that he basically got fired, though. He pushed against his forehead. Too much negativity. He didn't want to think about Val right now. He squinted at a photograph of a Porsche logo.

Mia leaned over the tiny counter next to a cash register. Behind it, a man with tattoos around his eyes, down his neck and on both arms, looked at her without amusement. She started flipping through a portfolio of previous customers' tattoos and Nathan looked over her shoulder. Flags, skulls, Chinese symbols, crosses, mermaids. Eventually, she pointed at two different images, claiming she couldn't make up her mind. The circus freak said it would cost her double, if she couldn't choose.

She wobbled as she turned her attention toward Nathan. "Which one do you like?"

"It matters where you're going to put it." Nathan raised his eyebrows twice, trying to be flirtatious. Somehow when he drank, he turned into a Casanova, a guy women wanted to sleep with, but nothing more. For a long while, he'd been satisfied with that. In fact, all of the guys at the shop had envied him and egged him on. When he'd actually made it to work, that was. Rod, a recovering alcoholic, had been more than patient with him. Not that Nathan was an alcoholic. He simply stopped cold turkey one day when he decided he needed to grow up.

"Any suggestions?" She seemed to flirt right back.

His mind went crazy, thinking about her exposed hip or butt or breast. He thought a woman's hidden tattoo, visible only to her lover was the biggest turn-on. Instead of risking sounding like a pervert, he shrugged. "It's up to you."

"Maybe you should go first. I'm afraid it might hurt."

The man behind the counter let out a short, guttural laugh. "If you want a manicure, you're in the wrong place, lady."

This was Nathan's chance to prove himself. Today he needed to feel like a man more than ever. "Alright. I'm ready."

CHAPTER TWENTY-TWO

When her cell phone rang a little while later, Val didn't want to pick it up. She was still angry at the bank. Angry at Nathan for not taking care of this for her. And even angry at herself. Why? Because she'd pushed for this house, never even asking about the building inspector's report. She didn't want to think about dollars and cents; she just wanted to live in that historical property. But a six-bedroom fixer-upper was apparently too much for them.

She answered the phone that rested on her desk at work. "Hello?"

"Mom?" Chip's young, unsure voice came over the line. "No one's home to let me in. The bus dropped me off and the door's locked."

She rose to her feet. "Are you sure? Nathan should be there. Ring the doorbell."

"I did, Mom. A bunch of times. Please come home. It's cold out here."

Clear as day, she could picture her seven-year-old son in his navy jacket, the wind whipping against his exposed ears, threatening to turn his sniffles into another ear infection. He'd had a million of them when he was a baby and now that he was older, he often had sinus infections. Either way, his illnesses dragged on for weeks, requiring an expensive trip to the pediatrician for antibiotics.

She grabbed her purse and coat off of the back of her office chair. "I'll be there as soon as I can. Go onto the screened back porch and sit in the corner. That will help block the wind."

"Hurry, Mom. I'm scared."

She cursed Nathan under her breath. On her frantic drive home, she realized what had gone wrong. Nathan was back at work, so Chip was supposed to stay for after-school care. He must've forgotten.

Fifteen minutes later, she sped into their driveway. Chip was sitting on the tile floor of the back porch, squeezing his knees into his chest. He shivered. She ran over to him and wrapped her arms around his lean body. He was going to be tall and thin like his dad, she figured.

"Come inside, Chipmunk. I'll make you some hot cocoa."

# # #

Nathan pulled his car into the driveway and tried to compose himself. What had started out as a miserable day had morphed into the most fun he'd had in a long time. So why did he feel bad? Just because he thought Mia was pretty? Well, he wasn't blind. And he hadn't done anything wrong.

He pulled up his sleeve to see his scorpion tattoo. Pretty cool. The guys down at the shop would be impressed. Most of them had at least one tattoo. They liked to razz him about being a square. Darkness clouded his thoughts. He shoved away the image of the shop.

Lowering his sleeve, he climbed out of the car and walked into the house. "Hi, honey. I'm home." He smiled, thinking he sounded like somebody in a 1950s TV show.

A few minutes later, Val came down the stairs with a sour expression. "The bank won't give us a loan. It's a good thing you're back to work. How's it going by the way?"

"Not so. . ." He looked into her imploring blue eyes fringed with thick lashes. God, she was beautiful. He didn't deserve her. "It's okay. A little rough, trying to remember everything. But it's coming back to me."

She sighed. "I'm glad." She opened the refrigerator. "Any chance Rod would give you a loan?"

He stumbled and caught himself on the countertop.

She straightened her back and looked over her shoulder. "Are you alright?"

He nodded. Could she smell the alcohol on his

breath? Just in case. . . "Had a beer after work with the guys to celebrate. That's all."

She closed the fridge. "Oh."

No anger. No yelling. That's what his ex would've done. He'd better leave the room before Val changed her mind. He mumbled something about checking his e-mail and headed for the hallway.

Her voice echoed its way to him. "Don't forget to ask Rod."

# # #

First thing the next morning Val charged into Kelly's office. Full steam ahead, as always. "Can I talk to you?"

Kelly looked up from her desk which was scattered with furniture catalogs and sketch pads. "Sure." Today she wore a suit the color of lime sherbet with a patterned silk scarf around her neck. Her boss, who almost always dressed in pastels, stood and gestured for Val to sit at her little round table.

Outside the window, Val noticed fog obscured her view of the city. "I was wondering if you could loan me some money."

Kelly closed the office door. She sat next to Val and crossed her legs. "What for?"

Maybe between her boss and Nathan's boss,

they'd get enough cash to stay afloat. Assuming Nathan wouldn't buy any more antique cars. "Our house needs a new roof and the bank won't give us a loan."

"You have those barrel roof tiles, don't you?"

Val nodded. "No one around here makes them."

Kelly fiddled with her hand-made beaded earrings. She made jewelry when it was her ex-husband's weekend with their twelve-year-old son. "I'm afraid I can't help you."

The air was sucked from her lungs. "What?"

Kelly looked away and removed her scarf. She rubbed the back of her neck. "This economy is killing us. People aren't spending money on extras and they see hiring an interior designer as a luxury."

Pushing her too-long bangs behind her ear, Val thought about the clients she'd lost while Nathan was in the hospital. No other new clients had come along since then, either. "I'm sorry to hear that. How serious is it?"

Again Kelly hesitated. "If we don't get some more business soon, I might have to declare bankruptcy."

Val gasped. "I had no idea it was that bad. What can I do?"

"We need more commercial clients. They provide a steadier source of revenue than residential work."

"That's a good idea. I'll call some of my former clients and see if they know anyone who needs to have work done."

Kelly's lips pursed together. She didn't look like she had faith in Val's strategy. "I'd appreciate that." She sighed and placed her hand on top of Val's. "I'm afraid I just don't have the money to help you and Nathan. I would if I could."

"I know you would." Val rose and reached around to give Kelly a hug. "I'd better start making some calls."

# # #

Joely walked into Anna's room and interrupted the game. Jake's fingers hovered over a rook as he turned toward her.

Joely put her hands on her hips. "I hate to say this, but it's Anna's bed time."

"Mommy, I almost have Daddy in checkmate." Anna's big blue eyes shined up at her.

"No, you don't," Jake said. He tousled her blond hair.

Anna pulled away from Jake and giggled. "Can't we play 'til the end, Mommy?"

"The end might not come until sunrise." Joely shook her head. "Give your daddy a hug and get your pj's on."

Jake reached his arms out and squeezed his little girl. This was one of those moments that would define their daughter's life. A bedtime routine that included two doting parents.

Sentiment flooded Joely. Her eyes brimmed with tears and she looked up at the ceiling in an attempt to stop them. Above her was the entire solar system painted in glow-in-the-dark paints. It was one of her favorite works because she'd done it especially for Anna. After years of painting Winnie the Pooh and Neverland scenes in other people's children's rooms, Joely had created a one-of-a-kind space for her own child. Okay, these thoughts weren't helping her regain her composure. She turned toward the door. "Tell me when you're ready and I'll tuck you in."

About twenty minutes later, Anna's room went dark except for the stars and planets above her bed. Anna quietly sang "Somewhere over the Rainbow" to her stuffed animals. Jake and Joely curled up together on the living room couch, her head on his chest.

Joely wrung her hands, trying to work up her nerve. "Jake?"

He stroked her long, curly hair. "Yes."

"Remember how you said whenever you see a family in the park, you wish you were them?" It had been part of his proposal.

He nodded, his chin gently bumping her crown.

"I was wondering how many children you saw."

"What?"

"How many children were in those families?"

He paused, thinking. "Usually two. That's kind of the American tradition, isn't it?"

"I suppose so." She swallowed. "Do you want another baby? A boy to carry on the Mahoney name?"

"Sure. Deep down I think every man wants a son." He touched her hair some more. "What about you?"

"I always dreamed of a girl and a boy. But. . . ."

"You have lupus." Heavy silence settled around them. "Can you have more kids?"

She chewed on her lower lip. "It's possible. I would need to go off my meds, though. They aren't good for a fetus."

"Is that what you did when you had Anna?"

She nodded. Her eyes landed on a baby picture of Anna lying on her back on a yellow quilt. Beneath her tiny body, patchwork pieces formed little rays of sun.

Joely could remember rocking Anna to sleep in the crook of her arm, she could remember bathing Anna's soft belly in the bathroom sink, she could remember Anna's smile the first time she'd tasted birthday cake. Babies gave life meaning. "I'd love for us to have another child."

He leaned down and kissed her head. "That's great news. I wasn't sure you could have any more."

Maybe she shouldn't get his hopes up. After all, Anna's birth had been a miracle. "I'll have to check with my doctor."

"Sure." He cleared his throat a few minutes later. "Things are still busy at work and I won't be able to come over for a while. In fact I'm heading back to the office tonight."

Her teeth dug into her raw lip. He was pulling away. She was glad he couldn't see her face. The tears had welled up again and this time she couldn't stop them.

# # #

Frogs leaped inside Nathan's gut. He ran his fingers through his hair, checking his reflection in the glass, before opening the door to the physical therapy clinic. He greeted the red haired receptionist and took a seat. His knee bounced in anticipation.

He loved his wife, but he definitely looked forward to seeing Mia.

After what felt like the longest wait, Nathan was called back. Alone in the small exam room, he cracked his knuckles. Energy charged his body. When Mia's silhouette entered the doorway, he broke into a sly grin. "Hi."

"Hi," she said. She closed the door behind her. She usually only did that when she tied the exercise bands onto the handle.

His leapfrogs went wild, hopping ecstatically.

"How are you?" she asked. She seemed coy. Did she feel the electricity between them, too?

"Good. How's your tattoo? I mean. . . does it still

hurt?"

She shrugged. She pulled the neck of her blouse to the side, revealing the little heart inked below her collarbone. She'd taken his advice on where to place it.

He couldn't help but read something into that. "Have you shown it to anybody?"

"No." Her cheeks bloomed pink. "No one to show it to."

He seemed to remember her saying something about her boyfriend cheating on her. "Your boyfriend was an asshole. You'll find someone better." Someone like me. I'd like to kiss your tiny heart tattoo and unbutton your blouse and. . . .

"Hey, let's keep our little drunken party quiet, okay? You're my patient and I could get in trouble for. . . ." For once, Mia was the one left searching for a word.

He rushed in to help her. "No problem. It might look bad even though we didn't do anything wrong."

Her shoulders seemed to relax at this. "Yes." She took a deep breath and slipped seamlessly into professional mode. "Lie on your side. Let's see how you're doing."

They made small talk throughout the visit, but his mind kept wandering. Did she feel it, too? Did she yearn to lock the door behind her and take advantage of him? God, he hoped so. That would be so hot.

# # #

Val read a few pages of the diary she'd found every night after dinner, searching for the secrets of the house. Wondering what the female spirit had to say. So far Val had learned that the original owner had been the president of a bank and had built this house as a wedding gift to his wife, Helen. She was from New Mexico and longed to return to its mild winters. In hopes of curing her homesickness, this house was built in the hacienda style she was used to.

Val's fingertips traced over the cursive words on the page. "It must break your heart to see your home neglected for so long."

The light turned off then back on. Val nodded. She heard Nathan and Chip talking downstairs about Ford Mustangs. It didn't sound as if Chip were reading, though, like Nathan said they would be. More like two guys having a lively discussion about something they both enjoyed.

The telephone rang. Since the boys were busy, she answered the upstairs extension. "Hello?"

"This is Mrs. Bean, Chip's teacher." The woman's voice rose at the end as if she were asking a question.

"Yes, this is his mom." Her heart sped up, even though she knew Chip was doing better in school. Teachers always made her nervous.

"I'm afraid we need to have another conference."

Val leaned against the hallway. She didn't have time to trot over to that school again. Tomorrow she had a meeting with a potential client and she couldn't cancel. "Why? Isn't Chip doing better?"

"I thought so, but it turns out Chip has been cheating. A student told me today that she saw Chip copying off of someone's paper during the spelling test."

Val's hand formed a fist and she pressed it against her forehead. "How do you know that student isn't making this up?"

Mrs. Bean cleared her throat, exerting her authority. "This student is very reliable. Besides, Chip's classroom work other than the spelling tests hasn't improved. He still won't read aloud when called upon."

"Well, what do you want me to do?"

"I thought you could come in and we could discuss it."

"No, I don't think so. Just punish him or whatever you normally do in a situation like this." The threat of Chip failing the first grade pierced her mind. Instant headache. "My husband has been working with Chip every night on his reading." Ever since the counseling session, she would come home to the two of them sitting in the living room reading *Car and Driver* magazines. Not exactly what Mrs. Bean hoped Chip would read, but who cared? It was great to hear Chip actually trying to sound out words. "He must be getting better. Maybe he's too shy to read in front of the other students."

"That's not how I see it. Chip is very outgoing most of the time. I'm afraid I will definitely recommend that he repeat the first grade."

Val chewed on her lower lip. "Mrs. Bean, I have to go." She hung up the phone, wondering if she had been too rude. Should she have thanked the woman for calling her son a cheater? She shook her head and listened to Nathan telling Chip about the glory days of auto manufacturing in Detroit. The Paris of the Midwest.

She stomped down the stairs. "Chip is supposed to be reading--not goofing around!" She hated the shrillness in her voice. She hated who she was becoming.

#

The sounds of terra cotta tiles tossed off the roof and shattering as they landed in the dumpster woke Nathan again. Ironically, Val claimed she took pleasure in the noises that came with her house's improvements. To him, the racket pounded in his head ominously. He'd gone through his savings and maxed out most of their credit cards to pay for the tiles required to maintain the integrity of the house, as Val explained. But she assumed he'd been given a loan by Rod. And he wasn't about to correct her.

On the way to physical therapy, he heard the foreman call out to him. Nathan considered climbing into his car, pretending he hadn't heard. Instead, he paused and waited for the middle-aged man in an unzipped windbreaker, a red plaid shirt and jeans, to approach.

"Is there a problem?" Nathan asked.

The foreman stuck his hands in his coat pockets to warm them. "Well, it looks like we need to order some more tiles. I'm afraid we underestimated the number needed. That's going to increase the cost a bit, I'm afraid."

Nathan shoved his hands in his pockets, fumbling for his keys. "How much?"

"I'm not sure. Maybe a thousand dollars more."

Shrugging, Nathan searched for his car key on his jingling key ring. "Do it. Do it fast. They're predicting rain next week."

The man nodded. "Just wanted to check with you first. You know, the balance is due before we finish."

Nathan opened his car door and waved to the man. "I'm well aware." Without waiting for the roofer to step back, Nathan started the car and threw it into reverse. He had to get away before his head exploded.

CHAPTER TWENTY-THREE

Mia walked in and saw Nate sitting on the cushioned exam table in the corner room. She clutched his chart to her chest and silently berated herself. She shouldn't have gotten a tattoo with a patient. Alcohol always made her do dumb things.

She forced herself to offer a pleasant, but restrained, "Hi. How are you?"

After he answered "just fine", he spotted a silver harmonica on the chair in the corner. "What's this?"

"Oh, a kid came in with his grandpa today and he must've forgotten it."

Nate hopped down and picked up the instrument. Thrusting one side into his mouth, he slid it up and down the notes. Just as quickly, he removed it. "Man, this takes me back."

She couldn't help but admire his twinkling eyes and dimpled chin. "Takes you back where?"

He studied the shiny silver rectangle in his palm. "I used to play in a band."

"You played harmonica? Not guitar or drums or something cool?"

"Hey, harmonicas are cool." He started to play a melody. After several bars, he stopped and checked her expression.

She clapped. "You're really good. Did you write that?"

A short guttural laugh. "You didn't recognize it? That was Blues Traveler. They've been on Letterman, Saturday Night Live, in a bunch of movies."

She shrugged. Must be an old band. But Nate wasn't much older than she was. She'd checked his chart. Eight years wasn't that big a deal.

He played a bit from another song.

She pictured him in a black T-shirt and faded, skin-tight blue jeans, playing on stage. "I guess harmonica players can be cool."

He nodded. Clearly vindicated.

She could listen to him play all day, but she patted the exam tabletop, indicating for him to lie face down. "Let's see if you've been faithful to your exercises."

Guilt flashed across his face. "I must confess I'm getting a little bored. Do I really have to do them every day?"

"Well, let's see how strong you are. Maybe we can cut some exercises out." This was a complaint she often heard from patients. It was her job to keep them motivated and make adjustments in their regimen. Her hands positioned themselves on his shoulder. "Put your arm out to your side." She pressed on different muscles to make sure the right ones were activating with every movement. "Good."

As she worked, they chatted easily. He talked about the mosaic tile floor he'd uncovered in his house and about his son whom he adored.

Nate cleared his throat. "I'm worried about Chip. I thought he was acing his spelling tests and I even rewarded him with a trip to a car show. Then we find out he's been cheating."

She winced involuntarily when he said "we". Hopefully he didn't notice. "I remember cheating in fifth grade. We had to memorize all fifty states and their capitals." She shook her head at the memory. "I didn't study because it just seemed too daunting."

"That's not it. Chip studies. I read to him every night. It's like he has a mental block or something. I don't understand it."

She directed him to stand. "Is it possible he has some kind of learning disability?"

"Wouldn't his teacher know if he did?"

She shrugged. "You would think so." Now Nate stood on his feet and faced her. As a therapist, she'd grown accustomed to invading people's personal space, but today she avoided eye contact. She hoped he couldn't hear her heart thumping. "But she doesn't know how much you've been working with Chip at home. Something doesn't add up."

"You're right. Maybe I'll get on the internet and try to figure out what's going on with Chip."

Ah-choo! A small sneeze escaped her, tossing her head forward.

Nate reached his fingers forward and pushed her stray curl back behind her ears. They stared into each other's eyes without speaking. She didn't trust herself if she opened her mouth. Her heart thudded even louder inside her chest.

This was wrong. This was so wrong.

# # #

Mia sat in her small Mazda parked across the street from Nate's place. It was like a Spanish mansion or something. She'd never seen anything like it around here. And she'd never been outside of Michigan to see this style of architecture either. Only in books. "Your wife is so lucky." Just a whisper. She was alone.

Her fingers danced across the steering wheel, tapping, as she watched. A couple of kids walked down the sidewalk and she hunched down in her seat.

"What are you doing here? Hoping for evidence

that his wife is a shrew?" She muttered to herself, knowing this type of surveillance wasn't healthy. "But you didn't imagine that spark when he brushed your bangs out of your eyes." Involuntarily, her hand touched her hair in the same spot. Sweet memories. She'd replay that moment over and over in her mind tonight as she lay alone in bed.

"John is nothing compared to Nate." Her hand fisted at the name of her ex. The one she'd been in love with for the past year. The one who accidentally announced in a text message that he loved another woman. "Nate has a house, not a run-down apartment over his parents' garage. Nate has a good job, Nate is the perfect combination of family man and. . ." She pictured him playing harmonica in a band. "Sexiness." Her lips closed and she swallowed.

Noticing her cell phone on the passenger seat beside her, she picked it up. Turned it on and clicked a picture of the beautiful home. His home. The one his wife didn't appreciate. Once the photo was taken, she dropped the phone and wondered which window went to his bedroom. Probably upstairs and to the left.

A familiar-looking golden retriever raced from the backyard into the front. Homer. He'd grown since she'd seen him last. Nate said that the dog had helped him bond with his son. How precious is that?

She wouldn't mind dating a man with a son. That

just meant he was mature. Something she was more than ready for in a mate.

Suddenly, a figure appeared--chasing the dog. He had long legs and square shoulders. Nate. Smiling and shrinking down even farther in her seat, she studied him.

"Come here, Homer!" he shouted. The dog circled back around as if he thought this were a fun game. When Nate stopped, the dog stopped a good distance away. When Nate lurched, so did Homer.

Grabbing her camera, she took a few more pictures. It would be nice to have his photograph. She checked the screen and saw that some shots blurred, but others turned out fine. Too bad she couldn't zoom in.

Homer ran behind the house, forcing Nate to disappear in his pursuit. Mia sighed. "If you bought me a house like this, Nate, I'd love you forever."

After physical therapy Nathan had driven around for a while killing time. He bought some AAA batteries because he had a nagging feeling that he needed them. He went to a matinee movie that he didn't even care about. When he got home, let the dog out. He hadn't had the time or money to build the fence he'd intended to install, so that Homer could roam free. Unfortunately, Homer went a little wild after being alone for a few hours. The silly dog took off running around the house.

"Homer! Come here, boy." Nathan was supposed to leave the dog on a long chain out back while everybody was gone during the day. Val thought that's just what Nathan did, but since he didn't have a job any more to go to, he liked to let the dog stay indoors where Homer had a soft place to lie.

Nathan circled around to the front of the house, catching a whiff of nearby lilac bushes. He noticed a small car across the street. It kind of looked like Mia sitting behind the wheel. Of course, that was ridiculous. He only imagined it was her. He spotted Homer and the dog took off running toward the back. When he circled around the house a few minutes later, the car had left.

Once he finally gave up on catching Homer, he went inside. He stood in the doorway and tried to charm the dog the way he used to charm women. "I don't care if you follow me or not. But I'm done chasing you." Homer tilted his head as if he understood. Or at least was trying to.

"Maybe I'll get a treat. Want a treat, boy?" Nathan headed into the kitchen and a moment later, Homer came inside. Nathan closed the door behind them before going to the shelf with the doggie treats.

"Mia had a good idea today, boy. Said I should do research on learning disabilities. See if I can figure out how to help Chip." He patted the dog on the head as it chomped its bone-shaped biscuit.

Up the stairs and to the computer. Nathan logged on and typed in "reading problems" and all sorts of websites filled the screen. The information was a bit overwhelming. He looked at his watch after a while and discovered he'd been lost in cyberspace for two hours. Yet he didn't feel as if he'd learned anything. His memory was like Swiss cheese.

He heard the men on the roof hammering, which reminded him. He didn't have the money to pay them when they finished the job. He closed out the web browser and decided he had one last resort.

Twenty minutes later he pulled into Rod's Garage. He parked his car, careful to leave the closest spaces open for customers. A couple of guys waved and shouted hello as he headed into the office. He nodded back.

Rod spun his lucky coin across his desk. He looked up when Nathan entered the doorway and offered a hesitant smile. "Hi there, old friend." He stood and they shook hands.

Nathan took a seat across from the desk. "I hope you're in the mood to give an old friend a second chance."

Rod pushed aside the paperwork blocking his view and sat. "What can I do?"

"Give me my job back. I'm sorry I messed up

before. I'll pay you back the money you lost." An anchor dropped in his gut. God knew he didn't have the money to do that. Deeper and deeper this hole grew.

"No worries." Rod waved his hand dismissively. "You came back too soon. That's all. Go home, take your medicine and come back when you're better."

Anger surged. Take your medicine? How condescending. "Rod, I'm telling you, I *am* better."

Rod's shoulders rose with a deep breath. "It hasn't been that long since you messed up, Nathan."

Out of nowhere, Nate's fist slammed on Rod's desk. The coin jumped. "Damn it! Don't make me beg!" A pen rolled across the surface and onto the floor.

Rod's eyes widened and he took another deep breath. "Nathan, I don't know why you're so upset. This isn't like you."

Nathan sprang from his chair and paced like a caged tiger. "I need the money, Rod."

"What's wrong? Are you in some sort of trouble?"

He couldn't help but roll his eyes. "No. I have a family to support, remember?"

"Doesn't Val work?"

Rage flared. "I want to work. I want my own paycheck." He punched the wall. The drywall caved in beneath his fist. Pain tore at his bloody knuckles.

Rod stood up. "Calm down. Are you drinking again?" He paused. "Because if you are, you should go to a meeting. There's one at St. Peter's downtown tonight."

Nathan stared at his injured hand. Somehow the physical pain distracted him from his fury. He shook his head. "I . . . I don't know what's wrong with me."

Coming closer, Rod looked at Nathan's torn skin. "I'll go get the first aid kit. You wait here."

Once Rod exited, Nathan noticed something shiny on the desk. Rod's lucky coin. Nathan's heart rattled against his ribs. He tried to swallow the lump in his throat. Staring. A thousand dollars would help. Who knew? Maybe it had gone up in value since Rod had had it appraised.

He walked over to pick it up off the wooden surface. It was gold with a man's profile on the front. Nathan licked his dry lips.

Rod would be back any minute.

Take it. This is your chance. You have no other options.

He caressed the antique coin with his thumb. Self-hatred spewed like venom inside of him. He couldn't help it. He shoved the coin inside his pocket and hurried out of there.

CHAPTER TWENTY-FOUR

Nathan knew he hadn't hesitated nearly long enough before grabbing Rod's coin. Now the gold rested in his open, no-longer-calloused palm. He hated what he saw. When had he gone soft?

The scruffy-looking pawnbroker picked it up, adjusted his red baseball cap and studied it. He closed one eye as if to get a better look. "What's this writing on the back?"

"It's Greek."

Baseball cap dude didn't speak before walking toward the back of the shop, where he opened an office door. Nathan could hear two deep-pitched voices conferring, but he couldn't make out their words.

He shifted his weight and ran his hand through his hair. His eyes scanned the jewelry and weapons in the glass display case in front of him. Guitars and a moose head were mounted on the wall. It had been a long time since he'd frequented a place like this.

The baseball cap man returned to the room. "I'll

give you one-hundred dollars."

"Are you kidding?" Nathan heard his voice grow loud. "It's worth at least a thousand."

The guy shrugged. "Put it on eBay if you want."

Nathan raised his hands and squeezed the sides of his head. "Damn." He couldn't list it on eBay. He wanted this dirty business over and done with as quickly as possible. Acid already swirled in his gut. "Can't you do better?"

The man turned the coin in his fingers, squinting again. "Alright. One-fifty."

Nathan slammed his palms on the glass counter, causing it to rattle. Baseball cap guy didn't look too pleased. Nathan started pacing a small area. What was he doing? His heart thump, thump, thumped. He swallowed, trying to alleviate his dry throat. "I'll have to think about it." He held out his hand.

The man seemed reluctant to hand it back. "If you come in tomorrow, I'll have time to confer with my coin guy. Might be able to do ya better then."

As soon as the precious gold touched Nathan's hand, he shoved it into his front jean pocket. Out the door he sailed and straight to his favorite bar.

# # #

Val recognized the pain in her lower abdomen. Most women weren't aware of their bodies the way she was. She might be the mother of an only child, but she'd given birth twice.

The first time had been a little scary, but mostly joyous. Her little chipmunk. The second time had knocked her down and she'd never seen it coming. Once you've been through nine months of pregnancy, labored and delivered with flying colors, it seemed almost routine. She'd had cravings for chocolate covered bananas, chatted about her due date with other women while standing in line at the grocery store, and had casually discussed baby names with her spouse. Nothing was quite as urgent the second time around. They would use the same crib, high chair and baby clothes. All they had to buy were diapers. She worried less about her weight gain and less about all of the scary genetic diseases she'd read about in books. But she'd be sorry.

Her baby had been born way too early and didn't live to see the sunrise.

The tragedy compounded a marriage already on the rocks. Her husband was an artist who couldn't make a living off his work. And he didn't want to make a living any other way. With a toddler waiting for her at home, she didn't have much time to grieve. Instead, she and her partner lashed out, blaming each other for their disappointment. They divorced within the year.

She checked her reflection in the design studio's

bathroom mirror. She seemed especially pale compared to her black locks. Toying with her bangs, she caught a glimpse of the pink strands. Maybe it was time to go natural and quit pretending. If only she remembered what that looked like.

Her hand rubbed the soft flesh beneath her belly button. She knew this feeling. Her body was ovulating. Ready to get pregnant. But was she?

Nathan wasn't sure how long he'd been there. Long enough to drink himself better. He noticed a flash of light when someone entered the bar. Turning to see who it was, he couldn't help but smile. It was Mia.

Instead of wearing her usual khaki pants, she wore a short denim skirt, which showed off her curvy legs. Her body jiggled in all the right places as she approached and hopped up on the barstool next to him. "Fancy meeting you here."

"Of all the bars in all the world, you had to walk into mine." He tried to quote "Casablanca", but wasn't sure he'd nailed it. It didn't seem to matter because she grinned, showing off her perfectly straight, yet tiny teeth. Everything about her was dainty and feminine. And youthful. Her face didn't have a line on it.

She reached into the little black purse slung over her shoulder and retrieved something. "Here." The silver harmonica.

"Shouldn't you give it back to the kid who lost it?"

She laughed and lightly touched her curly hair. "I did. This one is for you."

He took it from her and slid up the notes quickly to try it out. A few guys turned their heads to see where the sound came from, but soon focused back on their own conversations or the basketball game on the overhead TV.

He felt his head wobble a little to the side. "You shouldn't have. What's the occasion?" Was it a holiday?

"It's just a gift. To thank you for being you."

Okay, that sounded a little corny, even coming from a hot Marissa Tomei look-alike. He caught a glimpse of her cleavage thanks to her low-scooped shirt. The little heart tattoo revealed itself, too. Time to turn on the charm. "So how can I thank you for being you?"

She touched her hair again. It was so damn cute. "No need to reciprocate."

"Reciprocate." The word sounded unusually long and complicated. "Re-cip-ro-cate." He laughed to himself. "Why are you so formal? I'm not your patient here." He dared to brush his fingers against her forearm. Her smile encouraged him. "We're just two friends getting a drink." He turned toward the bartender. "The lady needs a drink." He searched his memory for what she'd ordered last time. A fuzzy navel? A screwdriver? He thought it had juice in it, but it could've been a Bloody Mary. Some kind of froo-froo girlie drink. He was pretty sure of that, anyway. "She'll have a Bloody Mary."

She shook her head. "I hate those. How about just a beer?"

He slung his arm around her shoulder. "A girl after my own heart." She didn't seem to mind his flirting, so he kept his arm in place. "Tell me about your day." Girls loved to talk about themselves. He couldn't go wrong with this line.

She shrugged. "My boyfriend came by--I mean, my ex-boyfriend came by to pick up his clothes and stuff. He even brought a woman with him. Can you believe that?"

"It didn't take him long to find someone new. Unless. . . ."

Her head tilted to the side. "Unless what?"

He pulled away. "Nothing." He took a drink. Why make her feel worse?

She shook his arm. "Tell me. What?"

They playfully argued back and forth for a couple of minutes, her hand gently touching his arm then knee as she leaned in for emphasis. Could she be coming on to him? This was like a fantasy. He took a deep breath, not wanting to hurt her. "Unless he was already dating her while he was still with you."

Her smile faded. "Yeah. She's probably the one he meant to text when he sent it to me." She fisted her hand and banged it against the side of her head. "I am so stupid, stupid, stupid."

He reached up and stopped her fist. "Don't do that to yourself. He's the jerk. There's nothing wrong with you at all."

Looking at him, she licked her lower lip. "Trust me. There's plenty wrong with me. That's why guys never stay."

Even though he didn't want to, he released her wrist. "That's the difference between men and women. If a man gets cheated on, he blames the woman. If a woman gets cheated on, she blames herself."

She bobbed her head in agreement and took a sip of her beer. "You're right. He's the one with a problem, not me." She drank some more. "Of course, I have to admit, I have terrible taste in men."

He couldn't resist the bait. "How so?" This conversation could prove insightful.

"I always choose men who are emotionally unavailable. I like the kind that drive motorcycles without helmets, spend Christmas alone, get tattoos. . . ." Their eyes met and they both grinned.

Doubt had left him. She felt the chemistry, too. He glanced at the heart-shaped ink near her collar bone. Before he realized it, he leaned in and kissed her neck. He planted kiss after kiss upwards until their lips met. Wow! The world fell away as they made out.

She opened her mouth and welcomed his tongue. His hands roamed up and down her back. He wanted more. So much more.

He hated to pull away, so waited until she did. They both panted, trying to catch their breath. Her lipstick had faded and he liked that he was to blame. He pressed his mouth against hers again. He pushed her back against the bar so that he was dominating her.

God, this was so hot. He had forgotten how great it was to French kiss a woman for the first time. It was so primal.

He heard knuckles rapping on the bar. He stopped kissing Mia and turned to see the bartender giving him an annoyed look. "Hey, either order another drink or get a room."

Nathan noticed their bottles were empty. He faced Mia who looked a bit flustered, but in a good way. "You want to get out of here?"

"Yeah." She stood up and reached for her purse.

He put his hand over hers. "My treat." He pulled out his wallet and paid the bill with the only credit card that wasn't at its limit. He kept it just for emergencies. He shook away the thought, clasped her tiny hand and led her out of the bar.

CHAPTER TWENTY-FIVE

"I'm not sure why you wanted to see me without Nathan," Val told the perky counselor. Blond Barbara had suggested they do individual sessions as well as joint ones. Val had intended to blow off the appointment, but at the last minute, she figured it couldn't hurt.

Barbara clicked the pen in her hand. "Sometimes couples end up recreating the patterns they witnessed in their own parents' marriages. It helps to work things out individually then come together."

She shrugged. "My parents are happily married. Have been for forty-some years."

"Tell me about what it was like growing up."

Leaning back against the chair, Val decided it couldn't hurt to open up a little. "It was stifling. My parents are conservative, religious people and I was this wild child. I've always rushed into things without thinking. In my twenties, I hitchhiked to New York when they wanted me to go to college. Unfortunately, I fell for an artist and rushed into marriage. What's funny is I've always been in a hurry, but in the end, I feel like I'm behind."

"You rush ahead but feel behind," Barbara repeated.

"Right. I'm in my thirties and I'm a newlywed. I should have everything figured out by now, but instead. . . ."

Barbara's eyes focused on the notepad in her lap as she nodded. "Sounds like you and your parents didn't get along. Did they argue about you?"

"They never argued. There aren't any deep, dark secrets from my childhood that are ruining my current marriage."

"That's interesting. You said they never argued. That doesn't seem healthy. And you also used the word 'ruin' when describing your relationship with Nate."

Fidgeting, Val scratched her nose and tossed her leg over her opposite leg. "His name is Nathan. I don't know who Nate is. And I'm really not sure I want to have a child with him."

At that revelation, Barbara scribbled something on a notepad. "Are you pregnant?"

Her hand automatically pressed on her abdomen. It had been aching off and on all day. "No, but I had been hoping to have more children. We bought that house with all of those bedrooms so that we could raise a big family."

Barbara nodded slowly as if she were thinking. "This is the house that needs renovating."

"Yes. I didn't think we'd be able to fix the roof, but Nathan came up with the money. Thank God, Rod loaned him some money." Val made a mental note that she needed to figure out a way to show Rod how grateful she was. "But our bank accounts are almost empty. We still need to refinish the floors and buy some more furniture. I guess that can wait. Either way, I'm not sure we can afford to add a baby to the household. Then again I'm running out of time if I do want to have more." She'd just turned thirty-three.

"Let's talk more about that. A baby."

Sadness washed over Val and she bit her lip to stop from crying. "I had another baby. After Chip. But he died." She pressed her lips together and took a deep breath. "Then my husband left me just when I needed him most."

Barbara reached for a box of tissues and handed them to Val. She made some kind of encouraging sound with her throat.

Val pulled a tissue loose and wiped her eyes. "I don't know if I want to risk it again. Risk bonding with another baby that might not survive. Risk my husband not being there for me again." She swallowed. She'd never talked about any of this before and it overwhelmed her.

"Relationships are always a risk. You love and you risk not being loved back."

"It's not supposed to be that way with Nathan. He was always Mr. Dependable. He might not have been adventurous and outgoing, like my ex, but that's what I liked about him. He was content watching a DVD and cooking dinner with me and Chip. He was ready for parenthood. Maybe he didn't quite know how to be a dad, but he wanted to learn. You know?" She dabbed at the corner of her eye.

Barbara nodded. That's pretty much all counselors did, apparently. Start the waterworks and nod away.

Val looked at the picture on Barbara's desk. It was a picture of a black Lab. "Do you have kids?"

"No."

"Are you even married?"

Barbara hesitated. "No."

Val sucked in her breath and let it out loudly. "Then how can you counsel me on whether I should stay with my husband or not?"

Barbara adjusted her position in her chair. First she glanced at her notes, then made eye contact. "I've been trained on how to help people work through things. It sounds as if you're considering a divorce."

Silence filled the room. Val uncrossed and crossed her legs on the other side. "Maybe. I don't want to, though."

"You're thinking about divorce, but you don't want one."

Val nodded. Thoughts raced through her mind. Why did she want to stay with Nathan despite his mood swings? Because she loved him. Parts of him anyway. Because Chip deserved a family. Because she didn't want to be a two-time loser. Her mom would just die if Val announced a divorce only months after the wedding. "Do the couples you see usually stay together or split?"

Barbara looked up as if searching the files inside her head. "I'd say it's about fifty-fifty. What matters isn't what other couples do. It's what you want to do. What would it take for you to make up your mind that this marriage is going to succeed?"

Val played with her manicure. "That's a good question."

"Because that's what it comes down to. I can give you two the tools to resolve your conflicts, which is something it sounds like you need, but you need to choose to soldier on when times get tough. If you're always looking for a reason to leave, you'll find one. The marriages that last are the ones where each one stays through the rough patches and keeps trying to make things better."

Did this chick actually know what she was talking

about? "I want this to work." A weight lifted from Val's shoulders. She glanced at the clock and saw the session was about to end. She stood. "Thanks for helping me figure that out."

# # #

Nathan and Mia kissed just outside of the bar, in the shadows not illuminated by the corner streetlight. He moved his hands all over her body. If she'd let him, he'd slip one hand underneath her shirt. Which she did. He felt her bra and envisioned black lace. Instinct told him to find the clasp and unhook it. But not here.

When two guys walked by and went into the bar, Nathan pulled his body away from Mia's.

She adjusted her shirt and looked at him with hungry, brown eyes. "Want to come back to my place?"

God, did he! Just then a Honda Accord parked across the street. He watched as a mother, father, and two boys climbed out and headed for a Chinese restaurant. Family dinner.

Even through the blur of alcohol, he knew he should stop this. "What time is it?" They both glanced at their watches. His--a cheap Timex and hers--a gold bracelet-style. Seven o'clock. His heartbeat slowed to a solid march inside his ribs. Val was off work by now. She'd pick up Chip at daycare and bring him home for dinner. They'd be worried if Nathan wasn't there.

He plunged his fingers through his hair. "Listen, Mia."

She stepped back. "Are you kidding me? We haven't even done anything and you're breaking up with me?"

Swallowing, he eased himself toward her. He wanted to press his lips against hers again. He'd kill to know if he'd been right about the color of her bra. But he couldn't. He picked up her hands in his and held them. "I don't know what I'm doing. Please don't hate me. But I've got to go."

She nodded. "Yeah. Sure. I get it." Her hands slithered out of his grip. "I'm a big girl."

His mouth hung slightly open, but words didn't come out. He leaned in and forced his lips against hers. She didn't fight back and he knew he could have her if he wanted.

At that thought, he broke their connection. He pivoted on his heel and headed home.

CHAPTER TWENTY-SIX

Val couldn't help believing the diary held the answer to why the ghost lingered in the house. Now that the leak above the four-poster bed had been repaired, she stretched out on her comforter and read the diary. So far, she'd learned that the woman who'd lived there, Helen, was consumed by grief after her baby died. Stillborn. Val shuddered at the similarities to her own history. After baby Rose was buried, Helen allowed the servants to care for her other three children while she sat crying or staring out the window. Val could picture the woman's rocking chair on the raised landing across the room, with the apple tree below.

After a few months of mourning, Helen's husband bought her a Steinway. Val figured that must be the old, black piano in the living room. Probably since it was so heavy, every owner had left it with the house when they moved out. Helen wrote in the diary that it was expensive and at first she told her husband she wasn't worth it. He insisted that it was a gift for her and someday the children would learn to play as well. Helen agreed when he added the part about their children. Soon she discovered that moving her fingers across the keyboard comforted her. Scales, then Beethoven and Bach soothed her. She left her room more and more every day in order to play music for herself and eventually to teach the children.

Val traced her fingers on the final sentences: *I am fortunate to have a husband that stood by me during my illness, although it was more mental than physical. I am indebted to him for helping me find happiness again.*

That must be what the spirit was trying to tell Val. That a good spouse stays even when the other is weak or injured. If she waited long enough, Nathan would return to his old self just as Helen had.

Nathan entered the room just then. "Hi, babe. Whatcha reading?"

Blushing, she closed the diary and tucked it in the drawer of her nightstand. "Nothing." As far as Nathan knew, she found ghost stories entertaining the way some people enjoyed sci-fi. He had no idea she believed in their existence.

The door closed behind him and he turned the lock. "Chip's finally asleep. And you look beautiful tonight."

She leaned up against the headboard to study him. "You've been flirting with me all evening." In fact, he'd bumped into her in the kitchen while they got out the silverware to eat the Chinese take-out he'd been so considerate to bring home for dinner. Each bump included a caress of her back, her hip, her behind. He even dared to nibble on her ear when Chip was in the room.

Now he sauntered over to her. He picked up her hand and kissed her knuckles. "That's because I've been dying to get you alone." His kisses trailed up her arm and to the special spot at the nape of her neck. Her nerve endings tingled.

She felt his tongue flick in the soft area between her collarbones and she knew she wouldn't be able to resist him. It had been a while since they'd been intimate and she missed it. Not counting his days in the hospital, this was the longest gap since they'd started sleeping together. They hadn't had sex since he threw the butter knife. Her senses turned cold.

He unbuttoned her top button and kissed the exposed skin. Then another button followed with a kiss. The third button and she felt his mouth between her breasts. Her body grew warm. Desperate, she tugged his T-shirt over his head.

Something dark on his arm caught her eye. "What's that?" She touched his bicep.

He smiled. "I got a tattoo. Do you like it?"

Her fingers traced the scorpion inked in black over his muscle. "I guess so. I'm surprised, though." A scorpion didn't seem like him. Not that she had any idea what tattoo did fit Nathan's personality. "When did you get it?"

He pulled away from her and sat upright. "My first week back at the shop. To celebrate." His demeanor shifted, almost as if he were ready for a fight.

"You've been celebrating a lot. Tattoos, drinks with the guys after work."

"I'm entitled to a little fun, aren't I?"

The counselor had mentioned that Nathan needed to unwind after going to so many doctors' appointments. "Of course. I'm not judging you. I have a tattoo myself, remember?" She'd been younger and more impulsive then. After seeing the way her skin stretched during pregnancy, she wasn't so sure she'd get one again.

"Now where was that?" Rather than finishing his slow descent down her torso, he unbuttoned and unzipped her jeans. He pulled them open to expose the pink and purple butterfly on her hip.

She giggled as he worked his warm lips over the spot. She needed him. They needed each other.

###

Nathan figured it didn't matter where he got his appetite, as long as he came home for dinner. Last night proved it. He thought Val's moans were going to wake the neighbors. Afterward, she stroked his scorpion tattoo and said that she thought it was sexy. For the first time in a while, she gave him a good-bye kiss before she left for work this morning.

Sober now, he sat in bed and looked at Rod's coin. He knew he couldn't sell it. He wasn't a thief. Just like he wasn't an alcoholic. He was simply a man trying to put a roof over his family's head. Who knew roofs were so damn expensive?

He put the coin on his night stand and pulled on a pair of jeans. The coin seemed to be staring at him. He couldn't leave it out or Val might ask about it. So, he stuck it in his front pocket.

What the hell was he going to do today to fill the time until Val came home? Then he remembered. He had physical therapy.

His heart sped up. Mia. He wasn't sure what to do about her. He didn't know if he could handle seeing her again. On the other hand, he wasn't sure he could handle *not* seeing her, either. He shaved and put on one of his nicer button-down shirts with his jeans.

Once at the office, he acted cool with the red-headed receptionist. He didn't want to get Mia in trouble. But it wasn't like she made out with all of her clients. Most of the people she worked with were on Social Security and walked with canes. She probably loved it when a muscular, younger man, like him, showed up.

He tried to read the newspaper someone had left in the waiting room, but his mind wouldn't focus. He kept re-reading the first few sentences without retaining any of the information.

Finally, Mia called him back to the room. She smiled warmly, but also seemed distant. He hopped up on the table quicker than he used to. His body had restored itself almost completely. He owed it all to Mia.

She looked at her clipboard and avoided eye contact. "How are you today, Mr. Sullivan?"

He chuckled. "Just fine, Miss. . . What's your last name?"

Her eyes narrowed. "You don't even know my last name?" She turned and closed the exam room door. "You grope a girl and you don't even bother to get her name?"

Panic kicked in. He hadn't expected her to be angry at him. After all, he hadn't slept with her. "I know your name, Mia. What's wrong?"

"What's wrong? Seriously?" She scowled at him. "Fine. Do you want to pretend nothing happened? Is that it?"

He squeezed the back of his neck. "I. . . No?" What was the right answer? The girls he'd been with before Val had never expected a call the next day or a serious relationship. Everybody knew it was just sex. Drunken sex. "I liked last night."

Her features softened. "Really?"

Glad to have tamed the beast, he nodded. "Last night was awesome. I was worried you had regrets."

"No. I mean, I'm risking my job for you. But you're worth it." She came close, wedged her body between his legs and kissed him.

All of those hours she'd worked on his muscles in here, he'd fantasized about this. Her fingers were soothing, massaging. Finally he could taste her lips. They did not disappoint.

They made out for a few minutes and he reached for the buttons on her blouse.

She pulled away, panting. "We can't. Not here."

What the hell? She got him all worked up for nothing? He sighed. "You're a tease."

Her pink lips pulled into a smile. "And you love it."

There was no denying it. He did love it.

CHAPTER TWENTY-SEVEN

The roofing company called Val at work with the bad news. "Mrs. Sullivan? I'm afraid the check your husband gave us for the additional tiles bounced. We won't send any workers to finish the job until proper payment has been made."

Val's throat dried. "I'm sorry. What did you say?"

"I know these are hard times, but I have to pay my workers. Would you like to put it on a credit card?"

She reached for her purse. "Yes. Just a minute." She pulled out her Visa and read the numbers.

For a moment, the man on the phone remained silent while processing the transaction. "I'm sorry. That card has been denied."

Val chewed on her pen. "Try it again."

The man did, but still said it didn't work. "You might want to contact the credit card company to make sure there isn't a mistake."

"I will. How much more do we still owe you?"

"One-thousand dollars for these additional tiles and then the final balance of $15,000."

Val started to cough. "My husband hasn't paid you? Nathan said he'd taken care of everything."

"No. He has paid $25,000 so far, but it was estimated at $40,000."

She nodded her head even though no one was in the room with her. "I know. Okay. Please keep working and I will call the credit card company to figure this all out. It's a mistake, I assure you."

After she hung up the phone, she called Visa. Unfortunately, they refused to admit their mistake. They said she and Nathan were at their limit. She stared at her bulletin board filled with pages ripped out of *Better Homes & Gardens*. Her dream was for one of her designs to one day be featured. She was starting to see that her dreams were out of reach.

A moment later, she called Nathan's work. The guy who answered the phone said Nathan wasn't there. He transferred her to Rod.

"Val. . . hi." Rod sounded strange. Not his usual jovial self.

"Rod, I'm trying to get a hold of Nathan. Is he out to lunch or something?"

He cleared his throat. "Val, Nathan isn't working today."

"What? He didn't say anything to me about taking the day off."

"He didn't tell you? He hasn't been working for a while."

The room started to spin. She rubbed her forehead. "I don't know what you mean. He just went out last night with the guys for a beer after work."

Rod remained quiet for a minute. "Maybe it would be best if you came over here. There's some stuff we need to talk about face-to-face."

But she didn't want to talk to Rod. She wanted to talk to her husband. "I'll have to get back to you." She hung up before he had a chance to say anything else.

For a moment she stared at the phone's ten digits. She dialed Nathan's cell. "Nathan? Where are you?"

He paused and she could hear people talking in the background. "At work. Why?"

"No, you're not. I just talked to Rod."

For a minute, Nathan didn't speak. "What did he say?"

"That you haven't been at work in a long time. So, I'll ask you again. Where are you?" She detected the shrillness she'd often heard in her own mother's voice, but she couldn't help herself.

"I'm. . .at home."

"Who's talking in the background?"

"Nobody." It sounded like a door opening and then the voices disappeared. "It's the TV."

She sighed, not believing him. "Whatever. I'm coming home. We need to talk." She hung up before he could protest. With a quick glance at the clock and her calendar, she slung her purse over her shoulder. Hopefully Kelly would understand. She stuck her head in her boss' office, but no one sat behind the desk. Her hand gripped the strap of her purse while she marched toward Joely's office.

Fortunately, her friend greeted her with a smile. "What's up?"

"Would you tell Kelly I had to go? Family emergency."

Worry lines formed across her brow. "Is Chip sick?"

Val shook her head. "It's Nathan. No time to explain. But I'll definitely need to talk to you later." She raced home, wondering if she'd beat Nathan there, which would mean catching him in another lie. Her heart pummeled her ribs. She and her ex argued all of the time about his half-truths, but she'd hated it. She didn't want to be the only grown-up in her marriage this time.

When she pulled into the garage, she was pleased to see Nathan's antique car in its spot. Even so, she still needed to confront him about his job. Her head started to throb as she walked past a stack of abandoned roofing tiles. Once inside the house, she heard the TV on in the library and she headed toward the noise.

Nathan sat stiffly in the leather club chair they'd purchased their first weekend in the house. A beer bottle sat on the table next to him. At Nathan's feet, Homer lay. The dog raised his head lazily.

Nathan looked at her, his face full of remorse. He flipped off the TV. "Hi."

"Hi." Silence hung in the air. She didn't want to scold him, but what else could she do? "Why didn't you tell me that Rod let you go?"

His spine straightened. "Is that what he told you? Because I did not get fired. He told me I should focus on my recovery is all."

"But why would he say that?"

Nathan stared at the floor. "I made some mistakes estimating repairs. Huge mistakes that cost the company hundreds, no--thousands, of dollars." His slanted eyebrows lowered. His face crumpled and his eyes watered. "I screwed up. Big time."

Sympathy surged through her. She crossed the room, sat on the chair's arm and hugged him. "It's okay." The last thing she wanted was to see him cry. She heard him sniff. "The doctor told you it might be hard to go back to work. I wish you would've told me."

He shook his head and the tears spilled down his cheeks. "I couldn't. I was so embarrassed." He wiped his nose with the back of his hand and refused to look her in the eye.

"If you would've told me. . ." What? They still wouldn't have the money to fix the roof or pay for their new furniture or the hospital bills. Anger shot through her. "We've been paying for Chip to go to after-school care when you could've been here watching him?" That wouldn't exactly pay for the repairs, but it wouldn't have been throwing money away either. "The roofing company called me and said the check you wrote bounced."

His eyes darted around the room as if he were looking for an escape route. Or another convenient lie. "I'll take care of it."

She rose and moved a few steps back. "Quit it! Quit pretending that you have everything taken care of. We owe them thousands of dollars that we don't have. Just admit it."

He slapped his hands against the leather and she jumped. Homer bolted from the room. Nathan stood and glared at her. "Fine. I'm a terrible husband. I bought you this house. . . I thought it would make you happy, but. . .

we can't afford it. I knew it. You knew it. Yet here we are."

She folded her arms and wished she'd never started this. On the other hand, he should be the one worried about upsetting her. "I don't know who you are anymore. You lied to me. You're the one who's supposed to fix things--not make them worse."

The veins popped in his neck. Something vicious flashed in his eyes. He reached for the beer bottle and threw it against the wall. She ducked. Heard the glass shatter, wet drops spilled on her arms.

She struggled to breathe, moving toward the doorway with her back against the wall. She'd intended to ask him to pick Chip up from school, but not now. Shut up and get out.

She ran to her car and shoved the key into the ignition. It took three tries. As she drove down the road, she realized her hands were trembling. In fact, her whole body was.

# # #

Nathan hopped into his car as soon as Val left. Before starting the engine, he pounded the steering wheel with his fists. "You're a loser. Rod knows it and now Val knows it, too." He slammed his fist one more time.

He reached into his pocket and pulled out the gold

coin. He needed to return it, but he was too embarrassed. After shoving it back into his jeans, he decided to head to his new, favorite place.

Even though he was speeding, the ride there took too long. He plopped on his usual bar stool and ordered a beer. Rod would probably say Nathan had a drinking problem, but he never hit the hard liquor. Just because he had a beer or two didn't mean anything. His life was going down the toilet. Everybody knows a man isn't a man if he can't provide for his family. That's why he didn't respect his brother.

He took a long swig. When he set it down, the glass thudded against the top of the bar. His shoulders slumped as he thought about Val. She'd rushed out of the room as if she were afraid of him. How could that be? He hadn't planned on losing his temper like that, but she had to know he'd never hurt her. He took another drink.

Once Val was back at Kelly's Designs, she rushed into Joely's office and closed the door behind her. She plopped down in the chair closest to Joely's desk. She tried to catch her breath.

Joely put down her pencil and pushed away the sketch she'd been drawing. "Oh, my God. What happened?"

At first, Val couldn't speak. Then the words burst

out like a geyser. "I don't know what to do. We owe all of this money. . .Nathan can't work. . .I feel sorry for him one minute, but then he's. . .shouting at me the next." For some reason, she didn't want to admit that her husband scared her. Tears flowed down her face.

Joely leaned forward and embraced her. Just what she needed. Val savored the comfort of her friend's touch. She cried and cried. She mourned the man she'd married and she mourned the future she'd imagined they'd have together.

Once Val's sobs faded, Joely released her and handed her a tissue.

Val dabbed at her eyes, sure that her mascara had run. She had a client meeting later today and she couldn't afford to cancel. She couldn't afford to do anything. She was broke. "You don't happen to have an extra $15,000 you could loan me, do ya?" Through her tears, she cracked a smile.

"Nope. Sorry." Joely gently tugged on her dangling earring. "Have you tried the bank?"

Nodding, Val pursed her lips. "I even asked Kelly. But she said she didn't have it."

Joely's eyebrows raised in surprise. "Really? You'd think if you owned your own business, you'd have lots of spare cash."

"Apparently not." She sighed. "I was hoping

Nathan's boss might be able to front us the money, but I guess that's out." She squeezed her temples. "What am I gonna do?"

"Have you thought about. . . I hate to even suggest it."

"What?" She looked at Joely while still rubbing her forehead. "Tell me. I'm desperate."

Joely took a deep breath. "Have you considered asking your parents for a loan?"

"Oh great." Val massaged in tiny little circles.

Shrugging, her friend looked innocent. "You did say you were desperate."

"If we don't come up with the money, they won't finish the roof. And it's supposed to rain in a few days." She slouched in the chair. "I feel like a little kid, asking my mom for money to go to the movies."

"But this isn't something frivolous. This is for their only daughter. Another way to look at it is this is for their grandson."

Most grandparents would do anything for their grandkids, but Val wasn't so sure. "They don't even bother to visit Chip on his birthday. Christmas is usually the only time we get together."

"They do live far away." Joely was trying to make her feel better.

She heaved another sigh. "You're right. They're my only hope." She stood, but didn't want to leave. "I guess I'd better make myself do it right away or I'll lose my nerve."

Joely patted her on the back. "You can do it."

Instead of opening the door, Val waited another beat. Her friend was so good to her. Especially considering Joely suffered most days in pain.

Dropping her chin, Val turned the doorknob and made her way back to her office. Time to call the number she rarely dialed. "Hello, Mom?"

"Is that you, Val? You're lucky you caught me." Her words dripped in a Southern drawl. "I was just heading out to the garden. I thought I'd bring strawberries to everyone in my Bible study group."

It would be another month before berries were in season here. Val pictured her mother in her straw hat and gingham Capri pants. The woman never wore jeans in the church.

Val's shoulders tensed. "Mom, this won't take long. Remember how you said at my wedding that I should've asked you for the money to get a nicer reception hall?"

"Uh-huh." Her mother was probably sliding on her gardening gloves to keep her hands from getting dirty.

"Well. . . I'm in a tight spot. I was wondering if you could loan me some money."

"What for, dear?"

Val wiggled her shoulders, trying to loosen them. It didn't help. "The house we bought needs a lot more work than we realized. I'm afraid we need several thousand dollars in order to fix the roof."

"Are these the fancy, handmade tiles you imported from Mexico?"

Val nodded. Why hadn't she realized she would regret bragging about her historic house in that last phone call? "Yes. No one makes them here in the US. We had to get them from Mexico."

"Well, it sounds to me like you made a poor choice. Your father and I aren't rich you know. We live within our means. That's how we raised you. Either get a cheaper roof or sell the house and buy one you can actually afford."

Her mother's words punched her in the gut. Val would never sell her hacienda. It represented success. The kind of success her mother never believed she could achieve.

"Val, are you there?" her mother asked. As if she were concerned.

"Fine, Mom. I knew I shouldn't even bother to ask."

"Don't speak to me in that tone. I'm still your mother and you should show me the proper respect."

The throbbing in her head increased. She pinched the bridge of her nose. "I've gotta go. Bye." She leaned back in her chair and stared at her bulletin board filled with beautifully decorated rooms. "Why do you always make me feel like crap, Mom? Can't you tell that my life is falling apart?"

I need help. Somebody please help.

CHAPTER TWENTY-EIGHT

Mia dialed Nate's number on her cell phone then twined a lock of hair around her finger. It rang and rang, but he didn't answer. Too bad. Her next appointment had just cancelled and she was hoping the two of them could meet up somewhere. Pick up where they'd left off.

She checked her makeup in the rearview mirror of her Mazda. If Nate picked up, she'd freshen her lipstick, but if he didn't, she wouldn't bother. She dialed one more time. He still didn't answer. She turned on the radio and decided to go for a drive. After all, the sun was shining and she deserved a break.

After taking a few random turns, she found herself parked in front of Nate's house. Again. She stared at the Spanish palace and wondered about his life.

"Why couldn't it be me? Why couldn't Nate be married to me?" She pictured them eating a picnic by the fountain in the front yard. Homer would jump in the water and splash them. They would laugh even though her sundress would end up soaked, sticking to her skin. Nate would grab her and kiss her like she was his oxygen.

# # #

That night Val lay in bed, staring at the damaged ceiling, both relieved and worried because Nathan hadn't come home. In the distance, she thought she heard a melody playing.

Sitting up, she listened harder. It sounded like the piano downstairs. She checked her alarm clock and saw that it was midnight. Surely Chip had been asleep for hours. And he was the only one in the house who liked to pound on the piano. This didn't sound like a child playing, though. This sounded like a real song.

She crawled out of bed and crept down the stairs, half expecting to see Chip or Nathan standing in front of the black piano. But when she reached the bottom of the stairs, the house grew silent. And no one was in the room.

She scratched her head and neared the piano. Her fingertips grazed the top of the keys without pressing them. After a minute, she decided she must've been dreaming and returned to the stairs. Then she heard classical music playing again. Her heart leapt into her throat. She whipped her head around to see who was there.

She watched as the ebony and ivory keys lowered while the piano seemed to play itself. Her palm pressed against her chest, trying to calm herself. Then she smelled apple pie. Just like on the day of the open house. And she knew. She knew it was the spirit of Helen.

"What are you trying to tell me? That I shouldn't worry that my house is falling apart? I shouldn't think about leaving my husband because he's changed?"

The keys started to play a soothing lullaby. But Val was not comforted. She shook her head. "It's not the same as with you. It's not the same."

#

Nathan dialed the familiar number from his cell phone outside the bar. Last call was over and he'd made his way to his car. He knew he shouldn't drive, though. That's where his logic ended.

"Hello?" a groggy, female voice answered.

Thankful, he closed his eyes. "Diane."

"Who is this? It's the middle of the night." She did not sound happy. She'd always struggled to sleep through the night, waking up to any little sound.

"It's Nate. Nathan." His head wobbled and thoughts swirled incoherently through his mind. "You've got to help me. I'm losing her."

"What?" She sounded more alert. He imagined she'd turned on her bedside lamp.

"My wife. She looks at me the way you used to. Right before you left."

She sighed loud enough for it to carry across the

miles. "Nathan, you've been drinking, haven't you? I told you I've moved on with my life."

He suspected she was about to hang up. "But wait. Just tell me what I did wrong."

"You know exactly what screwed up our marriage. And you're doing it right now."

He was confused. How could he be ruining his marriage right now? "Just tell me what I could've done differently. I love her. I loved you. I can't take losing her."

"Nathan, don't ever drunk call me again. In fact, don't call me period." The phone line disconnected.

He stared at his cell phone. Then he started his engine and pulled out without checking for traffic.

CHAPTER TWENTY-NINE

The phone next to Mia's bed rang at two-forty-eight in the morning. She answered it mid-yawn. "Hello?"

"Uh, Mia. It's Nate. Can you come get me?"

His voice stimulated her like a cup of coffee. She glanced at her Snoopy T-shirt and matching boxer shorts. Not exactly what she'd normally wear for a booty call. "Why do I need to get you?" She didn't want to leave her cozy bed if she didn't have to.

"I'm. . . in jail."

She gripped the phone tight. "What happened?"

"Nothing. I'll tell you when you get here. . . Bring your checkbook."

Mia didn't bother to put on a bra, just pulled on a pair of jeans and rushed out the door. The streets were vacant at this time of the morning, with some of the traffic signals blinking yellow rather than going through their normal cycle. During the drive, she wondered if he'd been in a bar fight or had an accident or what. More importantly, why had he called her instead of his wife? She smirked a little. This was a good sign.

She went into the quiet police station and told the clerk at the desk she was there to pick up Nate Sullivan. The twenty-something man eyed her chest a little too long. She crossed her arms.

The man picked up the phone and spoke in short, incomplete sentences. "Nate Sullivan. Send out." He hung up the phone and smiled at her.

She didn't encourage him. After all, she'd dated plenty of guys his age and they weren't worth her time. Sure, they were good in bed, but they freaked out if you ever mentioned getting engaged. "What exactly happened?"

"DUI. Your dad was swerving all over the road. It's a wonder he didn't get himself killed."

Mia locked her arms together even tighter. Nate didn't look old enough to be her dad. That guy was just being mean. She paid the bail and didn't relax until she saw Nate shuffling toward her. She reached out and hugged him. "Thank God you're all right."

He broke their embrace and headed for the exit. "Thanks for bailing me out." He pushed the glass door open.

The cool night air caused her to shiver. "No problem." He wasn't the first guy who'd asked her for bail money. But he definitely was the last guy she ever expected to. "They told me you were arrested for DUI."

His head hung low as he shook it. "I'm such an idiot. Val and I had a big fight today and I figured we both needed some time apart to cool off."

She stiffened at the mention of his wife. "Is that why you called me instead of her?"

He nodded. "She'd kill me if she knew about this. I know it's a lot to ask, but. . .can I crash at your place tonight?"

She shivered again, this time with a thrill. "Of course." She unlocked her Mazda and they both climbed in. She could tell by the way he looked around her vehicle that he wasn't impressed. "It's not exactly a classic like your car is, but it runs."

He chuckled, then rubbed his forehead. "Beggars can't be choosers. Please tell me you have aspirin at your place."

"I have everything you could possibly want at my place." She tried to say it in her sexiest voice.

"Good."

Once they made it to her one-bedroom apartment, she darted to pick up the empty sweet potato chips bag in the living room. She didn't have an eat-in kitchen, so the couch served as her dining room table. "Are you hungry?"

"No. Just some aspirin please." He plopped down

on her couch and the dog put its chin on his leg. He petted the golden retriever. "Homer."

"No. That's Homer's momma." Boy, was he out of it.

Nate's head rolled to the side, near a pizza stain on her couch. One of her boyfriends had left the couch when he moved out. Mia was waiting until she got married and had a house before she invested in new furniture. Right now, she had tons of student loan debt to pay off and since she currently lived alone, she didn't need anything fancy.

As she passed through her bedroom on the way to the medicine cabinet, she wished her bed actually had a headboard. She didn't want Nate to think she was too young for him.

Quickly, she straightened her floral comforter and tossed yesterday's work clothes and her sweatshirt into the hamper. She surveyed the room, decided it would have to do, and brought Nate his medicine.

He tossed the pills into his mouth and drank a little of the bottled water she brought him. After he swallowed, he looked at her chest. "Snoopy, huh?"

Blushing, she looked down at her top. "Yeah." Not knowing whether to sit next to him or invite him to bed, she remained standing. Even his five o'clock shadow made him look sexy.

Unfortunately, the room's silence emphasized her awkwardness. She walked over to her CD player and put in the disk she'd just bought.

Almost immediately, Nate's face brightened. "Blues Traveler? Do you like them? They're one of my favorites."

She returned his smile. "I know." Unsure of what to do with her arms, she folded them, then released them. Finally, she decided to sit next to him. Apparently, he wanted her to seduce him. She wasn't used to this role reversal, but that was okay. "You played some of their songs for me when you found that harmonica in the office."

"That's right. I forgot."

She scooted a little closer to him so she could massage his shoulders.

He closed his eyes and the lines across his forehead relaxed. "That feels good. Almost makes me forget that I'm a total screw-up."

She continued working her fingers into his tense muscles. "You're not a screw-up. I think you're great."

His eyes opened and he gave her a quizzical look. "You must be blind then."

"Not at all." Her hands crawled their way up the back of his neck and into his hair. Her body grew warm as she touched his sexy, thick hair. God, she had wanted to cross that line between therapist and patient so many times with him. Stroking his hair was definitely doing that. She leaned down and kissed his scruffy cheek. He didn't resist, so she moved in for what she really wanted. His mouth. In one fluid motion, she moved her body so it pressed against his.

They kissed and fondled each other with their clothes on until she couldn't take it any longer. She stood and held his hand, leading him to her bedroom.

He walked slowly behind her. "I don't know if we should. . . ."

"You know you want to," she whispered. She'd just die if he turned her down now.

The band provided background music on their short trip to the next room. She pushed him down on the bed and stripped his shirt off. Then she smothered his muscular chest with kisses. Finally, all of her fantasies were coming true.

# # #

The next afternoon, Val was glad to have work to distract her from her personal life. She sat at her desk and tried to figure out how they could get more business clients. If Kelly Designs went under, she might never find another job. Certainly not one where she loved her boss and her best friend was her co-worker. Speaking of her friend, Joely had been out of the office most of the day, working on-site. As soon as Val heard her come in, she poked her head into Joely's office. "Want to take a little break?"

Joely's head whipped up from the newspaper on her desk. "Are you okay?"

Val took a swig of the pop with twenty-three flavors. But she only cared about two ingredients right now. She couldn't wait for the caffeine and sugar to kick in. Make her feel better. But this was her fourth one of the day and so far they weren't helping. "Do I look that bad?"

Joely shrugged. "You don't look that good." They both laughed for one second. "Did you see the paper?"

"No. Nathan usually reads the news and tells me if there's anything I might be interested in." Nathan. She didn't even know if he'd be there when she came home tonight. Sighing, she sat down. "Is there something juicy in there?"

Joely pushed the newsprint toward her. "I hate to be the one to tell you this, but. . .Nathan was arrested last night."

"What?" Val jerked the newspaper up. "For what?"

Joely chewed on her lower lip. "Driving under the influence."

Val scanned the police beat and couldn't believe it

when she read Nathan's name. "Great. Just great. I hope none of my clients see this."

"I doubt they will. But more importantly, what's going on with you and Nathan?"

Val shook her head. "I don't know. He took off yesterday and to be honest, I'm not sure if I care." Her eyes stared at the paper without reading it. "I don't mean that. I do care. He's my husband."

"Is the counseling helping?"

Val took a deep breath before answering. "The counselor wants us to talk about when we first fell in love, but Nathan doesn't even remember."

"Val, most guys don't remember things. That's not because of the head injury, that's because he's a man."

She pretended to laugh it off, but worry clawed at her. "Nathan is definitely different since the accident. My problem is, I don't know how long I can wait for my old Nathan to come back."

Softly, Joely touched Val's hand.

Tears sprang to Val's eyes. "I know I said for better or for worse, but I never expected this. I feel so guilty, but. . . . who he is now, after the accident--I never would've married him." Saying the words out loud flooded her with both relief and guilt.

"Only you know what's right for you." Her friend

twisted her mouth and her tiny mole to the side. "How strongly do you feel about your wedding vows?"

Her belly churned. "Before I walked down the aisle, I swore this marriage would work. I'd do whatever it took. For Chip's sake if nothing else."

Joely opened her arms and raised her palms. "There's your answer."

#

Val parked her car in the empty garage and told Chip to go inside and grab a granola bar for a snack. She walked to the mailbox, wondering what to do. Was Nathan coming home tonight? Did he have a drinking problem or was all of this a result of the accident?

She opened the black metal door of the mailbox and pulled out a bill from the hospital stamped "second notice" and a large manila envelope. "What could this be?" It was stamped "requested material" and addressed to Mr. and Mrs. Sullivan. Her stomach clenched. In fact, she thought she might throw up.

Rushing into the house, she made it to the bathroom just in time. *I hope I'm not getting the flu.*

As she rinsed out her mouth at the sink, she heard the back door open. Nathan. Her pale reflection in the mirror froze. She splashed cold water on her face and forced herself to open the door so she could face her husband.

Nathan leaned against the kitchen counter, looking wiped out. In the adjacent breakfast nook Chip sat eating his snack, oblivious to his parents' tenuous relationship.

She looked at her son who, in between bites, pretended the granola bar was a toy car. "Chip, why don't you go eat up in your room?"

"Why?"

"Just go," Nathan said. Chip grabbed the wrapper and "drove" his granola bar through the air and up the stairs. Homer followed the boy as if he were on an invisible leash.

Val's stomach lurched and she hoped it was just nerves and not more vomit. She crossed her arms and leaned against the opposite wall. "Did you have fun last night?"

Nathan's face drained of all its color. He shifted his weight and fidgeted.

"You made the paper." She couldn't believe her husband had been arrested. Her only hope was that her clients didn't remember her married name. "A DUI. Nice."

For some reason, his posture seemed to relax when she accused him. He shoved his hands in his pockets. "I don't remember much about last night."

"Well, there's a permanent record of it at the police station." When she'd been talking to Joely, she'd wanted to find a way to fix things, but this was too big to ignore. "Nathan, you never used to drink. I don't understand what's going on with you."

His chest expanded with a deep breath. He lowered his head and shook it. "I'm sorry. I don't want to be this guy. I'm such an ass."

Her heart softened just a tad, like hardened butter left out on the counter. She toyed with her shiny wedding band, not knowing what to say.

Just then Chip bounded down the stairs and came into the kitchen. "Look, Mom! Look, Nathan!" Homer's dog tags jingled as he followed his favorite person. Chip wore his gym shoes on his hands--their rubber soles flapping like the mouths of a puppet. "I need new shoes for school."

Nathan pulled his hands out of his pockets and stood to his full 5'11". "How did that get ripped? I know you're used to getting whatever you want, but those days are over. You need to. . .take care of what you have!"

Chip's mouth frowned. "But it's not my fault."

Nathan moved closer to Chip's little body and wagged his finger. "It's never your fault. Well, guess what. . . we don't have any money!" He took the shoes off of Chip's hands and threw them on the floor. "So you'd better find some duct tape. . . and fix these. . . unless you want to go. . . barefoot tomorrow."

Chip burst into tears. He took off running down the hall and up the stairs. Homer chased him and Val hoped the dog would comfort him until she got the chance.

She scowled at Nathan. "You're not home five minutes and you're yelling. That's not okay. No one yells at my son. Why'd you even bother to come back?"

Nathan's eyes widened. He was probably shocked at the way she stood her ground with him. His voice lowered in volume. "The kid has to learn the value of a dollar."

"You know what? You were right. You are an ass." She stormed out of the kitchen and up the stairs to check on her son. When she heard the back door slam, her muscles clenched even tighter.

# # #

Mia called in sick to work so she could thoroughly clean her apartment. Then she went to the grocery store and bought the ingredients to make a special dinner. She picked up an extra toothbrush and even cleaned out a drawer in her bureau for Nate. The whole time, she listened to Blues Traveler, her new favorite band. It helped her to replay every minute of their night together.

Once the Stouffer's lasagna and garlic bread were in the oven, she called Nathan. She'd expected him to come by already, but this was okay. Her heart leapt when she heard his deep voice. "Hi! I just wanted to let you know that dinner will be ready in forty-five minutes."

"Dinner? Did I say I was coming to dinner?"

She giggled. "Well, I thought it was implied. You're not the kind to sleep with a girl and blow her off, are you?" He hesitated and acid slid down her throat. Oh, God. He regretted last night. She needed to say something quick. "It's just dinner. You gotta eat, don't you?"

"Um. . .I'm not sure."

"You're not sure if you need to eat? Are you drunk again? Boy, you were really wasted last night."

"I know." He didn't say anything more.

Was he going back to his wife? If so, hadn't last night meant anything to him? "Nate, just come over. We'll eat, we'll talk. I promise you, we'll have a good time."

"Mia, I'm sorry. But I can't." The line went dead.

CHAPTER THIRTY

Val had completely forgotten about the large envelope that had arrived in yesterday's mail until she saw it the next afternoon on the foyer table. She sat on the bottom stair and ripped open the envelope. She skimmed what must've been ten pages of information. It had some bullet points that attracted her attention.

Is your child left-handed? Does your child have frequent ear infections? Was your child slow to choose a dominant hand? Was your child speech delayed? Does your child seem bright, yet struggle to read? Does someone in your family have dyslexia?

Her hands started shaking. She could answer "yes" to every one of these questions except the last one. She didn't know of anyone who had dyslexia.

She read the materials thoroughly now, anxious to find information on getting Chip help. She scanned statistics and numbers, searching for answers. Eventually, she found a part that suggested seeing a neurologist for a diagnosis.

She sprang to her feet and went to the kitchen. Rummaging through the junk drawer, she pulled out the phone book and flipped to Physicians--Neurology. She read each name. When she read Dr. Chesney's name, she smiled briefly. The man who had saved her husband's life.

She dialed his number and a female receptionist answered. "I am wondering if Dr. Chesney can examine my son and determine if he's dyslexic."

"I'm afraid Dr. Chesney doesn't do that. I could ask him for a referral, though."

Val nodded. "Yes. Please do." She paced between the kitchen and the foyer, stepping over the jagged line that separated orange and brown tiles. The border between scraped tiles and dirty ones had spread toward the kitchen like a slow-moving puddle. Once Nathan went back to work, however, the edge hadn't budged.

"May I ask how did you choose to call our offices?" the woman asked. "We are doing a survey."

"He was the neurosurgeon who operated on my husband after an accident."

"Oh. How is your husband doing?"

Val stopped moving. She swallowed. "Not so good." Her voice cracked. "He's started drinking and he's gotten violent." She'd never admitted that last one to anyone. Tears of shame sprung to her eyes.

"I'm so sorry. Unfortunately, those are typical outcomes of brain injuries. Are you seeing a counselor?"

"We tried counseling, but it didn't work."

"I'm sorry." The woman was full of sorries, but that didn't help Val. "Was it someone who specializes in brain injuries? Because a lot of therapists aren't trained to address the unique needs of patients and their families."

Val thought about Barbara and how she kept trying to remind them of why they fell in love in the first place. "I picked someone out of the phone book."

"I think you'd be much happier if you worked with Dr. Shouse. She's amazing. Her own husband suffered a frontal lobe injury and she's very compassionate and very knowledgeable."

"I don't know. . . I think it might be too late." Val squeezed her eyes shut, trying to stop the tears. The fear in Chip's eyes when Nathan was yelling was just too much. "No, thanks."

# # #

The piano woke Val up that night. It was a beautiful classical piece that she'd heard before. "Brahm's Lullaby," she thought it was called. She stayed in bed and spoke to the spirit. "I'm trying to be patient with Nathan, but it's so hard."

The melody continued. She wished she could

afford to get Chip piano lessons. It seemed such a waste that they had an antique Steinway that only a spirit could play.

The phone rang and the piano went silent. Val answered it and heard a young woman's voice ask for Nate.

Val squinted at the time on her alarm clock. Midnight. "Nathan isn't here. Who is this? Why are you calling this late?" The woman hung up without answering. Val's heart jolted. A woman calling in the middle of the night and hanging up could only mean one thing. Nathan was cheating on her. Val's hormones flared and she threw the phone across the room.

She wished it weren't so late, so she could call Joely. Instead, she looked at the phone on the scuffed hardwood floor. It wasn't like her to lose her temper. Nathan was stressing her out. She tried to imagine how Joely would try to comfort her. She would say, "No one said marriage would be easy" or she would say, "Nathan isn't the kind of man to cheat." Which he wasn't. But why did some young girl call asking for him? Joely would point out that if the woman was calling for him in the middle of the night that meant Nathan *wasn't* in her bed, either. Val nodded her head and lay back down. "Thanks, Joely." She smiled to herself. The piano downstairs started playing again, eventually lulling her to sleep.

#

Nathan sat on the opposite end of the beige couch from Val. Across from them in a wing back chair, sat their new therapist. This woman was older than Barbara, with a few laugh lines permanently etched on her face. She had short, gray-streaked hair that looked like it wouldn't move if the wind blew. Her name was Dr. Shouse.

Yesterday his wife had called him, explaining that thanks to a referral from Dr. Chesney, this counselor agreed to see them right away. Apparently, Dr. Shouse had a medical license and could prescribe anti-depressants if necessary. As if he would ever agree to that.

Dr. Shouse crossed her legs and looked at Val. "Tell me what brings you in today."

Val toyed with her cuticles. "As you know, my husband suffered an injury to his head. I'm afraid it has completely changed his personality and. . . I don't know what to do."

"What to do?" the woman prodded.

"Yes." Val sounded impatient. "I keep waiting for the old Nathan to return, but I don't think I can hold out much longer."

He wondered what she meant by the "old" Nathan. He hoped the counselor would ask, but she didn't. Instead she looked at Val. "Tell me about Nathan's current personality."

Val took a deep breath and glanced at him. "He's different. He doesn't think things through, he forgets things, he gets angry easily."

He studied his wife, unable to tell whether she still loved him or not. "What did I forget?"

Val shook her head and picked up the brown throw pillow between them. She placed it in her lap and picked at it. "I don't know. You forgot to finish cleaning the tile in the foyer. You forgot to rent a floor sander. You forgot to tell me you lost your job."

The room went silent. The counselor made eye contact with him and then with Val. She waited for someone to speak.

He shifted in his seat. He stood and walked over to the bookshelves. "I'm sorry I got fired. I begged Rod to give me another chance, but he wouldn't. It's not my fault."

Dr. Shouse turned so she could watch him as he pretended to read the titles of her books. "It's not your fault."

"No!" He faced her. "Nothing's my fault. I do things and I don't even know why. It's like I can't control myself. Especially when Val corners me."

At that, Val squeezed the pillow across her chest. "Corner you? I have to tiptoe around you--worried that you're going to attack me." She averted her eyes and studied her cuticles again.

Her words stabbed his heart. His own wife was afraid of him. He hated himself. "I would never hurt you."

Val's lips pressed together into a straight line. "I don't know that. I don't think you know that for sure, either." She released the pillow from her grip.

They all paused a beat to collect their thoughts. Fortunately, Dr. Shouse took the lead. "Is there domestic violence between you two?"

Val shook her head. "No. But when Nathan gets mad, he turns into this crazed person. It's scary more than anything. He throws things." She pushed her black bangs out of her eyes. "I don't think he'd ever hurt me. But. . .he's done a lot of things I never thought he would."

"Such as?" Dr. Shouse asked.

"I don't know. Buy an antique car, take Chip out of school, get a tattoo, get a DUI." She rubbed her temples as if she were getting a headache.

Part of him wanted to put his arm around her and tuck her head against his shoulder. But he knew better. Instead he fought back. "You have a tattoo. So what?"

Val nodded. "I didn't say everything was bad. I just said you're not yourself." She took a deep breath. "The fact that you bought me that house wasn't like you, but I love it."

Dr. Shouse scribbled something on her notepad,

then looked at Val. "Some of Nathan's personality changes have been difficult to accept and some have been welcome."

Val raised her eyebrows as if she were having a light bulb moment. "I guess so. Here's the thing. I want to be the impulsive one and he's supposed to be the one who thinks things through. We used to balance each other out. Now we're drowning in debt. We can't afford to pay the roofers, the medical bills have started coming in and we don't have the money to pay them either."

The counselor cleared her throat. "It sounds like you had what I call a parent-child relationship. Val liked being the one who had fun and Nathan was the one who would do all of the worrying."

Val had never thought of herself as a child. Although she'd liked having someone else balance the checkbook and pay the bills. "I guess so. I used to be fun, but all that changed when I became a single mom. I was hoping that Nathan could take over the worrying for me."

Scratching her salt-and-pepper hair, Dr. Shouse watched Nathan nod in agreement. "For some reason, married couples sometimes reenact their childhood with one person stuck in the child's role and the other, the grown-up. The problem is it's not healthy. In those kind of relationships, you're not equals."

Val's blue eyes shimmered with tears. "But this isn't working, either. I'm afraid we're going to have to sell the house."

At that statement, Nathan couldn't resist. He sat next to her and rubbed her knee. "But you love that house. It was my gift to you."

She nodded. "I don't want to, but I don't see any other options."

"It has a backyard for Chip and Homer to run around in. It's your home."

Dr. Shouse tilted her head at him. "It's your home, too, isn't it?"

He shrugged. "I don't think Val wants me to live there anymore."

Val looked at him, still fighting the tears. "I do want you to live there. But I need you to help me figure things out, not blow up all the time."

He put his arms around his wife and hugged her. "God, it feels good to hear you say that." But guilt oozed through his system. Mia. He'd broken his wedding vows with Mia. He pulled away from Val. "I don't deserve you."

Val scrunched up her face in confusion. "I used to feel that I didn't deserve someone as wonderful as you."

Dr. Shouse chimed in. "You used to feel that way?"

Nathan watched Val impatiently push her hair behind her ears. No one spoke for a moment. Finally, Val looked up at Dr. Shouse. "Please help us. I don't want a divorce. But I don't want to live like this either."

His heart stretched like a serpentine belt that was about to snap. He longed to make his wife happy again, but he knew he'd gone too far. Kissing another woman was one thing, something he'd done without too much remorse. Something he could live with. But actually having sex was unforgivable. Val was right. He wasn't dependable, upstanding Nathan Sullivan anymore.

He'd become a monster.

And no one hated him more than he hated himself.

CHAPTER THIRTY-ONE

After their counseling session, Nathan and Val lingered in the parking lot. He didn't know where to go next. He kicked a rock near his tire and swallowed. "What do you think of Dr. Shouse?"

Val twisted her mouth to the side. "I'm not sure. I thought she might give us some great ideas on how to cope since she has personal experience with brain injuries. But it's a little early to tell."

He nodded. The wind blew and he caught a glimpse of her pink locks hidden beneath her black bangs. How he missed his creative, spunky wife. "She did suggest that I carry a notebook and write things down so I don't forget."

She leaned against her car. "Are you going to do that?"

"Sure. It's frustrating that I can remember the name of my third-grade teacher, but I forget what you asked me to do five minutes ago." What really sucked was that he forgot to add labor to estimates for repairs at work. How could he be so dumb? "What made you decide to try counseling again?"

"I can't call it quits until I know I've exhausted every option." She crossed her arms. "So, are you coming home tonight?" It didn't sound like she really wanted him to.

He studied the pavement beneath his feet. "Maybe I should find some place to stay until. . . ." Until what? She filed for divorce? She settled for a pathetic, unemployed husband? She found out about his fling with Mia?

"Until we work some things out?" she offered.

"Right." He dared to look at her big, blue eyes. How he longed to tell her everything and have her forgive him! But that was unlikely. She was mad he'd kept his work situation a secret. She'd totally lose it if she found out he'd been with another woman. And he wouldn't blame her.

"Where are you going to go?" Her face softened and she looked concerned. "The same place you've been staying?"

"No." He squeezed the back of his neck hoping that she didn't suspect where he'd stayed the first night. "I'll ask Rod if I can crash with him. If not, I'll find something."

"What about your mom's house?"

He shook his head. "I don't want her to know I lost my job."

"She would understand."

"I'm not like my brother. I hate how he runs to Mom to bail him out whenever he does something irresponsible." He paused, realizing he, too, had been irresponsible. He was more like his brother than he'd like to admit.

She didn't respond. The night air blew a few strands of her ebony hair across her face. He started to reach for them, but stopped himself. Instead, she tucked them back into place.

The two of them stood there, as ill-at-ease with each other as if they were on a blind date. He wanted to talk more, but his confession lodged in his throat.

She looked at her watch. "I'd better go pick up Chip. Joely's babysitting him."

Chip. Nathan wanted to be the father the boy never had. The kind of father who would not only bring home a puppy, but stick around long enough to train it how to fetch. The kind of father who not only built shelves for his Matchbox cars, but got down on the floor with his son and raced them. The kind of father who not only took him to antique car shows, but taught him how to drive a stick shift when he was sixteen.

Instead he was the kind of father Chip didn't need.

The kind who cheated on his mom and broke up the family. He was no better than Chip's biological father, a man so self-involved they'd never even met.

Nathan sighed. "Tell Chip 'hi' for me." He watched Val climb into her car. She waved halfheartedly as she drove away.

God, he needed a drink.

#

After work, Mia staked out Nate's house. He hadn't been returning her calls and he'd skipped his last PT appointment. From across the street, she saw a Honda Accord pull in, driven by a woman she assumed was Nate's wife. She had short, dark hair and looked as if she never smiled. Poor Nate.

Mia could be the perfect match for him. If he liked antique cars, she did, too. If he liked harmonica music, she did, too. And if he liked to get drunk before they made love, then she did, too.

It hit her. Why she hadn't seen Nate's car come home. She turned the key and drove to the bar.

Once she found a nearby parking spot, she headed into the dark establishment. Several men turned and gave her the once-over when she entered. One guy even winked, but she looked away, scanning the stools for Nate. Bingo! He sat on the far end today.

She licked her lips and tried to walk like a model, exuding femininity. He didn't notice because he was busy peeling the label off of his beer bottle. She hopped up on the barstool next to him. "Hi there. I missed you." She leaned close to him, hoping he'd catch a whiff of her vanilla perfume. He'd mentioned how much he liked it that night in her bedroom.

His head turned her way, but he offered only a fading smile. "Hi." He finished off his beer and ordered another one. Then, as if he'd forgotten his manners, he asked what she'd like.

What was going on with him? He'd called her when he'd needed to be bailed out of jail and he'd gone back to her place all worked up and ready for action. And now, he was lukewarm. She stroked the hairs on his forearm. The tail of his scorpion tattoo peeked out from underneath his shirt sleeve and she fondled it. "Want to do something crazy again?"

He shook his head. "I've done too much already."

"Sounds like you had a bad day. Want to come back to my place and talk about it?" She raised her eyebrows a couple of times. Guys never said 'no' to guaranteed sex. And if that's what it took to get someone to keep her warm at night, she was glad to do it. Nate was different only in the fact that he wasn't afraid of commitment. He might become so infatuated with her that he'd decide he needed her around for the rest of his life.

His eyes squeezed closed. "No thanks, Mia."

"What's the matter?"

"I've screwed up my life, that's what. My wife doesn't like me anymore. . . and I don't blame her."

She put her arm around his shoulders and squeezed. "I like you." He didn't even smile. She thought about the stern look on his wife's face as she pulled into that awesome house. That woman did not appreciate what a prize she had in Nate. "You've had some bad luck, but I understand you." She studied his drooping eyelids. "I promise if you come with me, your luck will change." She smiled and squeezed his shoulder again.

He kept his eyes on his drink. "I can't."

Her arm returned to her side. This was starting to get embarrassing. "Was I just a one night stand?" Her voice grew loud and finally Nate looked at her. A couple of other guys in the bar also stared at her, but she didn't care.

Nate held his hand out flat signaling for her to shush. "Mia, keep your voice down. I'm sorry if you thought we were dating or something, but. . . ."

"But what? You're suddenly devoted to your wife now that you've slept with me?"

His Adam's apple moved as he swallowed. His voice remained low. "Mia, it's not like that. I was drunk. I didn't mean to. . . ."

"Oh, that's so much better. Now it was an accident that you slept with me. Thanks a lot!" She hopped down from the bar, ready to storm out. Hoping he'd come chasing after her.

He reached into his wallet as if he were going to pay his bill, but it was empty. His mouth fell open and he stared at his billfold.

She leaned in and kissed his lips. Maybe this would remind him of the good time they'd had before he'd passed out. "You know where to find me." She turned and marched out the door, knowing that all eyes were on her.

# # #

Within half an hour after Mia left, Nathan's friend walked in. Rod stood behind Nathan and patted his back. "Hi, buddy. I'm glad you called."

Nathan hung his head in shame. If he started talking, he was afraid he might cry. And real men don't cry--especially in front of other men. "Can you loan me twenty bucks to pay my tab?"

Rod pulled a bill out of a wallet full of green and placed it on the bar.

Envy flashed through Nathan, but only for a

minute. Then he remembered that Rod was here to help. "Thanks. I owe ya one."

Rod gripped Nathan's arm. "Let's get you out of here."

At first he waved away Rod's support, but when he almost tripped on his own two feet, he allowed Rod to escort him through the bar. Once outside, he couldn't remember where he'd parked his car. Turning his head, he searched up and down the street.

"Nathan, you're in no condition to drive. I'll take you home." Rod walked toward his Mercedes and unlocked the passenger-side door. He assisted Nathan into his seat, much more gently than the police had the night he'd been arrested.

Nathan tried to shake his head, but it moved all over the place. "No. I can't go home. Val doesn't want me there."

Rod walked around the vehicle and climbed behind the wheel. "Are you sure?"

"Yes. I no longer have a home."

Rod checked his rearview mirror before pulling out of his parallel parking spot. "You can crash at my place then. We have a lot to talk about once you sober up."

Nathan thought of the coin. He reached into his jean pocket where he always kept it. He pulled the gold piece out and held it between his thumb and forefinger. "I need to give you this."

Rod glanced over at the coin and his eyes grew wide. But only for a second. Then his gaze returned to the road. "I was wondering where that went."

"I took it. I'm a horrible friend, I know. . .because I saw that you dropped it. . . and I stole it." Confession didn't make him feel better, but he didn't seem able to stop. "I'm sorry. I meant to give it back. . . I don't know what's wrong with me. . . . Val hates me. Did I tell you that? Oh, and I cheated on her."

# # #

Knowing she couldn't count on Nathan, Val finally refinished the upstairs floors herself by laboring each night after work. A company Kelly Designs did a lot of business with loaned her the sander. Chip filled in the gouges with wood putty and helped to rub on the stain. The two of them were a good team.

The heartbreak was that she had to fix up the house in order to put it on the market. She'd done everything on the inside herself, but the roof remained unfinished. That would certainly hurt her chances of getting a good price for the place, but she didn't know any other way to dig herself out of this hole.

She wanted to blame Nathan, but she knew it was her fault, too. She'd longed for this house even though they couldn't afford it. It wasn't very responsible of her to close her eyes to reality.

Saturday morning she was forced to take a break. She drove Chip to his father's apartment and rang the doorbell. It didn't work. She pressed the button again. Still no sound. Her hand curled into a ball and she knocked on the door.

Chip smiled up at her while they waited. "Dad said he's going to take me to the figure-eight racetrack and let me watch the drivers practice."

She returned his smile, thinking that was the last thing she'd want to do on a Saturday. Boys needed their dads. When no one answered the door, she pounded it. "Darrin! It's your weekend with Chip. Darrin, open the door!"

The door across the hall opened and an old woman with her white hair in curlers stuck her head out. "He's not home. I saw him leave last night and he never came back."

Val didn't know whether this woman knew what she was talking about or not. She shook her head, hoping the neighbor was wrong.

The woman pointed toward the parking lot with a crooked finger. "Look for yourself. His car isn't here."

Following the woman's directions, Val headed toward the lot out back. She searched the small paved area and quickly realized defeat. The yellow Mustang wasn't there. Poor Chip. His dad had blown him off again.

Waving at the old lady, Val hoped she would go back inside her apartment and give them some privacy. The neighbor lingered for only a moment before doing just that. Val crouched down to Chip's eye level. "Looks like your dad got tied up at work."

The little boy's brown eyes shone with disappointment. "You don't have to cover for him, Mom. I know he forgot." He crossed his arms across his chest. "Like always."

"He probably just got his dates mixed up." She flipped open her phone and dialed Darrin's cell. It went to voicemail. She exhaled a little too loudly. Darrin had flaked out for the millionth time. How could he do this to a child who idolized him?

And what was she going to do with Chip? "Looks like you get to come to an estate sale with me and Joely." Her voice tried to make it sound like fun, even though they both knew that it probably wouldn't be.

"What's that?" He held her hand as they made their way back to her Honda.

Pushing the curse words that she wanted to yell at Darrin out of her mind, she searched for the right details. "Well, it's when someone is selling everything they've collected over a lifetime. Sometimes you find real neat stuff, like old comic books or toys."

"Will there be Matchbox cars?"

Her spirits rose. "Maybe. It's a good thing you're coming with me because it's kind of like a treasure hunt. I'm going to need your help to find the good stuff."

His head still hung low. They climbed into her car and she drove toward Joely's place to pick her up. Usually it was a treat how she could hang with her friend while they searched for items to decorate their clients' homes. But she worried Chip would grow bored and pressure them to rush. She flipped on the radio, hoping it would cheer them both up.

"Do I really have to go?" Chip whined from the backseat.

Glancing at his reflection in the rearview mirror, she nodded. "I'm afraid you do." She searched her mind for the week's spelling words. "How do you spell 'because'?"

"Aww, Mom. It's the weekend. That means no school."

"We need to practice, Chip. Spell 'because'."

In the rearview mirror, she saw him silently mouthing the letters before saying them out loud. Why did Mrs. Bean give the students such difficult words anyway?

Chip finally spoke loud enough for her to hear. "B-e-k-o-z."

Swallowing, she shook her head. Not even close. "It's b-e-c-a-u-s-e."

"That doesn't make sense. Zzzz. It sounds like it ends with a 'z'."

"I know. It doesn't really follow the rules." She wondered if the upcoming meeting to determine if Chip was dyslexic would prove helpful or if she would be left without answers. If he had a learning disability, then surely the school would have someone trained to tutor him in reading. Because she'd been pushing him to read almost every night, but it was torture. He could read a word correctly one time and not recognize it in the next sentence.

Her shoulders tensed. Just thinking about it stressed her out. The poor kid deserved an easier life. Not only were his parents divorced, but just as he was warming up to his stepdad, that man moved out, too.

As if he were reading her mind, Chip piped up. "Mom. Mom! I know. I don't have to go with you to your sale. What about Nathan? He could watch me."

She kept driving. "I don't know about that." Who knew what Nathan was up to these days? He'd called to tell her that he'd moved in with Rod, but that was the extent of their contact outside of their counseling sessions.

"Pleeeeease, Mom. Don't make me go to your boring thing."

A minute later, she pulled into Joely's apartment complex. She didn't get out of the car, though. Instead, she located her phone and dialed Nathan's cell. It probably wouldn't work, but she could try. When he answered, her voice left her.

"Hello?" he said again.

"Nathan, it's me. Val. . . Um, I was wondering what you have going on today."

"Nothing really. Rod is making me go to an AA meeting tonight, but otherwise, I was just going to watch TV."

AA. She'd tried to talk Darrin into going, but he never would. How did she end up married to another alcoholic? Beads of sweat formed above her lip. She wiped them off before speaking. "Have you been drinking?"

"No. It's not like I have to drink. The bar just gave me some place to go during the day when the house was empty."

Was she supposed to feel sorry for him now? She rolled her eyes. "Any chance Chip could hang out with you today?"

"Uh--you mean here?"

"Or you could hang out at the house. Give Rod and his family a break."

"Sure. I miss the kid. Maybe I'll take him to a movie. They're playing Cars at the old theater downtown."

So he'd been keeping track of kid movies. She smiled to herself. "That would be great."

CHAPTER THIRTY-TWO

After he'd thrown on jeans and a T-shirt, Nathan drove exactly the speed limit to pick up Chip. He didn't want to attract any attention since his license was suspended for that dumb DUI. And he didn't want to remind Val that he wasn't supposed to drive. He wanted to make her life easier--swoop in and be the hero. Be everything that Chip's real father wasn't.

When Nathan pulled up to Joely's place, Chip opened the front door and ran toward the car. Since when was Chip happy to see him? Nathan climbed out of his MG, unsure of what to do. He crouched down to Chip's level. "Hi, buddy." Seeing Chip's smile warmed Nathan like a day at the beach.

Chip squeezed him tight for a minute. "Thanks, Nathan. You saved me!"

When they separated, Nathan realized that was the first time they'd ever hugged. His heart jumped. He mussed Chip's hair the way his grandfather used to do to him. "Climb in. Prepare for an adventure."

Val approached, holding out her keys. "Take my car. It has seat belts."

Chip skipped to his mom's car. "Can we go to the race track?" He climbed in the backseat.

Nathan took Val's keys and sat behind the wheel of her Honda. He looked over his shoulder at the boy he thought of as a son. "We could go see a movie or if you want to go to the track, we can do that."

Chip grinned, exposing three gaps.

Nathan waved bye to Val. He started the car and carefully merged into traffic. He glanced at Chip's reflection in the rearview mirror. "Did you lose another tooth?"

"Yep." He wiggled a tooth on the bottom row. "Pretty soon this one's gonna come out, too."

"Did the tooth fairy come?"

"Gave me a dollar. Can we go to the store so I can spend it?"

Nathan loved the fact that he could devote the entire day to Chip's whims. "No problem." They went to the race track, but there wasn't anything to see. They hit the Dollar Store and then the library.

Chip stuck out his lower lip. "Aww. Why are we going to the library?"

"I thought we'd get some books on how to train Homer to do tricks." Nathan hoped this would inspire Chip to try to read.

Chip nodded. "That sounds cool!"

They found some books and returned to the house. Even though Chip seemed motivated, he struggled to sound out every word. He didn't know when to say a long vowel sound or a short one. He had no idea how to divide up multisyllabic words, either. Unfortunately, he soon gave up and asked Nathan to finish reading.

The poor kid was really trying, but to no avail. Nathan wondered if that information he sent away for about dyslexia had arrived yet. He'd have to ask Val.

They grabbed some doggie treats out of the pantry and called Homer. The not-so-small pup wagged his tail and happily followed them into the backyard. Nathan shook his head. Homer had grown in the short time Nathan had been gone. Chip seemed a little taller, too. Nathan tried to swallow the horrible taste in his mouth.

If he didn't get his act together, he'd miss everything.

# # #

Val dreaded telling Joely her decision.

The two of them made their way through the bungalow past hard-sided suitcases, a hefty 1950s TV, and an art deco bedroom set. Val tried to avoid thinking about what she needed to tell Joely. "Thank God Chip didn't come with us. I haven't seen one toy or comic book in the whole house."

Joely sniffed and wiped her nose with a tissue. "If Nathan couldn't watch Chip, Jake might've been able to."

Shrugging, Val didn't know what to say. Jake was Anna's father, but it was a little much to ask him to watch Chip. "It sounds like you're getting a little bit of a cold."

"Yep. No big deal. How are things going with you and Nathan?" Joely picked up a ceramic angel which was part of a large collection on the dresser.

Glancing around to make sure no one was listening, Val lowered her voice. "I don't know. I never would've guessed he'd start drinking. I mean, he'd never even order a glass of wine when we went out to dinner before."

Joely made eye contact. "Maybe that's why. He knew he wouldn't be able to stop once he started."

Val tugged on one of her three earrings. Was she that naïve? She'd assumed he didn't like the taste. "He said he's not an alcoholic, but I don't know. Do regular people get behind the wheel after they've had too much to drink?"

"Unfortunately, some do."

"He said he's going to a meeting tonight, so maybe that will help. Plus, we're seeing a new marriage counselor. I think I like her."

"That's good. I know you have a hard time trusting counselors."

That's because it seemed like every time she told her counselor something as an adolescent, somehow her mom found out. Her mom had found the cigarettes and condoms hidden under her mattress and had grounded her so that she missed her senior prom. But why had her mom even thought to look there? So much for patient-therapist confidentiality. In the end, Val always felt like a disappointment to her overly-religious mother. Just for being a normal teenager. Just for being herself.

But Dr. Shouse had a point. Val no longer was a child. She needed to be a grown-up in this marriage, even if Nathan no longer was.

Something on the bureau across the room caught her eye. She walked over toward what appeared to be a carved elephant, but just when she got close, a man with glasses picked it up. Sticking her hand in her pockets, she stood and waited for him to put it back down. After all, her client loved elephants because they were the symbol of her sorority. Val would score points if she could add this beautiful piece of art to her client's décor.

The man who held her treasure had a receding hairline and was dressed in business casual.

Val shifted her weight. "Are you going to buy that?"

He looked at her. "Yes, I think so. My youngest daughter loves elephants."

Disappointed, Val fiddled with her wedding band. Funny how she was still getting used to it. "Well, she's a lucky girl. That looks like it was hand-carved."

Nodding, he turned the piece over in his hand. Val joined back up with Joely and decided to continue searching on behalf of her clients. She'd keep an eye on the man, though, just in case he changed his mind and set down the elephant.

Joely opened the bedroom closet and ran her fingertips across an array of colorful dresses. "Oh my gosh. Look at these!"

Val came closer to see the collection of old cocktail dresses. They weren't her style, but Joely loved vintage clothes. Her friend liked to mix old and new, much like Val enjoyed decorating her historic home with both modern and antique pieces. "You could double the size of your wardrobe in one fell swoop."

Joely held the skirt of a black and white polka-dotted dress. "I could throw on a belt or scarf in any color and this would be fresh." She continued digging through the clothes, coughing off and on. When she reached the dark corner, she gasped.

"What is it?" Val craned her neck to see.

On a hanger way in the back, Joely pulled out a wedding gown. It went straight down and was covered in elegant white lace. It seemed more 1960s flower child than the other dresses. "It's perfect." She walked over to the nearby dresser mirror and held it in front of her body as if trying to imagine how it would look.

"What size is it?"

Peeking at the tag, Joely smiled. "I might have to take it in a little." Still clutching the dress, she danced in a circle. "Finally! I've found the perfect dress!"

Val wanted to catch some of Joely's happiness, but she worried about telling her the bad news. She offered to help carry any other dresses that she wanted. After Joely selected a few, Val knew she couldn't put it off any longer. She drew in a breath. "Joely, I'm afraid you won't be able to get married at my house after all. I'm putting it on the market."

Joely clutched the wedding gown tight. Disappointment fell in shadows under her brown eyes. "Isn't there anything else you can do?"

"No. We bit off more than we could chew. The place was over our budget and we didn't realize how costly repairs would be."

Trying to be selfless, Joely reached her arm around Val's shoulders. "I'm heartbroken more for you than for me. Jake and I can get married anywhere, so don't worry about us."

"Thanks."

After scanning all three bedrooms, she and Joely

passed through the hallway toward the back of the house. When she saw the tall bench with coat hooks and a mirror on top, she stifled the urge to sing. This was the kind of piece that she loved to find. It was an antique, which meant it was solid wood, yet it was so practical. Her hand reached inside her purse to pull out her tape measure. She made her way closer, only to see that same man with the glasses rubbing his hand over the finish.

"Don't tell me you're buying this, too," she said.

He nodded. "I don't see a price, but it doesn't matter. This will be perfect in the mudroom for when my daughters come home from school. They can hang their coats and backpacks and sit down to take off their shoes."

Val wanted to scream, "Yes, of course. That's why I want it," but she didn't. "I guess we have the same taste-- first the elephant and now this."

He looked at the wooden elephant in his hand. "I should've brought a bag or something. I think I'm going to be buying a lot of stuff here."

Val's curiosity was piqued. "Why is that?"

His mouth twitched. "My wife and I just divorced. She's staying in the house with all of the furniture and I bought a new house. It's so stark and empty, though, I'm worried my daughters won't feel at home there."

She understood completely. That's why she loved shopping at estate sales. Some of her clients wanted their homes to look like they'd been assembled over time rather than everything shiny and new. That announced, "I hired a decorator."

She swallowed her bitterness at having lost two treasures to this man in one day. He was a divorced dad trying to do right by his kids. She couldn't help admiring him for that. She reached into her purse, pulled out an extra plastic bag and gave it to him. "I won't be needing this."

If she and Nathan divorced, would he worry about making his new home comfortable for Chip? He wasn't even Chip's real dad. Maybe he wouldn't want to be a part of Chip's life anymore. Maybe today was the last day they'd ever see each other.

A pain bore into her heart. She'd failed as a mother and as a friend.

CHAPTER THIRTY-THREE

Alternating chills and sweat tormented Joely all night. She coughed and her chest hurt. When her alarm buzzed, she could barely move her swollen hand to flip the switch off.

Damn! This was going to be a bad one. She could tell.

"Anna." She hoped her daughter could get herself ready for school.

No response. Joely tried to push the air with her diaphragm. She couldn't quite get enough. "Anna." *Sweetie, time to get up*. She didn't have the energy to say the words.

Anna walked into Joely's bedroom, rubbing her eyes. "Mommy, why are you still in bed?"

Joely coughed. Even that hurt. "My lupus is acting up. I need you to be a big girl today. Can you get yourself dressed and eat some Cheerios?"

Her daughter's blond head nodded. She smiled at the suggestion of being grown-up. "Is today a long sleeve day or short sleeve day?"

The weather. Had Joely watched the news last night? She squeezed her eyes shut, willing herself to remember. Lately, the weather had been fairly nice. Why not hope for more of the same? "Short sleeves."

"Yea!" Anna clapped and darted out of the room.

Joely lay there, trying to work up the energy to call in sick. She closed her eyes and considered her options. It had been so long since she'd had a terrible flare, she'd been spoiled. But this was how it worked. A constant push-pull. Fighting a cold one day, and lying in bed unable to move, the next. Inside her head she chuckled.

Because if she didn't laugh, she'd cry.

After ten minutes, Anna re-appeared in Joely's bedroom. She twirled, showing off her pink and white striped pants, polka-dotted socks and flowered shirt ensemble. "What do you think, Mommy?"

Not exactly what she'd pick out, but no need to fuss over the little things. At least they all had pink on them. Joely offered a weak smile. She breathed fast and shallow. The oxygen didn't seem to reach her lungs.

Anna's eyebrows pulled together. "Are you okay, Mommy? Should I call the doctor?"

Joely's head shook. She didn't want to scare her daughter. If she could just get Anna off to school, Joely could stay in bed all day, trying to fight this off. Whatever it was. She started coughing. Every contraction tore at her chest. She couldn't stop.

The coughing continued until she felt something in the hand covering her mouth. She looked down and saw mucus tinged with blood.

Anna saw it and screamed.

Joely reached for the box of tissues on her nightstand and wiped her hand. "Anna. It's all right. I need you to get me the phone." Her daughter reached for the nearby phone and gave it to Joely. She hit speed dial, but Val didn't answer. Next, she rang Kate. "Hey, sis. I'm pretty sick. Any chance you could come up here for a couple of days?"

"Oh, no. What's wrong?" Kate sounded like a nervous mother.

Joely's body jerked with another painful coughing fit. "I'm not sure." Something about this seemed familiar. "I think I need to go to the hospital."

"I'll be there as soon as I can. But you know, I'll have to find someone to watch Brianna first. Call 911 if you need to."

Joely closed her eyes. She wanted her sister now. But she knew even if Kate left immediately, it would be at least two hours before she could make it. Beads of sweat formed on Joely's face. A fever. She'd had plenty of those.

She'd coughed up blood before, too. How quickly she'd forgotten. She shouldn't have pushed herself so hard. Shouldn't have ignored her body's warning signs.

Kate's breath sounded rushed, as if she were running frantically around her house. "You should call Jake."

Joely shook her head against the pillow. "He's swamped at work." Jake had told her as much. Right after she said she'd have to check with her doctor about having more kids.

"Now listen. If Jake Mahoney claims that he'll be there for you in sickness and in health, then he'd better prove it right now. Either you tell him you need a ride to the hospital or I will."

"You call." It hurt too much to talk. "Please hurry." At that, she hung up.

Anna took the phone out of her hand and placed it in its cradle. Then she reached her arms around Joely's shoulders and hugged her. "I love you, Mommy! Do you want me to get your medicine?"

Joely thought of the rows of amber prescription bottles in the kitchen that she'd been ignoring lately. She needed to eat before she took them or she'd get sick. "No." She hated to ask Anna to be her nurse. She hated to ask anyone. But she had little choice. "Maybe you could bring me a piece of bread and a glass of orange juice first."

"I could toast it if you want."

Joely shook her head. She didn't want Anna using any electric appliances without supervision. No doubt, Anna could easily operate a toaster. But Joely didn't want to risk anything. It took several trips for Anna to assemble all of Joely's medicines. By the time she had, Joely glanced at her alarm clock. "The bus." Cough, cough. "You'd better go."

Anna froze. Joely waved her away. Anna reached over and hugged her mother again. "I'm not leaving you."

Guilt piled on top of her chest. Her daughter shouldn't miss school over this. "Go." Her firmest voice.

Anna shook her head. Her six-year-old face so determined. "Not 'til Aunt Kate or Daddy get here."

A sigh of resignation.

That was Anna's cue. She climbed into bed and snuggled up next to her mother. Joely couldn't help but smile at her daughter's compassion.

About fifteen minutes later, Jake showed up. He let himself in with the spare key Joely had given him. He rushed into Joely's bedroom and placed his palm across her forehead. "You're burning up."

Anna slid out of the bed. "And she coughed up blood!"

Jake reached under Joely's back and knees. He lifted her in his arms like a fireman. "Why didn't you call me? Kate said you didn't think I could be bothered." He carried her out of the bedroom. "I'm taking you to the ER."

Joely looked at her faded T-shirt and sweatpants. She didn't want people to see her like this. A deep cough ripped through her lungs. Her throat raw. Who cared what she was wearing? She closed her eyes and rested her head on his shoulder. Safe. Jake made her feel safe.

The hospital smelled familiar. Not good, just familiar. A faint chemical odor. An orderly placed her in a wheelchair as soon as Jake carried her into the ER. Someone whisked her off for a chest X-ray, a blood draw, and to see a doctor who listened to her lungs. In between coughs, she rattled off all the names of medicines she could remember that she was on.

Jake must've seen the bewildered look in the doctor's eyes because he said, "She has lupus." Anna clutched her father's hand.

"But I stopped taking everything." She chewed on her thumbnail, dreading a lecture from the doctor. "I was feeling so good. . . I wanted to see if I could make it without all of the drugs." She'd hoped skipping the steroids would help her weight loss and she could give a trial run to see if she might be able to have another baby.

After a short reminder about the importance of lupus meds, the doctor declared that Joely had pneumonia.

He gave her antibiotics and steroids and other prescriptions. Then he ordered her to stay overnight.

Overnight turned into a week.

# # #

"Hi, I'm Rod and I'm an alcoholic."

Nathan studied his friend's face as the introductions zigzagged through the folding chairs in the basement of the First Presbyterian Church. Rod didn't look like an alcoholic. He looked like he was at peace. When it was Nathan's turn, he said the words, but didn't quite believe them.

After everyone said their name, a balding man asked if anyone wanted to share their story.

A man about Nathan's age raised his hand and walked to the front of the room. "Hi, I'm Lex and I'm an alcoholic."

"Hi, Lex," the audience replied without enthusiasm.

Lex seemed to struggle with where to place his hands. He crossed his arms, then scratched his chin and finally shoved his fists into his jean pockets. "I was first sent to AA by a court order. I'd been arrested at the scene of a horrible accident. I'd run into a tree and killed my best friend, Barney." He pulled out his hands and they trembled as he cracked his knuckles. "For the longest time, I insisted that I wasn't drunk. I hadn't had that much to drink—three or four beers was all--and I was way more sober than Barney. That's why I was the one driving. But the cops didn't care. They gave me a breathalyzer and sent me to jail." He took a moment to crack the knuckles on his other hand, one by one. He glanced at the crowd, but quickly returned his gaze to the Berber carpet. "My friend died in the hospital that night and I wasn't even there because I was locked up."

Bitterness tainted his words. Nathan wasn't sure if Lex was mad at the police or mad at himself. He surveyed the man from head to toe and figured he was working class, just like him. Maybe even a mechanic.

Lex coughed a few times. "For years, I maintained that I wasn't an alcoholic. In fact, I'd driven Barney and me tons of times after a couple of beers without any problem. But now. . .I realize that I'll never know if it was just an accident or if. . ." He inhaled in short staccato breaths, trying to compose himself. "What if the alcohol really did cause me to hit that tree? What if Barney would still be alive. . . ?" He squeezed his eyes shut and pinched the bridge of his nose.

The leader of the group walked up and put his hand on the man's back. Lex pulled himself together and addressed the crowd. "All I'm saying is alcohol ruined my life. Alcohol maybe killed my friend. Alcohol is a bitch." He quickly made his way back to his seat.

Nathan rubbed the back of his neck. He felt sorry for the guy, but. . . he didn't know about admitting that he was powerless against alcohol and turning it over to a higher power. He'd quit drinking before. After his divorce. He could quit again.

Acid pooled in his stomach. Was Val going to divorce him? It wasn't so much alcohol's fault as it was that damn fall down the stairs. That's when his life got screwed up. Alcohol just helped him feel like less of a loser. He swallowed.

Unfortunately, because of alcohol, he'd slept with Mia. Thus, making things even worse. He could never complete Step Nine: making amends to those harmed.

He did not deserve forgiveness.

CHAPTER THIRTY-FOUR

Val tapped her fingers against her thigh while Chip sat in the next room being tested. She could barely hear some of the questions through the door. "Do you know what ancient means?" Chip said no. "Try to remember this list of words, then repeat them back to me." He didn't do so well with that one, either. "Can you read this word?" He stood up and asked about the toy car on the doctor's bookshelf.

Shaking her head, Val wanted both to scold Chip and rescue him. This was difficult for him. She worried about what the neurologist would tell her in the end. That Chip was unmotivated or had ADD or had a low IQ? She chewed on her lower lip.

She wished Nathan were here so she could talk about her anxiety. He was the one who must've requested that material on dyslexia. If he were here, he could hold her hand and remind her that she'd done her best with Chip. That he was smart in his own way. That he knew the names of the last ten Indy 500 winners and eventually, he'd figure out how to memorize his spelling words, too.

But telling herself these things did little to comfort her. She wanted a partner in raising Chip. Now that she'd had a little taste of how good it could be, she didn't want to go back. Sure, she'd hoped Nathan would not only provide emotional support, but financial support, as well. But if he couldn't work because of his head injury, she didn't hold that against him. And if he had trouble remembering things, she'd have to be more patient is all. The poor guy. The doctor had said it could take a while for Nathan to return to his "pre-morbid personality." Maybe a year or two. But then again, he'd said maybe never.

She flipped through a magazine, but couldn't do much more than look at the pictures.

After two hours, the doctor opened up the door to the testing room. Out ran Chip, who gave Val a hug. "She said I did good."

Val smiled at him and gave a pleading look to the medical expert. "Well?"

The doctor, a woman with long, braided hair smiled sweetly. "He was a very good test-taker." She held up a stack of papers. "I will need a few days to compile all of these results into a report. Then I'll call you so we can discuss them."

"Can't you tell me something?"

The woman's thumb stroked the corner of the

papers. She glanced at Chip and lowered her voice. "If I had to guess, I'd say he is dyslexic. The good thing is you're catching this early and once I look everything over, I can tell you specific things to do in order to help."

Val had hoped the heaviness in her chest would be eased. Unfortunately, the pressure remained.

# # #

For the first few days, Joely actually felt worse rather than better. Her lungs wrestled for oxygen. The weight of a brick on her chest. Pain stabbed at her back. Even lying in bed hurt.

She turned her head to see Jake sitting next to her. He'd brought his laptop and briefcase full of papers to the hospital.

When he noticed her staring at him, he put his work aside. He stood and held her hand. "I had no idea you'd stopped your medicine. I don't ever want you to do that again. It's too dangerous."

She shook her head. "This could've happened anyway. Any time I catch a cold it can snowball into something catastrophic."

"Can I get you anything? A blanket? Something to eat?" Worry lined his forehead. Dark circles discolored the skin beneath his blue eyes.

"No. I'm fine."

"You are not fine. Don't ever hesitate to call me

when you're sick. I can't believe you called your sister who lives two hours away instead of me."

"But you said you didn't have time for me."

He caressed her cheek. "I'm busy. That's true, but if you need me, I'll be there. Promise me you'll let me be."

Tears stung her eyes. Her chest hurt. "I promise." Bad news barged into her thoughts. "Val's selling her house. We don't have any place to get married now."

He kissed her cheek where his thumb had been. "Maybe I can get the hospital priest to marry us right here in this room. That would be memorable, wouldn't it?" He smirked.

She tried to laugh, but it hurt.

"Just kidding. Don't worry about it. Things have a way of working out."

# # #

At their next counseling session, Val studied her husband, trying to figure out if he was ready to come home. She wanted to talk to him about Chip's testing and how she thought maybe it was her fault. Was it because she smoked when she was young? Was it because she'd put Chip in daycare where he'd gotten sick so often? Was it because she hadn't read to him enough? The neurologist said none of this was true, but Val couldn't help but blame herself. As his mom, it was her job to stop anything bad from happening to him. And dyslexia would be something he'd struggle with for his whole life.

She also wanted to tell Nathan about putting the house on the market. Even though her life was falling apart and some of it was his fault, she felt compelled to talk to him. Back when they'd been dating, he'd always been so logical, coming up with solutions to her problems. She needed him now more than ever.

Dr. Shouse sat across from them and turned to a blank page in her notepad. "Val, you need to put your relationship before the accident up on a shelf. Nathan might not ever be the man you remember. He has a better chance of recovery with your support, but you need to accept who he is now."

Val looked at Nathan with his slanted eyebrows and forest green eyes. He looked like the man who kissed her on each cheek before meeting her lips. He looked like the man who gave his old Matchbox cars to Chip the first time they'd met. He looked like the man who grilled her French toast the morning after their wedding. He might've been a little tight with money, but he'd made up for it by his actions. He paid attention to the details of her life and she'd fallen in love with him. "The other counselor kept asking about what brought us together in the first place."

Dr. Shouse leaned forward and laced her fingers together. "That's traditional counseling, but head injury cases are different. The two of you need to choose to build a new relationship together. Are you willing to do that?"

Val noticed Dr. Shouse staring at her. "I think so. I miss having Nathan in my life."

Nathan cocked his head as if he were surprised by this.

Dr. Shouse nodded, looking pleased. "And Nathan, are you committed to making this marriage work?"

Nathan fidgeted. "Um. I'm such a screw up. I'm pretty sure Val wishes she'd never married me."

Val knew deep down he was right. She tried not to let it show in her eyes. "The truth is, things worked better before, but I still want to try." She wanted to hold his hand, but he was too far away.

He looked at his scuffed up work boots. "Thanks to me we're on the verge of bankruptcy."

The counselor faced him. "Are you willing to make this work?"

He shook his head.

Val tried to understand the creases forming across his forehead. Instead of looking relieved to hear that she wanted him back, he appeared troubled.

She felt as if she were losing him. Like an open can of pop lost its fizz. Their marriage had gone flat and she worried he was going to pour what was left down the drain. Why wasn't he thankful that she'd forgiven him? She'd forced herself to overlook his DUI arrest. It helped, of course, that none of her clients had mentioned it. Kelly had asked if everything was okay, but hadn't held it against her. And Nathan said he hadn't had anything to drink since moving in with Rod.

He pressed on his temples. "I'm afraid I can't do this. Val. . . ." He made eye contact. "I think it's over."

Val's heart tumbled down.

Dr. Shouse's mouth opened a bit too far, then closed. "Nathan, help me understand where you're coming from."

He splayed his hand through his hair. "I'm no good. Val deserves to be with someone who can contribute. Someone who can take care of her. She deserves a real man."

At this, Dr. Shouse stroked her chin. "Tell me about a 'real man'."

He looked at the bookshelves against the wall. "A man without brain damage. A man with a good-paying job and a man who is dependable."

"And that's not you." Dr. Shouse's voice softened.

"Not anymore. I can tell I've changed. I fly off the handle one minute and am ready to cry the next. I'm like. . ."

Lately, Val had been feeling especially emotional herself. She had to admit, she missed Nathan's touch as they passed by each other in the hall or when he fell asleep spooning with his hand on her hip.

"You're like?" Dr. Shouse encouraged him.

He shrugged. "I don't know. I'm like a car that only has two speeds—first and fifth. There's no in-between."

"Would you say that's accurate, Val?"

"Yes. He used to be even-tempered all of the time, but since the accident, he's bouncing between two extremes. He's lost his middle."

"How do you feel about that?" the counselor asked.

Studying her stubby fingernails, Val noticed that wood stain had left a light brown patina on them. Pride swelled in her chest for the work she'd been forced to do. "I like how he isn't afraid to kiss me when Chip's in the room anymore. He's much more spontaneous." Another breath. "But he loses control so easily, it scares me. It's like I can't ever disagree with him."

He straightened his back. "But you never used to disagree with me. Before the accident, we never fought. You and I always saw eye to eye."

Dr. Shouse asked if Val remembered it that way. Val crossed her legs. "Well. . . when we were dating, I tried to get along. I don't like to fight." When she felt strongly about something, she'd flirt and cajole until she got her way. "But now that I found out you lied to me about money and we're losing the house. . . I can't keep quiet any more."

"So, you avoided conflict, but that didn't work very well in the long run," Dr. Shouse said.

Val shrugged. She'd never thought of it like that before. "I guess so. Are you saying that we would've ended up fighting even if Nathan hadn't been injured?"

Dr. Shouse leaned back and raised her eyebrows. "It's pretty hard to be married to someone and never have an argument."

Val mulled that over. She blamed all of her problems on Nathan and his brain injury. Was she to blame, too? "All I know is that I want Nathan to come home." She studied his face, hoping that he'd say he couldn't live without her either. But he remained quiet.

Nathan closed his eyes for a moment. He let out a loud gush of air and pushed on his knees to stand. "None of this is Val's fault. It's all mine. And. . .I want a divorce."

CHAPTER THIRTY-FIVE

Mia watched as a brown-haired boy played in the front yard with Homer. He must be Nate's son. Tapping her fingers against the steering wheel, she considered motherhood. She wouldn't mind raising Nate's child if that's what it took to get him to marry her.

Nate had blown off his physical therapy appointment with her and she was starting to panic. After all, she was in love with him.

Memories of rejection seeped into her mind. She'd been a late bloomer, ignored by the teenaged boys in her high school. Until her senior year. Suddenly, her hips rounded, her chest developed and guys couldn't wait to get her into their cars. And she'd been overwhelmed with the new-found attention. Kissing soon led to touching which led to sex. She'd been thrilled to discover that she loved it almost as much as the guys did. Because this was her true gift. Sex was power.

Unfortunately, she'd never made it past the "let's live together" level of commitment. She'd done everything she could to please John and the string of men before him—cooking dinner, offering massages, never saying no to sex. But she could tell Nate was better than all of her previous boyfriends. He was the marrying kind. She just had to convince him that she was his soul mate.

The golden retriever jumped in the fountain and splashed around. The boy laughed and stood by when the dog climbed back out and shook himself dry. A moment later, the dog took off running across the lawn and down the sidewalk. The child chased after him, yelling, "Homer! Stop! Come back." But the dog didn't listen and he could run much faster than the boy.

She watched as the kid sprinted a few blocks before giving up.

This was her chance. She started her car and drove down the street along the dog's path. Soon she spotted Homer and she putted along until the dog stopped to roll in the grass. Boy, did he look like his mommy.

She parked and slowly approached the dog. "Hi, Homer. Remember me?" She made her way close enough to pet the large pup. After a few strokes, she grabbed his collar. He reluctantly climbed into her car. She drove back to Nate's place and pulled into the drive.

Smiling, she looped her finger through Homer's collar and headed to the front door. She rang the bell, hoping Nate would answer. In her mind, he would smile and be pleased to see her. He'd invite her in for a glass of lemonade and show her the place. Maybe take her up to his bedroom and fool around. . . . That would be so hot.

The front door opened and a woman with a pink streak of hair stared back at her. She had red-rimmed eyes as if she'd been crying. Mia couldn't find her voice.

"Yes?" the sad woman asked. "Oh. You found Homer. Chip said he ran off. Thanks for bringing him back."

Mia led the dog into the house. "No problem." She peered into the foyer, trying to catch a glimpse of the grand house's interior. "Is Nate here?"

The woman furrowed her brow. "I don't think I've met you. Do you live down the street?"

Mia searched for a lie. But why should she lie? "No. I'm a friend of Nate's and I just happened to be in the neighborhood."

The woman squinted at her as if trying to place her. "Well, I'm Nathan's wife, Val. I don't believe we've met." She reached her hand out to shake.

Mia didn't like this. She didn't want to make nice with Nate's wife. She was the enemy. Mia ignored Val's outstretched hand. "I saw a For Sale sign in your yard. Mind if I take a look around?" She couldn't wait to see where Nate slept when he wasn't with her.

Val dropped her hand. "Now isn't a good time. Call the realtor to schedule a viewing."

Mia tried to hide her disappointment. "Is Nate home?"

"No." Squinting at Mia again, Val placed her hand on her hip. "Who are you exactly?"

"Just someone who cares about Nate more than you do. Someone who thinks his snoring is cute." At that, Mia knew she'd gone too far. Crimson filled Val's face followed by a scowl.

Mia turned on her heels and made a quick escape. She climbed into her car and sped off down the street. Her heart beat as if she'd just run a race. At a stoplight, she caught her breath. Through her panting, her face broke into a grin.

Nate wouldn't be able to ignore her anymore.

# # #

After the creepy woman left, Val noticed her hands trembling. Shell-shocked, she leaned against the pillar between the foyer and the living room. So Nathan had cheated on her.

Somehow she managed to make her way to the phone to dial Joely's number. "If you're not up to it, just say so. Can I come over? I could really use a friend." Within fifteen minutes, Val knocked on Joely's apartment.

Val hugged Joely gently and told Chip to go play with Anna. Chip complied and Joely suggested they sit in the living room, near her painting of a sunset.

Val's stomach lurched and she placed her palm over it. Before sitting, she made them both a cup of tea in her friend's kitchen. She knew her way around since she often stopped by to help when Joely was having a flare. Finally, Val rested on the couch with Joely. "I'm so freaked out. This woman brought Homer back, asked to see the house and then mentioned that Nate snored."

Joely patted Val's free hand. "I'm so sorry. Maybe that woman was crazy. After all, Nathan is nothing if not loyal. I've never even seen him look at another woman."

"I haven't either. But it's strange that he announced he wants a divorce and then this young woman shows up insinuating that she's slept with him." Val stared at the murky brown of her drink. How naïve she'd been. "I figured once I decided to stay with Nathan, then that would be that. It never occurred to me that he might want out. I mean, why would he want a divorce?"

Joely shook her head. "I don't know. Maybe he's feeling sorry for himself. He thinks you'd be better off without him."

"Sometimes I think that I would." Joely's face flinched as if wounded by Val's words. Val spoke quickly, trying to fix things. "But now that he's moved out, I realize how much I miss having him around." Her insides percolated.

"Have there been any other signs that he might have cheated?"

"No." Then she remembered the phone calls in the middle of the night. "There have been a few hang-ups and a female asked for Nate--not Nathan--but Nate." She put down her cup and fiddled with her ring. "Could she be the reason he likes to be called Nate? She's younger and prettier than me."

Shaking her head, Joely murmured some words of comfort, but they didn't help. A wave of nausea overcame Val. She bolted for the nearby bathroom.

On top of everything else, she was sick. All thoughts ceased while she emptied her stomach.

Afterwards, she hoped that Chip wouldn't catch it. The last thing she needed was a kid with the flu. Or even worse, Joely could catch it. She splashed cold water on her face and returned to her friend. "Sorry about that. I shouldn't have come over. I don't want to expose you to anything."

Joely chewed on her lower lip. "Is there any chance. . . ." She didn't finish her thought.

"What?" Val feigned cluelessness. The truth was, even though Chip caught every bug that passed through the city, Val remained healthy. She hadn't thrown up since three years ago when she'd had food poisoning. And before that, when she'd been pregnant. She shook her head. "I can't be pregnant."

"Well, that's a relief." Joely pretended to wipe sweat off her brow.

She did some calculating in her head. "I mean, it's technically possible, but. . . I can't be. I just can't." Out of nowhere, she burst into tears.

Joely scooted closer. She rubbed soothing circles on Val's back.

Val cried and cried. "This can't be happening. I'm pregnant and my husband wants a divorce. I'm going to have a baby and the father isn't going to be around." Worried that she was soaking Joely's shirt with her tears, Val pulled back. She went to the bathroom and grabbed a box of tissues. "Looks like I should buy stock in these." A half-smile touched her lips.

"It's going to be all right. Do you have any pregnancy tests--just to make sure?"

Val nodded. "You wouldn't happen to have one here, would you?"

Joely shook her head, her expression turning sad.

In the distance Val could hear Chip and Anna discussing the rules of alien drag car racing. A sentimental smile formed as she considered that her son might finally have a sibling. God, if she were to have another baby, she wanted to raise it in her hacienda. To use the nursery down the hall that she'd recently painted yellow.

Suddenly, she needed to get home. Once alone in her master bath, she did what she had to do. Then waited.

# # #

Nathan looked around Rod's two-story Colonial and saw the signs of a happy family. School pictures of his three kids (two girls and a boy) in silver frames on the fireplace mantel, American Girl dolls and a baseball mitt strewn across the floor, books about fairies and unicorns and dinosaurs on the coffee table. In the evenings, the house vibrated with chatter and laughter. Both Rod and his wife worked full-time and the kids were all in school. During the day, like now, the place was eerily quiet.

God, he needed a drink. Why did Rod get to have all of this? Not only did he have a Norman Rockwell family, but he also owned a successful business. At one time, Nathan had hoped to follow in Rod's footsteps, but that dream had died. Nathan no longer had thousands of dollars in savings. He no longer had the brains to run his own shop. And he certainly had screwed up any chances he had of staying married to Val.

Spotting Rod's wedding picture across the room, Nathan tried to remember what Val looked like on their wedding day. But he couldn't. He could, however, see her spunky, pink-streaked hair. He could see her ocean blue eyes and her easy smile. He hadn't given her much to smile about lately, but somehow he knew that she was a glass half-full kind of girl. He didn't remember marrying her, but he did know that he loved her.

Even though he knew it was pointless, he went to the kitchen and started searching all of the cabinets for alcohol. He climbed up on a chair to check above the fridge. A lot of people kept their liquor there. Especially if they had kids. But there was nothing. Clearly, Rod took this AA stuff seriously.

He got in his car and drove to the bar. His bar. He parked his car, but didn't get out. Instead, he stared at the door. The sign said "Must be 21 to enter." His breath drew in slowly.

If he just had a few drinks, his life wouldn't feel so shitty. He watched a man wearing a hat and dark glasses go into the bar. That man was on his way to forgetting his worries and Nathan couldn't help envying him.

An image of him and Mia in bed formed. She'd done most of the seducing that night, but he hadn't exactly resisted. Why had he thrown his marriage away like that?

Closing his eyes, he felt the tug to chase his troubles away with booze. Yet part of him wanted to figure things out. If he kept his mind clear, would he be able to fix any of his mistakes?

He stared at the door to the bar. *I've been there before and it didn't do me any good.*

Just then his cell phone rang. He looked at the caller i.d. and saw that it was Mia. He didn't answer. When it rang a few minutes later, he almost didn't even check. He did, though, and saw that it was Val. "Hello?" His heart thudded inside his chest.

"I need to talk to you."

CHAPTER THIRTY-SIX

Val met Nathan at a coffee shop. Neither of them could commit to a meeting that lasted longer than the time it took to drink eight ounces. She sat across from him at a round table, barely big enough to hold their mugs.

Cupping her hands around her decaf, she tapped her foot nervously. Her uterus ached. Behind her, the espresso machine whirred loudly.

"How are you?" he asked.

"Fine."

"How's Chip?"

She hesitated. A group of teenagers laughed at a faraway table. "I had him tested. . . . It turns out he's dyslexic."

Concern lined his face. "I'm sorry. So that's why he's having such a hard time learning to read."

She nodded and crossed her ankles. "I guess it's kind of bad news and good news. It turns out there are certain techniques that have been proven to help dyslexic kids learn to read. I'll need to get him a tutor, but it'll be worth it."

"Of course it will be. I'll help pay. . . ." Misery filled his eyes. He must've realized he didn't have any money for such an offer.

She appreciated his generous instincts, though. She swallowed, not anxious to talk about her situation. "I'll figure something out. The house is in pretty good condition, except for the roof, of course. If it sells, then I'll have the money for tutoring."

He took a sip of his coffee and scrunched up his face as if disappointed with the taste.

She struggled to get comfortable in the hard-back chair. "I need to tell you something. But first I want to know why you said in counseling you want a divorce."

He scratched the stubble on his chin. "I think it's inevitable. Let's just get it over with."

"But why? Is it because you've met someone else?" Her body stiffened with fear. Did she really want to hear this?

He shook his head. "No. Definitely not." But something in his demeanor made her doubtful. His green eyes held a mystery.

"You can tell the truth. She came by the house yesterday."

He sat up straight, his eyes intent on hers. "What?

Who?"

Val knew she'd been right. He knew exactly who. "She's attractive. I can see why you like her."

"I don't like her." He fumbled for words. "I can't believe she came by the house."

A sharp pain poked her chest. "Did you sleep with her?"

His eyes darted away.

That was her answer. She dug her fingernails into her palm. *Don't cry--don't cry*. Her other hand cupped her belly. "I think we should continue with counseling."

"Why?"

"Because I'm pregnant." When he didn't respond, she bumped the table as she stood, spilling some of her coffee. Too bad. She got into her car and drove away from the coffee shop.

Then the tears came.

# # #

Once she arrived home, Val dried her eyes and glowered at the stack of newspapers on the checkered kitchen floor. Nathan's newspapers. "I guess there's no point in saving these." She reached down, grabbed as many as she could and stuffed them into the trash. Then she kept going until she realized she was going to puke.

She grabbed her gut as she leaned over the toilet.

This poor baby. When her stomach felt void, she washed up and returned to the kitchen. A headline about a local business expanding caught her eye. She pulled the top paper out of the trash. When she read the details, she discovered they already had an interior decorating firm. A sigh escaped her lips.

She moved to a chair in the breakfast nook and flipped through the paper for other articles of interest. Her gaze landed on an ad for a Parents-Without-Partners mixer.

Her hand caressed her belly. She was going to be a single mother once again. Disgusted with her bad taste in men, she shook her head. Unlike most wives, she wouldn't even get to keep the house after the divorce.

An idea came to her. She remembered that divorced dad she met at the estate sale. He'd said his house was stark and white. Considering about half of all marriages end in divorce, that meant an awful lot of people starting over from scratch. That meant lots of dads who needed help decorating their new homes.

It was too late to save her own house, but at least she could save Kelly Designs.

# # #

Nathan didn't show up for their next marriage counseling appointment. Val decided to stay and talk anyway. She really needed some advice.

"It looks like I'm destined to be a single mom."

"Nathan isn't interested in reconciling?" Dr. Shouse asked.

Val gestured to the empty seat beside her on the couch. "As you can see, he's not. Maybe he's doing me a favor. I mean, he's the reason I have to sell the house."

"He's also the reason you had the house in the first place."

Yes, it was all very confusing. Nathan had screwed up and yet he'd always had her best interests at heart. Until he cheated on her. "He slept with another woman. I'm not sure either of us will be able to forget that."

"You don't have to forget. You only have to forgive."

Counselors had lots of clichés, but it wasn't so easy in the real world. "How can I forgive him when he won't forgive himself?"

Dr. Shouse nodded. "I think Nathan has a lot of anger about the fall-out from the accident. Our society defines men by their jobs and by getting fired, Nathan lost a big part of who he was. That's probably why he started drinking."

"You asked me last time how he's different now than before his fall. I started thinking that he reminds me of this calico cat my grandmother used to have. You could pet it and it would purr, but a moment later, it would turn around and bite you. That's how Nathan is now."

Pondering that analogy, the counselor rubbed her chin. "Why do you think your grandmother kept the cat?"

"Hmm. That's a good question. I guess she'd had the cat for a long time and felt attached to it."

"Even though it bit her grandchild, she kept that cat. Interesting."

Is she insinuating that Grandma cared more about that cat than me? That's ridiculous. "It only bit me a couple of times before I figured him out. He only liked to be petted for a few minutes before he'd had enough."

"Can you learn something from that which you can apply to Nathan?"

Growing impatient, Val shifted in her seat, then touched her belly the way pregnant women often did. "I don't know. I'm having his baby. What about that? Shouldn't he offer to do whatever it takes to make this marriage work?"

As usual, Dr. Shouse remained calm. "If you can get Nathan to come in with you next time, I'd be glad to see if I can help you re-negotiate your relationship." She paused. "My question to you is what do you want that relationship to look like?"

Did she want to stay married to someone who'd cheated on her? Would she always wonder if Nathan would run to that other woman when things got tough? Did she want to raise another child with a man who was unpredictable? "I don't know."

"You have to clarify your wants and needs. Once you know your goal, then you have a better chance of reaching it."

# # #

When he'd heard that Val was pregnant with his child, Nathan's mouth fell open. Just when he'd permanently destroyed his marriage, a baby came along. But it was so unfair. That baby didn't deserve a screwed-up, brain-damaged man for a father.

He showed up for his physical therapy appointment and saw the glee in Mia's eyes. He followed her into the corner room.

She closed the door behind them. "Too bad we don't have locks on these." She leaned in to kiss him, but he turned his head away.

He crossed his arms.

She touched his knee. "I'm glad you came today. I thought you were blowing me off."

"Did you come to my house?"

"Maybe." She tossed her curly, brown hair flirtatiously.

Sure, she was pretty. But she wasn't worth

throwing away a marriage for. He fiddled with his wedding band. Val was pregnant with his child. She'd asked him to meet her at the counselor's office this week. That seemed promising, right?

He pushed Mia's hand off his knee. "I'm sorry if I led you on, but I'm married. You knew that."

She trailed her finger lightly down his jawline. Her long lashes fluttered. "But you always talk about her like she's a pain."

"Do I?" He hadn't realized.

She continued stroking his cheek. She leaned in and brushed her lips over his face.

Something about it felt familiar, but he couldn't put his finger on it. He pulled away. "Mia, please stop."

Nodding, she stayed close enough that he could smell her vanilla perfume. "You're right. Not here. I could meet you at my place on my lunch hour."

He tried to ignore her wonderful scent. "I can't. I'm sorry if I hurt you, but I'm not this guy. I'm not a cheater."

She backed away from him. "You *are* this guy. You've made out with me more than once. I'm the one you called when you were in trouble. Not her. She didn't bail you out of jail. I did." Her brown eyes turned cold.

"I know." He didn't really remember much about that night, but he knew it'd been a mistake. "I was drunk. I wasn't thinking straight."

"Are you telling me you're happily married? You're going back to your wife now?" Her voice sounded mocking.

He shook his head. "All I know is that you and I can't be together."

She pointed her finger at him. "You're a self-centered jerk."

He stared at the floor. There was no denying it. He hurt every woman that dared to care for him. He regretted that Mia had so quickly grown fond of him, but he really regretted that Mia had been the vehicle that crashed into his marriage. He made eye contact. "I'm trying to do the honorable thing here. I came to tell you that it's over and that I'll be finding a new physical therapist."

Tears pooled in her eyes and he felt the urge to comfort her. He took a deep breath and restrained himself. "I wish you all the best." He stood and headed toward the door.

"You want to know something? This is stupid. You and I never even did the deed."

His head whipped around to catch her expression. "But I remember going into your bedroom. . . ."

"Yeah. As soon as your head hit the pillow, you passed out." She licked her lips. "I was hoping you'd be able to satisfy me when you were sober, but somehow I doubt that. I bet you're boring as hell in the sack. You're a boring, old man."

Her words didn't even sting. He opened the door, marched out of the office and out of Mia's life forever.

CHAPTER THIRTY-SEVEN

The doorbell rang and Joely called from her bedroom for Anna to get it. Joely slipped the strap of the black one-piece suit over her shoulder, but didn't look in the mirror. Instead, she gazed at the other two suits she'd ordered from the catalog that lay on her bed. All were in supposedly slimming black, but each a different size. She hadn't wanted to worry about it not fitting her.

Her thumb pulled at the leg cut-outs as she heard Jake and Anna say their hellos. It felt a little tight, but swimsuits always did. She cracked open the bedroom door and stuck her head out. "Jake, could you come here a minute?"

She watched Anna do a little dance in her pink, ruffled swimsuit as Jake made his way to her door. Joely hesitated to let him see her.

His eyebrows pulled together. "Yes?"

A gulp of air. She opened the door quickly and ushered him in. "Okay. I need to know what you think."

His gaze rested on the other black tanks on the

comforter and he seemed to understand. "It looks good."

She stood back as if wanting him to view her from head to toe. "I want you to be honest. This is what I look like."

"You do know that I've seen you naked, don't you?" He smirked.

"That's different. The lights were out." And she always made sure she hid under the covers. "I was hoping I could exercise enough to get my old figure back, but I can't. The doctor said if my joints hurt for more than two hours after a work-out that I overdid it. Well, they hurt for days." Even if she warmed them before the gym and iced them afterward.

Compassion spread across his face. "I told you that I understand. I love your body the way it is."

Her arms crossed self-consciously over her voluptuous chest. "Since when do you like fat girls?"

He came toward her, his arms open. She stiffened as he hugged her. For all the years that she'd known him, he'd never dated anyone with an ounce of pudge. Even his ex-wife had been a former Calvin Klein model.

His hand stroked her hair. "Joely, we're not twenty anymore. Neither of us can go back and I, for one, don't want to. I was so shallow and full of myself then. Now I'm nearly forty and all I want is to share my life with you and Anna. Stop beating yourself up and let me take care of you." He kissed her forehead, nose, lips.

It still amazed her that he'd called off work just to be with her in the hospital. Often, she fell asleep to the memory of his carrying her out of bed. Her hero.

She giggled as his lips descended her body. Collarbone. Belly. In the end, he kissed her thighs. First the dimples on the right one.

"Stop it." Giggling louder, she swatted at his hair.

"I love every inch of you." Then the left thigh. He stood back to his six-foot-two height and his cool, blue eyes implored her.

Inside, her heart pounded. God, she was lucky. Her palm stroked his blond five o'clock shadow. "I probably can't give you another child."

He nodded. "I know. That's all right." A smile crinkled the corners of his eyes. "This way I can divulge all of my fatherly advice to Anna."

Her lips darted forward and captured his. She kissed him long and hard, as if he were providing her life. Neither of them seemed to want to separate. If circumstances were different, they'd move over to the bed. Instead, they kissed and touched and savored each other.

Anna knocked on the bedroom door. "Mommy? Can I come in?

Joely's lips reluctantly left Jake's. She turned her head toward the door. "Just a minute." She stepped back as if it would help her resist him. Deep breath. She focused on Jake. "I'm not giving up on exercise all together, though, because it can actually help with the lupus. I need to do something low-impact. So. . ." Her heart galloped. "I was wondering if you would teach me how to swim. Like you did Anna."

Again, a smile spread across his lips. "I'd be honored." And like teenagers, they stole another kiss.

# # #

Val heard Chip run to open the front door with Homer on his heels. Kelly walked in the house and greeted them. "Hi, guys. It's a bit drizzly out there today."

Val came into the foyer and saw her boss, Kelly, petting the dog. "Thanks for coming out in this." Val leaned Kelly's umbrella against one of the pillars between the foyer and living room. She helped her remove her trench coat then draped it over the banister. "I hope it stops soon. I'm not sure how much the roof can take."

Beneath her trench, Kelly wore a lilac dress with silver and gold necklaces. She shook out her brown bob and gazed around the entry. "I can't believe how gorgeous this place is."

"Thanks. Chip and I have been working hard." In fact, she hated herself for waiting for Nathan to do everything. It felt amazing to work up a sweat while restoring this place. "I don't want to sell, but. . . ." Sadness rose to her chest, but she tamped it back down. "Come in. Let me show you around."

Chip ran back up to his room, the stairs creaking beneath his feet. Homer, of course, followed.

Her boss had her real estate license and had offered to make suggestions for the upcoming sale. Val led her through the house counter-clockwise. First the library, dining room, breakfast nook and kitchen. Skipping the living room, they went up the stairs, past the hallway buckets strategically placed to catch leaks, to the six bedrooms and the bathroom with the chandelier over the tub. She saved her favorite room for last.

They went back down the stairs to the grand living room with its arched doors leading to the patio. A sigh escaped her. She'd let Joely down now that she was unable to hold the wedding here. She'd never host that wine party she'd envisioned on that patio either. For sure, she'd never open her own interior design studio.

Kelly admired the marble fireplace on the opposite wall. "This must be worth a fortune."

Val nodded. Most of the historic details would be too expensive to put in a house built these days. A lump clogged her throat. She knew she'd never live in a house this special ever again.

Kelly crossed the twenty-five foot room, looking out the windows. "I've been working on your idea to cater our services to divorced dads. I think it's brilliant."

"I'm glad."

"I've started spreading the word and am taking out some ads." Kelly stopped when she reached the piano tucked into the corner. "Wow. Did this come with the place?"

"Yes. I have the original owner's diary and she mentions it. It was a gift from her husband." Val winced. Helen and her husband had a stronger bond than she and Nathan. They'd survived post-partum depression before it had a name. Back when it was a crime for a woman to withdraw into herself and shirk her parenting duties. Her husband stood by her, tried to cheer her up, and eventually Helen remembered life's little pleasures. Like playing the piano and baking apple pies for her children. So why had her spirit failed to cross over?

Kelly played a scale up and down the keyboard. "It needs to be tuned."

Val shrugged. "Well, it is almost a hundred years old." She watched as Kelly's fingers touched the gold "Steinway" letters.

Kelly turned and looked at her. "Have you had this appraised?"

"No."

Kelly's fingertip graced the carved music stand. "I think it's worth a lot of money."

"I figure I'll leave it here for whoever buys the house."

Kelly shook her head. "No. I mean it's worth *a lot* of money. Maybe enough that you wouldn't have to sell the house."

The room started to spin. Val dropped onto the piano bench. "Are you serious?"

"I was watching 'If Walls Could Talk' the other day--"

"I love that show!"

"Me, too. Anyway, I think they had a square grand like this one and it was worth fifteen to twenty thousand dollars."

Val slapped her chest. "Oh, my God! If that's true, I could afford to fix the roof *and* keep the house!" She stood, grabbed Kelly's manicured fingertips and jumped up and down.

# # #

"I'm Nathan and I'm an alcoholic." Nathan stood in front of the room and settled his gaze on Rod. "I haven't had a drink in thirty days." The men and women in folding chairs applauded, but to Nathan it was a hollow victory.

He shifted his weight and stuck his hands in his jean pockets. "I never thought I was an alcoholic because I can make myself stop. But because of alcohol I don't know if I cheated on my wife or not. I mean, I kissed another woman and I feel bad about that. But maybe Val could forgive me for that. . . I don't know. The thing is I was so drunk, I went into another woman's bedroom and I can't even remember. . . ."

Someone coughed, but otherwise the room remained still. Quiet. Everyone listened to Nathan's confession. "I don't know what's the worst thing I did that night. I also got behind the wheel." His eyes moved to the second row and to Lex, who killed his best friend when he drove drunk. As if unable to stand the shared connection, Lex looked down at his folded hands in his lap.

Nathan squeezed the back of his neck. "Fortunately, the cops arrested me before I did any damage or hurt anyone." He swallowed. "I easily could've killed an innocent person that night." Blinking back tears, he shook his head. He sniffled and the floodgates opened. He sobbed in front of all of these strangers. "I'm sorry." His cheeks burned with embarrassment.

He wiped his nose with his knuckle. "Ever since I fell down the stairs, my life has been out of control. That's why I can't stop crying right now." He chuckled. "My wife doesn't like who I've become, I don't remember how to be my old self, and. . ." Another short laugh. "Now she's pregnant."

A gasp from the crowd. He looked at Rod whose eyes grew wide.

Nathan's nose continued to run, but he forced himself to go on. "I don't know if I can fix my marriage, but I know that I have to pull myself together for the sake of this baby. . . " Sniff. "All I know for sure is that alcohol doesn't help. I'm brain damaged enough as it is. From now on, I'll never take another drink."

Applause. Then a few people mumbled, "One day at a time. One day at a time."

CHAPTER THIRTY-EIGHT

Rows of white-painted, wooden chairs facing the fireplace filled Val's living room. With the grand piano gone, they easily fit thirty people in there. Val stood and watched Chip descend the stairs holding his ring bearer's pillow in front as if it were an offering to the gods. Beside him, Anna clasped a small basket of daisies, tossing their petals as she went.

Anna stumbled on one of the steps. Val's heart jumped. Chip grabbed Anna's hand and caught her. A collective sigh filled the air.

Chip bent over and picked up the pillow he'd dropped. They continued holding hands the rest of the way down. Murmurs of "how cute" traveled around the room.

From the back corner, Nathan's harmonica started playing "Here Comes the Bride." Val shivered with anticipation and memories.

Joely, dressed in her vintage, plain white dress, climbed down the stairs, her hand gripping the wrought iron banister for support. Daisies encircled her upswept brunette curls.

Val gasped at how gorgeous her friend looked. Joely's skin glowed and her rosy smile revealed all: this was truly the happiest day of her life. Right behind her, Kate followed, though there wasn't much of a train for her to carry. Even Joely's sister seemed pleased about this union.

Dark thoughts seeped into Val's head. *You might think you know what's to come, Joely, but you don't. After all, I'd thought Nathan and I would be together forever.* Too quickly their flame had burned out.

The aroma of fresh-baked apple pie filled her senses. She glanced around to see if anyone else smelled it, but they didn't seem to. *Helen.* Last night Val had read the last page of the diary. It said that Helen would always treasure this house as a testament to her husband's faith and love. All who lived here needed to treasure it, too. Now that Val had saved it from foreclosure, Helen should be able to rest easy.

Val squeezed her eyes shut and pushed all negativity aside. At one point Helen's marriage had seemed doomed, but it had worked out. At that thought, Val smiled, wishing Joely and Jake all the best. That's all anyone could hope for.

Joely made her way to the marble fireplace where Jake stood, waiting. He looked almost too perfect with his blond hair slicked back and his tall frame in a tux. His expression mimicked Joely's. They both had waited for this moment for too long.

As the minister conducted the ceremony, Val's mind wandered. Chip sat next to her during what seemed like the perfect celebration for Joely. Simple elegance surrounded by friends. Val watched as Joely and Jake grinned at each other. She was glad her friend had decided to quit fighting with her body and take her exercise regime slower. Jake was a great match for her. He stepped up to the plate whenever Joely's lupus flared. He'd even suggested Joely stop working at Kelly Designs and do commissioned artwork from home. Val hated the idea of not seeing her friend every day, but she understood. Joely hadn't made up her mind yet.

Chip pulled a piece of paper out of his pocket and studied it, his lips moving. Joely turned toward the boy and motioned that it was time. Chip hopped up and took center stage. He shifted from his left foot to his right, clasping the wrinkled paper. "Love is p-p-patient. Love is kind. It does not en-vy, it does not. . .boast." He coughed. "It is not proud." He wadded the paper up and shoved it into his pants pocket. Everyone laughed and applauded. Chip looked at Val and beamed. He'd been practicing that with his tutor for weeks.

After the brief ceremony, everyone moved out

onto the adjoining covered patio. The air smelled clean and sweet, like freshly mown summer grass. Val flipped on the ceiling fan before helping Kate pour the champagne. This was even better than the wine tasting party she had envisioned inside these arched doors. She chatted and laughed easily with the small crowd as she made her way through.

When she reached Nathan, she froze. She clutched the half-full champagne bottle tight.

He shook his head. "None for me. Thanks." His eyes looked olive today. Dark and sad.

Touching her protruding belly, she felt as if the world stopped. "I'm not drinking either." Her heart thudded. Her throat dried. She struggled to breathe.

He placed his palm over the hand covering their unborn child. "How is our little one today?"

One shoulder jerked up. "Okay, I guess." She didn't want his warm hand to move. Bittersweet time lingered. But she knew this couldn't last. She swallowed. "Well, I'd better get back to work." She gestured toward the champagne bottle.

His hand stayed put. His eyes locked on hers. "I asked Rod for my job back. No, that's not true. I can't do my old job. I told him I'd do anything. Oil changes. Wash cars. Simple stuff that I can't mess up."

"Nathan. . . ." Words failed her. She glanced at their two hands, fitting together like spoons. The way their bodies once had. "I'm happy for you."

His broad shoulders rose with his breath. "Once I've proven myself again, I'll ask him to re-train me on the more complicated stuff. I'll write it all down in my notebook." He removed his hand and a chill came.

She nodded, tears forming in her eyes. She wiped them away with her fist.

He reached in his breast pocket and handed her his handkerchief.

He could be so gallant. *Take it. Take it.* She accepted his offer and dabbed at her tears. "Thanks." Now what should she do? Hand it back to him or wash it first?

He held up his palm. "You keep it."

"We should talk. Maybe later."

He shook his head. "Now." He took the champagne bottle out of her hand and placed it on the table. Gently, he gripped her elbow and led her outside into the backyard, where it was less crowded. He looked around as if he expected to see Homer rolling in the grass, but Val had locked the dog away for the wedding.

Nathan returned his attention to her. "Is there any chance you could forgive me?"

She sucked in air. She didn't want to think about the past. All she wanted was for this baby to grow up in a happy home with two parents who adored it. Her hand rubbed her abdomen. "You really hurt me. I don't know if I can trust you." The words wrestled with her heart. Her insides screamed in protest. *You love him. He's the father of your child.*

His eyes glanced at her belly and then back at her face. "I'm in AA. I'll never see. . ." He didn't seem to want to say the woman's name. ". . .her again. I'm even going to take some anger management classes that the counselor recommended. I've got to learn how to. . ." He shook his head and stared at the ground.

She lifted his chin. "I'm sorry you have to work so hard. I'm sorry you fell down the stairs and hit your head."

"It's not your fault. You don't need to be sorry."

"But you tripped while you were doing me a favor." She shifted her weight, getting tired standing for so long. The heat seemed a bit much for her today.

"That's what husbands do for their wives." He gazed up at the orange barrel tiles. The roof was finally complete. "How did you come up with the idea to sell the piano?"

"Kelly helped me realize its worth." Her arms crossed over her chest. "The truth is I should've figured it out sooner." She thought of Helen playing the piano at night. Hinting that it held the key. Did Val dare tell him the truth? If they were going to try and work things out, there could be no more secrets. Her heart beat faster. "The house has a ghost and she tried to tell me."

He burst out laughing. A full belly laugh, his head tossed back.

She stepped away. Horrified. She turned and walked toward the crowd. Her hands shaking. Why had she told him? First her own mother scoffed and now him.

He grabbed her shoulder and spun her around. "I'm sorry. I'm sorry. I can't believe I laughed. I've seen your books about ghosts, but I didn't know you believed in them."

"Well, I do. And I don't think it's funny."

"I don't either. I don't know why I laughed. Sometimes my brain makes the wrong connection and my emotions get mixed up. I was surprised, but I didn't think it was funny." Now he started to cry. "Oh, Val. My sweet Valentine. I love you and I don't ever want to hurt you again."

His tears caught her off guard. This was who he was now. Hot and cold. Happy one minute and sad the next. And it wasn't his fault. He was trying everything he could to be the man he once was. But he probably never would be. Just like the counselor said.

She heaved deeply. With his handkerchief, she blotted his eyes. The corners of her lips pulled up. "I love you, too." Not that that was enough. Marriage was more complicated than that.

He sniffed. "I didn't sleep with her, you know. But I did do some stuff I shouldn't have. . . . Can you forgive me?"

It took a moment for that to sink in. He hadn't slept with that young woman. That was something.

"I'll even go on anti-depressants or whatever Dr. Shouse thinks will help."

The recent ceremony replayed in her mind. *For richer for poorer. In sickness and in health.* Did those words really mean anything? She swallowed. It was up to her to give those words power. "Better than that. I accept you for who you are." Just like Jake accepted Joely.

He pushed his lips against hers. Hard. Too hard.

She pulled back. She saw his forehead wrinkle in confusion. "There's something I want to show you." Her lips kissed his left cheek, then his right. For the third kiss, she gently touched their lips together. "Do you remember that?"

His eyes looked up and to the side, searching his brain. He shook his head.

"That's all right." She rubbed her thumb against his scratchy cheek, just as she had while he was lying in that coma. She had prayed to God to let him wake up and here he was. She'd promised that she'd be a devoted wife. "That's the way you kissed me on our first date. You told me later it was because you were trying to work up the nerve to kiss me on the lips." She smiled at the memory.

He cocked his head. "Is that how you prefer me to kiss you?"

She shrugged. "Not all the time. But sometimes."

"That's fair." His Adam's apple bobbed. He leaned in and kissed her left cheek. Softly, sweetly. A moment later his lips caressed her right cheek with equal care. Then he looked her in the eye and hesitated.

She longed for him to complete the sequence.

She licked her lips. Her breath shallow. Her soul on fire.

Her eyes studied his. Silently urging him to keep going. One, two, three. Three had to follow one and two.

Until at last. . .

He plunged his mouth forward onto hers. Her heart crescendoed with joy. Endorphins exploded throughout her body. Her eyelids fluttered closed. All of her senses shut off so she could focus solely on touch.

Oblivious to the people celebrating nearby, their embrace went on and on. It was the most passionate, intense kiss she'd ever experienced.

As their lips danced together, she knew he'd be sleeping in her bed tonight.

Tonight and always.

THE END

Coming soon on Amazon by Karen Lenfestey:
Made for Two:

History teacher Diane Solier was only acting on instinct when she broke up a fight at her inner city high school. When the principal suspends her until things get sorted out, Diane returns to her hometown of Foxworth. Almost immediately she finds herself tracking down her old boyfriend, Tim. Just seeing him brings back how much she loved him and she realizes that her life, just like her tandem bike, was made for two. Unfortunately, Tim keeps pushing her away, claiming it will never work out. After all, she still wants to live in the city and he can't imagine leaving his family's bakery. But there's more to it than that. Tim has been hiding in this small town because he has a secret.

ABOUT THE AUTHOR

Karen Lenfestey, a Midwest Writer's Fellowship winner, studied communication at Purdue University and counseling at Indiana University. She has two other novels, *A Sister's Promise* and *What Happiness Looks Like*. She is about to release her first novella, *Made for Two*, so watch for it on Amazon. When she isn't writing, Karen enjoys speaking to readers at libraries, conferences and book clubs.

Visit her webpage at **www.karensnovels.com**
and check out her semi-humorous "Thoughts on Motherhood" blog.
You can also follow Karen Lenfestey on Facebook, Twitter and GoodReads.com

Book Club Discussion Questions:

1. In the beginning, Chip wanted to go to Mexico with Val and Nathan. If you had a child when you got married, would you take him or her with you on your honeymoon?

2. Would you have stayed with someone you'd just married if his/her personality changed drastically? Would it be different if you'd been married for a long time?

3. Do you think a man or a woman is more likely to stay if their partner becomes gravely ill?

4. At what point did you feel that Nathan had crossed the line into unforgivable territory?

5. Which couple is more like you and your partner: Val and Nathan or Joely and Jake?

6. Do you think Joely and Jake should try to have a baby? Should they adopt?

7. Do you believe Nathan will be able to control his anger in the future?

8. Do you think Val's pregnancy influenced her decision to stay with Nathan?

9. Was Val a better mother, wife, or friend? Why?

10. What did Helen's spirit need to communicate to Val? Have you ever felt like there was a ghost in the room?

11. Do you think Val and Nathan will make it in the long run?

Made in the USA
Lexington, KY
05 March 2017

Why Do You Need This New Edition?

If you're wondering why you should buy the third edition of *Making Reading Relevant*, here are five good reasons!

1. The new **"Writing Like a Reader" feature** will help you connect your reading skills with your writing skills and become a better writer.

2. A **new Check Your Learning feature** at the end of each chapter provides a quick way to make sure you've mastered the learning objectives and to identify sections you need to review.

3. Chapter 6, "Patterns of Organization Strategies," has been expanded to include more patterns of organization. It includes several new readings that provide interesting, concise, and relevant examples of the patterns.

4. Chapter 8, now called "Information Literacy Strategies," has been updated to reflect current terms and methods of finding information via the Internet.

5. The entire book now **corresponds closely to MyReadingLab**. *Making Reading Relevant* now uses the same terminology and topics that you'll find in MyReadingLab, and throughout the text, you'll find prompts to visit MyReadingLab for further practice.

MAKING READING RELEVANT

RELEVANT

THE ART OF CONNECTING

Third Edition

MAKING READING RELEVANT

THE ART OF CONNECTING

Teri Quick
Melissa Zimmer
Diane Hocevar
Metropolitan Community College
Omaha, Nebraska

PEARSON

Boston   Columbus   Indianapolis   New York   San Francisco
Upper Saddle River   Amsterdam   Cape Town   Dubai London   Madrid
Milan   Munich   Paris   Montreal   Toronto   Delhi   Mexico City
São Paulo   Sydney   Hong Kong   Seoul   Singapore   Taipei   Tokyo

Senior Acquisitions Editor: Nancy Blaine
Editorial Assistant: Jamie L. Fortner
Assistant Editor: Amanda Dykstra
Executive Media Producer: Stefanie Snajder
Senior Digital Editor: Julia Pomann
Production Manager: Meghan DeMaio
Creative Director: Jayne Conte
Cover Designer: Suzanne Behnke
Cover Art: © mypokcik/shutterstock
Project Coordination, Text Design, and
    Electronic Page Makeup: Nitin Agarwal/Aptara®, Inc.
Printer/Binder: Edwards Brothers Malloy
Cover Printer: Lehigh-Phoenix Color

Credits and acknowledgments borrowed from other sources and reproduced, with permission, in this textbook appear on the appropriate page within text.

Library of Congress Cataloging-in-Publication Data

Quick, Teri.
    Making reading relevant : the art of connecting/Teri Quick, Melissa Zimmer, Diane Hocevar.—3rd ed.
        p. cm.
    Includes bibliographical references and index.
    ISBN-13: 978-0-321-88866-2 (student version)
    ISBN-10: 0-321-88866-9 (student version)   1. Reading (Higher education)
I. Zimmer, Melissa.   II. Hocevar, Diane.   III. Title.
    LB2395.3.Q53 2014
    428.4071'1— dc23

                                                                            2012036307

Student Edition
ISBN-10: 0-321-88866-9
ISBN-13: 978-0-321-88866-2

10 9 8 7 6 5 4 3 2 —16 15 14 13

Annotated Instructor's Edition
ISBN-10: 0-321-87930-9
ISBN-13: 978-0-321-87930-1

Contents

Preface

Sometimes less is more. In this age of information overload, it seems imperative that students learn to become better, more efficient readers—and not by reading volumes on *how* to read, but by exposure to essential reading strategies with a major focus on application practice. This practice can be done using "real-life" materials (primary reading sources, such as textbooks, newspapers, and magazines) and/or by using a computer-based program such as MyReadingLab. This text addresses all reading topics necessary for success in college reading, as well as those assessed on state-wide reading tests (including Texas and Florida). It's intended for use in any college reading course, from college prep to higher level, within a variety of contexts, which are as follows:

- Reading courses that incorporate MyReadingLab and/or primary reading sources, such as newspapers, news magazines, novels, textbooks, and the Internet. Essential reading strategies are presented, but the choice of practice materials should be consistent with the reading level of the course.
- Reading courses that will use this as a stand-alone text.
- Reading courses "paired" or "linked" with a content-area course. Students would use the content course textbook as their primary reading source, and would be truly *"making reading relevant."*
- Paired reading and writing courses or a combination reading/ writing developmental class. When reading is paired with a writing course, this text helps students see the strong connections between reading and writing. It includes a thorough chapter about patterns of organization strategies, which coincides well with most developmental writing courses. The text offers extended writing practice in the Learning Activities sections of the Instructor's Manual, in addition to the new "Writing Like a Reader" feature in every chapter.
- Online reading modules or courses. Due to the increasing demand for online courses, the text lessons and Learning Activities (included in the Instructor's Manual) are structured to be easily adapted for the development of online reading modules.
- Reading courses on a quarter system because of the brevity of the text.
- Reading courses on a semester system that focus on the application of strategies, using primary reading sources and MyReadingLab.

FEATURES NEW TO THE THIRD EDITION

- Addition of the *Writing Like a Reader* section in each chapter. This new feature helps students connect their reading skills to their writing skills, which helps them become better readers and writers. The addition of a writing component makes *Making Reading Relevant*, 3/e, an excellent choice as a textbook for paired reading/writing classes.
- Close alignment with MyReadingLab. The following new features make *Making Reading Relevant*, 3/e, the perfect companion textbook for MyReadingLab.
  - Topics and terminology in *Making Reading Relevant*, 3/e, now match closely with those in MyReadingLab.
  - MyReadingLab prompts throughout the text. Each chapter contains prompts to tell the student when to go to MyReadingLab for further practice.
- Addition of specific Learning Objectives (LOs) for each chapter or chapter section.
- Check Your Learning feature. We've added a quick way for students to do a self-check to make sure they've mastered the LOs for each chapter. If they can't check each objective, it suggests that they go back and review the section(s) they haven't mastered.
- Expanded Chapter 6, Patterns of Organization Strategies. New patterns and terminology were added to align with MyReadingLab. Several example readings for the patterns were changed to provide more interesting, concise, and relevant examples.
- Chapter 7 title changed to "Visual Literacy Strategies" to reflect the addition of a wider variety of graphic organizers and other ways to organize information in a visual format.
- Chapter 8 title changed to "Information Literacy Strategies." This chapter has been updated to be in line with current terms and methods of accessing information via the Internet.

ADDITIONAL FEATURES

The text and Instructor's Manual are structured to help students and instructors work through the lessons *quickly* and meaningfully.

Each chapter includes the following:

- Stated Learning Objectives followed by a readiness quiz. The readiness quiz isn't meant to be a true pretest; its purpose is to help gauge the prior knowledge of the students and to serve as a bridge to the chapter.
- Learning strategies with featured *QUICK* Tips to highlight some of the more important strategies

- Practices using a variety of concise real-life content within the text
- Writing Like a Reader feature
- Check Your Learning feature
- MyReadingLab connections and prompts
- Suggested learning activities called "*Quick* Connections" at the end of each chapter

In addition, *Making Reading Relevant*, 3/e, is strongly supported by the following supplements:

Annotated Instructor's Edition (ISBN 0321879309). Includes solutions to the exercises in the student edition and links to helpful resources in the Instructor's Manual.

Instructor's Manual (ISBN 0321888677). Features ideas for teaching the text strategies, extended practice activities, chapter check-up quizzes, Latin and Greek quizzes, and much more. Available for download from the Instructor Resource Center.

MyTest Test Bank (ISBN 0321888693). Pearson MyTest is a powerful assessment generation program that helps instructors easily create and print quizzes, study guides, and exams. Select questions from the test bank to accompany Making Reading Relevant, 3/e, or from other developmental reading test banks; supplement them with your own questions. Save the finished test as a Word document or PDF or export it to WebCT or Blackboard. Available at www.pearsonmytest.com.

Answer Key (ISBN 0321888685). Contains the solutions to the exercises in the student edition of the text. Available for download from the Instructor Resource Center.

This text is designed to be consumable. For maximum benefit, students need to actively respond to the passages and practices in the book by reading, writing, annotating, and highlighting as needed. Most reading texts currently available are much longer, more expensive, and require a greater commitment of students' time. We believe that reading courses that stress the use of primary sources and MyReadingLab for application practice are more effective than courses that have prechosen, often outdated reading selections for application practice.

This text can easily be read outside of class in preparation for classroom practice. The brevity of the text may encourage more (not less) outside reading by today's students, who are often reluctant to read extensively and/or whose busy lives limit time available for homework assignments. When introduced to new concepts, students benefit from instruction that connects the learning to the place(s) in their environments (work, school, home) where they can use it. Real-life materials might include chapters from content area textbooks, current event and editorial resources (such as magazines and newspapers), novels, college catalogs, recipes, written directions, websites, and computer practice like MyReadingLab. Current brain research indicates that "students are natural learners, are energized by learning, and apparently, love to learn when they can start learning something new from where they are, using what they already know, and can do their own exploring, thinking, and discovering" (Smilkstein, 2003). This research supports the use of active learning using real-life materials to foster authentic and lasting learning.

For several years, we searched for a simple, concise text to use in our reading classes. We didn't find a brief text that addressed all of the topics we wanted to include. Neither did we find anything that stressed the application of reading strategies using primary reading sources and proven computer practice sites (MyReadingLab) as the basis of the content. This text was written to fill those needs.

TO THE STUDENT

How important is reading to you?

As a student, reading serves as a major tool for learning. You probably have discovered that *how well* you read can and will determine the degree of success you achieve in your classes. Whether you're taking courses in business management, nursing, welding, or any other subject area, you'll be required to read for information, to follow directions, to understand what you read, and to think critically.

Whatever your current reading level, you're taking a positive first step in reaching your academic and career goals by taking a reading course. Actually, reading is much more complex than many students realize. Effective reading requires various levels of thinking. While it's necessary to determine what a passage *says,* it's also crucial to interpret what it *means.* Simply recalling facts differs from making inferences. However, both processes benefit from guided practice. Basic reading strategies cover what is obvious and clear in a passage. More challenging reading strategies cover those parts of a passage that require deeper reflection. In the college reading classroom, the instructor may verbally model both the literal and interpretive processes involved in reading a selection. Students should observe this verbalization and then actively participate in the learning process by sharing and discussing their own "reading thinking."

Making Reading Relevant: The Art of Connecting, 3/e, will introduce you to a comprehensive set of reading strategies. You can use these strategies as tools for learning in your college courses and for managing reading tasks you'll meet on the job and in daily living. The text was designed to minimize the number of practice passages so that you can apply the text strategies to real-life reading materials that are interesting and relevant. Good reading is an art, much like playing baseball or playing the piano. A teacher can show you how to hold the bat or how to put your fingers on the keys, but in order for you to hit home runs or become a concert pianist you need to practice. Our hope is that you'll read this text, complete the practices, apply the strategies to real-life materials, and go on to become a highly successful student!

Teri Quick
Melissa Zimmer
Diane Hocevar

Acknowledgments

Making Reading Relevant, 3/e, is dedicated to all of our family and friends who offered encouragement and support.

> ***From Teri, special appreciation goes to:*** The late Tom Markin, my dad, for his lifelong teaching and belief in me.

> ***From Melissa, special appreciation goes to:*** Scott Zimmer, my husband, a true partner. Kaleb and Chloe, my children, who make my world go round. Janet Riordan, my late mother, whose love for reading forged my path. Jennifer Rumer, my sister, whose belief in me sustains me. Jeremiah Riordan, my dad, who saved our lives.

> ***From Diane, special appreciation goes to:*** Bob Mancuso, my uncle, who encouraged me to become a teacher. The late Joseph (Chic) and Josephine Mancuso, my parents, who taught me so much about life.

Thanks also to the following people for their roles in making the book happen: Nancy Blaine, our editor, for her guidance and support; Amanda Dykstra, our assistant editor, who's amazing and has helped us tremendously; Laura Mann for encouraging us to write the book; and Craig Campanella, our past editor, for his patience and wisdom.

And also thanks to the following reviewers: AnaLaura Gonzalez, Laredo Community College; Agnes Kubrak, Henry Ford Community College; Denise Clay, Fullerton College.

Teri Quick
Melissa Zimmer
Diane Hocevar

One

Vocabulary Strategies

Chapter Preview

Vocabulary Strategies Overview

LEARNING OBJECTIVES (LOs)

Upon completion of this chapter, you will be able to:

▪ LO1—Define an unknown word by using context clues

▪ LO2—Define an unknown word by using word analysis strategies

▪ LO3—Use denotation and connotation to determine the author's meaning of a word

A good vocabulary . . .
          always speaks well for you.

Readiness Quiz   ⚙ Complete this Exercise at MyReadingLab.com

Section 1: Match the underlined word on the left to the best definition on the right.

1. _____	Because _hyperactive_ children often become distracted, teachers should provide a calm environment.	**A.** rule by royalty
2. _____	He is _resilient_, not a weak person.	**B.** loud
3. _____	That man drives me crazy; he is so _vociferous_! I wish he would be quiet.	**C.** overactive
4. _____	Queen Elizabeth is the head of England's _monarchy_.	**D.** opposed
5. _____	Instead of supporting me, he is _averse_ to my position.	**E.** able to recover strength

Section 2: Mark each statement below **T** for true or **F** for false.

6. _____ I know how to sound out a word.

7. _____ I know what the Latin root **aqu** means.

8. _____ The connotation of a word is its dictionary definition.

9. _____ The suffix comes at the beginning of a word.

10. _____ Word analysis involves looking at word parts.

VOCABULARY STRATEGIES OVERVIEW

Improving your vocabulary is important to your success in college, as well as to your success in life. In college, you need a well-developed vocabulary in order to comprehend and learn information presented in your textbooks and to write papers that will earn high grades. In life, you need a good working vocabulary that allows you to succeed in your career and communicate well with others. Vocabulary is associated with educational level and intelligence. Most educated, intelligent people have broad vocabularies, and like it or not, we are often evaluated by our ability to communicate effectively through the use of the oral and written word.

There are two common strategies for finding the meaning of unfamiliar words: context clues and word analysis. This chapter will describe both. A reader can determine the meanings of many words without having to stop to look them up in a dictionary. The use of context clues and word analysis improves reading comprehension and enhances retention of new words because we tend to remember words we figure out for ourselves.

This chapter will also explain the difference between a word's denotative and connotative meanings. It's important to understand how an author uses words to suggest certain meanings or to evoke emotion in the reader. Understanding denotation and connotation will enable you to notice a writer's word choices and more effectively discern what they are meant to convey. Learning and using the strategies in this chapter will get you well on your way to becoming a more capable reader and communicator!

A. Context Clues

Context clues are the words and sentences around a word that can give clues to its meaning. Writers sometimes knowingly use words that may be unfamiliar to their readers. Therefore, they may use other clarifying words or phrases to help with the understanding of new words. These words or phrases are called **context clues.** If readers are aware that such clues often exist in words or sentences surrounding the unknown words, they can save time and improve comprehension. Context clues enable the reader to make valid guesses about the meanings of many unfamiliar words.

Review the chart below for an explanation and example of each of the four main types of context clues.

Now practice using the four clues.

Clue	Explanation	Example
Definition or Synonym	A definition or synonym (i.e., word that means the same) is in the sentence with the word	**Hypochondria is** abnormal anxiety about one's health.
Example	Examples or illustrations that clarify the word's meaning	He has many **idiosyncrasies, such as** the inability to cross a bridge, holding his feet up across a railroad track, and not letting his food touch on his plate.
Contrast or Antonym	The word's antonym, or opposite, appears in the sentence	The bride was **elated** on her wedding day; however, her parents were very heavy-hearted.

Clue	Explanation	Example
Inference or General Sense	You must apply your background knowledge to the information the context offers	The classroom was **commodious** enough to hold 30 desks, 30 computer stations, an entire technology center for the instructor, and several large bookcases.

1. DEFINITION/SYNONYM   Sometimes the context in which an unfamiliar word appears contains a definition in the form of a synonym or a longer explanation. A reader needs to look for a stated definition or synonym in the sentence containing an unfamiliar word.

USING THE CLUE

Read the sentence and circle the definition of the bold-printed word.

1. A **stamen** is the pollen-producing male organ of a flower.

2. Mary **commiserated,** or sympathized, with a friend who had lost her job.

3. To **harass** someone means to continuously annoy him.

4. Those born in the United States have **suffrage** (the right to vote).

5. The study of how people think and learn, **cognition,** is a field that attracts many psychologists.

Look for the following to help locate a definition in the sentence containing an unfamiliar word:

Clues	"refers to," "is defined as," "means," or "is"
Words in italics	Partitions are *dividers* for rooms.
Words set off by parentheses, dashes, or commas	I have a disorder, vertigo, that leaves me feeling dizzy and confused.
Synonyms	My new neighbor is a sot, or drunkard.

QUICK TIP

Commas, parentheses, and dashes often set off a word from its definition.

2. EXAMPLE Writers often use examples to clarify the meaning of unfamiliar words and terms. Examples are vivid illustrations or explanations that define, either by creating familiar images in your mind or by recalling familiar objects, ideas, or situations.

Using the Clue

Read the sentence and answer the questions.

1. To get along with your partner, do your share of **chores,** for example, sweeping, dusting, cleaning the bathroom, doing laundry, and putting the dishes in the dishwasher.

   What are the chores? _____

   _____

   What words let you know "here comes the list"? _____

2. Coughing, runny nose, scratchy eyes, red splotches on your skin, and sneezing illustrate a few **ailments** that are usually associated with allergies.

   What are the ailments? _____

   _____

   Ailments must be _____

3. Jim is a **malcontent** because he has such a negative attitude and finds fault with everything.

   What two things do a malcontent do? _____

   _____

4. I would not mind being locked up with a **docile** animal (cat, goldfish), but I would mind a **predatory** (lion, tiger) one!

   What are two examples of docile animals? _____

   Docile must mean _____

5. The museum owner was trying to **authenticate** the portrait from the 1800s and the vase from King Henry's collection.

   What two things were the owner trying to authenticate? _____

   _____

   Authenticate must mean _____

   _____

Example clue words	for example, such as, consists of

3. CONTRAST/ANTONYM Sometimes the context in which an unfamiliar word or term appears contains an antonym, or opposite word, that helps define the word. Look for words like *but, on the other hand,* or *however* to signal an opposite word from which you can gain meaning for the unfamiliar word.

Using the Clue

Read the sentences and define the words.

1. The climate in the Midwest is never **static;** on the contrary, it changes daily.

   Define static _____

2. In Darwin's day, his theory of evolution was **iconoclastic,** but today many people think it is a reasonable theory.

   Define iconoclastic _____

3. Although he was gone an **eon,** when she saw him, it seemed like only yesterday they had parted.

   Define eon _____

4. Everyone was pleased to discover that the bus driver was **circumspect,** unlike his brother the taxi driver, whose driver's license had been revoked for recklessness.

   Define circumspect _____

5. My teacher has been called **altruistic** because he gave up his professional baseball career to serve as a teacher in a village in Africa. On the other hand, he has been called **egocentric** because he constantly boasts about what he does for others.

   Define altruistic _____

   Define egocentric _____

Contrast clue words	however, on the other hand, in contrast, but, yet, unlike, different

---

4. INFERENCE/GENERAL SENSE   An inference is an informed guess based upon what you already know and the information available. Sometimes you have to make a guess about a word based upon prior knowledge combined with the information given.

Using the Clue

Read the sentence and answer the questions.

1. The maniac concocted a **diabolic** plan to end the world.

   Define diabolic _____

2. The elementary teacher's **buoyant** manner made the children feel welcome and at ease on the first day of school.

   Define buoyant _____

3. The **deft** hands of the artist created a beautiful portrait of the queen.

   Define deft _____

4. It was an **enigmatic** situation, and, as the detective, I had to work overtime to put the facts together.

   Define enigmatic _____

5. Living alone for years, the man developed strange and **eccentric** habits.

   Define eccentric _____

QUICK TIP

Read the words and/or sentences around an unfamiliar word to find clues that help you connect meaning to the word.

QUICK TIP

Look for signal words like "for example" (to illustrate), "however" (to contrast), "means" (to define), and "therefore" (to infer).

USING THE CLUES IN PARAGRAPHS

Use context clues to determine the meaning of each underlined word in the following paragraphs.

Advertising for tobacco products is the most <u>pervasive</u> evidence of company efforts to keep their products in the public eye. Full-page ads in magazines and on billboards portray young, healthy, successful, physically fit people enjoying tobacco products in a variety of circumstances ranging from <u>opulent</u> restaurants and apartments to rafting, boating, and wind surfing.

_____ 1. pervasive

      a. pertinent   b. common   c. perfected

_____   2. opulent

> a. bizarre   b. cheap   c. expensive

In today's society, all people have the freedom to explore and develop their potential. We each carry with us responsibility to pursue emotional well-being. During our lifetime we each will be faced with choices to grow or choices to <u>stagnate</u>. Our emotional growth depends upon our ability to take active roles in its development.

_____   3. stagnate

> a. commence   b. stand still   c. endure

Addictions <u>evolve</u> gradually, often from very <u>innocuous</u> beginnings. A person who feels unhappy, overwhelmed, threatened, or bored finds a subject or behavior that produces a state of being the person desires, or that <u>suppresses</u> what the person wants to forget. <u>Moderate</u> use of these behaviors, for example, having an occasional drink or partying with friends, does not <u>constitute</u> an addiction. Some people, however, reach a point where they can experience security or pleasure only when they are involved with this object or behavior. Withdrawal of the object produces anxiety and despair. At this point, when the person has lost control and cannot function without the object, he or she is considered addicted.

_____   4. evolve

> a. develop   b. shrink   c. evade

_____   5. innocuous

> a. carefully planned   b. harmless   c. mysterious

_____   6. suppresses

> a. contradicts   b. subdues   c. combines

_____   7. moderate

> a. reasonable   b. secluded   c. numerous

_____   8. constitute

> a. contain   b. abolish   c. establish

Key: 1. B, 2. C, 3. B, 4. A, 5. B, 6. B, 7. A, 8. C

How did you do? Were you able to figure out the meaning of the words by using context clues? Being aware of, and looking for, context clues to word meaning is the first step in building a better vocabulary. The second step, word analysis, will be explained next.

⌐MyReadingLab ─────────────────────────────

For more help with **Vocabulary,** go to your learning path in
MyReadingLab at www.myreadinglab.com.

B. Word Analysis

Word analysis is breaking a word into parts to find meaning. When a reader comes across an unfamiliar word, there are several options available: skip the word, stop and look it up in a dictionary, reread the paragraph containing the word and use context clues to try to figure it out, or use word analysis to try to find its meaning. You've just learned how to use context clues, and when you combine those strategies with word analysis, you're well on your way to more effective vocabulary building.

What does "use word analysis" mean? Word analysis is done using two processes in combination. The first one, breaking the word into syllables and looking for familiar prefixes, root words, and suffixes, may already be a familiar step. The other part of the process, looking for Latin and Greek word parts, may be less familiar. If so, this section will explain how to learn and use common Latin and Greek roots to help analyze and bring meaning to unknown words. The two processes, syllabication and looking for Latin and Greek word parts, can be done at the same time to quickly find meaning for an unfamiliar word.

Consider, for example, the word **immovable.** If you don't know this word, you can start by dividing the prefix, root word, and suffix. Thus you would have the prefix **im,** the root **mov,** and the suffix **able.** Think about what each part means. **Im** is a common prefix meaning "not." The root word **mov** is a Latin root meaning "move." The suffix **able** means exactly what it looks like—able to do whatever comes before it. Put the three meanings together and you have *not move able*—or not able to be moved—which is what immovable means.

Many words don't have a prefix, root, and suffix, and many don't contain a Latin or Greek part. Even so, any word can be broken into syllables, which makes it easier to see if there are prefixes or suffixes, or a Latin or Greek part. If there aren't, dividing words into syllables may help with pronunciation. Since our listening vocabulary is much greater than our reading vocabulary, we recognize many more words by sound than by sight. Thus, if readers can pronounce and hear a word, there's a good chance they will recognize the word and know its meaning.

Using context clues in combination with word analysis strategies enables the reader to quickly determine meaning for many words that are unfamiliar when first encountered. Being able to find meaning for unknown words is a great way to increase vocabulary, which in turn increases comprehension.

QUICK TIP

If you don't remember the long and short vowel sounds, ask your instructor to review them. Many college students have forgotten long and short vowel sounds, but you need to know them to be able to pronounce words.

1. ROOT WORDS, PREFIXES, SUFFIXES Once you've divided a word, look at the first and last parts to see if they include a common prefix and/or suffix. Prefixes come at the beginnings of words and change or modify the meaning. Suffixes do the same thing, but they're added at the ends of words. Prefixes generally have more meaning than suffixes. Many suffixes are used to change the tense (*ed* or *ing*), or to show the state or condition of the root word (*ar, al*). Other suffixes do carry meaning, such as *able/ible* (able to), or *ful* (full of).

Some of the most common prefixes mean *not,* or the opposite of what the word means without the prefix. You may recognize the ones in the list below:

un	unhappy
in	inadequate
il	illegal
im	immeasurable
ir	irrational
a	asexual

Train yourself to immediately recognize these prefixes and know that they mean *not,* or the opposite of what the word would be without the prefix. Other common prefixes you should immediately register meaning for are *re*—again, *pre*—before, *co* or *con*—together, and number prefixes such as *uni*—one, *bi*—two, and *tri*—three. Studying common Latin and Greek word parts will teach you the meaning of many more prefixes.

The core of a word is the part we call the root. This is the part that has the main meaning. Because many words are made by adding prefixes and suffixes, the root of the word is often in the middle. Most long words are just a root word with several prefixes and suffixes added. That's why breaking words apart can often show you quickly what they mean if you know the meanings of the separate parts. For example, a word like *irreplaceable* may look long and unfamiliar to you. But if you break it into syllables, starting by dividing off the prefixes and suffixes, you end up with this: ir-re-place-able. Look at each of those parts and substitute the meaning for the prefixes, root and suffix, and you see this: not-again-place-able. This is what the word means: not able to place again, or not able to be replaced. Many longer words are just a string of prefixes and suffixes, so separate those from the root word, and you'll see that long words can be easy to pronounce.

As previously mentioned, suffixes come at the end of words, and they also change, or modify, meaning. Suffixes often change the part of speech of the word as well. For example, *dirt* is a noun, but when the suffix *y* is added, *dirt* becomes *dirty*, which is an adjective. Below is a chart of common suffixes that readers need to know in order to use word analysis to help determine the meaning of unknown words.

Noun Suffixes

Suffix	Meaning	Example
-al	act or process of	refusal, removal, approval
-acy, -ance, -ence	state or quality of	privacy, maintenance, eminence
-er, -or, -ist	one who	trainer, protector, chemist
-ism	doctrine, belief	communism, socialism, materialism
-ity, -ty	quality of	simplicity, duplicity, elasticity
-ment	condition of	contentment, resentment, improvement
-ness, -sion, -tion, -dom	state of being	heaviness, concession, transition, freedom

Verb Suffixes

-ate, -en	become	authenticate, enlighten, duplicate
-ify, -fy, -ize, -ise	make or become	solidify, terrify, civilize, expertise

Adjective Suffixes

-able, -ible	capable of being	presentable, certifiable, edible
-ful	full of	meaningful, playful, resentful
-ic, -ical, -al	pertaining to	authentic, mythical, musical
-ious, -ous, -y	characterized by	nutritious, portentous, messy
-ish, -ive	having the quality of	fiendish, brownish, creative
-less	without	endless, fearless, shameless

QUICK TIP

Most long words are made up of a root word with added prefixes and suffixes—take words apart to make them easy to define.

Of course, since the root of a word is the basic part with the most meaning, you have to know what the root means to get meaning for an entire word. Some words, called **compound words,** may contain two roots, or two words put together, such as doghouse. Knowing the meaning of the root or roots is where Latin and Greek come into the process of word analysis.

2. LATIN AND GREEK   Because of the far-reaching influences of the ancient Roman and Greek societies, over half of the English language is based on Latin and/or Greek word parts. Learning some of the most common Latin and Greek parts is a fast way to build a better vocabulary. Once you know the meaning of the parts, you will start recognizing them in unfamiliar words, and you will be able to use your knowledge of the word parts along with the context to figure out meanings of unknown words. The Latin and Greek word parts must be memorized (in your long-term memory) in order for them to permanently help you with your vocabulary.

QUICK TIP

Flash cards are a great way to memorize the word parts and their meanings. Remember to draw pictures on them!

Following are five lists of the most common and widely used Latin and Greek prefixes and root words. There are 20 prefixes or roots in each list. Think of these lists as your Top 100 vocabulary builders. The prefixes and roots need to be memorized and placed in your long-term memory in order for them to be of benefit to you. We suggest learning 20 words a week for five weeks, reviewing all words weekly as they're learned, and taking a final test over all 100 parts. This process will ensure that you'll remember the meanings when you encounter the roots or prefixes in words. Knowledge of these Latin and Greek parts will make a significant improvement in your vocabulary.

Latin and Greek Prefixes

Word Part	Meaning	Examples	
1. anti	against	antiaircraft	antiabortion
2. co, com, con	together	coworkers	conjoined
3. contra, counter	against	contradict	counterclockwise
4. ex	out	exit	extract
5. hyper	excessive	hyperactive	hyperventilate
6. hypo	under, less	hypodermic	hypothyroid
7. inter	between	interrupt	interstate
8. intro, intra	within	introspective	intramural
9. mis	wrong	misspell	mislead
10. multi	many	multiplication	multilingual
11. peri	around	perimeter	periscope
12. post	after	posttest	postoperative
13. pre	before	prenatal	pretest
14. re	again	redecorate	retake
15. retro	back	retro fashions	retrorockets
16. sub	under	subway	submarine
17. super	above	superintendent	superman
18. syn, sym	together	symphony	synchronize
19. tele	far	television	telescope
20. trans	across	transcontinental	Transportation

Latin and Greek Number and Negative Prefixes

Word Part	Meaning	Examples	
1. uni	one	uniform	unisex
2. mono	one	monopoly	monolog
3. bi	two	bisexual	bicycle
4. tri	three	tripod	tricycle
5. quadr	four	quadruplets	quadrangle
6. quint	five	quintet	quintuplets
7. penta	five	pentagon	pentameter
8. hex	six	hexagon	hexagram
9. oct	eight	octopus	octagon
10. dec	ten	decade	decimal
11. cent	hundred	century	centipede
12. kilo	thousand	kilometer	kilogram
13. semi	half	semiconscious	semester
14. un	not	unhappy	unconscious
15. in	not	incapable	incomplete
16. im	not	impossible	immovable
17. il	not	illegal	illiterate
18. ir	not	irregular	irrational
19. a	not	asexual	atypical
20. dis	not	discontent	Disable

Latin and Greek Roots

Word Part	Meaning	Examples	
1. am, amat	love	amative	amorous
2. ann, enn	year	annual	anniversary
3. aqu	water	aquarium	aquaplane
4. astr	star	astronomy	astrology
5. aud, audit	hear	auditory	audition
6. auto	self	automatic	autobiography
7. bibli/o	book	bibliography	Bible
8. bio	life	biology	biography
9. capit	head	capital	decapitate
10. chron	time	chronological	chronic
11. cred, credit	believe, trust	credibility	credentials
12. cycle	circle, wheel	cycle	bicycle
13. dem	people	democracy	demographics
14. derm	skin	epidermis	dermatologist
15. dict	say	dictate	diction
16. dyn	power	dynamite	dynasty
17. fid	faith	confidence	fidelity
18. frater	brother	fraternity	fraternal
19. gram, graph	write	autograph	telegram
20. greg	flock	congregation	Gregarious

Latin and Greek Roots

Word Part	Meaning	Examples	
1. hetero	other	heterosexual	heterogeneous
2. homo	same	homosexual	homonym
3. hydr	water	hydrant	hydroplane
4. loc	place	location	locale
5. log	word, study	biology	apology
6. mal	bad	malnutrition	malpractice
7. man	hand	manual	manicure
8. mater, matr	mother	maternity	maternal
9. metr, meter	measure	thermometer	speedometer
10. mit, miss	send	transmit	missionary
11. mor, mort	death	mortuary	mortality
12. mov, mot, mob	move	motion	mobility
13. pater, patr	father	paternity	patriarch
14. ped	foot	pedestrian	pedicure
15. phil	loving	philosophy	philanthropist
16. phon	sound	phonics	telephone
17. prim	first	primary	primitive
18. psych	mind	psychology	psychiatrist
19. pyr	fire	pyromaniac	pyrotechnics
20. reg	rule	regulations	Regulate

Latin and Greek Roots

Word Part	Meaning	Examples	
1. rupt	break	rupture	interrupt
2. scrib, script	write	scripture	inscribe
3. seg, sect	cut	section	bisect
4. sol	alone	solo	solitaire
5. soph	wisdom	sophisticated	sophomore (wise moron)
6. spect	look	spectator	spectacle
7. tard	late	tardy	retarded
8. tempor	time	temporary	tempo
9. the	God	theology	atheist
10. therm	heat	thermometer	thermostat
11. tract	pull	tractor	extract
12. turb	whirl, agitate	disturbance	turbulence
13. urb	city	urban	suburb
14. vac	empty	vacant	vacuum
15. vers, vert	turn	reverse	convert
16. vid, vis	see	vision	video
17. vit, viv	life	vital	vivacious
18. voc, vocat	call	vocal	vocation
19. xeno	stranger	xenophobia	xenobiotic
20. zoo	animal	zoology	Zoologist

Once you've memorized the Latin and Greek word parts, you need to be able to apply that knowledge by determining meaning for words containing Latin and Greek parts when you see them in sentences. Let's see how that works. Below are 10 sentences containing a word based on Latin or Greek. Refer to the lists (if needed) and determine the meaning of the words in italics. Then indicate whether each sentence is True **(T)** or False **(F)**.

_____   1. *Postoperative* procedures occur before an operation.

_____   2. An *intravenous* needle goes within the vein.

_____   3. A *decade* lasts twenty years.

_____   4. An *illiterate* person is a good reader.

_____   5. Your *audio* system needs a big screen for maximum effect.

_____   6. *Demographics* show statistics about people.

_____   7. A *hydroplane* needs a paved landing strip at least 200 yards long.

_____   8. A *biped* has two feet.

_____   9. An *urbanite* lives in a small town.

_____   10. A *soliloquy* is a speech by one person.

By combining the knowledge of word parts with the context of the sentence, you can see how it's possible to determine meaning. Often you don't need to know the exact meaning of unfamiliar words, but if you get a general meaning, it's enough for comprehension. Let's see how you did. Here are the answers:

1. F, 2. T, 3. F, 4. F, 5. F, 6. T, 7. F, 8. T, 9. F, 10. T

Your instructor may give you more application quizzes that will increase your ability to determine meaning by using context clues, syllabication, and Latin and Greek word parts. In addition to using these strategies, there's another vocabulary concept you should find helpful. It's described next.

C. Denotation and Connotation

There is a difference between how a word is defined in a dictionary—its **denotation**—and what a word may suggest or how it makes the reader feel. The suggested meaning of a word is called the **connotation,** and this meaning is not found in a dictionary. Connotations are learned as we hear words spoken, or as we read how they're used, in context. Connotation may also result from cultural differences, or how words are used in particular cultures.

Due to connotative meanings, many words create a positive or negative reaction in the reader. For example, one dictionary definition of the verb *travel* is "to go from one place to another" (*Webster's New World Dictionary,* 1995). This word and its meaning are neutral in the sentence below, not really evoking a positive or negative response:

> *He* traveled *all summer.*

However, if a writer wanted to create a more positive image, she might say:

> *He* toured *all summer.*

And if she wanted to communicate a more negative image, she could state it this way:

> *He* drifted *all summer.*

It's important for readers to notice a writer's word choices to more fully understand what the writer is trying to convey.

See if you can identify the more positive connotation in each of the following word pairs:

1. smirk   smile
2. aroma   odor
3. lady   female
4. cram   study
5. desire   lust

The more positive words above are *smile, aroma, lady, study,* and *desire.* For more practice on positive and negative words, see Chapter 4, Critical Reading Strategies.

You often hear that the best way to improve your vocabulary is to read, read, read, and this is true! But doing all that reading takes time, and as a college student, your time is limited. The strategies we've included in this chapter are shortcuts that can help you increase your vocabulary quickly. Here are a few other tips to help in your quest for a better vocabulary:

- Buy a good college-edition dictionary to use when other strategies aren't enough.
- Buy a thesaurus to supplement your dictionary, particularly for writing.
- Use mnemonics (memory tricks) to help memorize word meanings.
- Make flash cards with pictures to help memorize word meanings.

- Keep a vocabulary notebook to record unfamiliar words, meanings, and sentences containing those words.
- Use new words as much as possible. Use it or lose it!

Writing Like a Reader

One of the most important aspects of good writing is word choice. Word choice means exactly that—you **choose** the best words to express your ideas. Think about the reader as you choose each word. Who is the audience for your writing? What is the purpose of your writing—what do you want to convey to the reader? As you increase your vocabulary by becoming a better reader, you will also improve your writing because you will be able to choose words that express exactly what you want to say to the reader. Good writers avoid vague, general language and clichés (overused words and phrases). Good writers have a large vocabulary from which to choose.

Suppose you want to write an essay calling for stronger regulation of offshore oil drilling. Which of the following two paragraphs would be more convincing to the reader?

Oil spills are bad news for birds. The oil harms their feathers so that they freeze to death. Swallowing the oil makes the birds sick.

Oil spills are devastating to coastal birds such as gulls and pelicans. Viscous oil destroys the insulating properties of their feathers, causing hypothermia that can be fatal. The birds inevitably consume some of the oil while grooming, which can lead to ulcers, diarrhea, anemia, and kidney and liver damage.

The second passage helps the reader visualize the harmful effects of oil spills. It makes a much stronger argument because of better word choices. Always keep the reader in mind when choosing words as a writer!

Chapter Summary

Vocabulary Strategies Overview: An educated vocabulary is important to academic, career, and life success. There are several strategies that enable a reader to quickly determine the meaning of unfamiliar words.

Context Clues
- *Definition:* Also called synonym. Look for a definition or synonym that is directly stated in the sentence containing the unknown word.
- *Example:* An example or examples of the word are given; these enable the reader to understand the unknown word.

Two

Basic Comprehension Strategies

Chapter Preview

Comprehension Strategies Overview

A. Identifying Topics
B. Identifying Main Ideas
C. Identifying Details
D. Improving Comprehension

LEARNING OBJECTIVES (LOs)

Upon completion of this chapter, you'll be able to:

- LO1—Identify the topic of a paragraph or reading
- LO2—Identify the main idea of a paragraph or reading
- LO3—Identify the major details in a paragraph or reading
- LO4—Use a checklist to improve comprehension

Comprehension equals understanding . . .
Understanding equals learning.

Readiness Quiz   ⚙ ─Complete this Exercise at MyReadingLab.com

Choose **T** for true or **F** for false after reading each statement below.

1. _____ Topic and main idea are the same thing.

2. _____ A topic can be stated in a word or two.

3. _____ The main idea tells the point of the entire passage.

4. _____ All of the details are equally important.

5. _____ There may be a main idea for each paragraph as well as for the entire passage.

6. _____ The topic contains supporting details.

7. _____ The main idea may be stated, or you might have to figure it out.

8. _____ I know what the 5 Ws and H are.

9. _____ The topic is longer than the main idea.

10. _____ I know what to do if I'm having trouble comprehending while reading.

COMPREHENSION STRATEGIES OVERVIEW

Comprehension, or understanding, is the ultimate goal of any reader. If a reader doesn't understand what is read, there's no point in reading. Many students say that comprehension is their biggest reading problem. This chapter shows the reader how to break comprehension down into four easy strategies. The first three strategies—being able to identify topics, main ideas, and details—are the key elements of comprehension. This text offers a fourth strategy for improving comprehension—a comprehension strategies chart that shows what a reader can do to remedy specific comprehension problems. Readers who can identify the three key elements of comprehension and who also have a reference chart to address specific comprehension problems should experience excellent comprehension.

A. Identifying Topics

In order to comprehend the meaning of what they are reading, readers must first be able to identify three key elements: the topic, the main idea, and the details. The first of these, **the topic,** is the most basic of the three—the subject of the entire reading. Who or what is the reading about? The topic is very general and can usually be stated in a word or phrase. If a reader is unable to identify the topic, he or

she will not be able to comprehend the reading. This lesson focuses on strategies for identifying the topic as the first step to the comprehension of any reading.

Consider the following paragraph:

> The cool-down period is an important part of an exercise workout. The cool-down involves reducing the intensity of exercise to allow the body to recover from the workout. During vigorous exercise such as jogging, a lot of blood is pumped to the legs, and there may not be enough to supply the heart and brain. Failure to cool down properly may result in dizziness, fainting, and in rare instances, a heart attack. By gradually reducing the level of physical activity during a cool-down period, blood flow is directed back to the heart and brain.

What did you just read about? That's the topic of this paragraph. Remember, it's who or what the entire paragraph is about. Did you come up with the topic "cool-down period"? If so, you're right!

QUICK TIP

Force yourself to state what you've read about (the entire reading) in a word or two. This is the topic.

Let's look at another paragraph to see if you can detect an easy way to identify the topic.

> One big difference between high school and college is the amount of studying needed. In high school, most students spend very little time studying outside of class or study hall. But in college, much more studying is required. They say, to be a successful college student, you should plan to spend two hours studying outside of class for every hour you spend in class. Many new college students have a difficult time learning to spend enough time studying.

What is this paragraph about? Did you say "studying"? That's correct, but how did you know? Often the word that expresses the topic will be repeated frequently throughout the paragraph or reading. If you see the same word many times, this is a good clue that the repeated word is the topic.

QUICK TIP

An often-repeated word is a clue to the topic.

Let's see how good you're at identifying topics in paragraphs. Read the following paragraphs and then state the topic on the line below each one. Remember—it should take only a few words to state what the paragraph is all about!

TOPIC PRACTICE ONE

1. You may be surprised to learn that the device we call a lie detector does not actually detect lies (Vrij, 2000). What we call a lie detector is really a polygraph (literally, "many writings"), an electronic device that simultaneously senses and makes records of several physiological indices, including blood pressure, heart rate, respiration, and galvanic skin response (GSR)—changes in the skin's ability to conduct electrical current that are associated with levels of perspiration. Computerized scoring systems have been developed for interpreting the results (Olsen et al., 1997).

TOPIC _____

2. School resource officers can benefit law enforcement, school districts, and the community in general. By having the officers in the schools every day, they can open lines of communication between school officials and the law enforcement community. Many times officers and school officials work on the same problems and have to handle the same "bad" kids, but are not able to work closely together for various reasons. The school resource officers help break down these barriers. (Oliver, 2001)

TOPIC _____

3. Whether you are a student, an instructor, a prospective author, or a bookseller, this site is the place to find a host of solutions to today's classroom challenges—ranging from traditional textbooks and supplements to CD-ROMs, Companion Websites, and extensive distance learning offerings. (Prentice Hall website)

TOPIC _____

4. Few economists doubt that current Bush tax cuts, $290 billion in this year alone, helped stimulate the economy at first. Those rebate checks that arrived in the fall of 2001 helped prop up the economy during a dark period, and consumer spending helped the United States make its way to recovery. Now that the economy is improving, the calculus for tax cuts is different. Will cutting taxes further make a meaningful difference to the economy? And even if it does, can we afford to increase the deficit for the sake of tax relief? (Thottam, 2004)

TOPIC _____

Now that you've practiced identifying the topic of a paragraph, do you've any questions about it? If you do, write your questions here to ask your instructor.

Next, let's see if you can identify the topic of a longer passage. Read the following passage and then write the topic on the line at the end.

Topic Practice Two

The more I observe the human condition, the more I'm convinced that boredom is the single biggest factor in the lives of billions of the people who dwell on this little ball of rock and mud. Here in this country boredom and its attendants, depression and unhappiness, are present in what could well be the overwhelming majority of our citizens.

This is again brought home to me when I read of the astronomical salaries we are paying sports figures and media stars. These people can command these salaries because they have the capacity to entertain millions of our citizens who will watch them in person or on TV and in the movies. This audience justifies the salaries from promoters and advertisers who use the media to sell tickets and merchandise to the multitudes.

The entertainment industry exists only because it relieves the boredom and brings temporary "happiness" to millions of its customers. This boredom is so deep and so pervasive in our people that they will tolerate even abysmally poor quality entertainment from the producers. Citizens' desires to escape their lives and themselves make them so desperate they will pay large sums of money for even momentary escape from the boredom they endure. (Tom Markin)

TOPIC _____

Remember—identifying the topic is the first step toward understanding, or comprehending, what you're reading. You've to know what you're reading about. Then you're ready to go on to the second step of comprehension, identifying the main idea.

B. Identifying Main Ideas

The term **main idea** has different meanings according to different instructors, and is often confused with the term *topic*. The topic, as you now have learned, is the general subject of the reading. The main idea, on the other hand, is **the point** the reading makes about the topic. The main idea of a passage or reading is the central thought or message. An easy way to understand the difference between main idea and topic is to imagine overhearing a conversation in which you hear your name mentioned often. You know the *topic* of the conversation is you, but you want to know what is being said about you. You probably wouldn't be satisfied until you knew the point they were making about you, or the *main idea*. The same principle applies to reading. The topic is not enough—you also need to know the main idea.

STATED MAIN IDEA   The topic can usually be stated in a word or phrase, while it takes a sentence or a complete thought to state the main idea. Whether you're reading a paragraph or a longer passage, you'll often find one sentence that best summarizes the entire paragraph or passage. This is your main idea statement, which is called a "topic sentence" in a paragraph, or a "thesis statement" if one sentence states the main idea of a longer passage. Since the topic sentence or thesis statement is most often stated toward the beginning of a paragraph or longer reading, look at the first few sentences to see if one seems to be a general statement that makes a point.

QUICK TIP

Topic = General subject (a word or phrase)

Main idea = Point made about the topic

Topic sentence = Main idea sentence in a paragraph

Thesis statement = Main idea sentence in a longer passage

Reread the paragraph below in which you identified the topic as being "cool-down period." As you read it now, see if you recognize a sentence that states the main idea of the entire paragraph. Remember, this sentence will tell you what point the writer is making about the cool-down period. What does the writer want you to know about the cool-down period once you've finished reading the paragraph?

The cool-down period is an important part of an exercise workout. The cool-down involves reducing the intensity of exercise to allow the body to recover from the workout. During vigorous exercise such as jogging, a lot of blood is pumped to the legs, and there may not be enough to supply the heart and brain. Failure to cool down properly may result in dizziness, fainting, and in rare instances, a heart attack. By gradually reducing the level of physical activity during a cool-down period, blood flow is directed back to the heart and brain.

Did you find the topic sentence, or main idea? It's the first sentence, which tells you that the cool-down period is an important part of a workout. The paragraph then goes on to explain why the cool-down period is important. But what you need to remember is that the cool-down period is important.

Another easy way to locate the main idea is to use the SQ3R (Survey, Question, Read, Recite, Review) textbook study method, which is discussed in the next chapter. One of the many benefits of using this method is that it often points you to the main idea. When using SQ3R, you form questions from each heading, and often the answer to your question will be the main idea for that section.

Let's say that there was a heading in your textbook above the paragraph you just read that said **Cool-Down Period.** If you were using SQ3R, you'd make a question from that heading. Since most people know what a cool-down period is, the question you might make from that heading would be something like, "What about the cool-down period?" Then the first sentence would tell you what you need to know about the cool-down period—that it's important.

QUICK TIP

The sentence that answers your SQ3R question is often the main idea sentence.

IMPLIED MAIN IDEA If you can't find a sentence that summarizes the point being made about the topic, the main idea may be only suggested or implied. In that case, **you** need to determine what the main idea is. If there's no stated main idea, determine your own main idea by asking yourself the following three questions:

1. What is the topic?
2. What are the details trying to show?
3. What is the **ONE** point being made about the topic?

The answer to question 3 is the main idea.

Read the following paragraph and see if you can determine the point, or the main idea, that the writer is making.

A news story in Washington, D.C. reports that, of 184 persons convicted of illegal gun possession in a six-month period, only 14 received a jail sentence. Forty-six other cases involved persons who had previously been convicted of a felony or possession of a gun. Although the maximum penalty for such repeaters in the District of Columbia is ten years in prison, half of these were not jailed at all. A study last year revealed that in New York City, which has about the most prohibitive gun legislation in the country, only one of six people convicted of crimes involving weapons went to jail.

(Goldwater, 1975)

Using our three-question method, see if you can answer the following questions:

1. What is the topic of the paragraph? If you determined that it's about illegal gun possession, you're right.
2. What are the details trying to show? Did you get the idea that people convicted of illegal gun possession aren't punished very often? Each of the examples used pointed out the lack of punishment for those convicted of illegal gun possession.
3. What is the **ONE** point being made about the topic (illegal gun possession)? If you concluded that laws against illegal gun possession in the United States aren't being enforced, give yourself an A+!

That's the point, or main idea, that Barry Goldwater was trying to make. He used examples to give details, but he never stated his main idea. It was up to you, the reader, to use your skills to determine the point the writer wanted you to know.

When the main idea is not stated by the writer in a topic sentence, your work as a reader is more difficult; you still need to identify the main idea in order to comprehend what you're reading. When you've to figure out the main idea for yourself because the writer has *implied* it, rather than directly stated it, remember that it's up to you to identify the topic, add up the details, and decide what point the writer is making. In addition to using information stated in the reading, you're also expected to use any background information you already know about the topic to help determine the main idea. Once you've done that, if you're reading from material you can write on, it's a good idea to write the main point in the margin. This will help you solidify the main idea in your mind, and it will help you when you review the material at a later date.

If you're not sure you've found the topic sentence, or that you've made the correct assumption about the main idea, here's an easy way to check yourself. If most of the details are related to the topic sentence you chose, or if they add up to the main idea you stated in your own words, then you're probably correct.

QUICK TIP

Most of the sentences in the reading should relate to the main idea. If they don't, you haven't found the correct main idea.

Let's try determining the main idea in paragraphs where there's no topic sentence. Read each of the following paragraphs. Using the details given, plus your background knowledge, determine the main idea for each paragraph and write it on the line below the paragraph. The first paragraph is taken from a dental radiography text, and the second is from a psychology text.

MAIN IDEA PRACTICE ONE

Dental Radiography

The operator should always wear protective eyewear, mask, utility gloves, and a plastic or rubber apron when cleaning the tank or changing the solutions. The tank and its inserts should be scrubbed each time the solutions are changed. A solution made up of 1.5 oz (45 ml) of commercial hydrochloric acid, 1 qt (0.95 L) of cold water, and 3 qt (2.85 L) of warm water is sufficient to remove the deposits that frequently form on the walls of 1 gal (3.8 L) inserts. Commercial solutions for cleaning are available. (Johnson, McNally & Essay, 2003)

MAIN IDEA: _____

Psychology

For nearly a century, researchers have agreed with the proposal that we are sensitive to at least four primary tastes: sweet, sour, bitter, and salty (Henning, 1916; Scott and Plata-Salaman, 1991). Hence it is reasonable to suppose that there are at least four different types (shapes) of receptor sites. The arrangement is like a key fitting into a lock. In this case, the key is the molecule and the lock is the receptor site. Once the sites are occupied, depolarization occurs and information is transmitted through the gustatory nerve to the brain. . . . A number of molecules can occupy a receptor site: The better the fit, the greater the depolarization (McLaughlin & Margolskee, 1994). Keep in mind, however, that the lock-and-key theory is not absolute. Even though a receptor signals a certain taste more than others, it can also contribute to the perception of other tastes (Erickson, DiLorenzo, & Woodbury, 1994).

MAIN IDEA: _____

Whether the main idea is stated in a topic sentence or merely implied, being able to find the main idea in what you read is **crucial** to your comprehension. If you don't know what the writer wants you to know when you're finished reading, you haven't *really* read the material because *reading is comprehension.*

Now that you know how to identify the topic and the main idea, you're two-thirds of the way to good comprehension. Knowing what the reading is about and knowing the main point the author is making are obviously important to comprehension. But you still need more information to comprehend fully, or understand, everything you need to know. The information that gives you complete understanding is contained in the details—the third element key to comprehension.

⌐MyReadingLab───────────────────────────────

For more help with **Stated Main Idea** and **Implied Main Idea,** go to your learning path in MyReadingLab at www.myreadinglab.com.

C. Identifying Details

Once a reader has identified the topic and main idea of a reading, the next step to comprehension is to find the details that will fill in and complete your understanding. Most readings have many details; some need to be remembered, others don't.

MAJOR DETAILS   The details that relate directly to the main idea are called major details; these are important and need to be highlighted or recorded in some way. Major details explain, develop, support, and give examples of the main idea. They back up the main idea or offer important new information.

A skilled reader starts to identify the major details by using the 5 W and H questions with the main idea. These questions ask *who, what, when, where, why,* or *how.*

Consider the following paragraph:

> Forty percent of children say the American Dream is beyond their reach. A quarter don't feel safe walking alone on the streets of their own neighborhoods. Almost a third of kids under 17 went without health insurance during the last year. Marguerite Sallee, 58, a blond Republican in a power suit, cites these figures to show one thing: America needs to do a better job of caring for its children.
>
> *Newsweek* magazine, October 3, 2005

To comprehend a paragraph, start by identifying the topic. Here, if you came up with "children" as the topic, you're right. Next, ask yourself what point is being made about the topic, and whether there's a sentence that states it. The last sentence nicely states the writer's main idea. Now you need your major details to complete your comprehension of this paragraph.

Let's try the 5 Ws and H.

Who? <u>Marguerite Sallee.</u>

What? <u>More caring for children.</u>

When? <u>Now (implied).</u>

Where? <u>America.</u>

Why? <u>Examples: American Dream beyond reach, don't feel safe, no health insurance.</u>

How? <u>Not stated in the paragraph, but you would expect the answer in following paragraphs.</u>

With this information, your comprehension of the paragraph should be complete, and you should understand what the writer wants you to know.

QUICK TIP

Start identifying major details by finding the answers to your 5 W and H questions.

After you've identified the most important details by answering your 5 W and H questions, there's another way to find major details if you're reading from a source with headings using SQ3R. Find the answers for your SQ3R questions, which may be different from your 5 W and H questions. The answers to SQ3R questions made from headings may also be major details. The last step is to look for details that directly relate to or support your main idea. If the detail doesn't tie in directly, it's not a major detail.

QUICK TIP

Check a detail against the main idea statement to see if it's a major detail.

MINOR DETAILS There are other details that could be left out and the main idea would still be clear. These are called minor details. These details explain a major detail. The minor details are used to add interest, but usually don't need to be remembered, and aren't necessary for comprehension.

To illustrate the difference between major and minor details, read the following paragraph and identify topic, main idea, and the major and minor details.

DETAILS PRACTICE ONE

There are a number of ways to get rid of hiccups. The first way, which many people try, is holding their breath and counting to ten. However, most people never make it to ten because the hiccups take over and interrupt the process. Another common method is to try breathing into a paper bag. I had a friend who tried this and it only made his stomach hurt and his hiccups get worse. Finally, there's the method of trying to scare the hiccups away. If you can get someone to sneak up on you and yell, that might make the hiccups stop. Hopefully one of these methods will work for you.

TOPIC: _____

MAIN IDEA: _____

Major Details	Minor Details
1. _____	1. _____
2. _____	2. _____
3. _____	3. _____

How did you do? Was it easy for you to see that the paragraph was telling you about three ways to try to get rid of the hiccups? That's what was important. Knowing that most people can't make it to ten when counting, or what happened to the friend, isn't what you need to know or remember from the paragraph. What you need to know to comprehend the paragraph are the major details, or the three ways to get rid of hiccups. Being able to identify the major details that support the main idea is the final piece to the comprehension puzzle.

Now that you've learned the three key strategies for comprehending your reading materials, you should be well on your way to good comprehension! Knowing how to identify the topic, main idea, and major details in your reading material leads to good comprehension. However, there still might be times when you find yourself losing attention and having difficulty understanding what you're reading. The last comprehension strategy addresses what you should do if this occurs.

⌐MyReadingLab────────────────────────────────────

For more help with **Supporting Details,** go to your learning path in MyReadingLab at www.myreadinglab.com.

Writing Like a Reader

Why do you write? You write to share information, thoughts, and ideas with a reader. Think about things you've read that have been difficult to understand—what made it difficult? The most common reason is that the paragraphs were hard to follow. Well-written paragraphs have two aspects that make them easy for the reader to understand: unity and coherence. Unity means that all of the sentences (details) in the paragraph support the topic sentence (main idea). Coherence means that the sentences flow smoothly and logically. The two together create comprehension for the reader. Since comprehension is the end goal for both the reader and the writer, be sure to consider unity and coherence as you write.

To see the difference unity and coherence make, read the following paragraph. Then reread the paragraph in Details Practice One that you just read. Which one is easier to understand? Why?

> I had a friend who tried this, but it only made his stomach hurt and his hiccups get worse. If you can get someone to sneak up on you and yell that might make the hiccups stop. Most people never make it to ten because the hiccups take over and interrupt the process. Try breathing into a paper bag. There's the method of trying to scare the hiccups away. Many people try holding their breath and counting to ten. There are a number of ways to get rid of hiccups.

D. Improving Comprehension

The following checklist is a great tool for improving comprehension that goes beyond being able to identify topic, main idea, and major details. Sometimes, you'll find yourself having difficulty comprehending a certain reading and becoming frustrated. That's the time to turn to the Comprehension Strategies checklist. It can help you determine why you're having problems, and how to correct them. To use the checklist, read through the possible problems on the left side. Once you've decided what your problem is, read through the suggestions on the right side and try them until you find a solution that works for you.

Comprehension Strategies

Problems	Strategies
Having difficulty concentrating	1. Take frequent breaks. 2. Read difficult material when your mind is fresh and alert. 3. Use guide questions (see SQ3R section in Chapter 3). 4. Stop and write down distracting thoughts. 5. Move to a quieter place. 6. Stand or walk while reading.
Words are difficult or unfamiliar	1. Use context clues. 2. Analyze word parts—look for Latin or Greek roots that will give meaning for the word. 3. Skim through material before reading. Mark and look up meanings of difficult words. Jot meanings in the margin or on 3 × 5 cards. 4. Use glossary or margin definitions if available.
Sentences are long or confusing	1. Read aloud. 2. Express each sentence in your own words. 3. Look for key words—subject and verb. 4. Break long sentences into shorter sections.
Ideas are hard to understand; complicated	1. Rephrase or explain each in your own words. 2. Make notes. 3. Locate a more basic text or video that explains ideas in simpler form. 4. Study with a classmate, discuss difficult ideas. 5. Search the Internet for simple explanations of the ideas presented in the text.
Ideas are new and unfamiliar; you've little or no knowledge about the topic and the writer assumes you do	1. Make sure you didn't miss or skip introductory information. 2. Get background information by: a. Referring to an earlier section or chapter in the book b. Referring to an encyclopedia c. Referring to a more basic text d. Referring to the Internet

(cont.)

Problems	Strategies
The material seems disorganized or poorly organized or there seems to be no organization	1. Read the Table of Contents—it's an outline of the book and each chapter. 2. Pay more attention to headings. 3. Read the summary, if available. 4. Try to discover organization by outlining or drawing a concept map as you read.
You don't know what is important; everything seems important	1. Use surveying or previewing. 2. Ask and answer guide (SQ3R) questions. 3. Locate and underline topic sentences.

Chapter Summary

Topic: General subject of passage; can be stated in a word or phrase.

Main Idea: Point being made about the topic. Stated main idea means that the main idea is stated in a sentence. Implied main idea is not directly stated, but is suggested or implied.

Details: Two kinds: major and minor. Major details support the main idea and are important. Minor details are less important and usually don't need to be remembered. Use the 5 Ws and H to find the major details.

Improving Comprehension: Use the Comprehension Strategies chart.

Use the Four Strategies above to Comprehend What You Read.

Check Your Learning (Learning Outcomes)

Have you mastered the Learning Objectives (LO) for Chapter 2? Place a check mark next to each LO that you're able to do.

_____ LO1—Identify the topic of a paragraph or reading

_____ LO2—Identify the main idea of a paragraph or reading

_____ LO3—Identify the major details in a paragraph or reading

_____ LO4—Use a checklist to improve comprehension

Go back and review the sections that cover any LO you didn't check.

Quick Connections—Chapter Two

NEWS SOURCE CONNECTION

Using a news source (news magazine or newspaper), choose an article to read. Keep in mind that you're looking for the topic, the main idea, and three important details. After reading the article, take three different colored highlighters and highlight the topic in one color, the main idea sentence in another color, and three important details in the third. If the main idea is not stated in a sentence, write your own main idea statement.

TEXTBOOK CONNECTION

Use a textbook from one of your other classes, and if possible, do this activity as you're doing a reading assignment for the other class. Choose a section of the text and write the heading for that section on a sheet of paper. Scan the section for subheadings, and write those below the heading, leaving three lines between each subheading. As you read that section, fill in each of the three lines with an important detail from the section. If you do this for the entire assignment, you'll have a complete set of study notes.

NOVEL CONNECTION

After reading each chapter of a novel, stop to write down the topic of the chapter, the main idea, and at least three major details, or important things that happened. If you're unsure about the topic and/or main idea, write the details first, then see what they all relate to (topic), and what point is being made (main idea).

WEB CONNECTION ⚙ ⌐Complete this Exercise at MyReadingLab.com

Go to a news source Website, such as *Time* magazine or the *New York Times* newspaper site. Choose an article that looks interesting and skim it to see what it's about. Write down what you *think* the topic and main idea of the article are. Read the article and then review what you initially wrote for the topic and main idea. Decide if your prediction was correct, and if not, rewrite what you now believe to be the topic and main idea. This is a good way to check your comprehension for any article you read.

MyReadingLab™ CONNECTION ⚙ ⌐Complete this Exercise at MyReadingLab.com

Visit MyReadingLab to take a review quiz testing your mastery of this chapter's topics.

Three

Textbook Strategies

Chapter Preview

Course information bottom line . . .
The Textbook

LEARNING OBJECTIVES (LOs)

Upon completion of this chapter, you'll be able to:

■ LO1—Identify and use textbook organizational aids

■ LO2—Use three textbook reading methods

■ LO3—Comprehend information found in graphs, charts, and tables

■ LO4—Take notes while reading

■ LO5—Use skimming and scanning

■ LO6—Use a textbook excerpt to practice textbook strategies

Readiness Quiz   ☼┌Complete this **Exercise** at **MyReadingLab.com**

Choose **T** for true or **F** for false after reading each statement below.

1. _____   Most textbooks are set up in a similar way.

2. _____   In college, a student needs to read everything thoroughly.

3. _____   I've used highlighting to mark important information in a textbook.

4. _____   The index is the place to find the meaning of words used in a book.

5. _____   I normally read the preface in my textbooks.

6. _____   Skimming and scanning mean about the same thing.

7. _____   A reader who thoroughly reads the material once can remember most of the chapter.

8. _____   I have a method I use when I read textbooks.

9. _____   Scanning is used to get a quick overview of the reading material.

10. _____   When reading from a textbook, a reader should begin on the first page of the chapter and read until the chapter ends without skipping anything.

TEXTBOOK STRATEGIES OVERVIEW

As a college student, it has been estimated that you'll receive approximately 70 percent of the information you need to know from your textbooks. Therefore, it's extremely important that you know how to read your texts, comprehend them, gain the knowledge needed to pass your classes, and ultimately, to be successful in your career.

To achieve your textbook reading goals, there are three simple strategies you can use. The first, identifying and using textbook organizational aids, is simply knowing what the aids are, being aware of them as you start each new textbook, and then using them to assure the most efficient reading of your textbooks. The five textbook aids you'll be learning about are the preface, table of contents, glossary, index, and appendix.

The second strategy you'll learn is to use at least one of three methods specifically designed for reading textbooks, which will enable you to get the most out of your book in the least amount of time. By now I'm sure you've discovered that trying to read a textbook the same way you read a novel or a newspaper just doesn't work! Because textbooks are fact dense, and because you're expected to remember much of the material, it takes an entirely different approach to read a text. Most readers have never been taught how to read textbooks. This results in a high rate of frustrated students and teachers. In this chapter, you'll learn three methods for reading textbooks that are easy and really work! Because students have different learning styles, we've included three methods: SQ3R (Survey, Question, Read, Recite, Review), 5C (Connect, Cards Vocabulary, Cards Main Points, Classroom, Commit to Memory), and triple highlighting. One of the methods, or a combination of them, will likely work for you.

The third textbook strategy that every college student can benefit from is a combination of two processes: skimming and scanning. You'll learn how to do both, and you'll also learn when to use these time-saving techniques.

Knowing and using the textbook strategies in this chapter can definitely make you a more successful college reader. Take the time to learn and practice these strategies until they become automatic. You'll be amazed at how much easier reading and comprehending your texts will become!

A. Identifying and Using Textbook Organizational Aids

There are five common parts of a textbook (called organizational aids) that can make you a more efficient textbook reader. The five organizational aids in a text that are most useful to the student are the **preface** (also called To the Student), **table of contents, glossary, index (indexes),** and appendix **(appendices).** In addition to knowing these five parts, it's important to check each textbook for other textbook aids such as chapter previews and reviews, chapter objectives, summaries, headings and subheadings, visual and graphic aids, margin information, chapter questions, and vocabulary aids.

QUICK TIP

Always read the preface or To the Student section of your texts to quickly see what aids the author has included that will help you use that text more efficiently.

Your instructor may have you participate in an activity that will allow you to discover for yourself the five parts of a text mentioned above, and how each part can help you use your textbooks more efficiently. If your instructor chooses not to use the following activity with your class, complete it on your own with a text, or several texts, available to you.

QUICK TIP

Start every school term by looking through each of your new textbooks to familiarize yourself with the five textbook organizational aids.

Textbook Organization and Aids

After being divided into groups and assigned one of the five text parts below, work as a group to fill in your section with a description of that part of a textbook. List the kinds of general information that would be found in that part of any textbook, not information specific to the text you're using. Complete your assigned part with your group and then fill in the others as each group presents.

Preface

_____

_____

_____

_____

_____

Table of Contents

_____
_____
_____
_____
_____

Glossary

_____
_____
_____
_____
_____

Index(es)

_____
_____
_____
_____
_____

Appendix (Appendices)

_____
_____
_____
_____
_____
_____

Other Textbook Aids

_____
_____
_____
_____
_____

B. Textbook Reading Methods

Reading a textbook is like playing a football game. You would never be able to win the game if all you did was show up and play. There's much time spent before the game preparing, there's a plan for the actual playing time, and there's follow-up to make sure you learn from that game so you can do better in the next one. In order to "win" at reading textbooks, you need a plan that includes pregame preparation, playing strategies, and postgame follow-up.

We've included three different game strategies, or textbook reading methods. You'll notice that each has a pregame (prereading) step, a playing (reading) plan, and a postgame (review) follow-up. Try each of them and see which one works best for you. You may want to combine parts of all three and come up with your own. What's important is that you've a method that works for YOU. Don't just show up to read and be a loser at the textbook reading game. Get your game plan, use it for every reading assignment, and be a winner at college textbook reading!

Here are brief explanations of the three text strategies. After you've read through them and have a basic understanding of how each one works, your instructor will provide you with several activities so you can try the strategies and determine which one, or which combination of the strategies, works best for you.

1. SQ3R (SURVEY, QUESTION, READ, RECITE, REVIEW)   SQ3R has been one of the most popular text-reading strategies since World War II, when it was widely used by soldiers to learn the material in their training manuals. Many studies have been done on the effectiveness of SQ3R, all showing that students comprehend and retain more information when using SQ3R. SQ3R is an excellent textbook reading method for most students because it's easy to use and it works! It works because it makes you *think* about what you're reading. Here's a brief explanation of the five steps in the SQ3R method.

Survey

Purpose: To become familiar with the overall content and organization of the material before you start reading. This enables you to comprehend faster and more thoroughly.

Method: Survey or preview the material by reading and **highlighting** the following:

- Title and subtitle
- Introduction (this can take several forms—chapter overview, chapter preview, chapter highlights, a list of main points in the chapter, or simply a paragraph)

- Headings and subheadings
- Bold or colored print, italics
- Margins
- Boxes
- Graphics (e.g., pictures, charts, graphs, diagrams, tables—and their captions)
- Vocabulary definitions
- Summary—End of chapter, end of sections—any summaries
- Questions—End of the chapter or sections—any questions
- Anything that catches your eye!

Result: A good survey gives you all of the most important information in a chapter and shows you how it's organized. This allows you to start comprehending as soon as you start to read.

QUICK TIP

Surveying, plus reading once, has been proven more effective than reading a selection twice. Don't skip the survey!

Question

Purpose: To give you something to think about before you start to read a section, and to give you something to look for as you read—the answer to your question. If you're looking for an answer, you stay more focused on the meaning of what you're reading.

Method: Make a question from each heading and subheading by using one of the W or H words (who, what, where, when, why, how). Write your W or H word lightly by the key word(s) in the heading. Most often your question will probably be "what is . . . ?" and then the heading. Your question should ask about the aspect of the heading that you're most curious about.

Result: You've created interest and now have a purpose for your reading— to find the answer to your question. Reading with interest and a purpose results in better attention to the content and improved comprehension.

QUICK TIP

Use the 5 Ws and H to form questions from the headings.

Read

Purpose: To gain information and knowledge by finding the answer to your question.

Method: Read through the section under the heading looking for the answer to your question. Read only until you come to a new heading, then stop.

Result: You find the answer to your question, and your mind doesn't wander like it does when you read without a purpose. Also, you should understand and remember what you read because you're paying attention to it.

Recite (Highlight)

Purpose: To get a permanent record of the information you need to remember.

Method: Start by reciting (saying) and then highlighting the answer to the question you made from the heading. Recite and highlight names, dates, definitions, key parts of topic sentences, lists—everything you think might be on a test. After you've highlighted key information, you may also want to write yourself some notes in the margin to clarify certain passages or to remind yourself of things you need to memorize or things you need to ask your instructor. Remember that the key to good highlighting is never to try to highlight as you read material for the first time. Wait until you finish a section, then go back and highlight using the suggestions above.

Result: You now have a permanent record of the information you need to study for the test. From this point on you'll only reread what you've highlighted, so make sure you think it's accurate and complete. If you aren't able to, or don't want to highlight in the book, use one of the alternative methods of recording such as taking notes, outlining or mapping (Chapter 7), or try the 5C method, which is explained next.

> ## QUICK TIP
>
> Read only from one heading to the next, and then STOP. Go back over what you just read and highlight the answer to your question plus any other important information.

Review

Purpose: To learn the material you need to know.

Method: Reread your highlighting at least three times. The first time to review is as soon as you've completed the reading. Check your highlighting at this time to make sure it's complete and accurate. The second time to reread your highlighting is every week, if possible, but at least once between finishing the assignment and starting to study for the test. The third time is before the test. Start rereading your highlighting several days before the test, and continue up to test time. Also memorize anything that you must know for sure from memory.

Result: You know everything you need to know from the text, and are ready to do well on your test.

> ## QUICK TIP
>
> Reviewing is easy—just reread your highlighting and margin notes! The more often you read over them, the less studying you'll need to do right before a test.

While SQ3R does not require the use of index cards, it may be helpful to students to include cards in the process. The following chart provides that option. Note the asterisks (*) both within the top two boxes of the chart and in the explanations below the chart.

SQ3R with Cards at a Glance

Step 1: Survey*	Go through the chapter: Read title, headings, and subheadings; **look at** and **read** captions for all pictures, charts, and graphs; note anything that stands out such as bolded vocabulary; read chapter overview, summary, and questions at start and/or end of chapter.
Purpose	To connect with prior knowledge, and to get an overview of chapter content and organization.
Result	You get more out of your reading when you do read the chapter, and you retain more of what you read.
Ask Yourself	Do I have a good idea of what this chapter is about and how it's organized?
	Do I have some background knowledge from previous experiences?
Step 2: Question**	Turn the title and each heading into one or more questions using the 5 Ws and H (who, what, why, where, when, and how); write questions above each heading or on a 3 × 5 card.
Purpose	To create interest and read with a purpose; to stay more focused on the content.
Result	You're better able to locate main ideas and major details.
Ask Yourself	Did I turn the title and all headings into appropriate questions?
Step 3: Read	Read from one heading to the next, looking for the answers to your questions.
Purpose	To locate and to begin to learn the chapter content.
Result	You find answers to your questions, stay more focused, and experience better comprehension.
Ask Yourself	Did I notice that reading with a purpose helped me to better understand the reading?

*VOCABULARY CARDS: (Complete this step right *after* the SURVEY step.)

• Identify key words in chapter which are bold-faced and/or listed
• Make a 3 × 5 (or larger) card for each word; place word on one side of card and the definition on the back side
• Add any pictures or other personalization (such as colors, shapes, designs) to each card

**COMPREHENSION CARDS: (Complete this step as you complete the QUESTION step; add your questions by each heading.)

• Identify chapter sections using main headings for the divisions; determine how many sections the chapter includes
• Write main headings and all subheadings on 3 × 5 (or larger) cards for each section. This will look like an outline of the section. Write on only one side of cards. If more space is needed per section, staple cards together. Each section is one CHUNK of information.

(*cont.*)

Step 4: Recite/ Highlight	AFTER reading each section, highlight the answers to your questions in the text OR write the answers in the margin of the text or on the same cards you used for the questions.
Purpose	To gain information by finding the answers to your questions.
Result	You've a better understanding and retention of information as well as a record of what you need to know for a test.
Ask Yourself	Did I find and mark or write the answers to the questions I formed in Step 2?
Step 5: Review	Reread your highlighting, notes, or cards as soon as possible, and then periodically and before a test.
Purpose	To move information from short-term to long-term memory, and to effectively prepare for a test without cramming.
Result	You learn the material you identified as important and perform well on the test.
Ask Yourself	Has this method helped me to learn my chapter information and commit it to memory?

2. 5C 5C was developed to give students a different way to break down and comprehend textbook material. This method uses 3×5 note cards, rather than highlighting, to record important information. It is based on the idea that the vocabulary and headings provide most of the key information in a textbook reading. There are times when you can't, or prefer not to, highlight in a book. Having your information on cards also makes studying more convenient because you can carry the cards with you and read over them whenever you have a few minutes of extra time. Hundreds of students have used 5C with a high degree of success.

Connect

Purpose: To connect with the content and organization of the chapter.

Method: Go through the chapter (it takes approximately 10–15 minutes) and **look at** and **read** everything that catches your eye. This will include the title, headings, bold or color print, boxes or items in the margins, captions for all pictures, and charts and graphs. Skim (quickly read for main points) the summary and questions at the end of the chapter.

Result: This step will make it quicker and easier for you to comprehend because you'll get a good idea of what the chapter is about and you can start relating your background knowledge to the chapter content.

Cards Vocabulary

Purpose: Much of the key information in a chapter is contained in the vocabulary words. Use 3 × 5 note cards to identify and define vocabulary words.

Method: Go through the chapter and write each vocabulary word on a separate card and write the definition on the other side. In addition to the definition, writing a sentence containing the word will help you understand and remember the meaning of the word.

Result: You've a set of note cards containing the key vocabulary terms and definitions from the chapter.

Cards Main Points

Purpose: The other source of key information in a chapter is headings. Use 3 × 5 note cards to write questions and answers from the headings. This results in better comprehension and a record of the important information.

Method: Go through the chapter and outline the information on cards using the font size of the headings. The chapter title will be the largest. The next size down will be the main points, the next size down will be the major details, and the next size down will be the minor details. Use colors to separate your outline. When you outline, make sure only one "chunk" of information goes on each card. One chunk would be one main point with its major and minor details. When you come to a new main point, it is time to start another card. If you've a section that takes up two cards, staple those cards together as one "chunk" of information.

Result: You've a set of note cards containing the main points from the chapter.

QUICK TIP

Draw a simple picture on the front (word and question) sides of your cards. The picture should be something that will trigger your memory of the definition or answer to your question. Your mind will remember the picture, and then the answer!

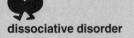
dissociative disorder

Characterized by a person having a disruption, split or breakdown in his or her normal integrated self

Classroom

Purpose: To add information to your cards from your teacher's lecture.

Method: Take your cards with you to class and add important points from your instructor. If there's too much information to fit on your cards, add more cards and staple them to the original cards. Keep all chunks of information about the same main points together.

Result: You now have a complete set of cards that contain the important information from the textbook and from your teacher.

Commit to Memory

Purpose: To learn the information for a test, for future courses, and/or your career.

Method: Carry your cards with you and read through them often. Take them out to review whenever you've a few minutes of time—while waiting, during slow time at work, during TV commercials—get in the habit of pulling out your cards several times a day!

Result: Frequent reading of the cards and self-testing will commit the information to your long-term memory and is easier and more effective than last-minute cramming.

QUICK TIP

Get in the habit of carrying your cards with you wherever you go and remember to read through them any time you have a few extra minutes. Painless and efficient studying!

5C Method at a Glance: Chapter-Card-Card-Classroom-Commit

Step 1: Chapter	Go through the chapter: **look at** and **read** the captions for all the pictures, charts, and graphs.
Purpose	In order for new information to stick in your brain, you need to access your background knowledge . . . things you already know about a topic.
Ask Yourself	Do I have a good idea of what this chapter is about? Do I have some background knowledge from previous experiences?

(cont.)

Step 2: Cards Vocabulary	On 3×5 note cards, create a list of the vocabulary words with their definitions. Add a picture of the DEFINITION to the front of your card for memory and understanding.
Take It A Step Further	Personalize your note cards. Add pictures, shapes, color, and designs. This helps both sides of the brain work together to retrieve information.
Purpose	The main points of your chapter center around the vocabulary. In the next step, you'll see a lot of the reading has already been done by defining the vocabulary words on your note cards. You'll recognize that the vocabulary words are actually parts of the main points.
Ask Yourself	Do I see how my vocabulary and main points go together in helping make the chapter information clear?
Step 3: Cards Main Points	**Outline your chapter using font size!** The title will be the largest. The next size down will be the main points, the next size down will be the major details, and the next size down will be the minor details. Lots of textbooks use color as a way of deciphering main points from major and minor details.
Purpose	You aren't expected to remember every written word within your chapter. Matter of fact, you're only expected to remember, or have an idea of, the main points and major details.
Ask Yourself	Did I notice that most of my main points were explained through the vocabulary definitions?
Step 4: Classroom	Bring your cards to class! Take notes on your cards! That is it!! You'll be amazed at how much of your instructor's lecture you'll already know.
Purpose	This keeps points of key information from your text and your teacher together. If you've to create a new card, make sure you staple it to the textbook card so all CHUNKS of information stay together and organized.
Ask Yourself	Do I recognize chapter words in my instructor's lecture?
	As my instructor brings up various topics from the chapter, am I able to locate a note card I created?
Step 5: Commit	Use your cards to study. Your information will be in chunks, therefore making it easier to remember.
Purpose	The brain loves many things, so it's important to remember when actively reading that the brain loves center, color, repetition, small organized chunks, and design.
Ask Yourself	Has this method helped me to learn my chapter information and commit it to memory?

3. TRIPLE HIGHLIGHTING   Triple highlighting is a method that has been successfully used in college classes and the military. Air Force trainees using triple highlighting were able to score at least 95 percent on a 100-question, closed-book test. Students in college classes found that the triple-highlighted areas accurately predicted quiz questions. Triple highlighting can be used with SQ3R and 5C if desired, or it can be used by itself. If you like triple highlighting better than the other two methods, be sure you still do some kind of survey, preview, or connection before you start reading. Also review and commit to memory the triple-highlighted areas before a test. Here are the three steps in the triple-highlighting method.

Yellow Highlight

Purpose: To record what you determine to be important information in the chapter.

Method: As you read, use a yellow highlighter to mark what you believe is important information.

Result: You have a record of the information you, the student, have determined to be important.

QUICK TIP

Don't try to highlight as you're reading for the first time. Wait until the end of a section, then go back and highlight the important points. Everything seems important as you're reading—it's easier to see what's important when you've the complete picture.

Blue Highlight

Purpose: To record answers to questions posed by the author at the end of the chapter.

Method: If there are questions at the end of the chapter, find the answer to each question. With a pencil, write the number of the question in the margin next to the answer, then highlight the answer with blue.

Result: You have a record of the information the author has determined to be important.

Pink Highlight

Purpose: To record important points made by your instructor.

Method: Follow along in your text during class lecture and discussion. Notice when your instructor repeats points or writes them on the board. Highlight this information with pink.

Result: You have a record of the information your instructor has determined to be important.

Triple Highlight

Purpose: Shows you which information is most important and most likely to be on your tests.

Method: Reread everything that you've highlighted with all three colors. These areas contain the key information in the reading. The student (you!) thought it was important enough to highlight, the author thought it was important enough to write a question about, and the instructor thought it was important enough to emphasize in class. This means the likelihood of seeing that piece of information again on a test, or in some graded form, is very high.

Result: You have the most important information triple highlighted and ready to study for the test.

QUICK TIP

Research has shown that triple-highlighted information shows up on quizzes and tests a high percentage of the time.

Triple Highlighting at a Glance

Step 1: Survey	Go through the chapter: Read headings; **look at** and **read** the captions for all the pictures, charts, and graphs; read chapter summary and questions.
Purpose	To become familiar with content of the reading.
Result	Shows you the most important points; helps you understand the organization of the chapter; activates your prior knowledge; comprehension begins as soon as you start reading.
Ask Yourself	Did I notice the same ideas repeated in the headings, chapter summary and questions at the end of the chapter? Do I have a good idea of what the chapter is about and how it's organized?

(cont.)

Step 2: Yellow Highlight	Use a yellow (or whatever color you want) highlighter. As you finish each section of the chapter, go back and highlight what YOU think are the most important points.
Purpose	To record what you think is the most important information in the chapter.
Result	You now have a record of what **YOU** think are the main points from the reading.
Ask Yourself	Did I highlight answers to questions I made from the headings? Did I highlight vocabulary words? Did I highlight the 5 Ws? Did I highlight points that I think will be on a test over the reading?
Step 3: Blue Highlight	If your textbook has questions at the end of the chapter, or anywhere in the chapter, scan back over the reading and find the answers to the textbook questions. Highlight the answers in blue (or any color different from your first color). Write the number of the question in the margin in pencil next to the answer you highlighted.
Purpose	To record what the author thinks is important in the chapter.
Result	You now have a record of what **THE AUTHOR** thinks are the main points from the reading.
Ask Yourself	Did I find the answers to all of the chapter questions? Were the answers to the questions already highlighted in my first color? If so, that means you did a good job of choosing important information to highlight in your first color.
Step 4: Pink Highlight	Take your textbook to class with you. When your instructor starts lecturing over the book, use a pink (or any color different from the first two you used) highlighter to highlight information the teacher is talking about or writing on the board.
Purpose	To record what your instructor thinks is important in the chapter.
Result	You now have a record of what **YOUR INSTRUCTOR** thinks are the main points from the reading.
Ask Yourself	Am I highlighting information that is already highlighted in one or two colors? Is my instructor giving new information that's not in the book? If so, you need to be taking notes in addition to your highlighting.

(cont.)

Step 5: Triple Highlighting	Reread everything that is triple highlighted as soon as you can after class. Continue to reread the triple-highlighted sections often.
Purpose	You're learning the important information from the chapter. You're also learning what you'll need to know for the test.
Result	You'll make a good grade on the test. Everything that is triple highlighted is almost guaranteed to show up on the test!
Ask Yourself	Has this method helped me to identify and learn the important information from my reading? Did I make a good grade on the test after using this method? If so, triple highlighting is an effective textbook reading method for you!

⌐MyReadingLab─────────────────────────

For more help with **Active Reading,** go to your learning path in MyReadingLab at www.myreadinglab.com.

Writing Like a Reader

One of the best ways to check and reinforce what you've learned from reading a textbook is to write a summary. You can stop and summarize after every paragraph, every heading, every section, or at the end of the chapter. The ability to write an effective summary is one of the most important writing skills a college student can possess. An important application of summary in a writing course is summarizing information from various sources in a research paper.

A summary has two key features: (1) it is shorter than the original and (2) it repeats the key ideas using different phrases and sentences. A summary must be written using the writer's own words without copying directly from the source. (Copying directly from the source is called plagiarism and is not acceptable. You can learn more about plagiarism in Chapter 8.)

To summarize any type of reading, read a section, then close the text and write the most important information from memory. When you've finished, skim that section again to make sure you didn't leave out any key points. Add anything important that you forgot, and then move on to read the next section. Below is an example summary for the section on Triple Highlighting in this chapter.

> Triple highlighting is a textbook reading method that uses three different colors of highlighters. One color highlights what the reader thinks is important. A second color highlights what the teacher says is important, and a third color highlights answers to questions at the end of the chapter. The most highlighted parts of the text are the most important and will probably be on the test.

C. Reading Graphs, Charts, and Tables

Graphs, charts, and tables are pictures of information. You've heard the expression "A picture is worth a thousand words." This is certainly true in reading. The picture provided by a graph, chart, or table can enable readers to see information more quickly than having to read a paragraph or more. Graphs, charts, and tables are often a summary of written text, but sometimes they present additional information. Either way, they are extremely important to the reader, so you need to know how to efficiently read graphs, charts, and tables.

Charts, including graphs, are graphic representations of information. Tables are lists of items. There are common elements involved when reading all three.

1. Read the title.
2. Read the labels.
3. Determine what type of information is being presented.

BAR AND LINE GRAPHS   A bar graph is a visual display used to compare groups of data and to make generalizations about the data.

Example   Given the graph "Enrollment in Introductory Courses at Union University," answer the following questions:

1. Which course has the most students enrolled in it?

2. Order the courses by enrollment from lowest to highest.

3. The enrollment in Econ is approximately how many times larger than the enrollment in Chem?

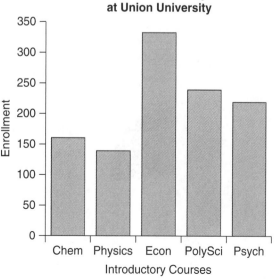

Enrollment in Introductory Courses at Union University

4. Approximately how many students were enrolled in the course with the most students?

5. Approximately how many more students are in Econ than in Physics?

Answers to Example

1. Which course has the most students enrolled in it?

   Answer: Econ

2. Order the courses by enrollment from lowest to highest.

   Answer: Physics, Chem, Psych, Poly Sci, Econ.

3. The enrollment in Econ is approximately how many times larger than the enrollment in Chem?

   Answer: 2 times larger

4. Approximately how many students were enrolled in the course with the most students?

   Answer: approximately 340 students (Econ)

5. Approximately how many more students are there in Econ than in Physics?

   Answer: approximately 200 more students in Econ than in Physics.

CIRCLE GRAPHS   A circle graph is used to show how the whole amount is broken into parts. The whole circle or pie graph depicts the entire sample space. The pieces of the pie in the circle graph are called sectors.

MOST POPULAR MOVIE GENRES

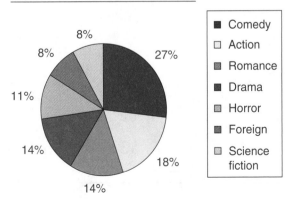

CHARTS   Charts are graphic interpretations of data.

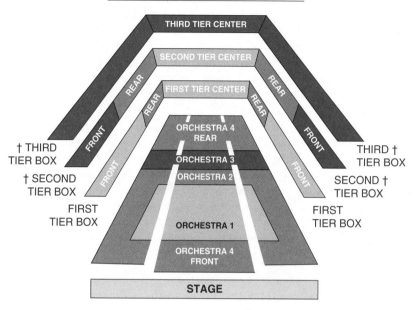

SEATING CHART FOR STAR THEATER

TABLES   Tables are lists of items organized into boxes, such as bus or train schedules.

Candy Sold Table

Candy Sold	M	T	W	T	F	Sa	Su	Total
M&M's	10	9	10	8	12	12	7	68
Snickers	12	11	14	6	13	16	12	84
Mars	15	17	20	14	18	20	15	119
Twix	14	15	18	10	8	18	16	99
Milky Way	13	14	10	8	14	19	9	87
Kit Kat	9	10	12	8	7	12	0	58
Total	73	76	84	54	72	97	59	515

Remember: Reading graphs, charts, and tables is easy:

- Read the TITLE.
- Read the LABELS.
- Determine what type of information is being presented.

D. Taking Notes While Reading

There are several reasons why you may want to take notes while reading. If you can't or don't want to make marks in a textbook or other sources, you need to get the important information recorded on paper. Many students find that they comprehend material better if they summarize it in their heads and write the important points. Written notes can be kept together in a notebook for easy studying later. Written notes are another textbook reading strategy which may be combined with other strategies like SQ3R and triple highlighting.

1. CORNELL NOTES To make written notes from your textbook or from a classroom lecture, a popular and proven method is Cornell Notes. Using the Cornell Notes method will help you take organized notes without much effort. The Cornell note-taking system divides an 8.5 × 11 page into three sections: (1) Key Points Column (left side of page), (2) Note-Taking Column (right side of page), and (3) Summary (bottom of page).

Here are the steps for using the Cornell Notes method.

1. Set up your note-taking pages:
   • If taking notes by hand, start by dividing each page in your notebook into three parts. Draw a dark horizontal line about five or six lines from the bottom. Use a marker or go over the line several times with your pen so the line is clear and easy to see.

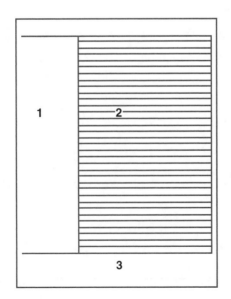

- Draw a dark vertical line about 2 inches from the left side of the paper from the top to the horizontal line.
- If taking notes on a laptop computer, you'll find a template online by typing "Cornell Notes template" into a search box.
- Place the text or course name, date, and topic at the top of each page.

2. Write the notes:
   - The large box to the right is for writing notes.
   - Skip a line between ideas and topics.
   - Don't use complete sentences. Use abbreviations whenever possible. Develop shorthand of your own, such as using "&" for the word *and*.

3. Review and clarify the notes right after reading, or as soon as possible after class:
   - Determine main ideas, key points, dates, and people; then write these in the left column.

4. Write a summary of the notes at the bottom of each page:
   - Use your own words to write a summary of the main ideas in the bottom section.

5. Study your notes for a test:
   - Reread your notes in the right column.
   - Then, spend most of your time studying the ideas in the left column and the summary at the bottom. These are the important ideas and will probably include most of the information you need to know for a test.

2. ANNOTATION   Another way to find and document important information in a textbook is to use annotation. Annotation is simply marking and writing notes directly in a textbook. The purpose of annotation is to be actively involved in your reading. Here are some of the techniques you can use to annotate your text.

- Underline important terms.
- Circle definitions and meanings.
- Write key words and definitions in the margin.
- Signal where important information can be found with key words or symbols in the margin (TQ = test question; * = important; RR = reread, etc.).
- Write short summaries in the margin at the end of major sections.
- Write a question in the margin next to the section where the answer is found.
- Indicate steps in a process by writing numbers next to each step or in the margin.
- Note anything that you don't understand or that you want to ask your instructor.

3. HIGHLIGHTING Highlighting is one of the fastest and most efficient ways to separate important information in a textbook chapter. Of course, you can't highlight in a book that doesn't belong to you, but in college you buy your textbooks, so highlighting is a method you may use if you choose. Highlighting may look easy, and it is if you remember the following points:

a. NEVER highlight as you're reading for the first time. Read through an entire section, or from one heading to the next; then go back and highlight. It will be much easier to determine what to highlight once you've an overview of the information.

b. Here is a list of things to highlight:
- Answers to your heading questions (if you're using SQ3R)
- Anything that stood out in your survey or preview
- Answers to chapter questions (which were read as part of your survey)
- Topic sentences
- Main points
- Names, dates, events
- Lists (number them too if they aren't already numbered).
- Anything you think you may be asked on a test

c. Review by reading **just** your highlighting. You don't need to reread everything!

4. "STICKY" NOTES This note-taking method is an alternative to taking notes directly in a textbook or on notebook paper. As you read assigned textbook material, write key terms and important facts, concepts, or ideas on the "sticky" notes. Then place these notes on appropriate spots in margins or blank spaces in the text. The "sticky" notes are a valuable tool for summarizing large quantities of information. They can also be easily removed from the text to use for class discussions, essay writing, or exam review.

5. ONE-SENTENCE SUMMARIES As you read, stop and reflect after each paragraph or section. Then create a sentence to sum up the information. As you progress through a passage, you'll gain a deeper understanding of the material while enhancing your retention. If you're a visual learner, you might even consider including quick drawings in your summaries.

─MyReadingLab─────────────────────

For more help with **Note Taking and Highlighting,** go to your learning path in MyReadingLab at www.myreadinglab.com.

E. SKIMMING AND SCANNING

The last of our textbook reading strategies is actually two processes: **skimming** and **scanning**. There are different kinds of reading for different situations, even with textbook reading. You need to consider your *purpose* for reading to be able to decide which strategy to use. To get detailed information, using a text-reading strategy like SQ3R works best. But sometimes you don't need detailed information. You might be previewing or reviewing material. Or you might be looking for a specific piece of information. If your purpose is to get a quick overview of the material, or to preview or review, then skimming is the best method. If your purpose is to quickly find a certain fact or piece of information, scanning is the way to go. Neither of these methods requires the reading of every single word in the material, so they also serve as ways to speed up your reading—which is a good thing for college students.

Read the explanations of skimming and scanning that follow. Be sure you understand the distinction between the two—both in the methods themselves, and also the purpose of each. Your instructor will provide you with several practice activities so you can become confident using skimming and scanning, and also confident that you know WHEN to use them.

QUICK TIP

Stop and ask yourself **why** you're reading the material (i.e., your purpose) and then determine which reading strategy is needed.

SKIMMING Skimming is used to quickly identify the main ideas of a text. When you read the newspaper, you probably don't read from front to back, word for word. Instead you read quickly over the headlines, and maybe the first few sentences of an article to get the main idea and/or to decide if you want to read the entire thing. If not, you continue to move your eyes quickly over the paper, reading the headlines and beginnings of articles. This is very similar to the techniques used in skimming. When you're done reading your newspaper, you've an overview of the news. When you skim an assignment, you've an overview of what it contains when you're done. This is often called a preview or, in SQ3R, the survey.

There are many strategies that can be used for skimming. Here are the most common ones—try them out and decide for yourself which ones work best for you.

How to Skim

- Read the title.
- Read the introduction or first paragraph.
- Read the chapter preview, overview, or highlights.
- Read the first sentence of each or every other paragraph.
- Read headings and subheadings.
- Notice pictures, charts, and graphs.
- Notice bold, italic or color words/phrases.
- Read the summary or last paragraph.

Now try skimming the Textbook Excerpt for Practice under Heading F to get an overview of the material. Skim it in 30 seconds or less and see if you can fill in the blanks below without looking back at the reading.

Main idea: _____

Who's theories are these? _____

Write any of the theories you remember—how many did you get?

_____

QUICK TIP

Skimming: **WHY?** To get a quick overview. **WHEN?** Before you start reading your assignment. **HOW?** See bulleted steps above.

SCANNING   Scanning is completely different from skimming. You use scanning when you need to quickly locate a specific piece of information. You're using scanning when you look up a number in the telephone book, or a word in the dictionary. When you're skimming, you don't know what you're looking for—you're trying to determine what the reading is about. When you're scanning, you **do** know what you're looking for—a specific piece of information. In scanning you have a question in your mind, and you read a passage only to find the answer, ignoring unrelated information. Scanning involves moving your eyes quickly down the page, seeking specific words, phrases or numbers.

How to Scan

- State the specific information you're looking for.
- Anticipate how the answer will look: Will it have capital letters at the beginning? Will it be a number? Is it one word or several words?

- Use headings and other aids to help you identify sections where your answer is most likely to appear.
- Move your eyes quickly down the page looking for the antici-pated type of information.

Scan the following paragraph to find out how many moons Sat-urn has.

> It's the start of a four-year tour, during which the ship will make at least 76 loops of the planet and engage a dozen cameras and instruments. NASA will be able to tweak the trajectory of the orbiter so it can slalom among nine of Saturn's 31 moons. The grandest of the satellites is Titan, which has long frustrated scien-tists because its dense atmosphere, laced with organic gases, obscures its surface.
>
> (*Time*, June 28, 2004)

How many moons does Saturn have? Did you find the answer of 31? Were you looking for numerals rather than words? Good job! Now scan the paragraph again to find the answer to this question: How long is the ship's tour supposed to last?

What answer did you find for that question? The correct answer is four years, but the number was written out, and it was hyphenated to the word year, making it harder to find. Remember: If you can't find the answer to your question in the anticipated form, try to think of other ways it might appear. You might also look for another key word in the question, which in this case was the word "tour."

QUICK TIP

Scanning: **WHY?** To find specific information. **WHEN?** Only when you need the answer to a question. **HOW?** See the bulleted steps above.

Skimming and scanning are two easy ways you can improve your reading comprehension, efficiency, and speed. Remember to vary your reading speed and strategies according to your purpose.

QUICK TIP

You don't need to, and shouldn't, read everything in college (or in life) word for word!

F. Textbook Excerpt for Practice

Instructors will find an additional copy of this excerpt in the Instructor's Manual (IM) so that the pages can be duplicated, if needed, for further practice.

The following textbook excerpt may be used as needed to practice the strategies discussed in this chapter.

Some Theories About Love and Loving

Why and how do we love? Biological explanations tend to focus on why we love. Psychological, sociological, and anthropological approaches try to explain how as well as why.

Lee's Styles of Loving

Canadian sociologist John A. Lee (1973) developed one of the most widely cited and studied approaches to love. Although not a full-fledged theory, Lee's approach was built on his collection of more than 4,000 statements about love from hundreds of works of fiction and nonfiction.

The sources ranged from the literature of ancient Greece (which recognized *agape* and *eros* as two kinds of love), the Bible, and medieval, Victorian, and modern writers. Lee administered a 30-item questionnaire based on this research to people in Canada and Great Britain. From the responses he derived six basic styles of loving: *eros, mania, ludus, storge, agape,* and *pragma* . . . all of which overlap and vary in intensity in real life.

Eros   **Eros** (root of the word *erotic*) is the love of beauty. Because it is also characterized by powerful physical attraction, eros epitomizes "love at first sight." This is the kind of love often described in romance novels, where the loves are immediately love-struck and experience palpitating hearts, light-headedness, and intense emotional desire.

Erotic lovers want to know everything about the loved one—what she or he dreamed about last night and what happened on the way to work today. Erotic lovers often like to wear matching T-shirts, identical bracelets, and matching colors, to order the same foods when dining out, and to be identified with each other as totally as possible (Lasswell and Lasswell, 1976).

Mania   Characterized by obsessiveness, jealousy, possessiveness, and intense dependency, **mania** may be expressed in anxiety, sleeplessness, loss of appetite, headaches, and even suicide because of real or imagined rejection. Manic lovers are consumed by thoughts of their beloved and have an insatiable need for attention and signs of affection (Lee, 1973). Mania is often associated with low self-esteem and a poor self-concept. As a result, manic people are typically not attractive to those who have a strong self-concept and high self-esteem (Lasswell and Lasswell, 1976).

Ludus   **Ludus** is carefree and casual love that is considered "fun and games." Physical appearance is less important to ludic lovers than self-sufficiency and a nondemanding partner. They try to control their feelings and may have several lovers at one time. They are not possessive or jealous, primarily because they don't want lovers to become dependent on them. Ludic lovers have sex for fun, not emotional rapport. In their sexual encounters they are typically self-centered and may be exploitive because they do not want commitment, which they consider "scary."

Storge   **Storge** (pronounced "STOR-gay") is a slow-burning, peaceful, and affectionate love that "just comes naturally" with the passage of time and the enjoyment of shared activities. Storgic relationships lack the ecstatic highs and lows that characterize some other styles; sex occurs late in this type of relationship, and the goals are usually marriage, home, and children. Even if they break up, storgic lovers are likely to remain good friends (Lee, 1973).

The storgic lover finds routine home activities relaxing and comfortable. Because there is mutual trust, temporary separations are not a problem. In storgic love, affection develops over the years, as in many lasting marriages. Passion may be replaced by spirituality, respect, and contentment in the enjoyment of each other's company (Murstein, 1974).

Agape   The classical Christian type of love, **agape** (pronounced "AH-gah-pay") is altruistic, self-sacrificing love that is directed toward all humankind. It is a self-giving love in which partners help each other develop their maximum potential without considering their own advantages or costs. Agape is always kind and patient, never jealous or demanding, and does not seek reciprocity. Lee points out, however, that he has not yet found an unqualified example of agape during his interviews.

Intense agape can border on masochism. For example, an agapic person might wait indefinitely for a lover to be released from prison, might tolerate an alcoholic or drug-addicted spouse, or might be willing to live with a partner who engages in illegal activities or infidelity (Lasswell and Lasswell, 1976).

Pragma   According to Lee, **pragma** is rational love based on practical considerations, such as compatibility and perceived benefits. Indeed, it can be described as "love with a shopping list." A pragmatic person seeks compatibility in such things as background, education, religious views, and vocational and professional interests. If one person does not work out, the pragmatic person moves on, quite rationally, to search for someone else.

Pragmatic lovers look out for their partners, encouraging them, for example, to ask for a promotion or to finish college.

They are also practical in divorce. For example, a couple might stay together until the younger child finishes high school or until both partners find better jobs (Lasswell and Lasswell, 1976).

Chapter Summary

Textbook Strategies: Approximately 70 percent of course information comes from the textbook. It's extremely important to know how to use textbooks and to have strategies for reading them.

Textbook Organizational Aids
- *Preface*—Author to reader, gives useful information about the book.
- *Table of Contents*—Like an outline of the book, gives chapter titles, sections, page numbers.
- *Glossary*—A mini-dictionary of words from the text with meanings as they are used in the text.
- *Index(es)*—Alphabetical listing of topics in the book with page numbers showing where they can be found. Many textbooks have more than one index.
- *Appendix(ices)*—Additional information in the back of the book. The text will refer you to the appendices. They're usually lettered A, B, C, and so on.

Textbook Reading Methods
- *SQ3R*—A five-step method involving surveying, questioning, reading, reciting or highlighting, and reviewing.
- *5C*—A five-step method using index cards to record key information and vocabulary words and definitions.
- *Triple Highlighting*—A three-step method using different color highlighters to mark important information as noted by the student, the author and the instructor.

Reading Graphs, Charts, and Tables—Read the title, read the labels, determine what type of information is being presented.

Taking Notes While Reading
- *Cornell Notes*—Main idea on the left side of page, details on the right.
- *Annotations*—Notes written *directly* in a text or book.
- *Highlighting*—Featuring information you want to remember in a text or book, using highlighters.
- *"Sticky" notes*—Placing "sticky" notes (containing key information) directly on book pages for easy removal.
- *One-sentence summaries*—Quick summaries written after reading each paragraph or section.

Skimming and Scanning

- **Skimming**—Quickly reading over material to get the main idea of the entire reading.
- **Scanning**—Quickly reading over material to find a specific piece of information.

Check Your Learning (Learning Outcomes)

Have you mastered the Learning Objectives (LOs) for Chapter 3? Place a check mark next to each LO that you're able to do.

_____LO1—Identify and use textbook organizational aids

_____LO2—Use three textbook reading methods

_____LO3—Comprehend information found in graphs, charts, and tables

_____LO4—Take notes while reading

_____LO5—Use skimming and scanning

_____LO6—Use a textbook excerpt to practice textbook strategies

Go back and review the sections that cover any LO you didn't check.

Quick Connections—Chapter Three

NEWS SOURCE CONNECTION

Using a news source (news magazine or newspaper), choose an article that has several headings to read. Apply a text reading method to your news article. Surveying, making questions from the headings, highlighting the answers, and reviewing are also effective strategies to improve your reading of news articles with headings.

TEXTBOOK CONNECTION

Use a textbook from one of your other classes, and if possible, do this activity as you're doing a reading assignment for the other class. Choose either SQ3R, 5C, or triple highlighting, and read your assignment using the chosen textbook method. After you've finished, write down at least three things you liked about the method you used, and three things you didn't like. Do the same for each of the other two methods, and then you can determine which method (or perhaps a combination of the methods) works best for you.

NOVEL CONNECTION

The first step of every textbook reading method involves a survey, or preview. Survey or preview the novel you'll read before you start reading. In addition to the sections you preview for a textbook, see what other information is available to preview with your novel (i.e., book jacket). As with a textbook, a novel preview can improve comprehension. It can also help you get into the novel more *quick*ly.

WEB CONNECTION ⚙️⟶⌐Complete this Exercise at MyReadingLab.com

Conduct a search and find a site on the Internet where you can read about textbook reading methods and possibly find practices. Write a brief description of a textbook reading method that is new to you and seems to be one that would work well. Your instructor may have everyone in the class share the new method each student found. If you find a site with good practice exercises, use them to improve your textbook-reading ability.

MyReadingLab™ CONNECTION ⚙️⟶⌐Complete this Exercise at MyReadingLab.com

Visit MyReadingLab to take a review quiz testing your mastery of this chapter's topics.

Four

Critical Reading Strategies

Chapter Preview

Part A: Critical Reading Strategies Overview

A. Predicting, Drawing Conclusions, and Making Inferences
   1. Predicting
   2. Drawing Conclusions and Making Inferences

LEARNING OBJECTIVES (LOs)

Upon completion of this chapter section, you'll be able to:

▩ LO1—Make **predictions** based on titles and passages read

▩ LO2—Make **inferences** based on information implied, but not stated, in passages

▩ LO3—**Draw conclusions** from information presented in one or more passages

Part B: Critical Reading Strategies Overview

B. Analyzing and Synthesizing
   1. Identifying the Writer's Purpose
   2. Fact and Opinion
   3. Judging Validity
   4. Identifying Author Attitude, Bias, Tone, and Assumptions

Reading can . . .
Take you places you might never go
and introduce you to people you might
never know.

LEARNING OBJECTIVES (LOs)

Upon completion of this chapter section, you'll be able to:

■ LO1—Analyze (break down or dissect) and synthesize (arrange or blend) information within a passage in order to:

• Identify the **writer's purpose**

• Distinguish between **facts and opinions**

• Judge the **validity** of a passage

• Identify **author attitudes, bias, tone,** and **assumptions**

Strategy Area A: Critical Reading—Predicting, Making Inferences, and Drawing Conclusions

Readiness Quiz A   ⚙ Complete this Exercise at **MyReadingLab.com**

Match the terms below with the best definitions on the right.

1 _____	critical	**A.**	decide, determine
2. _____	imply	**B.**	decide from suggestion
3. _____	infer	**C.**	forecast or foretell
4. _____	conclude	**D.**	evaluative
5. _____	explicit	**E.**	suggest
6. _____	predict	**F.**	clearly stated

Questions for Discussion

What is critical reading?

How do you read critically?

PART A: CRITICAL READING STRATEGIES OVERVIEW

A. Predicting, Drawing Conclusions, and Making Inferences

While the word *critical* has various dictionary definitions, when used in the context of critical reading, the term generally involves higher order thinking strategies such as analyzing, comparing, and judging. It is *evaluative* and reflective in nature. As used in the context of this chapter, it refers to any higher order thinking and reading strategies.

Critical thinking and reading are challenging and complex processes. There are entire courses devoted to these topics. This chapter isn't meant to thoroughly cover this area. It is merely a starting point. **Critical reading** requires consistent practice and continual exposure to a variety of written materials. The practices in this text should be followed up with ongoing practice. Participating in classroom discussions can also be helpful to you as you're exposed to the various perspectives and backgrounds of experience shared among your classmates. Broadening your own background of experience and expanding your perspectives will allow you to read and think more critically.

The first part of this chapter focuses on the critical reading strategies of **predicting, making inferences,** and **drawing conclusions,** which require higher level thinking. The latter two strategies often overlap. It's generally necessary to draw a conclusion in order to make an inference. However, not all conclusions require you to make an inference. We'll begin with strategies for predicting.

1. PREDICTING   Effective readers are active readers. They begin making predictions about what will come next—right from the beginning of a reading, starting with the title if there is one. Being aware of a writer's pattern of organization (see Chapter 6) may help you to anticipate the direction a reading will take. Test questions sometimes ask the reader to extend (extrapolate or project on the basis of known information) into the future or into a new situation. To make such "predictions," you must first have a clear understanding of the passage. Next, build upon this information by analyzing the logic used by the writer and/or the sequence of events described. Then, make choices that are consistent with the passage but that do not *over*extend, or stretch, the ideas expressed there.

QUICK TIP

Notice the way people are described. Use information about their personalities, thoughts, or feelings to determine how they might act or react.

QUICK TIP

After reading and analyzing a passage, ask yourself what might happen as a result of the stated actions or events.

Using the previewing strategy while reading can serve as a major step toward making more accurate predictions. Another great tool involves treating the reading as if it were a two-way conversation. In other words, after each statement a writer makes, the reader can practice an internal dialogue, responding to each point. This strategy simulates what happens in a face-to-face conversation. When you're listening to someone, you generally respond in some way to demonstrate that you've listened and understood. You may ask questions along the way to encourage the speaker to clarify or amplify (expand) what has been said. Active reading, much like active listening, enables you to get much more out of the communication and also to retain it more effectively.

Consider This Title: *The Story of an Hour*

When you read this title, what expectations do you have for the information that will follow? You may or may not be accurate, depending upon many factors, but you'll be more prepared for what follows if you at least attempt to anticipate or predict what lies ahead. You would obviously expect some type of story that takes place within an hour. Your internal dialogue might go something like this: "The Story of an Hour . . . hmm, good, that might mean it's not going to be very long. I wonder how someone can make much of a story out of something that only takes an hour. Well, I guess I'll find out."

Don't underestimate the importance of starting to predict by questioning or reflecting upon the title. Sometimes students are in such a hurry that they neglect to pay much attention to the title, or to do a quick preview of the reading. Taking the time to predict can save time later because you get more out of what you read. Continue the active internal dialogue throughout a reading, and you'll be well on your way toward making better predictions.

Now complete a brief practice as you read this short excerpt from Yann Martel's 2001 novel, *Life of Pi*. Pi, the main character in the book, is giving some advice to those who might happen to fall into a lion's pit at a zoo. Try writing short responses where indicated (by the blank lines) within the passage. Then check suggested answers below. To get you started, one possible response for question 1 below might be: "If I fall into a lion's pit? How would that happen? Maybe during a visit to the zoo." Now see if you can come up with your own thoughts and write them on the lines below.

1. So you see, if you fall into a lion's pit,

_____

2. the reason the lion will tear you to pieces

_____

3. isn't because it's hungry—

_____

4. be assured, zoo animals are amply fed—

_____

5. or because it's bloodthirsty,

_____

6. but because you've invaded its territory.

_____

Answers will vary, but the following are some possibilities:

1. Well, I don't intend to ever do that, but if I did, what should I know?
2. Tear me to pieces? Does the lion need a reason? Isn't that just what lions do?
3. Oh, I didn't really think the lion would need to be hungry to tear me to pieces, but what would his reason be, according to you?
4. Yes, I suppose they are, so go on . . .
5. It's not? I guess I thought lions were bloodthirsty. Now you've really got me curious.
6. Oh, yes, I would have invaded its territory. Lions are just protecting their territory then . . . like some people do. Interesting!

FINAL PRACTICE ON PREDICTING

Now you're ready for the last practice exercise for this section. Try predicting, using an excerpt from the textbook _Keys to Business Success_ by Martha Doran (2000). Consider the following heading from the chapter "Business Communication":

How do Nonverbal Clues Give Meaning in Communication?

1. Can you predict what minor headings might be included under a heading on nonverbal clues?

_____

_____

2. A paragraph under the heading _GESTURES_ begins with this sentence: "We usually consider gestures as obvious, yet they are culturally bound."

    What would you predict to follow this introductory sentence? Write your thoughts below. Then read the entire paragraph which follows.

_____

_____

We usually consider gestures as obvious, yet they are culturally bound. An American's friendly wave with the left hand to say "hi" may be an insult in some cultures where the left hand is considered unclean (the hygiene or toilet hand). The American "thumbs up" gesture to indicate OK is an obscene gesture in other cultures. While Americans may nod their heads up and down to indicate agreement, people in another culture nod the head to indicate no; while Americans shake their heads left to right to indicate no, in another culture the head turns to the left to indicate yes. Differing interpretations of gestures lead to the cultural aversion to foreigners who appear insulting and uncouth to the host culture. Since Americans frequently travel abroad, they may unwittingly communicate a poor image of themselves with wrong gestures. Most likely, they will not realize the wrong message, since that message is what the host culture perceives, not the intended message of the gesture.

How did you do? Discuss possible answers with your class.

2. DRAWING CONCLUSIONS AND MAKING INFERENCES When what you're reading includes information that isn't clearly or directly stated, it may be necessary for you to **draw a conclusion.** This means that you combine your prior knowledge, or what you already know from past learning or experience, with the new information you're reading to come to a decision.

Here is an example of drawing a **simple conclusion:** John is leaving his home in ten minutes for a meeting that requires him to wear a suit. John owns three suits. However, two of those are at the cleaners. Therefore, you would logically conclude that John will wear the one suit that isn't at the cleaners.

Sometimes, you can draw a conclusion by applying your prior knowledge to stated facts alone. Other times, you'll need to make a judgment based on an idea that is clearly suggested or implied by a writer, although not explicitly stated. This is called an **inference.** When making inferences, keep in mind the main idea and details of a passage. You should be able to defend your inference by first pointing to clearly stated information in a passage, and then reading "between the lines."

Making inferences is a natural part of the thinking process. For instance, if you pass a friend or acquaintance in a hallway and greet that person, but fail to get a response to your greeting, you probably infer something like "she must not have seen me" or "he must be preoccupied right now" or "gee, she's really stuck up!" The tricky thing about inferences is that, because they are implied, it's possible to be wrong. Perhaps the acquaintance didn't recognize you. Or possibly the friend had just received traumatic news and was too emotional to respond. The more evidence or clues you have to make an accurate inference, the better.

QUICK TIP

Use the "if–then" test to verify your inference. Does it make sense that if *X* (information stated in the passage) is true, then *Y* (your inference) is probably true?

When attempting to draw conclusions (including inferences), be sure you first understand the main idea and details of a passage. Also use context clues, other vocabulary strategies, and a dictionary to clarify any difficult terminology. Keep in mind the sequence of events and/or logical reasoning. Determine what might result from the actions or events the writer has described. Allow your own background of experience or prior knowledge to help you draw a conclusion without reading *too* much into a passage, or *overextending* its content.

QUICK TIP

Draw conclusions that are consistent with the content of the passage by mentally adding your own thoughts or reflections to what you've read. Any inferences you make should be supported by the passage itself in order to be considered logical conclusions.

For example, consider the following passage from the beginning of Dave Pelzer's (1995) autobiographical novel:

> SMACK! Mother hits me in the face and I topple to the floor. I know better than to stand there and take the hit. I learned the hard way that she takes that as an act of defiance, which means more hits, or worst of all, no food. I regain my posture and dodge her looks, as she screams into my ears.

A Child Called "It"

What logical inferences can you make regarding the situation described above? The passage doesn't need to tell us directly that this is an ongoing, abusive relationship between a mother and her son. We quickly infer these things. We might also infer that the child is perceptive enough to have learned how best to deal with the abuse. We get a glimpse of the importance of food to this child since "no food" is worse than "more hits." These inferences all fit the context of the passage. We might begin predicting what will follow, but any serious predictions at this point in the book would overextend the information given. As the story unfolds, we can begin to more accurately draw conclusions and make predictions because we have a stronger base of context from which to do this.

Now read the following excerpt:

> Stacey's story is enough to make any parent sick with worry. Sadly, her experience is growing more common. Over the last year, local and federal law-enforcement officials say they have noted a marked increase in teen prostitution in cities across the country. Solid numbers are difficult to come by—a government-sponsored study puts the figure in the hundreds of thousands—but law-enforcement agencies and advocacy groups that work with teen prostitutes say they are increasingly alarmed by the trend lines: the kids are getting younger; according to the FBI, the average age of a new recruit is just 13; some are as young as 9. The girls—many fewer are boys, most experts believe—are subjected to more violence from pimps. And, while the vast majority of teen prostitutes today are runaways, illegal immigrants and children of poor urban areas, experts say a growing number now come from middle-class homes.

> *Newsweek,* "This Could Be Your Kid," August 2003

Since this passage is taken out of context, the reader might logically infer that "Stacey's story" either came before . . . or would follow. The information seems to indicate that Stacey may be one of those teens involved in teen prostitution. However, without more information, it's possible, for example, that Stacey was merely approached by a pimp. We can also logically infer that parents who need to be the most concerned are those whose children have run away, are illegal immigrants, live in poor urban areas, or come from middle-class homes. While it is logical for the reader to draw this conclusion, it wouldn't be logical to draw the conclusion that *only* these parents need be concerned. Such a conclusion would overextend the content of the passage.

Inferences Practice

Try a paragraph from a developmental psychology textbook. Read the passage, then answer the questions that follow:

> Newborns appear to respond differentially to all four of the basic flavors (Crook, 1987). Some of the clearest demonstrations of this come from an elegantly simple set of early studies by Jacob Steiner (Ganchrow et al., 1983; Steiner, 1979). Newborn infants who had never been fed were photographed before and after flavored water was put into their mouths. By varying the flavor,

Steiner could determine whether the babies reacted differently to different tastes . . . babies responded quite differently to sweet, sour, and bitter flavors.

(Bee, 2000)

Place a check mark in front of the inferences that are logical to make from this passage:

1. _____ Responses to taste are merely learned responses.

2. _____ Newborn babies probably display a negative reaction to a bitter taste.

3. _____ It's likely that the passage will go on to address newborns' reactions to smell.

4. _____ Since this research began in 1979, it is probably outdated.

5. _____ The flavored water used posed danger to the newborns.

Note the following reasoning:

#1: This statement directly contradicts the evidence presented in the passage.

#2: Prior experience combined with the final statement that babies responded quite differently to sweet, sour, and bitter flavors would support this inference.

#3: The paragraph discusses only sense of taste; there are no headings, titles, or transitional sentences that indicate other senses will be discussed.

#4: By citing this study, the author implies that it is still important research and consistent with current theory.

#5: There's nothing in the passage that indicates any danger to newborns; while a critical reader might consider that possibility, it isn't a logical inference to make, given the content of the passage.

DRAWING CONCLUSIONS PRACTICE

For the final exercise in this section, compare two passages from separate websites which comment on the celebration of Columbus Day. Read both passages and then answer the questions that follow.

Passage 1

Historically, Columbus was not the first to discover America, nor was he the first European to land at America. He was the first to exploit, kill, and enslave the Arawak Indians of Haiti. The myth of

Christopher Columbus and the discovery of America is due to Washington Irving. His "biography" of Columbus was popularized in a dramatic and embellished account. In recent years, the holiday has been rejected by many people who view it as a celebration of conquest and genocide. In its place, Indigenous Peoples Day is celebrated.

(www.bright.net/~jimsjems/columbus.html)

Passage 2

The politically correct view is that Columbus did not discover America, because people had lived here for thousands of years. Worse yet, it's claimed, the main legacy of Columbus is death and destruction. Columbus is routinely vilified as a symbol of slavery and genocide, and the celebration of his arrival likened to a celebration of Hitler and the Holocaust. The attacks on Columbus are ominous, because the actual target is Western civilization.

Did Columbus "discover" America? Yes—in every important respect. This does not mean that no human eye had been cast on America before Columbus arrived. It does mean that Columbus brought America to the attention of the civilized world, i.e., to the growing, scientific civilizations of Western Europe. The result, ultimately, was the United States of America.

(www.aynrand.org/objectivism/columbus.html)

Now answer the following questions:

1. Would you conclude that these two writers agree or disagree?

_____

2. Which passage would most likely support the celebration of Columbus Day?

_____

3. List words that enable the reader to "hear" the emotion of the writer in passage 1. In other words, which words may have been used by the writer to trigger an emotional response from the reader? (Example: "exploit" has a negative connotation. Refer to discussion on connotative language in Chapter 1, Vocabulary Strategies.)

_____

4. List words that enable the reader to "hear" the emotion of the writer in passage 2.

_____

⌐MyReadingLab⎯⎯⎯⎯⎯⎯⎯⎯⎯⎯⎯⎯⎯⎯⎯⎯⎯

For more help with **Inference,** go to your learning path in
MyReadingLab at www.myreadinglab.com.

Strategy Area B: Critical Reading—Analyzing and Synthesizing

Readiness Quiz B1   ⚙⌐Complete this Exercise at MyReadingLab.com

Write an **F** before the statements which are facts and an **O** before the
statements which are opinions.

1. _____ Jennifer Lopez is beautiful.

2. _____ George Washington was the second president of the
United States.

3. _____ College tuition rates in Nebraska are on the rise.

4. _____ Nebraska state taxes are too high.

5. _____ A U.S. president was impeached.

6. _____ Investing in the stock market is risky.

Readiness Quiz B2

Part a: Match the terms below with the correct definitions on the right.

1. _____ valid   **A.** the act of taking for granted without
proof

2. _____ evidence   **B.** a position or manner indicative of
feeling, opinion, or intention toward
a person or thing

3. _____ attitude   **C.** foretell

4. _____ assumption   **D.** the means of proving or disproving
an assertion

5. _____ predict   **E.** subjective point of view

6. _____ bias   **F.** well supported by fact

Part b: Choose **T** for true or **F** for false after reading each statement below.

1. _____ A writer's attitude must be either positive or negative.

2. _____ Readers should always refrain from making predictions based upon a reading unless the prediction is stated within the passage.

3. _____ It's possible to recognize unstated ideas a writer accepts as true or takes for granted.

4. _____ A writer may present evidence that is true, but does not actually support his/her argument.

5. _____ The tone of a reading is the underlying feeling the writer creates.

6. _____ It's impossible to determine a writer's purpose unless it is directly stated.

PART B: CRITICAL READING STRATEGIES OVERVIEW

B. Analyzing and Synthesizing

In addition to predicting, making inferences, and drawing conclusions, readers are often required to **analyze** (break down or dissect) and **synthesize** (arrange or blend) information. It may be necessary to determine a **writer's purpose,** separate **facts** from **opinions,** judge the **validity** of an argument, and/or identify an **author's attitudes, bias, tone,** and **assumptions,** based on information presented.

1. IDENTIFYING THE WRITER'S PURPOSE A key element of better comprehension is for the reader to discern the writer's purpose and intended audience. Writers usually have a specific purpose and audience in mind when writing. The purpose will determine how a reading is organized and will also influence the writer's word choices.

Sometimes clues to the writer's purpose will be evident in the title of a reading. Some writers will directly state the purpose. Often, however, the purpose isn't stated, but merely implied. The reader's careful attention to word choices in the titles, headings, and reading will usually pay off in improved understanding of the writer's purpose. And understanding the purpose will greatly enhance the reader's comprehension of the main idea and details of the reading.

Main purposes of a reading may include the following:

- To inform (give facts or clarify)
- To describe (provide word pictures)
- To persuade (change someone's mind and/or behavior)
- To entertain (amuse or provide enjoyment)
- To narrate (tell a story)

It's important to realize, however, that, although a reading usually has one main purpose, the writer may include a variety or mix of minor purposes as well. For a more detailed analysis of some of these (and other) purposes, see Chapter 6, Patterns of Organization Strategies.

WRITER'S PURPOSE PRACTICE

Read the short passages below, and try to determine which of the following is the writer's main purpose: to inform, describe, persuade, entertain, or narrate.

> The young woman was tall, with a figure of perfect elegance on a large scale. She had dark and abundant hair, so glossy that it threw off the sunshine with a gleam, and a face which, besides being beautiful from regularity of feature and richness of complexion, had the impressiveness belonging to a marked brow and deep black eyes. She was ladylike, too, after the manner of the feminine gentility of those days . . .

> (Hawthorne, 1959)

MAIN PURPOSE: _____

> Think you might have HIV? Several sites around Omaha will offer free, confidential testing for a virus that is particularly affecting blacks and Latinos and is making a comeback in white gay men. "It's on the rise in all communities," said Rosey Higgs, HIV testing and counseling coordinator at the Nebraska AIDS Project. Federal health experts estimate that 180,000 to 280,000 HIV-positive people in the United States do not know their status . . . Free tests are available Friday, Saturday, and Monday.

> (Adapted from the *Omaha World Herald,* 2005)

MAIN PURPOSE: _____

2. FACT AND OPINION Critical readers need to be able to differentiate between facts and opinions. A fact is an idea that can be proved or disproved. An idea can be a fact even if it is untrue, as long as it can be either proved or disproved (see Readiness Quiz B1, question 2). Opinions usually include words which **interpret** (*explain or show the meaning of*) or **evaluate** (*judge the value of*) something. Sentence number one below is a clear statement of fact; the second sentence reflects an evaluation.

1. The woman who applied for the job had blue eyes and shoulder-length brown hair.
2. A beautiful woman applied for the job.

It's someone's opinion that the woman is beautiful. While there are numerous examples of interpretive words, here are a few more: loving, dangerous, bad, attractive, gentle, improper, brilliant, and finest. Note that all of these words are adjectives, or words used to describe a noun (person, place, or thing).

QUICK TIP

Look for words that **interpret** or **evaluate.** These often indicate an **opinion.**

Some words clearly indicate that an opinion follows. Examples: *I feel, I think, I believe, in my opinion.* Other words like *possibly, probably, usually, sometimes, often,* or *perhaps* may be used to limit a statement and to allow for the possibility of other viewpoints. Opinions may be valid when properly supported, and *facts* may actually be false.

Some people think that in order for something to be a fact, it must be proven scientifically. The scientific method, however, can only be used to prove repeatable observations. Another method for proving a fact is called legal-historical proof. This kind of proof depends upon exhibits, oral testimony, and written testimony. An example of this type of fact would be that George Washington was the first president of the United States. Such a statement cannot be proved scientifically, yet is a fact based on legal-historical proof.

One other caution when distinguishing between facts and opinions relates to making predictions. Since the future can't be proved by any method, predictions are regarded as opinions.

FACT AND OPINION PRACTICE

Consider the following statements in light of the discussion above. Write **F** for *facts* and **O** for *opinions* and **underline any words that signal evaluation or prediction:**

1. _____ American children watch too much television.

2. _____ Abraham Lincoln was the sixteenth president of the United States.

3. _____ Women are better communicators than men.

4. _____ The state of California will one day fall into the ocean.

5. _____ Mount Rainier in Washington State is 14,410 feet high.

Even experts' opinions may vary. For instance, some doctors promote a high protein, low carbohydrate diet, while other doctors remain skeptical. Some opinions are so widely accepted that they may seem like facts. However, when interpretation or evaluation is involved, statements are generally considered opinions.

The following passage is from an editorial. Identify as many of the interpretive or evaluative words (or phrases) as you can find, and mark or underline them in the passage. Then check the key below it.

> The rules for who must be paid overtime in America are more complicated than they need to be, and many of the job categories are hopelessly outmoded, having been crafted in some cases as long as 65 years ago. Few could doubt that such a situation needed clarifying.
>
> But in regard to the foreign workers, a terrible message is being sent, asking Congress to endorse law-breaking by millions of people. They sneak across the borders, usually entering a shadowy world of shabby housing, tax evasion and fear of almost all law enforcement. Most deserve better than that.
>
> _Omaha World Herald_ ("Straight Talk on Jobs," January 8, 2004)

KEY: The following words should be marked or underlined: complicated, outmoded, needed clarifying, terrible, sneak, shadowy, shabby, fear, deserve better.

3. JUDGING VALIDITY   A crucial component of judging the validity of evidence (that is, evidence well supported by facts) is to examine the _source_ of the evidence. Determine whether or not the source represents expertise, research, and/or appropriate data. Next, look at the evidence itself. Evidence that supports a conclusion strengthens an argument, while evidence that contradicts or casts doubt on a conclusion weakens an argument. Review a writer's claim as well as the evidence used to support it.

QUICK TIP

Ask yourself if a new piece of evidence strengthens the writer's claim, weakens the writer's claim, or is irrelevant to the validity (soundness) of the claim.

It's important to determine if a writer has used sound reasoning to develop a logical argument. Do the thoughts flow logically, or are there missing connections between ideas presented? Has the writer been complete in supporting a conclusion? Do any of the writer's claims contradict each other?

How about the author's use of language? Are words chosen to appeal to the reader's emotions rather than one's sense of logic? Is the language ambiguous (vague or unclear)?

Another important strategy for judging the validity of an argument is to look for common **fallacies** (false or erroneous ideas) in the reasoning. **While there are at least hundreds of fallacies in logic and they may often overlap, several of the most common are described below. Just as it's essential for a reader to recognize fallacies in an argument, it's important to avoid such fallacies in one's own writing to maintain credibility.**

> *Emotional appeal:* Words, phrases, slogans, or images are used to arouse a favorable response from the reader. Such tactics can be used in advertisements and political campaigns, or in any kind of persuasive writing. Readers need to look beyond the emotional appeal to consider the true validity of the argument.

Examples

A politician uses terms like *freedom* and *the American way* in a persuasive essay. Controversial issues like gay rights and abortion are discussed using positive or negative terms (e.g., *homophobic, pro-life, antichoice*) to sway the reader, apart from the facts. (See discussion on connotative language in Chapter 1, Vocabulary Strategies.)

> *Attack the person, or name-calling:* A person's conclusion is ignored or attacked on the basis of something the person has (or has not) done or said, rather than on the basis of that person's argument. Such fallacies are rampant during political campaigns, but can occur frequently whenever people differ in their perspectives. Attacks on a person and name-calling are used to divert the reader's attention from the real issue.

Examples

Senator X is a left-wing liberal, so why should we listen to anything he has to say?

Mrs. Y claims that teachers aren't doing their jobs, but since she's never been a teacher, how would she know?

Hasty generalization: A conclusion is drawn without sufficient evidence or from too small a sample.

Examples

Several police officers in Los Angeles beat up a black man during an arrest. Therefore, the L.A. Police Department is racist.

A pro-life activist shoots and kills an abortionist. Therefore, pro-lifers are dangerous right-wing extremists.

All or nothing: Opinions that state or imply the word *all* are generally stereotypes (and similar to hasty generalizations). They often ignore individual differences or relevant data.

Examples

Lawyers are greedy.

All men are insensitive.

Women are more emotional than men.

Children today are spoiled and lazy.

False cause: Many issues are complex. In an attempt to arrive at a conclusion, events are often erroneously linked as having a cause–effect relationship. The fact that one event follows another does not necessitate such a relationship. An outcome may also be the result of multiple causes, not just one.

Examples

No wonder crime is on an upswing; look at all the violence on TV. While violence on TV *may* contribute to the crime rate, the issue is more complicated. Also, it's important to determine if the initial claim—crime is on an upswing—is true before looking at the validity of the causes.

When some children get taller, they get worse grades in school. The lower grades could actually be caused by factors such as increased activities, hormonal issues, higher expectations, or peer pressure.

> *Testimonial:* A famous person endorses a product (or service). People can be swayed by the fame of the person, rather than by the merit of the product.

Examples

Michael Jordan advertises a particular brand of athletic shoes.

Candice Bergen promotes a cellular phone.

FALLACY PRACTICE

Which **fallacy** (i.e., mistake in reasoning) presented in this chapter can you identify for each statement below?

1. Mr. Smith's thoughts on this tax bill don't really matter since he wouldn't be affected by the tax increase.

   _____

2. I'm sure a new law which would lower the drinking age would pass because every single one of my friends thinks it's a great idea.

   _____

3. There's a high rate of breast cancer in Nebraska. This must be due to the use of pesticides and herbicides which contaminate the drinking water.

   _____

4. IDENTIFYING AUTHOR ATTITUDE, BIAS, TONE, AND ASSUMPTIONS Careful readers will attempt to discern a writer's attitude toward a subject, as well as to *uncover* assumptions a writer has made. The attitude a writer takes toward a subject is often expressed through the use of positive or negative words. (See discussion on connotative language in Chapter 1, Vocabulary Strategies.) A reader's awareness and analysis of word choices will be a major step toward exposing any bias the writer has expressed toward a topic.

When the writer is objective, word choices will often be neutral and/or both sides of an issue will be covered. When the writer expresses his or her own ideas or feelings about a topic, or covers only one side of an issue, the point of view is biased. This type of writing is considered subjective, rather than objective. Besides enabling the reader to pick up on any bias the writer has expressed, word choices used by the writer also help the reader to interpret the tone of the message. The tone may vary throughout a message, and involve an underlying feeling such as humor, anger, or fear.

QUICK TIP

Look for clue words in a passage that signal a writer's attitude toward a subject.

Examples of positive words: enthusiastic, patriotic, sympathetic, admirable, brave, caring, excellent

Examples of negative words: nasty, sarcastic, unfortunate, inadequate, inept, disapproving, substandard

Writers might express, for example, anger, humor, respect, impatience, sympathy, or disapproval. Or they might exhibit a neutral attitude. Pay close attention to word choices.

Opinions often flow from a writer's assumptions. Assumptions are ideas or perspectives that underlie a writer's claim. They sometimes result in stereotypes. Since assumptions are usually unstated and implied, they can be challenging to uncover. Consider the following example:

Orca whales mate for life and travel in family groups.

Science has demonstrated that Orca whales are intelligent.

Therefore, Orca whales should be saved from extinction.

The underlying assumption is that *an animal that displays such human qualities warrants special protection.* Unless the reader agrees with the underlying assumption, the evidence presented may not be valid for that reader.

QUICK TIP

Sometimes, you might identify a *missing* piece in the writer's logic that helps uncover an assumption.

Picking up on an author's attitudes and assumptions usually requires the reader to make inferences and draw conclusions (see the beginning of the chapter). Consider the following statement from a passage comparing human and animal cultures:

Our culture lets us make up for having lost our strength, claws, long teeth, and other defenses.

What assumption has the writer made?

___

The underlying assumption is that *humans evolved from animals*. If the reader agrees with this assumption, it may be more difficult to uncover the assumption. However, for a reader who does not accept the theory of evolution, such a statement may stand out and cause the reader to question the validity of the argument.

Writing Like a Reader

How does a good debater prepare for a debate? The process involves gathering not only information which supports the debater's stance on a topic, but also gathering information for the opposing point of view. When an audience sees that the debater has considered all of the facts, not only those that support his or her position, they will trust the debater more. When preparing to write persuasively, a critical thinker will take a similar approach.

A related factor in the writing process is modifying one's tone according to the intended audience. If you enjoy rap music and read a passage that takes an overtly negative tone toward rap, chances are that you wouldn't be very receptive to the author's argument. Likewise, when you write, you should consider your own audience's attitude toward the topic. You don't want to adopt a tone that will alienate your audience. Notice that the more neutral tone of the second paragraph below might be more well-received by a group of public high school students than the first.

> I'm disgusted by rap music, and you should be too. It's the devil's music. If you listen to it, you are just as guilty as the ones who write and produce it. The twisted and mindless lyrics should repulse any thinking human being. I hope you will join me in a boycott of such perversion.

> While rap music is both prevalent and popular in today's culture, its effects have become a matter of controversy. Although some critics claim that rap has contributed to teen pregnancy and unprotected sexual activity, others view it as an art form not so different from poetry.

ATTITUDE, BIAS, TONE, AND ASSUMPTION PRACTICE

The following is a paragraph from the 1960 novel, *Night,* by Elie Wiesel. Wiesel is struggling with his faith in God as a result of his experience in concentration camps during the Holocaust. These are his thoughts.

> "Blessed be the Name of the Eternal!"

> Why, but why should I bless Him? In every fiber I rebelled. Because He had had thousands of children burned in His pits?

Because He kept six crematories working night and day, on Sundays and feast days? Because in His great might He had created Auschwitz, Birkenau, Buna, and so many factories of death? How could I say to Him: "Blessed art Thou, Eternal, Master of the Universe, Who chose us from among the races to be tortured day and night, to see our fathers, our mothers, our brothers, end in the crematory? Praised be Thy Holy Name, Thou Who hast chosen us to be butchered on Thine altar?"

1. What assumptions is Wiesel making in this passage?

   _____

   _____

   _____

   _____

2. How would you describe Wiesel's attitude toward God in the passage above? What words or phrases used in the paragraph support your response?

   _____

   _____

   _____

   _____

3. What other words might you use to describe the overall tone of this passage?

   _____

4. Is Wiesel expressing a biased or a neutral point of view?

   _____

⌐MyReadingLab───────────────────────────────────

For more help with **Critical Thinking** and **Purpose and Tone,** go to your learning path in MyReadingLab at www.myreadinglab.com.

Chapter Summary

Critical Thinking: Generally involves higher order thinking skills such as analyzing, comparing, and judging. It is *evaluative* and reflective in nature. As used in the context of this chapter, it refers to any higher order thinking and reading skills.

Predicting: Previewing a reading, beginning with the title, is a major step toward making more accurate predictions. Notice the way people are described, and after reading and analyzing a passage, ask yourself what might happen as a result of the stated actions or events.

Making Inferences: An idea that is clearly *suggested* or *implied* by a writer, although not *explicitly* stated. When making inferences, keep in mind the main idea and details of a passage. Use the if–then test to verify inferences.

Drawing Conclusions: It's generally necessary to draw a conclusion in order to make an inference. However, not all conclusions require you to make an inference. Determine a consequence that is consistent with the content of the passage by mentally adding your response to the end of the reading and asking if it fits logically.

Analyzing and Synthesizing: Readers are often required to analyze (break down or dissect) and synthesize (arrange or blend) information.

Writer's Purpose: Writers usually have a specific purpose and audience in mind, which often determines the organizational pattern and word choices used. Main purposes of a reading may be to **inform,** to **describe,** to **persuade,** to **entertain,** or to **narrate.**

Fact and Opinion: A fact is an idea that can be proved or disproved. An idea can be a fact even if it is untrue, as long as it can be either proved or disproved. Opinions usually include words which **interpret** (*explain or show the meaning of*) or **evaluate** (*judge the value of*) something.

Judging Validity: First determine whether the source represents expertise, research, and/or appropriate data. Then decide whether the **evidence** strengthens the writer's claim, weakens the writer's claim, or is irrelevant to the validity of the claim. Make sure that arguments used flow logically and avoid contradictions. Look for common **fallacies** such as emotional appeals and all-or-nothing thinking.

Identifying Author Attitude, Bias, Tone, and Assumptions: Look for **clue words** in a passage that signal a writer's attitude toward a subject. Begin with titles and headings. Be on the lookout for assumptions (ideas or perspectives that underlie a writer's claim). These are often challenging to uncover because they tend to be unstated or implied.

Check Your Learning (Learning Outcomes)

Have you mastered the Learning Objectives (LOs) for Chapter 4? Place a check mark next to each LO that you're able to do.

PART A

_____ LO1—Make predictions based on titles and passages read

_____ LO2—Make inferences based on information implied, but not stated, in passages

_____ LO3—Draw conclusions from information presented in one or more passages

PART B

_____ LO1—Analyze (break down or dissect) and synthesize (arrange or blend) information within a passage in order to:

* _____ Identify the writer's purpose
* _____ Distinguish between facts and opinions
* _____ Judge the validity of a passage
* _____ Identify author attitudes, bias, tone, and assumptions

Go back and review the sections that cover any LO you didn't check.

Quick Connections—Chapter Four

NEWS SOURCE CONNECTION

Using a news source (news magazine or newspaper), choose a persuasive article or an editorial to read. Find and mark (or list) two to three conclusions or claims the writer has made. Then try to identify supporting evidence the writer has used, and evaluate the validity of the claims. Also attempt to identify any assumptions the writer has made.

TEXTBOOK CONNECTION

Use a textbook from one of your other classes, and if possible, do this activity as you're completing a reading assignment for the other class. Choose a section of the text you haven't yet read, and write the heading for that section on a sheet of paper. Based solely on that heading, identify two or more questions you expect the following section of text to answer. Then continue reading to find out if your _predictions_ were accurate.

NOVEL CONNECTION

After reading at least one chapter of a novel, identify two main characters. Draw conclusions about these characters, and list four or five character traits for each. (Examples might include words like _humorous, outgoing, stubborn, angry,_ and _loving._) For each trait listed, identify a line or passage in the chapter that supports your conclusions.

WEB CONNECTION ⚙️—[Complete this **Exercise** at **MyReadingLab.com**

Go to a news source website, such as *Newsweek* or the *New York Times* site. Choose an article that looks interesting, and skim it to make sure it includes both facts and opinions. List three statements of fact and three statements of opinion that you found (or print the article and highlight or mark them).

MyReadingLab™ CONNECTION ⚙️—[Complete this **Exercise** at **MyReadingLab.com**

For more help with any of this chapter's topics, go to your learning path in MyReadingLab at www.myreadinglab.com.

Five

Figurative Language Strategies

Chapter Preview

Figurative Language Strategies Overview

A. Metaphor and Simile

B. Personification

C. Hyperbole

LEARNING OBJECTIVES (LOs)

Upon completion of this chapter, you'll be able to:

- LO1—Recognize and interpret *metaphors* and *similes* in written context, and differentiate between them
- LO2—Recognize and interpret *personification* in written context
- LO3—Recognize and interpret *hyperbole* in written context

True Story . . .
A mother asked her young son to "keep an eye on" his baby brother. The son looked confused and asked, "but mommy, how do I take it out?"

Readiness Quiz A ⚙️ Complete this Exercise at MyReadingLab.com

Match the terms below with the correct definitions on the right.

1. _____ simile	**A.**	human qualities attributed to an object, animal, or idea
2. _____ metaphor	**B.**	a deliberate overstatement or exaggeration
3. _____ personification	**C.**	using *like* or *as* to make a comparison between two things
4. _____ hyperbole	**D.**	symbolical, not literal
5. _____ figurative	**E.**	making a comparison between two things without using *like* or *as*

Readiness Quiz B

Now match the terms below with the correct examples on the right.

1. _____ simile	**A.**	The tulips danced in the breeze.
2. _____ metaphor	**B.**	She's as lovely as a bright spring day.
3. _____ personification	**C.**	He's at least a thousand years old.
4. _____ hyperbole	**D.**	We peered out upon a fluffy, white blanket of snow.

FIGURATIVE LANGUAGE STRATEGIES OVERVIEW

This chapter focuses on four common types of figurative language: **simile, metaphor, personification,** and **hyperbole.** Figurative language is frequently used in poetry and other types of literature, but may show up in any kind of writing. It can greatly enhance the imaginative element of the reading process and, therefore, create some challenges in interpretation. At the same time, figurative language can assist the reader in understanding and making connections between the writer's thoughts and the reader's world of experience. Figurative language often invokes imagination rather than literal interpretation. Recognizing and understanding common forms of figurative language improves the reader's ability to make appropriate interpretations and applications of the language. You may rarely need to identify the actual figurative language terms, so focus on recognizing these common figures of speech and allowing them to help you draw connections the writer is implying.

QUICK TIP

When you recognize a writer's use of figurative language, attempt to create pictures in your mind of images the writer is "painting" for the reader. This is a form of visualization.

A. Metaphor and Simile

In one line of a poem entitled "We Are a People," the writer mentions a "moccasin path." When readers see the word "moccasin," a picture may take shape in their minds, triggering an association with a specific group of people, Native Americans. Being able to create such mental pictures and form such associations will enable readers to more accurately interpret the other lines of the poem. In some writings, one picture like this may be the foundation for understanding the entire piece. In the poem "We Are a People," the people group is never identified . . . except through the use of implied metaphors and images. Be sure to pay careful attention to titles and headings, where clue words often show up.

QUICK TIP

Sometimes, one word or phrase may be the foundation for understanding an entire reading. Clue words often show up in titles or headings.

In an essay titled *The Attic of the Brain,* Lewis Thomas helps the reader create a mental picture of an attic in an old house and then begins to describe how the brain has its own kind of "attic." An astute reader will begin to create her own images simply by reading a few words presented in an intriguing title. The brain does not have a physical "attic," but the **metaphor** enables the reader to draw relevant and enlightening comparisons. Such comparisons are sometimes signaled by such clue words as *like, as,* or *similar* to introduce a simile. For example, Thomas makes the following two direct comparisons, or **similes,** toward the end of his passage:

> Attempting to operate one's own mind, powered by such a magical instrument as the human brain, strikes me as rather like using the world's biggest computer to add columns of figures, or towing a Rolls-Royce with a nylon rope.

Here the human brain is compared to a magical instrument, and "attempting to operate" one's mind is compared to two other unlikely tasks.

Since **similes** are usually easier to recognize than **metaphors,** let's practice a few of those.

> A quarrelsome wife is like a constant dripping on a rainy day.
>
> (*Proverbs* 27:15)

What two things are being compared here? A quarrelsome wife and a constant dripping of rain. The writer is attempting to communicate some things about a quarrelsome wife using constant dripping as the "picture." What do you think of when you picture a constant dripping? While some people might actually enjoy the sound of rain, we know from the writer's choice of the word *quarrelsome* that he is creating a negative comparison. Use of the word *constant* implies something that might be repeated to the point of irritation. The reader may identify constant dripping as being tiresome, annoying, or even exasperating—not a glowing comparison for a quarrelsome wife.

Here's another **simile:**

> Like clouds and wind without rain is a man who boasts of his gifts falsely.
>
> (*Proverbs* 25:14)

In this verse, the gifts of a man who boasts falsely are compared to clouds and wind without rain. Since clouds and wind often result in rain, the picture of clouds and wind *without* rain helps the reader understand that a braggart's gifts may not live up to what is expected.

Now look at one more **simile:**

> Some people view the commitment of marriage as an alligator from some murky swamp.
>
> (Albom, 1997)

In this sentence, the commitment of marriage is compared to an alligator from a murky swamp. Let's first think of the pictures the word *alligator* calls up. Alligators might be seen as frightening and dangerous. In addition, a murky swamp could be described as dark or gloomy—a place you wouldn't want to enter. The reader gets the impression that some people see the commitment of marriage as something frightening, dangerous, and forbidding. Just as a murky swamp makes it hard to see what's ahead, it might be difficult for some to commit to a relationship when what will happen in the future is impossible to predict.

Here's one more sentence which includes both a **simile** and a **metaphor:**

> ALS* is like a lit candle; it melts your nerves and leaves your body a pile of wax.
>
> (Albom, 1997)

1. What is the simile? <u>ALS is like a lit candle</u>

2. What is the metaphor? <u>your body a pile of wax</u>

SIMILE/METAPHOR PRACTICE ONE

The practice exercise below is taken from the following website: http://volweb.utk.edu/Schools/bedford/harrisms/1poe.htm

First identify each sentence as a **simile** (S), or a **metaphor** (M), by writing the appropriate letter in the blank preceding each number. Remember that a **simile** is using words such as *like* or *as* to make a comparison between two things, while a **metaphor** makes a comparison between two things without using *like* or *as*.

_____ **1.** The baby was like an octopus, grabbing at all the cans on the grocery store shelves.

_____ **2.** As the teacher entered the room she muttered under her breath, "This class is like a three-ring circus!"

_____ **3.** The giant's steps were thunder as he ran toward Jack.

_____ **4.** The pillow was a cloud when I put my head upon it after a long day.

_____ **5.** I feel like a limp dishrag.

_____ **6.** Those girls are like two peas in a pod.

_____ **7.** The fluorescent light was the sun during our test.

_____ **8.** No one invites Harold to parties because he's a wet blanket.

---

*ALS, or amyotrophic lateral sclerosis, is a disease of the nerve cells in the brain and spinal cord that control voluntary muscle movement. ALS is also known as Lou Gehrig's disease. (http://www.ninds.nih.gov/disorders/amyotrophiclateralsclerosis/detail_ALS.htm)

_____   **9.** The bar of soap was a slippery eel during the dog's bath.

_____   **10.** Ted was as nervous as a cat with a long tail in a room full of rocking chairs.

Now go back through the 10 sentences above, and in the blanks below, identify the two items being compared. The first one is done for you.

1. baby	octopus
2.	
3.	
4.	
5.	
6.	
7.	
8.	
9.	
10.	

SIMILE/METAPHOR PRACTICE TWO

The next practice on **similes** and **metaphors** lists expressions used in the novel _Tuesdays with Morrie_ by Mitch Albom. Identify each thought as a **simile** (S), or a **metaphor** (M), in the blanks below:

_____   **1.** The newspaper had been _my lifeline, my oxygen._

_____   **2.** He had created a _cocoon_ of human activities—conversation, interaction, affection . . .

_____   **3.** . . . and it filled his life like an _overflowing soup bowl._

_____   **4.** Morrie had become a _prisoner of his chair._

_____   **5.** Sometimes he would close his eyes and try to draw the air up into his mouth and nostrils, and it seemed as if he were _trying to lift an anchor._

Now reread each thought above, and try to rewrite each italicized word or phrase in a more literal way on the lines below. The first one is done for you.

A. something needed to live or to stay alive _____

B. _____

C. _____

D. _____

E. _____

SIMILE/METAPHOR PRACTICE THREE

The final practice on **metaphors** is a more challenging reading in which **metaphors** are implied, though not directly stated. Read the following poem and then answer the questions that follow.

Of One Self-Slain

By Charles Hanson Towne
When he went blundering back to God,
His songs half written, his work half done,
Who knows what paths his bruised feet trod,
What hills of peace or pain he won?
I hope God smiled and took his hand,
And said, "Poor truant, passionate fool!
Life's book is hard to understand:
Why couldst thou not remain at school?"

Some students understand the main point of this poem immediately, while others struggle. It's often a good idea to begin to bring meaning to a reading by starting with the title.

1. What do the title and the first line of the poem suggest about the person in the poem?

   _____

   _____

2. What might "bruised feet" in line 3 represent?

   _____

   _____

3. List at least three more **metaphors** from the poem and what each represents:

   - _____

   - _____

   _____

   - _____

   - _____

   _____

4. How would you describe the **tone** of the poem?

B. Personification

Personification is a writing technique that attributes human qualities to an object, animal, or idea. While this technique is often used in poetry and other forms of creative writing, it is also commonly used in other types of writing. For instance, when describing the music of Elvin Jones and John Coltrane, in 2004 the magazine *Newsweek* had this to say:

> Coltrane's saxophone was the soaring, often tormented soul; Jones's drums were the beating heart—and a constant storm of commentary and suggestion.

Obviously, a saxophone isn't a soul, much less a tormented one. Nor are drums a beating heart. However, music (or in this case, musical instruments) may help convey thoughts and feelings normally ascribed to people.

When **personification** is used, it may bring life and meaning to a description—much like a picture or video may "breathe life" (another example of personification) into the words on a page. The technique helps us, the readers, to form our own mental pictures based on prior knowledge or past experiences. Consider this line from poet Kahlil Gibran (1923):

> But let there be spaces in your togetherness,
> And let the winds of the heavens dance between you.

The first half of the thought is literal and clear, while the second half is poetic and helps us to "see" the truth of the literal half.

QUICK TIP

As with other forms of figurative language, **personification** often helps the reader to form mental pictures based on prior knowledge or past experiences.

Now read the following passage from *20/20 Hindsight*, an essay by Jay Ford (1996), and answer the questions that follow.

> In Kenya I felt more free than I have ever felt before. The only thing holding me captive was the earth which would grow the food, the sky which would quench the earth of its thirst, and the

sun which would warm and help all things to grow. But these
masters were sure to give back all that you have put in.

What three objects were holding the writer *captive?*

1. Earth
2. Sky
3. Sun

What are your thoughts on how these objects might hold someone captive, and why does the writer call them *masters?*

Though answers may vary, you might have considered the need
for these aspects of nature in order for one to live.

PERSONIFICATION PRACTICE

The following sentences were used in a business article entitled "Quit-
ting Time" (*Newsweek,* 2004). Underline each specific example of **personification** below and then identify their meanings in your own
words.

Or maybe we'll catch a glimpse of that telltale <u>stationery peeking
out</u> from his desk—the heavy, ivory stock that's a give-away he's
been printing resumés.

_____

_____

Companies hired briskly in March and April, and economists predict
the unemployment rate will continue its steady downward march.

_____

_____

That's largely because <u>companies</u> spent the past few years <u>squeezing</u>
more and more work out of ever-smaller staffs, and many workers
aren't happy about it.

_____

_____

We're still a long way from the days when every <u>worker bee felt
like the king of the jungle</u>. But in the months ahead, there's hope
of hearing at least a few <u>roars</u>.

_____

_____

_____

_____

_____

_____

C. Hyperbole

A **hyperbole** (pronounced hy-peȓ-bò-lē) is a deliberate overstatement or exaggeration.

Examples of Common Types of Hyperbole

He was _scared to death_.

Don't go out without a coat; you'll _catch your death_ (of cold).

I'm so hungry, _I could eat a horse_.

We're _starving!_

She's _as big as a house_.

I've told you _a thousand times_ to pick up those toys!

I thought that sermon would last _forever!_

In the 1982 book _And More by Andy Rooney_, humorist Andrew A. Rooney includes a chapter entitled "Living is Dangerous to Your Health." The title and chapter are both exaggerations meant to make fun of the constant bombardment of news indicating how many things are bad for us. **Hyperbole** is often used to provide humor or special effect. The overstatement makes an impression on the reader.

QUICK TIP

As with other forms of figurative language, **hyperbole** isn't meant to be taken literally. The overstatement or exaggeration is used to make an impression on the reader. It may provide humor or some other special effect. Ask yourself what effect the writer may be trying to produce.

You may have seen or heard the common phrase "blazing inferno." According to writer and lexicographer Betty Kirkpatrick (_Clichés_, 1996), the phrase is used often by journalists in headlines such as "man leaps from roof in blazing inferno." Kirkpatrick asserts that the term would "properly be used to describe a very large and dangerous fire, but is in fact often used to describe anything bigger than a small garden rubbish fire, the tabloid press having a weakness for exaggeration, which sells more copies of newspapers."

Another well-known hyperbole is included in the following stanza from Ralph Waldo Emerson's *Concord Hymn*, written for the dedication of the Obelisk, a battle monument commemorating the valiant efforts put forth by citizens of Concord, Massachusetts on April 19, 1775. The event described marked the start of the Revolutionary War.

> *By the rude bridge that arched the flood,*
> *Their flag to April's breeze unfurled;*
> *Here once the embattled farmers stood;*
> *And fired the shot heard round the world.*

Given that a shot couldn't be heard *round the world*, how would you interpret the **hyperbole** underlined in the above stanza?

_____

_____

_____

_____

Did your answer include the idea that the shot had far-reaching consequences or interest? If so, you're on the right track! Great!

HYPERBOLE PRACTICE

Now write a more literal alternative for each of the **hyberboles** in italics below:

   1. He made *a ton of money* in the stock market.

   _____

   2. He has *a million relatives.*

   _____

   3. *Her beauty could launch a thousand ships.*

   _____

   4. *She is a giant in this industry.*

   _____

   5. *His mouth could rival the Grand Canyon.* I can never get a word in when "we" talk.

   _____

While this chapter focused on four common types of figurative language, there are many more types.

Three additional forms of figurative language frequently encountered include **analogy, irony,** and **understatement.**

Analogy

Definition: Finding likeness in two or more things that are seemingly dissimilar

Note that analogies are similar to metaphors and similes. However, analogies are a bit more complex. Analogies help to explain the similarities in the relationship between two things, while metaphors and similes tend to replace the meaning of a word with another word or phrase.

Example: "The universe is like a safe to which there is a combination. But the combination is locked up in the safe." (DeVries, 1965)

Irony

Definition: Using words to suggest the opposite of what the words literally mean or the opposite of what might be expected

Examples: A fish drowns; An attempt is made to ban a book, but due to the negative attention given to the book, more people read it.

Understatement

Definition: Using words that are purposely restrained or limited for effect

Example: "Not bad, eh?" (after a baseball player hits two consecutive home runs)

Writing Like a Reader

While writing, attempt to "flavor" your thoughts with figurative language and descriptive words, if appropriate. Besides adding interest, the use of figurative and descriptive language creates mental images that "paint" pictures for readers and trigger their imaginations. Instead of merely *telling* readers about something, *show* them. The first paragraph below *tells* the thoughts of an expectant mother while the second paragraph *shows* those thoughts.

> As I felt those first signs of life inside of me, I felt happier than I'd ever felt before. I prepared your room months before you even came home from the hospital. I cleaned and decorated just for you.

As I felt those first flutters of life, signs of the precious gift growing inside me, my heart nearly exploded in anticipation. Months before my due date, a small, sun-lit bedroom sparkled and anxiously awaited your arrival. The bright walls and soft furnishings whispered a welcoming lullaby.

⌐MyReadingLab──────────────────────────────

Interpreting figurative language is making a type of inference. For more help with **Inference,** go to your learning path in MyReadingLab at www.myreadinglab.com.

Chapter Summary

Figurative Language: Frequently used in poetry and other types of literature, but may show up in any kind of writing. It isn't to be taken literally, but is used to add interest and stimulate the imagination. While knowing the specific terms for common forms of figurative language may not be necessary, the reader's awareness and recognition of these forms should help create mental pictures that bring meaning and depth to a reading.

Metaphor: Draws comparisons between two things without using words such as *like, as,* or *similar.* These also help the reader to see how things are alike but may be more challenging to recognize or interpret than similes, since the comparison word clues aren't directly stated.

Simile: Draws comparisons between two things, using words such as *like, as,* or *similar.* These help the reader to see how things are alike. One word or phrase may sometimes provide the foundation for understanding an entire reading. Pay special attention to titles and headings.

Personification: Attributes human qualities to an object, animal, or idea. As with other types of figurative language, personification may bring life and meaning to a description and help readers to form mental pictures based on prior knowledge or past experiences.

Hyperbole: A deliberate overstatement or exaggeration. As with other forms of figurative language, hyperbole isn't meant to be taken literally. The exaggeration is used to make an impression on the reader. It may provide humor or some other special effect. Ask yourself what effect the writer may be trying to produce.

Check Your Learning (Learning Outcomes)

Have you mastered the Learning Objectives (LOs) for Chapter 5? Place a check mark next to each LO that you're able to do.

_____ LO1—Recognize and interpret *metaphors* and *similes* in written context, and differentiate between them

_____ LO2—Recognize and interpret *personification* in written context

_____ LO3—Recognize and interpret *hyperbole* in written context

Go back and review the sections that cover any LO you didn't check.

Quick Connections—Chapter Five

NEWS SOURCE CONNECTION

Using a news source (news magazine or newspaper), skim the source, looking for examples of the four types of figurative language covered in this chapter. Find and mark (or list) at least two examples of each. Then identify how each example could be stated in a literal way.

TEXTBOOK CONNECTION

Some textbooks lend themselves more to locating figurative language than others. If you're reading a textbook for another course, and the text does incorporate figurative language, write the title of the text and then list at least four figurative expressions you're able to find. Also write a short response, explaining why that subject area might lend itself to expressions of figurative language. If you have a textbook for another course that does not incorporate figurative language, write a brief response explaining why literal language is more appropriate for that text. Then list at least five general courses that probably would use textbooks which incorporate figurative language.

NOVEL CONNECTION

Using a course novel, or any novel acceptable to your instructor, skim for examples of the four types of figurative language covered in this chapter. Try to find at least two examples of each. Then prepare a matching game for another student in the course by folding a clean sheet of paper into eighths and writing one example (you've found) on each section. On a separate sheet of paper, also folded into eight sections, restate each example in a literal way. Number each section on both sheets so that the matches have the same numbers. Then cut each sheet, clipping all the figurative expressions together and all the literal restatements together. You'll have two separate piles. Be sure they are scrambled, so that they are ready to be matched by another student.

WEB CONNECTION ⚙️⚙️—[Complete this Exercise at **MyReadingLab.com**

Using Google or another search engine, type *figurative language* in the search bar. Find sites that end with *.edu* and that are also connected with a university or college. Search until you find at least four types of figurative language that aren't included in this chapter. List the four types you found, and at least one example of each. At the bottom of your paper, be sure to identify the sites you used as well.

MyReadingLab™ CONNECTION ⚙️⚙️—[Complete this Exercise at **MyReadingLab.com**

Visit MyReadingLab.com to take a review quiz testing your mastery of this chapter's topics.

Six

Patterns of Organization Strategies

Chapter Preview

Patterns of Organization Strategies Overview
A. Narration (Time Order)
B. Description
C. Process Analysis
D. Classification
E. Comparison/Contrast
F. Definition and Example

LEARNING OBJECTIVES (LOs)

Upon completion of this chapter, you'll be able to:

- LO1—Recognize different patterns of organization
- LO2—Identify the organization within each pattern
- LO3—Analyze information from each pattern
- LO4—Understand the purpose of each pattern

A writer uses patterns to organize writing; a reader must use them to organize reading.

Readiness Quiz ⚙️ [Complete this Exercise at MyReadingLab.com

Section 1: Match the following terms on the left with the definitions on the right:

1. _____ Narration (Time Order)   **A.** to explain parts, or to sort into categories

2. _____ Description   **B.** to relate an event or a series of events

3. _____ Process Analysis   **C.** to define a term or clarify the meaning

4. _____ Classification   **D.** to explain how to do something

5. _____ Comparison/Contrast   **E.** to create a vivid mental picture

6. _____ Definition and Example   **F.** to show how things are alike and different

Section 2: Match the following statements on the left with the terms on the right:

1. _____ The first thing you need to do to organize your closet is to get some shelves. Second, you need some boxes and pens for labeling.   **A.** Description

2. _____ Feng shui is the ancient Chinese art of harmony and balance.   **B.** Narration (Time Order)

3. _____ I can't wait to tell you about the father-daughter dance at my wedding!   **C.** Classification

4. _____ Movies have various genres such as horror, comedy, romance, or drama.   **D.** Comparison/ Contrast

5. _____ The dark, sleek shark moves effortlessly through the misty-blue water.   **E.** Definition and Example

6. _____ Country music and rock 'n' roll are alike in some ways, but they can be very different.   **F.** Process Analysis

PATTERNS OF ORGANIZATION STRATEGIES OVERVIEW

Why does a reader need to understand the author's pattern of organization? A pattern of organization refers to how a paragraph's sentences are structured or arranged. Understanding how to recognize the different patterns improves your reading comprehension. When authors write, they choose a structure or style that fits the topic. As readers begin to recognize the various patterns, relationships among ideas become clearer. This clarity improves comprehension because the reader is better able to follow the development of an idea from start to finish. When reading, look for the controlling idea, a word or thought that is repeated within the passage. The sentences of a paragraph are said to be *united* when they work together to support the main idea.

Readers should ask the following questions when reading:

1. How are the author's details organized? Is he or she telling a story, describing something, showing a process?
2. What unifies or ties together the author's writing? Are key words or ideas repeated, and/or are transitional words used?

Writers often mix patterns in their writings. This approach provides the reader with various ways to understand the subject. For example, the subject may first be described and then a story may follow. Being aware of these patterns enables the reader to make more connections among the details and improves comprehension.

This chapter addresses the following six patterns of organization:

1. Narration (Time Order)
2. Description
3. Process Analysis
4. Classification
5. Comparison/Contrast
6. Definition and Example

Purpose of Organizational Patterns

Pattern	Purpose
Narration (Time Order)	To relate an event or series of events leading to an outcome
Description	To create a vivid mental picture
Process Analysis	To explain how to do something or how something occurs
Classification	To explain parts of a whole or to sort into categories or groups
Comparison/Contrast	To tell how two things are similar or different, or both
Definition and Example	To define a term, either to clarify its meaning or to suggest a new meaning

Important Aspects of Each Organizational Pattern

Pattern	Important Aspects
Narration (Time Order	Story, told in first or third person; tells who, what, why, when, where, and how; sequence of events is important. **Transition words (after, later, during, never, suddenly, last)**
Description	Details that appeal to the five senses and create a visualization for the reader. **Transition words (for example, such as)**
Process Analysis	Describes a method of doing something; sequence is extremely important; look for steps and order. **Transition words (first, next, after, before, following, stage, secondly)**
Classification	Divides a subject into various parts or identifies a member of a group based on similar characteristics; look for part-to-whole relationship or various categories into which a large number of things can be sorted. **Transition words (part, type, group, category, class, member)**
Comparison/Contrast	Shows how two things are alike or different. Can be organized subject by subject, or point by point. **Transition words (in comparison, similarly, like, in contrast, on the other hand, whereas)**
Definition and Example	Defines a person, place, thing, or idea by explaining the characteristics that distinguish it from others in its class. **Transition words (for example, to illustrate, such as, means, is defined, can be seen as)**

Transition Words

Transitions or signal words are words or phrases that allow the reader to follow a writer's ideas. They assist in *bridging* or connecting the ideas in a passage and create a sense of unity. To learn more about important transitions that can help you verify the pattern of organization the author has chosen, refer to the previous charts. The charts above contain a list of common transitions or signals for each pattern of organization. The charts also summarize the purposes and important aspects of each pattern to aid in identification of the pattern.

QUICK TIP

Transition words create a powerful link between ideas in a writing. Think of them as a bridge.

The best way to learn to recognize patterns of organization is by reading and practicing. The following pages provide examples of each of the patterns. Read the examples and answer the questions that follow. Make sure you do not skip the Preparing to Read introductions, which will guide your understanding of each pattern.

A. Narration (Time Order)

PREPARING TO READ Can you recall special memories from your childhood? You know the memories that seem to stand out from the others? Maybe it was nothing spectacular, but just warm memories that still make you smile. Chic Mancuso is sharing his memories of what a day was like with his grandfather who was an Italian immigrant. As you read, notice it is a retelling of a specific event. Notice the relevance in the sequence of events in understanding the progression or how one thing leads to another. Look for transition words that help the reader follow the sequence of events.

"THINGS I REMEMBER GROWING UP"

From the Memoirs of Joseph (Chic) Mancuso

I remember in 1935 when I was 10 going with my grandfather (my mother's father) to the city market. At the back of his house on South 11th Street, he had a barn. He had a horse and wagon that he hitched to the horse in the barn. Before the weather got cold in early spring, he would go to the city market around 5:00 a.m. to buy fruits and vegetables. He bought so much it filled the back of his wagon! He would then take the wagon filled with fruits and vegetables through the alleys on the route where he sold the produce to his customers. It was a treat for me to go with him when school got out in mid-June. I would sleep over at their house, and we would get up at about 4:00 a.m. We would have a great big breakfast before we headed to 11th and

Jackson, the location of the city market, to buy fruits and vegetables. We rode into the alleys selling our produce around 7:30 a.m. My grandfather worked until all the fruits and vegetables were sold, usually around 3:30 p.m. If he had a few things left that wouldn't spoil, he would save them to sell the next day. It always amazed me that we would ride in the wagon all of that time and neither of us ever said a word! He couldn't speak any English, and I couldn't speak any Italian. Also, I still don't know how the customers knew how much the fruits and vegetables cost, how he was able to make change, and how he made a living doing that job. Once we got home, his wife and daughters would help him put the wagon in the barn and take care of the horse. He would immediately go sit in his rocking chair in the living room. One aunt would have his pipe filled and lit for him. Another aunt would bring him something to drink, and Nana would take off his shoes and rub his feet. Then, he took a nap until 4:30 p.m. When he woke up, he had his supper, and would leave for a pool hall called LaFerla's on 13th and Briggs. It was a meeting place for all of the Old Italian immigrants. There, they would play cards and have some drinks. I didn't get to go with him, so I anxiously awaited his return home. He usually left LaFerla's around 8:30 p.m. My aunts and Nana had fresh doughnuts and rolls waiting for him. After enjoying the baked goods, he just got up, went to bed, and never said anything to anyone. Some nights he grunted at his wife. That meant she had to come to bed with him. The women today think they have it rough!

Questions

1. This reading is mainly about two people. Who are they?

   _____

2. What was the author's purpose for writing this memoir?

   _____

   _____

   _____

3. Make a short list of the sequence of events.

   _____

   _____

   _____

   _____

4. What transitions words or phrases did you notice?

_____

_____

B. Description

PREPARING TO READ   Have you ever had the opportunity to see ocean life up close? In *The Great Tide Pool*, John Steinbeck *shows* with words what ocean life looks like. As you read, look for words and phrases that evoke the five senses.

THE GREAT TIDE POOL

John Steinbeck

Doc was collecting marine animals in the Great Tide Pool on the tip of the Peninsula. It is a fabulous place: when the tide is in, a wave-churned basin, creamy with foam, whipped by the combers that roll in from the whistling buoy on the reef. But when the tide goes out the little water world becomes quiet and lovely. The sea is very clear and the bottom becomes fantastic with hurrying, fighting, feeding, and breeding animals. Crabs rush from frond to frond of the waving algae. Starfish squat over mussels and limpets, attach their million little suckers and then slowly lift with incredible power until the prey is broken from the rock. And then the starfish stomach comes out and envelops its food. Orange and speckled and fluted nudibranches slide gracefully over the rocks, their skirts waving like the dresses of Spanish dancers. And black eels poke their heads out of crevices and wait for prey. The snapping shrimps with their trigger claws pop loudly. The lovely colored world is glassed over. Hermit crabs like frantic children scamper on the bottom sand. And now one, finding an empty snail shell he likes better than his own, creeps out, exposing his soft body to the enemy for a moment, and then pops into the new shell. A wave breaks over the barrier, and churns the glassy water for a moment and mixes bubbles into the pool, and then it clears and is tranquil and lovely and murderous again. Here a crab tears a leg from his brother. The anemones expand like soft and brilliant flowers, inviting any tired and perplexed animal to lie for a moment in their arms, and when some small crab of little tide-pool Johnnie accepts the green and purple invitation, the petals whip in, the stinging cells shoot tiny narcotic needles into the prey and it grows weak and perhaps sleepy while the searing caustic digestive acids melt its body down.

Then the creeping murderer, the octopus, steals out, slowly, softly, moving like a gray mist, pretending now to be a bit of weed, now a rock, now a lump of decaying meat while its evil goat eyes watch coldly. It oozes and flows toward a feeding crab, and as it comes close its yellow eyes burn and its body turns rosy with the pulsing color of anticipating and rage. Then suddenly it runs lightly on the tips of its arms as ferociously as a charging cat. It leaps savagely on the crab, there is a puff of black fluid, and the struggling mass is obscured in the sepia cloud while the octopus murders the crab. On the exposed rocks out of water, the barnacles bubble behind their closed doors and the limpets dry out. And down to the rocks come the black flies to eat anything they can find. The sharp smell of iodine from the algae, and the lime smell of calcareous bodies and the smell of powerful protean, smell of sperm and ova fill the air. On the exposed rocks the starfish emit semen and eggs from between their rays. The smells of life and richness, of death and digestion, of decay and birth, burden the air. And salt spray blows in from the barrier where the ocean waits for its rising-tide strength to permit it back into the Great Tide Pool again. And on the reef the whistling buoys sit like a sad and patient bull.

Source: *A Writer's Workshop,* McGraw-Hill, 2002.

Questions

1. Fill in the chart below with words and phrases that appeal to your senses.

Taste	Touch	Smell	Hear	See

2. What transition words or phrases did you notice?

C. Process Analysis

PREPARING TO READ Have you ever thought about the steps involved in bathing a dog? As you read, notice how the author lays out the steps in the process within his essay.

HOW TO GIVE A DOG A BATH

Have you ever tried to bathe a dog? Well, it isn't easy. First, you need to gather all your supplies; especially towels! Then, you need to thoroughly saturate the dog's body (avoid the head) with water before adding the shampoo. If you don't, the shampoo won't go anywhere. Next, rinse the body with warm water. Don't rush this step. If you rush it, as the dog dries, his fur will be matted and sticky. After you've washed and rinsed the body, it is time for the head. Some dogs will display good behavior during this process, but most won't! Tip the head in a downward position and use a cup full of water to saturate the dog's head. Try to cover the eyes as you do this. Quickly, add the shampoo and rinse using the same process used to wet the dog's head. Finally, use a towel to "towel dry" the dog as much as you can before allowing him/her to run loose. If you'd like, you can add another step. You can blow-dry your dog's fur with your hair drier! It may sound crazy, but you'd be amazed how many people do it!

Questions

1. According to the author, what are the steps in giving a dog a bath?

_____

_____

_____

2. Why is the sequence of the reading so important?

_____

_____

3. What transition words or phrases did you notice?

_____

D. Classification

PREPARING TO READ Think of any topic and how you would break it down into *categories*. The following article is divided into categories of family violence. As you read, notice that the format is similar to that of a textbook.

FAMILY VIOLENCE: WHY WE HURT THE ONES WE LOVE

Sandra Arbetter

When the lake waters swirled over the car holding Susan Smith's two little boys, the ripple was felt around the nation. How could the sweet-looking mother from the peaceful town of Union, South Carolina, drown her own children? Wake up, America. There are 600 cases every year of mothers killing their children, according to the U.S. Department of Justice. The Smith case jolted folks out of the numbness created by daily headlines of beatings, rapes, shootings, stabbings, and torture—all in the family. Maybe it was the news photos of the two handsome little faces. Maybe it was the murders coming so soon after O. J. Simpson was charged with stabbing to death his ex-wife, Nicole, and her friend Ron Goldman. How could a national sports hero be associated with such messy business as spousal abuse and murder?

The facts about family violence are coming out of the closet, and they reveal that children and wives are not the only family members mistreated. The web of family violence entangles husbands abused by wives and sisters abused by each other.

The statistics on family violence are staggering: Every 15 seconds a woman in this county is battered. Almost 2 million women are severely assaulted every year. One-third of female homicide victims are killed by a husband or partner.

Spousal abuse occurs in families of every racial, ethnic, and economic group. In a recent study at the University of Rhode Island, for example, nearly 20 of every 1000 women with family incomes over $40,000 reported being victims of severe violence. Last year more than 1 million teens ran away from home. Most left, not for the excitement of the streets or to be grown-up, but to escape beatings and sexual abuse and worse at home. One in 25 elderly persons is victimized. Almost one-third of the maltreatment is by adult children of the elderly, according to the U.S. Department of Health and Human Services. Three million cases of child abuse or neglect were reported in 1994. About half involve neglect, which means that adults are not providing a safe environment with adequate shelter, clothing, food, and sanitation. Abuse includes physical or emotional injury or sexual abuse.

Effects on Victims

But the numbers don't tell the whole story. It's the suffering of each victim that matters most. "I can't trust anyone," says 21-year-old Dan. "I feel lonely all the time." When the people who're supposed to take

Source: *Building Strategies for College Reading*, Prentice Hall, 2001.

care of you're hurting you instead, then nothing is safe. It can be hard to get along with friends and coworkers, or to have a long-term intimate relationship.

Children who witness (or are victims of) abuse are at risk for school problems, drug abuse, sexual acting out, running away, suicide, and becoming abusers themselves. Their self-esteem is shattered by feelings of powerlessness to protect themselves or the parent who's being abused. Girls from abusive homes tend to become victims. Boys tend to see violence as the way to deal with frustration.

Children from abusive families learn a false lesson: Love and violence go together. The person who loves you hits you, so you hit the person you love.

An Old Story

The violence is nothing new, but until recently there was an unwritten conspiracy to ignore it. Americans wanted to hold on to the image that families were all sweetness and light. When there was abuse, often a husband beating a wife, it was dismissed with a knowing smile as part of being in love.

Sweetness and light? Tell that to the 3.3 million children between the ages of 3 and 17 who're at risk from parental violence, according to Peter Jaffe, author of *Children of Abused Women*. Tell that to the thousands of children who have been wrenched from their abusive home to live in shelters or foster care. . . .

Why Men Abuse

More than 90 percent of the reported battering is done by the male partner, although the whole story of abuse by women is yet to be told. The shame of it keeps many men from reporting it, according to experts; men abuse by:

Physical abuse

Emotional abuse

Economic abuse (taking her money, making her ask for money)

Sexual abuse (making her do things against her will)

Isolation (controlling her activities, who she sees, who she talks to)

What causes men to abuse women they say they love? Experts say it has a lot to do with feelings of powerlessness. A man who abuses may look tough on the outside, but he often has low self-esteem and is very dependent on the woman. He expects her to meet all his needs, solve his loneliness, and make him feel good about himself. If she wants to go out with friends or make some decisions of her own, he feels abandoned. Violence steps in to keep the woman fearful of going against his wishes. The man often puts down his partner, calling her dumb or ugly or useless. Heard often enough, that wears down the woman's self-esteem so that she questions her ability to leave and make it on her own. . . .

Child Abuse

Every day in this country, children are killed by parents and caretakers. Men more than women tend to shake babies to stop them from crying, according to a report from the U.S. Advisory Board on Child Abuse and Neglect. This can cause death: Neck muscles aren't fully developed; the baby's head moves violently; the brain is pulled different directions, and brain cells tear. The problem is how to get untrained parents to understand that babies do not cry to irritate their mothers and fathers. Their crying communicates some need, and they can't stop just because someone is angry at the noise.

Women kill most often through severe neglect—like the mother in Memphis who left two toddlers in the car last June in 90-degree heat while she partied with friends. Temperatures in the car soared, and the children died.

Now statistics show an increase in the rate of abuse of adolescents. Teen abuse has been underreported, possibly because adults see teens as able to protect themselves. . . .

Elder Abuse

Grandparents are for hugs and I-Love-You drawings and visits on holidays. But did you know that some are abused? The elderly who're abused are often too frail to defend themselves and too ashamed to report mistreatment. Dr. David Finkelhor of the University of New Hampshire has identified three kinds of elder abuse:

Psychological abuse (name calling, insulting, ignoring, threatening)

Financial abuse (illegal or unethical use of the elderly person's funds)

Physical abuse (hitting, pushing, confining, sexual abuse)

Most elderly are abused by those they live with—partly the result of the stress of caring for a person who's ill or disabled, who needs to be fed and toileted, and who provides little satisfying companionship. Abusers usually have a history of substance abuse or mental illness. Two-thirds of them are financially dependent on the victim. There can even be an element of the adult child "getting even" for past abuse by the parent. . . .

Between Brothers and Sisters

If we have ignored spousal and elder abuse, we have all but denied the existence of sibling abuse, which often is chalked up to normal sibling rivalry. "I begged my parents not to go out and let my sister, Lila, baby-sit," said Sam, now 17. "She'd sit on me and put a pillow over my face and punch my head. She'd tickle me until I wet my pants, and then threaten to tell everyone at school about it. Once she pointed my father's gun at me and said she'd kill me if I didn't do what she asked."

Sam's mother and father thought his complaints were just childish squabbles between brother and sister. It turned out that Lila's behavior was a call for help. When Sam got a concussion after Lila tripped him, the whole family went for counseling. As they all learned to communicate their feelings verbally and to express praise and appreciation of one another, Lila's abusive behavior lessened. . . .

Getting Help

If you're being abused, tell someone. Some people are afraid to tell for fear they'll be sent away, the family will be torn apart, or that other family members will be angry. But what is the alternative—to continue to live with an abuser, to have your self-esteem plunge to zero, to risk getting into trouble, to be badly injured? . . .

Of course, many children from abusive homes go on to have successful lives with loving relationships. While some studies say 80 percent of abusers were abused as children, other research puts the figure closer to 30 percent. While that is still higher than the base rate of 5 percent for abuse in the general population, it means that up to 70 percent of children who were abused do not grow up to be abusive to their family members.

In many ways, family violence remains a terrible puzzle. But now that personal histories are being made public and problems are being recognized as such, we have a chance to put some of the pieces together.

Questions

1. What are the categories of the subject "Family Violence"?

   _____

   _____

2. What are the characteristics of the following?

   Child Abuse

   _____

_____

_____

Men Who Abuse

_____

_____

_____

4. What transition words or phrases did you notice?

_____

_____

E. Comparison/Contrast

PREPARING TO READ Compare (same) and contrast (different) readings show how two or more subjects are the same and how they differ. As you read, look for the similarities and differences between the traits of successful students and traits of struggling students.

WHAT MAKES STUDENTS DIFFERENT?

Have you ever wondered why some students succeed and some students don't? As they come through the door of the college, they are all equipped with their backpacks, supplies, and skills. What changes when the due date of the assignments come? Could it be their backpacks? No. Could it be their supplies? Maybe. If a student chooses not to buy a course book, that could change things. Could it be skills? Yes. Some students have what I like to call "stick with-it-ness." And sadly, some students have what I like to call "make-an-exception-for-me-ness." What is the difference between the two?

Students who possess "stick with-it-ness" have a secret. They value education and understand its purpose for their adult life. They are committed to coming to class. When they come to class, they are prepared and organized. If they have a personal problem, they leave it outside the classroom door. They look up information they don't understand and ask appropriate questions when needed. They try to pull together their new knowledge with their old knowledge to make informed decisions. Lastly, they have an "I CAN" attitude.

Students who possess "make-an-exception-for-me-ness" lack the secret. They have ambitions just like the successful students, but what they lack is the knowledge of how a college education gets them to where they see themselves in their adult life. They do not understand the steps that will help them achieve their ambitions. Often, these students are late for class on a regular basis. They also struggle with poor attendance. They struggle with priorities and sometimes have so much going on outside of school that they can't keep up with the demands of the classroom. Their lack of preparation shows an instructor that they don't understand the value of being in a college classroom. They tend to want to memorize information instead of thinking about and analyzing a situation. They have an "I CAN'T" attitude.

In conclusion, successful students try to understand and grasp college culture whereas unsuccessful students struggle to figure out the system and what is going on around them. If the "I CAN'T" students could just change their mantra to "I CAN," it is my belief that we would see a marked improvement in college entrance courses.

Questions

1. What traits do successful students possess according to the author?

_____

_____

_____

2. What traits do unsuccessful students possess according to the author?

_____

_____

_____

3. What are similarities between the two groups?

_____

_____

F. Definition and Example

PREPARING TO READ What would you say is the role of a wife? What is the role of a husband? As you read, notice the definitions Judy Brady gives to the word *wife*.

NOTE: This passage was written in the 1960s as satire (i.e., use of wit and/or sarcasm to make a point).

I WANT A WIFE

Judy Brady

1. I belong to that classification of people known as wives. I am A Wife. And, not altogether incidentally, I am a mother.

2. Not too long ago a male friend of mine appeared on the scene fresh from a recent divorce. He had one child, who is, of course, with his ex-wife. He is looking for another wife. As I thought about him while I was ironing one evening, it suddenly occurred to me that I, too, would like to have a wife. Why do I want a wife?

3. I would like to go back to school so that I can become economically independent, support myself, and, if need be, support those dependent upon me. I want a wife who will work and send me to school. And while I am going to school, I want a wife to take care of my children. I want a wife to keep track of the children's doctor and dentist appointments. And to keep track of mine, too. I want a wife to make sure my children eat properly and are kept clean. I want a wife who will wash the children's clothes and keep them mended. I want a wife who is a good nurturing attendant to my children, who arranges for their schooling, makes sure that they have an adequate social life with their peers, takes them to the park, the zoo, etc. I want a wife who takes care of the children when they are sick, a wife who arranges to be around when the children need special care, because, of course, I cannot miss classes at school. My wife must arrange to lose time at work and not lose the job. It may mean a small cut in my wife's income from time to time, but I guess I can tolerate that. Needless to say, my wife will arrange and pay for the care of the children while my wife is working.

4. I want a wife who will take care of my physical needs. I want a wife who will keep my house clean. A wife who will pick up after my children, a wife who will pick up after me. I want a wife who will keep my clothes clean, ironed, mended, replaced when need be, and who will see to it that my personal things are kept in their proper place so that I can find what I need the minute I need it. I want a wife who cooks the meals, a wife who is a good cook. I want a wife who will plan the menus, do the necessary grocery shopping, prepare the meals, serve them pleasantly, and then do the cleaning up while I do my studying. I want a wife who will care for me when I am sick and sympathize with my pain and loss of time from school. I want a wife to go along when our family takes a vacation so that someone can continue to care for me and my children when I need a rest and change of scene.

5. I want a wife who will not bother me with rambling complaints about a wife's duties. But I want a wife who will listen to me

when I feel the need to explain a rather difficult point I have come across in my course studies. And I want a wife who will type my papers for me when I have written them.

6. I want a wife who will take care of the details of my social life. When my wife and I are invited out by my friends, I want a wife who will take care of the baby-sitting arrangements. When I meet people at school that I like and want to entertain, I want a wife who will have the house clean, will prepare a special meal, serve it to me and my friends, and not interrupt when I talk about things that interest me and my friends. I want a wife who will have arranged that the children are fed and ready for bed before my guests arrive so that the children do not bother us. I want a wife who takes care of the needs of my guests so that they feel comfortable, who makes sure that they have an ashtray, that they are passed the hors d'oeuvres, that they are offered a second helping of the food, that their wine glasses are replenished when necessary, that their coffee is served to them as they like it. And I want a wife who knows that sometimes I need a night out by myself.

7. I want a wife who is sensitive to my sexual needs, a wife who makes love passionately and eagerly when I feel like it, a wife who makes sure that I am satisfied. And, of course, I want a wife who will not demand sexual attention when I am not in the mood for it. I want a wife who assumes the complete responsibility for birth control, because I do not want more children. I want a wife who will remain sexually faithful to me so that I do not have to clutter up my intellectual life with jealousies. And I want a wife who understands that my sexual needs may entail more than strict adherence to monogamy. I must, after all, be able to relate to people as fully as possible.

8. If, by chance, I find another person more suitable as a wife than the wife I already have, I want the liberty to replace my present wife with another one. Naturally, I will expect a fresh, new life; my wife will take the children and be solely responsible for them so that I am left free.

9. When I am through with school and have a job, I want my wife to quit working and remain at home so that my wife can more fully and completely take care of a wife's duties.

10. My God, who wouldn't want a wife?

Source: Strategies for College Writing, Prentice Hall, 2003.

Questions

1. According to the author, what are the characteristics of a wife?

2. What transition words or phrases did you notice?

There are other commonly used patterns of organization. Three more are briefly described below and include cause and effect, spatial order, and simple list.

Cause and Effect

Definition: This pattern explains the causes or reasons for an effect or the result of an event or situation.

Example: What happened to families sitting around the dinner table at dinner time? Baseball games, dance classes, and swim lessons and meets are all part of what we are trying to fit into our day. However, so are work, school, errands, and doctor appointments. Parents are struggling to fit everything into a 24-hour period. So what has taken the back seat? Sit-down, home-cooked, healthy meals have been sacrificed. Ask any mom and she will tell you, there simply isn't time.

Spatial Order

Definition: This pattern tells you where things are physically positioned and/or how the area is arranged.

Example: There are many things I love about our neighborhood, but the one thing that stands out most is the way the developer created that down home, yet affluent, feeling. As you drive into our neighborhood, there's a huge fountain with iron gates on each side of it. The entrance is paved with bricks. As you continue to drive down the main street you see beautiful landscaped yards on either side of the road. Halfway down, there's a gazebo, a fishing pond, and a huge green field with a walking track all the way around it. This is a congregational area for all of the neighbors. The kids fish while the parents walk around the track and visit with one another. As you exit our neighborhood on that same main road, you drive right into a gas station, with a sub sandwich shop on the left, a coffee shop on the right, and a great big carwash behind it all!

Simple List

Definition: This pattern uses words and sentences instead of numbers for items that are listed. The list actually becomes the details.

Example: There are several ways to get your dogs to stop barking. One way is to use a shock collar. Some people think it is cruel, but the next-door neighbors love the idea! Another way is to fill a can with pennies and shake it by the dog's ears when he is consistently barking. This actually works wonders rather quickly. Lastly, you can put hot sauce and water in a spray bottle and spray the dog when his barking becomes offensive. We do not recommend this one, though we have heard of several people using the method.

Writing Like a Reader

In this chapter, you learned how an author uses "patterns" to write. When a reader can recognize the author's pattern, comprehension is easier because the reader knows how to follow the author's message. Remember that often patterns are mixed throughout any piece of writing. When you're writing using different patterns, the glue that holds it all together is transition words, which are also called signal words. Without these words, the reader has a more difficult time comprehending. Transition words are often a single word, but sometimes they can be several words used in a phrase. Transition words are like signs along the reading road, so when you write, be sure to give your readers the signs they need to follow the road to comprehension!

For example, read the short paragraph below without any transition or signal words. Then read it with transition or signal words.

Registering for college classes is simple. Fill out your forms. Turn them in to the appropriate people. Print your schedule. Go get your books. Go to your classes. Pay the bill.

OR

Registering for college classes is simple. First, fill out your forms. Second, turn them in to the appropriate people. Then, print a copy of your schedule and take it to the bookstore to get your books. Next, go to your classes. Finally, pay the bill.

The second paragraph is much more unified than the first because of the use of transition words.

⌐MyReadingLab

For more help with **Basic Patterns of Organization,** go to your learning path in MyReadingLab at www.myreadinglab.com.

Chapter Summary

Patterns of Organization: A pattern refers to how the sentences or ideas in a reading are structured or arranged. Recognizing the different patterns leads to improved comprehension.

Transition Words: Provide a bridge from one idea to another.

Narration: A story or event usually told in first person. Tells who, what, why, when, and where. The sequence of events is important.

Description: Uses details that appeal to the five senses. Creates visualization for the reader.

Process Analysis: Shows with words a method of doing something. The sequence is extremely important. Look for steps and order.

Classification: Divides a subject into various categories. Identifies a member or group based on similar characteristics. Look for part-to-whole relationships or various categories into which a large number of items can be sorted.

Comparison/Contrast: Shows how two things are alike and/or different. The two things may be compared and contrasted subject by subject, or be compared and contrasted point by point.

Definition: Defines a person, place, thing, or idea by explaining the characteristics that distinguish it from others in its class.

Check Your Learning (Learning Outcomes)

Have you mastered the Learning Objectives (LOs) for Chapter 6? Place a check mark next to each LO that you're able to do.

_____ LO1—Recognize different patterns of organization

_____ LO2—Identify the organization within each pattern

_____ LO3—Analyze information from each pattern

_____ LO4—Understand the purpose of each pattern

Go back and review the sections that cover any LO you didn't check.

Quick Connections—Chapter Six

NEWS SOURCE CONNECTION

Narration: Using a newspaper or news magazine, locate a narrative selection. Make sure to remember that in news reporting the patterns are often intermixed, and a narrative is a retelling of an event. Clip the article from the newspaper or news magazine (print, if an online article) and highlight the example.

Description: Using a newspaper or news magazine, locate an article or part of an article that is describing an event, person, or place. With description, you're reading to find words that are intended to give a mental image of something experienced. Clip the article from the newspaper or news magazine (print, if an online article) and highlight the example.

Process: Using a newspaper or news magazine, locate an article describing a process. As you read, you're looking for gradual steps or changes that lead to a final result. Clip the article from the newspaper or news magazine (print, if an online article) and highlight the example.

Classification: Using a newspaper or news magazine, locate an article which includes an example of classification. You're reading to find information that has been divided into categories. Clip the article from the newspaper or news magazine (print, if an online article) and highlight the example.

Comparison/Contrast: Using newspapers or newsmagazines, locate two stories related to the same topic. Create a chart or diagram to compare and contrast their similarities and differences.

Definition: Using a newspaper or news magazine, locate an article that defines a person, place, thing, or idea. You're reading to find information that identifies someone or something by distinct, clear, and detailed essential qualities. Clip the article from the newspaper or news magazine (print, if an online article) and highlight the example.

TEXTBOOK CONNECTION

Narration: Using one of your own textbooks, locate a narrative selection. A narrative is retelling of an event. Mark the section within the text. Show your teacher to confirm.

Description: Using one of your own textbooks, locate a passage describing an event, person, or place. With description, you're reading to find words that are intended to give a mental image of something experienced. Mark the section within the text. Show your teacher to confirm.

Process: Using one of your own textbooks, locate a passage describing a process. As you read, you're looking for gradual steps or changes that lead to a final result. Mark the section within the text. Show your teacher to confirm.

Classification: Using one of your own textbooks, locate a passage which includes an example of classification. You're reading to find information that has been divided into categories. Mark the section within the text. Show your teacher to confirm.

Comparison/Contrast: Using two of your own textbooks, compare and contrast them based on various factors such as: Where are the chapter words defined? What types of visuals are included (pictures, graphs, charts, etc.)? Are there chapter summaries?

Definition: Using one of your own textbooks, locate a passage that defines a person, place, thing, or idea. You're reading to find information that identifies someone or something by distinct, clear, and detailed essential qualities. Mark the section within the text. Show your teacher to confirm.

NOVEL CONNECTION

Narration: Choose a particular event, told in narrative style, that happened within a novel. Retell the event to the class, or you may choose to write it.

Description: Using a novel, choose a character to describe. This may be done as a verbal or written exercise.

Process: Using a problem from a novel, identify steps a character could use to solve the problem.

Classification: Using a novel, create a category chart for the characters, events, problems, emotions, heroes, villains, and so on.

Comparison/Contrast: Using two characters from a course novel, compare and contrast them.

Definition: Choose an idea or topic from a novel. Create a list of characteristics the author uses to define it.

WEB CONNECTION

Using an online magazine or newspaper, read to locate examples of each of the six patterns described in this chapter.

MyReadingLab™ **CONNECTION** ⚙️—[Complete this **Exercise** at **MyReadingLab.com**

Visit MyReadingLab.com to take a review quiz testing your mastery of this chapter's topics.

Seven

Visual Literacy Strategies

Chapter Preview

Visual Literacy Strategies Overview
A. Cluster Diagram
B. Five Ws Concept Web
C. Venn Diagram

LEARNING OBJECTIVES (LOs)

Upon completion of this chapter, you'll be able to:
- LO1—Organize pertinent information in a reading
- LO2—Extract main ideas from a reading
- LO3—Use graphic organizer strategies to enhance comprehension

*A graphic organizer is worth
a thousand words . . .*

Readiness Quiz

1. Read the article below. After reading, fill out the informational organizer.
2. As a class, go over the organizer. Discuss how to extract pertinent information.

ASIAN LADY BEETLES CAN BE SERIOUS HOUSEHOLD PESTS

Dennis Ferraro

Several of the common species of lady beetles, or ladybugs, will wander indoors during the fall. However, this is a distinctive and annoying trait of the Asian lady beetle, a relatively new species imported to the United States from eastern Asia.

The multicolored Asian lady beetle has become common in many areas of the eastern United States and Nebraska. This ladybug is beneficial and used as a natural control. It can also be a serious household pest in areas where it is well established.

Asian lady beetles, like boxelder bugs, pine seed bugs and elm leaf bugs, are accidental invaders. They wander indoors during a limited part of their life cycle, but they do not feed or reproduce indoors. They cannot attack the house structure, furniture or fabric. They cannot sting or carry disease. Lady beetles do not feed on people, but they might pinch exposed skin. Lady beetles may leave a slimy smear and they have a distinct odor when squashed.

As with other accidental invaders, the best management is to seal cracks, gaps and openings on the outside before the beetles wander in. A synthetic pyrethroid insecticide, such as permethrin, can be applied to the outside of the building. But to be effective, treatment must be applied before the beetles begin to enter buildings. Other home-use insecticides are ineffective.

What happened? _____

_____

Who was there? _____

Why did it happen? _____

_____

When did it happen? _____

_____

Where did it happen? _____

VISUAL LITERACY STRATEGIES OVERVIEW

There are many kinds of visual images that can be used to represent information, and there are various ways information can be organized, depending upon the material being read. One of the most common types of visual literacy is some form of graphic organizer. A graphic organizer works well to simplify and organize material visually in one or more of the following ways:

- According to topics, main ideas, and details
- In sequential order
- To show relationships between or among different things
- To show similarities and differences between two or more ideas or things
- By story elements
- . . . and many others!

Graphic organizers come in numerous forms. We will present three of the most widely used examples in this text, but there are many more examples on the Internet if you search for *graphic organizers.*

How Do They Work?

Graphic organizers provide visual representations of ideas, facts, theories, and concepts. They consist of circles, boxes, and other shapes, along with lines, to show connections. Creating a graphic organizer not only assists you in preparing and studying for a test, but it can also provide you with a memorable visual *during* the test. Two features of an effective graphic organizer are **elaboration** and **personalization.** *Elaboration* is the use of colors, designs, and pictures to aid in memory. *Personalization* involves creating associations to the information on your graphic organizer with personal pictures or designs that make sense to you. These images will help you remember what is important. Following are descriptions of three common graphic organizers.

1. THE CLUSTER DIAGRAM   A cluster diagram has many uses, but is best used for organizing main ideas and details from textbook chapters. To complete a cluster diagram for a textbook chapter, the student would begin with the title of the chapter near the center of the page. Each additional line from the center with a circle at the end would represent a main idea from that chapter. Lines added from each main idea circle would represent major details the student should remember from the chapter. Use of colors and small pictures or graphics may also enhance memory. A cluster diagram allows students to see the "chunks" of information they need to know.

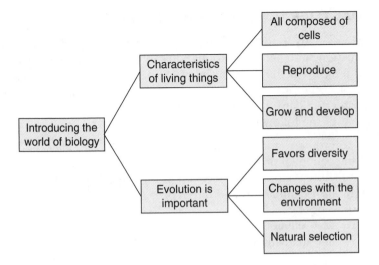

2. THE 5 WS CONCEPT WEB   The concept web is a gathering place for information. It is most effective when used with a narrative or news article. The five "Ws" concept web is a graphic organizer that consists of circles or squares and branches to other circles or squares. Each circle represents a specific "W." The center circle represents the title. The additional lines with circles and/or squares represent specific "Ws." The great thing about graphic organizers is that you can add lines and shapes to suit the material you're reading.

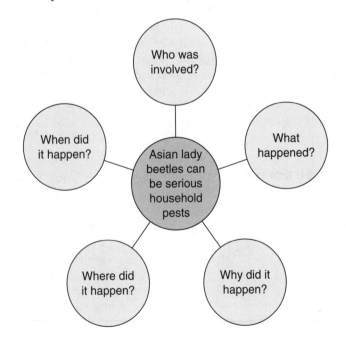

3. THE VENN DIAGRAM   A Venn Diagram is a set of two intersecting circles. It is a way to display information in a visual format and to categorize information into groups: most commonly, similarities and differences. You can use this diagram as you read to separate two ideas. The center is where you would write what the ideas have in common. Another way to use this tool is as a thought organizer before you write a compare and contrast paragraph or essay.

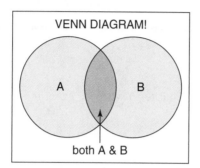

TO PRACTICE

Use the following readings and graphic organizers for practice.

- Cluster Diagram: Obsessive-Compulsive Disorder
- 5 Ws Concept Web: He's My Son!
- Venn Diagram: High School and College

QUICK TIP

Remember information by using **elaboration** (designs, colors, patterns) and **personalization** (association to something familiar, pictures).

QUICK TIP

When material seems disorganized or poorly organized, pay more attention to the headings, and read the summary first (if one is provided).

QUICK TIP

Font size is generally an important clue to organizing information. A main heading in large font often indicates a main point. Each sub-heading in smaller font is an important point supporting the main point. When the font reverts to large again, you have a new idea, or the next main point.

FOR EXTRA PRACTICE

Use the readings in Chapter 6 with the graphic organizers provided in this chapter.

A. Cluster Diagram

Use the cluster diagram that follows the article "Obsessive-Compulsive Disorder."

1. Before reading, place the title of the reading in the center circle.
2. After and during reading, place the main ideas of the reading in the circles directly linked to the title.
3. After and during reading, place the major details in the circles directly linked to each main idea.
4. Remember that you can add as many lines and circles/squares as you need when you create a cluster diagram.

OBSESSIVE-COMPULSIVE DISORDER

Mary Lynn Hendrix

What Is OCD?

In the mental illness called OCD, a person becomes trapped in a pattern of repetitive thoughts and behaviors that are senseless and distressing but extremely difficult to overcome. The following are typical examples of OCD:

> Troubled by the repeated thoughts that she may have contaminated herself by touching doorknobs and other "dirty" objects, a teenage girl spends hours every day washing her hands. Her hands are red and raw, and she has little time for social activities.
> A middle-aged man is tormented by the notion that he may injure others through carelessness. He has difficulty leaving his

home because he must first go through a lengthy ritual of checking and rechecking the gas jets and water faucets to make certain that they are turned off.

If OCD becomes severe enough, it can destroy a person's capacity to function in the home, at work, or at school. That is why it is important to learn about the disorder and the treatments that are now available.

How Common Is OCD?

For many years, mental health professionals thought of OCD as a very rare disease because only a small minority of their patients had the condition. But it's believed that many of those afflicted with OCD, in efforts to keep their repetitive thoughts and behaviors secret, fail to seek treatment. This has lead to underestimates of the number of people with the illness. However, a recent survey by the National Institute of Mental Health (NIMH)—the Federal agency that supports research nationwide on the brain, mental illness, and mental health— has provided new understanding about the prevalence of OCD. The NIMH survey shows that this disorder may affect as much as 2 percent of the population, meaning that OCD is more common than schizophrenia and other severe mental illnesses.

Source: Building Strategies for College Reading, Prentice Hall, 2001.

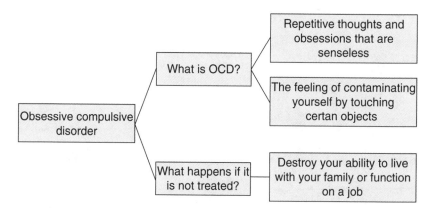

B. Five Ws Concept Web

1. Read "He's My Son!" by John Macionis.
2. After reading or as you read, use the concept web following the passage to fill in the who, what, why, when, and where of the short story.
3. Can you figure out the answer to the riddle at the end of the reading?

HE'S MY SON!

John Macionis

The automobile roared down the mountain road, tearing through sheets of windblown rain. Two people, a man and his young son, peered intently through the windshield, observing the edge of the road beyond which they could see only a black void. Suddenly, as the car rounded a bend, the headlights shone upon a large tree that had fallen across the roadway. The man swerved to the right and braked, but unable to stop, the car left the road, crashed through some brush, turned end upon end, and came to rest on its roof. Then a bit of good fortune: The noise of the crash had been heard at a nearby hunting lodge, and a telephone call from there soon brought police and a rescue crew. The driver, beyond help, was pronounced dead at the scene of the accident. Yet, the boy was still alive, although badly hurt and unconscious. Rushed by ambulance to the hospital in the town at the foot of the mountain, he was taken immediately into emergency surgery.

Alerted in advance, the medical team burst through the swinging doors ready to try to save the boy's life. Then, with a single look at his face, the surgeon abruptly exclaimed: "Oh, no! Get someone else to take over for me—I can't operate on this boy. *He's my son!*"

Answer to riddle (how can the boy be the surgeon's son?) _____

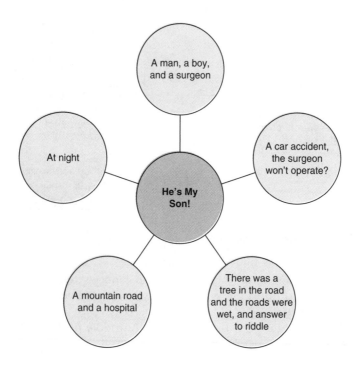

C. Venn Diagram

1. Read the essay "High School and College."
2. After reading or as you read, use the Venn Diagram graphic organizer that follows the story to list similarities and differences.

HIGH SCHOOL AND COLLEGE

When students graduate from high school, they are ready to make their college debut. As arrangements are made to enter the chosen college, students often wonder if college will be like high school. Some students are excited about this impending new adventure, while others are nervous and apprehensive. No matter which category applies, one thing is sure. While there are many similarities between high school and college, there are incredible differences.

In high school, a bell rings, and students fill the hallways on their way to first-period class. In college, a class begins at a certain time; you either are there or you're not. While one instructor may allow you to enter class late, another instructor may decide not to let you in at all. If you have a pattern of tardies in high school, you usually receive an after-school detention. If you're habitually tardy in college, however, your instructor may drop you from the course or lower your grade. If you're absent in high school, your parents may need to call and inform the school. And if you're *excessively* absent, your parents may receive a letter in the mail from the school district. In college, although you generally can be absent a certain number of times, once that predetermined number has been reached, the instructor may drop you from the course.

In high school, there's often a person in charge of student discipline. Students may be sent to an in-school suspension room for not completing assignments, for disrupting class, or for fighting with other students. In college, students simply are expected not to create any of these problems. Additionally, while high school teachers may be responsible for writing referrals, sending students out of the room, and explaining an issue to a student's parents, college instructors merely may ask a student either to get the work done or to drop the class. If a student does not comply, the *instructor* is able to drop the student from class. Also, if college students disrupt a class, or fight, they may be asked to leave the classroom. If students resist, a college instructor has the option of calling campus security to receive help in removing them.

In conclusion, good attendance habits, timely completion of work, and responsible classroom behavior are factors that enable students to be successful *both* in high school and in college. High school students, however, receive much more direct support from teachers, counselors, and administrators to ensure that they graduate and receive their high school diplomas. College students, on the other hand, must learn to take full advantage of available guidance, opportunities, and assistance in order to graduate and earn a college degree. While much support is still attainable, the ultimate responsibility for college success lies with the student.

Now that you've read "High School and College," fill in the Venn Diagram that follows.

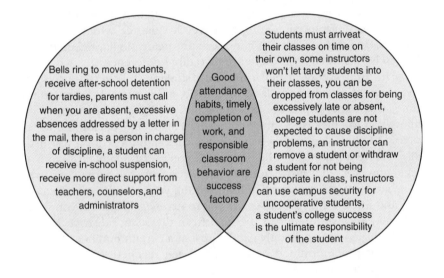

Bells ring to move students, receive after-school detention for tardies, parents must call when you are absent, excessive absences addressed by a letter in the mail, there is a person in charge of discipline, a student can receive in-school suspension, receive more direct support from teachers, counselors, and administrators

Good attendance habits, timely completion of work, and responsible classroom behavior are success factors

Students must arrive at their classes on time on their own, some instructors won't let tardy students into their classes, you can be dropped from classes for being excessively late or absent, college students are not expected to cause discipline problems, an instructor can remove a student or withdraw a student for not being appropriate in class, instructors can use campus security for uncooperative students, a student's college success is the ultimate responsibility of the student

Writing Like a Reader

In Chapter 2, you learned how to identify main ideas and details. What you actually did was sharpen your skills in "destructing" a paragraph. That is what a reader does. As a writer, you're "constructing" paragraphs. A well-written paragraph should have three things. The first is a main idea, which is the point the writer wants to get across to the reader. Second, it must have some major details. The major details support the main idea or the point the writer is making. Think of major details as "evidence." Most paragraphs also have a third component called minor details. A minor detail tells the reader more about the major detail it follows. The writer uses minor details to help the reader understand the "evidence" better. Use the **Paragraph Plan** graphic organizer below to create your own paragraph.

Focus on learning the difference between destructing (reading) and constructing (writing).

Main Idea _____
   (Point the author is making) _____
     Major detail _____
         (Evidence to support the author's point) _____
      Minor detail _____
          (Stories, reason, examples that support the Major detail) _____
     Major detail _____
         (Evidence to support the author's point) _____
      Minor detail _____
          (Stories, reason, examples that support the Major detail)
     Major detail _____
         (Evidence to support the author's point)
      Minor detail _____
          (Stories, reason, examples that support the Major detail)
     Major detail _____
         (Evidence to support the author's point)
      Minor detail _____
          (Stories, reason, examples that support the Major detail)

Once you're able to see the connection between how the author constructs a paragraph and how the reader destructs it, your reading comprehension will increase dramatically, and so will your writing skills!

⌐MyReadingLab

For more help with **Graphics and Visuals,** go to your learning path in MyReadingLab at www.myreadinglab.com.

Chapter Summary

> ***Graphic Organizers:*** Graphic organizers are used to create visual representations of ideas, facts, theories, and concepts.
>
> ***Elaboration:*** Elaboration is the use of colors, designs, and pictures to aid in remembering information.
>
> ***Personalization:*** Personalization is creating associations to the information on your graphic organizer with personal pictures or designs that makes sense to you.
>
> ***Cluster Diagram:*** A cluster diagram has many uses, but is best used for organizing main ideas and details from textbook chapters.
>
> ***5 Ws Concept Web:*** A graphic organizer that helps to identify who the reading is about, what happened, why it happened, when it happened, and where it happened.
>
> ***Venn Diagram:*** A graphic organizer that helps organize information according to similarities and differences.

Check Your Learning (Learning Outcomes)

Have you mastered the Learning Objectives (LOs) for Chapter 7? Place a check mark next to each LO that you're able to do.

_____ LO1—Organize pertinent information in a reading

_____ LO2—Extract main ideas from a reading

_____ LO3—Use graphic organizer strategies to enhance comprehension

Go back and review the sections that cover any LO you didn't check.

Quick Connections—Chapter Seven

NEWS SOURCE CONNECTION

Using the concept web format located within the chapter, choose a newspaper or news magazine article. Read the article and complete a 5 Ws concept web.

TEXTBOOK CONNECTION

Choose one of your own textbooks. Use the cluster diagram located within this chapter. As you read the chapter, place the main ideas in the circles directly connected to the title. Place the major details in the circles directly connected to the main idea circles.

NOVEL CONNECTION

Using a novel, select two characters and create a Venn Diagram that lists their similarities and differences.

WEB CONNECTION

Go to a news source website such as Time or the New York Times website. Find an article and create your own graphic organizer. Personalize it! Add color! Feel free to place information in ways that give meaning to you.

MyReadingLab™ CONNECTION ⚙️ [Complete this Exercise at MyReadingLab.com

Visit MyReadingLab.com to take a review quiz testing your mastery of this chapter's topics.

Eight

Information Literacy Strategies

Chapter Preview

Information Literacy Strategies Overview

A. How to Search the Internet
   1. The World Wide Web
   2. Four Key Components
   3. How to Begin

LEARNING OBJECTIVES (LOs)

Upon completion of this chapter section, you'll be able to:

- LO1—Conduct an Internet search using the World Wide Web
- LO2—Differentiate between the four key components of an Internet search
- LO3—Begin a purposeful Internet search

*Ability to use a computer to read
and write in college . . . Priceless*

B. Evaluating and Citing Web Sources
 1. Does the Site Meet the Purpose of Your Search?
 2. Is the Site Easy to Use? (Design and Navigability)
 3. How Valid Is the Information Found?
 4. When and How to Cite Web Sources

LEARNING OBJECTIVES (LOs)
Upon completion of this chapter section, you'll be able to:

▨ LO1—Determine if a site meets the purpose of your search

▨ LO2—Evaluate a site's design and navigability (ease of use)

▨ LO3—Assess the validity of website information

▨ LO4—Correctly cite Web sources

C. Word Processing Basics—A Reference Guide

LEARNING OBJECTIVES (LOs)

Upon completion of this chapter section, you'll be able to:

▨ LO1—Review, as needed, some of the basic concepts of word processing using the reference guide in this section.

Strategy Area A: How to Search the Internet

Readiness Quiz A ⚙️┤Complete this Exercise at MyReadingLab.com

Choose **T** for true and **F** for false after reading each statement below.

1. _____ A browser is a page that contains information, pictures, and video clips about a specific topic.

2. _____ A search engine is a computerized index to find information on the WWW.

3. _____ WWW is a math symbol, not a computer term.

4. _____ Opening a link from a Web page takes concentration and memory.

5. _____ Plus signs can help you narrow your search.

6. _____ Boolean searching involves the use of the words: AND, OR, AND-NOT.

Note: If you're a beginner in the area of computer basics (especially word processing), you may want to check out the readiness quiz and accompanying reference guide in Strategy Area C of this chapter before starting Strategy Areas A and B of the chapter.

INFORMATION LITERACY STRATEGIES OVERVIEW

Today, we acquire information in a broadening variety of ways. To adapt to our ever-growing digital environment, we also need to broaden our reading strategies. Strategy Area A of this chapter will help you learn how to search for information, and Strategy Area B will help you determine which sites and sources contain reliable information. Once you know how to do both, you'll be able to use technology to find valid information on just about any topic. Strategy Area C covers some word processing basics and is a reference guide for those who might need that kind of assistance.

A. How to Search the Internet

The first strategy involved in reading on the Internet is searching for the information you want to read. You may need information for class assignments such as a research paper, a speech, or a presentation. In addition to class assignments, you also use the Internet for personal purposes such as researching colleges, career paths, or job opportunities. To find relevant information quickly, you need to know how to effectively search the Internet. The first section of this chapter will show you how to conduct an efficient Internet search.

1. THE WORLD WIDE WEB4 The World Wide Web (commonly abbreviated as "the Web," "WWW," or "W3") is an interconnected, hypertext-based network that allows you to browse a variety of Internet resources organized by home pages. The Web is incredibly vast. This is positive because there's so much information available, but it can be negative because anyone with a little computer knowledge can create a Web page. When you do a search, you must realize that there's an extensive amount of unreliable, as well as reliable, information.

2. FOUR KEY COMPONENTS There are four basic components you'll use to locate information on the Web.

> *Browser:* A browser is a computer program that provides a way of viewing the information on the Web. Major browsers include Microsoft's Internet Explorer, Safari, Google Chrome, and Mozilla Firefox.
>
> *Search Engine:* A computerized index to information on the Web.
>
> **Four Popular Search Engines**
> www.google.com
> www.bing.com
> www.ask.com
> www.yahoo.com

Web Page: A document location or site that provides information on your search topic(s). It may contain pictures, video clips, audio clips, charts, graphs, links, and more.

QUICK TIP

Remember, anyone can make a Web page. When you search, use the strategies in Strategy Area B to make sure you find valid information.

Hyperlink (also called a hotlink): An automatic "address jump" to another site containing similar or more information on your search topic. Often a hyperlink will be in blue and underlined. However, the real defining feature is that the appearance of the text in a hyperlink changes when the cursor hovers over it. Just click on the hyperlink, and you're at a new website!

3. HOW TO BEGIN

1. Formulate a question based on your class assignment or personal research need.
2. Choose the important words from the question or topic sentence.

   Question: What was the Revolutionary War and who was involved?
   Important words: Revolutionary War

3. Type the important words into your search box located on your search engine home page.
4. Look at your results. Choose and open the Web page you think will best help you answer your question.

QUICK TIP

You may open and close several Web pages from your results until you find the one with the reliable information you're seeking.

Tips for Narrowing Your Search

Quotation Marks	Use around words that must appear together, in a specific order within your search	"Social Justice"
Plus Signs	Use before all words you want to appear in your results	+ "Social Justice" + environment
Minus Signs	Use before terms you do not want to appear in the results	+ "Social Justice" + environment — animals
Boolean Searching	Use AND, OR, AND-NOT AND: use between all words you want to appear in your results OR: use when more than one term will work in your search AND-NOT: use to limit the topic to a more specific result	"Social Justice" AND environment NOT animals

Now you should be ready to try a search! Search the Internet to find answers to the questions that follow. Fill in the important words that you'll need to type into the search box, do the search, and then fill in the answer to each question.

1. Question: What is the difference between an isosceles triangle and a right triangle?

Important words: _____

Search It!

Answer from results: _____

_____

2. Question: Who wrote the classic novel *To Kill a Mockingbird?*

Important words: _____

Search it!

Answer from results: _____

3. Question: Define, describe, and draw the three major rock types in earth science.

Important words: _____

Search it!

Answer from results:

Rock Type	Definition	Drawing
1.		
2 .		
3.		

4. Question: Compare and contrast Vegetarian and Vegan diets.

   Important words: _____

   Search it!

   Answer from results:

Vegetarian and Vegan Diets

Similarities	Differences

Strategy Area B: Evaluating and Citing Web Sources

Readiness Quiz B   ⚙️ [Complete this **Exercise** at **MyReadingLab.com**

Choose **T** for true or **F** for false after reading each statement below.

1. _____ Information found on the Internet is always current.

2. _____ It is primarily the instructor's responsibility to check the reliability and validity of information used in students' course assignments.

3. _____ The government regulates all Internet websites, so we know they're factual.

4. _____ Anyone can create a website and have it on the Internet.

5. _____ You can tell certain things about a website from its address.

6. _____ It's difficult to tell whether a website is someone's personal page.

Consider the following three questions when evaluating Internet websites:

1. Does the site meet the purpose of your search?

2. Is the site easy to use?

3. How valid is the information found?

1. DOES THE SITE MEET THE PURPOSE OF YOUR SEARCH? Don't just start your search by going to Google or Yahoo! and typing in a couple of words! You need to start by asking yourself, "What is the purpose of this search?" or "What is my research goal?" Once you've determined a research goal, you can screen sites by comparing them with your research goal. To determine your research goal, ask yourself questions like these: Do I want facts, opinions, reasoned arguments, statistics, narratives, eyewitness reports, or descriptions? Is the purpose of my search to find new ideas, or is it to find either factual or reasoned support for a position? Do I want to survey opinion? Do I want graphics, photos, or illustrations? Determine exactly what kind of information you need for your assignment. If you're not sure, check with your instructor before you determine your research goal.

> ## QUICK TIP
>
> Always set a research goal before you start your information search!

Here are some reliable academic databases that are accessible through most college libraries. Unlike a general search engine such as Google, databases provide information management in terms of accuracy and reliability.

- GENERAL ACADEMIC RESEARCH
  - EBSCOhost (Academic Search Premier)
  - eLibrary
  - LexisNexis Academic

- POPULAR AND CONTROVERSIAL ISSUES
  - SIRS Researcher
- VOCATIONAL/TECHNICAL
  - EBSCOhost (Vocational and Career Collection)
- EDUCATION
  - EBSCOhost (ERIC)
- BUSINESS
  - EBSCOhost (Business Source Elite)

Databases aren't the only acceptable sources for academic research. Online journals, magazines, podcasts, documentaries, and videos are other acceptable information resources. Just make sure you cite these sources according to your teacher's instructions. And don't forget—there are still the good, old print materials!

QUICK TIP

Many people use Wikipedia as a quick, easily accessible source for information. However, it is not considered a scholarly, credible or authoritative source. Why not? One reason is that anyone can edit the page. Also, there's no guarantee that the writer is an expert on the topic or that the content has undergone rigorous editorial review. It's perfectly acceptable to read a Wikipedia entry to get a quick overview of your research topic, as long as you follow it up by reading more scholarly sources. Often, such sources are among the references that Wikipedia articles cite, so make sure to read the "Notes" and/or "References" sections!

Once you've set your research goal, you can begin your search using the strategies in Strategy Area A of this chapter. As you open up sites that you're considering for your research, skim over each one to see if it seems to meet your research goal. If it appears to have the information you're looking for according to your goal, then you're ready to apply the next two strategies to see if the site is one you want to use.

2. IS THE SITE EASY TO USE? (DESIGN AND NAVIGABILITY)   There are several factors which should indicate rapidly how easy a site will be for you to use. The two major ones are the site's *design*, or set-up and appearance, and its *navigability*, or how easy it is to get around in the site. If the site appears confusing to you, you may want to look at alternative sites that are more user-friendly.

A site's design includes factors such as colors, background, size and font of print, and graphics. Are these things pleasing to the eye and easy to see? Or are they jumbled and distracting? Is there a clear order for finding information, or does it seem confusing?

Navigability of a site is how easy it is for the user to get around in, or use, the site. The design of the site contributes to its navigability. Are the different sections of the site clearly marked and easy to find? Is there always a link back to the home page? Are links to other sites easily identified? Are the links "hot," meaning you can click on them and be taken to the linked site? Are the links up-to-date?

QUICK TIP

Quickly skim over the home page of a site to get a feel for it. Is it pleasing to your eye? Does it make sense to you? Does it seem easy to start finding information?

If your impressions of the site are favorable so far, continue on to the third strategy for evaluating the site: Is the information found on the site valid and acceptable for use with your assignment?

3. HOW VALID IS THE INFORMATION FOUND?   Determining the validity of the information on a website is the most important part of the evaluation process. If the information isn't reliable and valid, it doesn't matter if it fits your research goal or is easy to use; the site is worthless to you! Often the most important part of a process tends to be the most time-consuming, but it doesn't have to be. Below are some quick ways to check the validity of a site. Start by finding the answers to these questions:

1. *Sponsor:* What kind of organization sponsors the site? The answer can be found by looking at the domain: the last three letters in the address, or URL (Uniform Resource Locator). Addresses which end with the letters .edu (education), .gov (government), .mil (military), or .org (nonprofit organization) are usually reputable sites. Addresses ending in .com or .net are commercial addresses, which mean they're generally trying to make money in some way. Information on these sites can be

reliable, but you need to do more checking than you would on the nonprofit sites. Sites which are personal Web pages set up by individuals are the least likely to be reliable. A site that ends with ~*name* (a personal name), % *name,* or a name followed by the words *people, users,* or *members,* indicates a personal website—which means, be careful!! These sites, while not necessarily unreliable, require more investigation from the reader because the information isn't backed by a domain owner or publisher.

QUICK TIP

The last three letters of the URL, also known as the "domain," are the quickest way to judge validity of a website.

2. *Author:* Who's responsible for the information? The top or bottom of the Web page should identify the person responsible for putting it up and maintaining it (the Webmaster of the site). Look for the author's institutional affiliation or other credentials. Is there documentation of the author or a bibliography of his work?

   What are the author's credentials and reputation? If the author is an expert and is qualified to write about the information contained at the site, it should be clearly stated. Look for a link to background information about the author, or better yet, a résumé. Make sure information is truly produced by this expert, and isn't posted erroneously or fraudulently.

3. *Date:* How old is the information? Remember, wide use of the Internet has been around for more than ten years, so you can't automatically assume that information you find on the Net is current. Look for the date that the site was last revised, which is usually found at the bottom of the home page. Even if the date is fairly recent, remember that it doesn't mean that all of the information on the site was revised on that date. However, a recent update may mean that the site is well maintained, which is a good indicator of current information.

4. *Content:* Where did the information originate? What seems to be the purpose of the site? Again, the last three letters of the address tell you a lot about the source of the information and if

the site is commercial or nonprofit. This is a good place to use your skimming skills. A quick skim of a few pages should help you begin to determine the comprehensiveness of the material, its accuracy, whether it contains more fact or opinion, if it's written from a scholarly point of view, if it seems to be promoting a particular viewpoint, or if it's advertising. Check to see if the information is documented in some way. Is there a bibliography or other list of sources? Has anyone reviewed the site? Keep in mind that there are specialized guide sites on the Internet to help you. These change frequently, so use your Internet searching skills to find the latest guides to Internet resources.

QUICK TIP

ALWAYS check the validity of a site before using it for academic purposes. Don't risk getting a low grade for using incorrect information.

5. *Corroboration:* Did you corroborate your sources? Corroboration, or finding the information in more than one place, is an important test of truth. It's a good idea to triangulate your sources—that is, find at least three sources that agree. If the sources do not agree, do further research to find out how wide the disagreement is before you draw your conclusions. If you can't find other sites with the same or similar information, be wary of trusting the validity of information.

A simple way to evaluate websites is to use a checklist (see next page). Once you've had enough practice finding and evaluating websites that fulfill your research goals, you won't need to use a checklist. You'll *automatically* find yourself checking the points mentioned to evaluate a site more rapidly. Won't that be great? The bottom line: Always evaluate any site you plan to use in your academic work, particularly the validity of the site. Don't skip this step to save time. You might be putting your college success in jeopardy. Try using the Website Evaluation Checklist on the following page. You can tear it out and make copies to use when you do Internet research.

QUICK TIP

Filling out a checklist sheet for each source you use makes it quick and easy to cite your sources on the Reference page of your written document.

Website Evaluation Checklist

Who sponsored the site?

Look at the domain at the end of the Web address for clues:

.edu = educational institution such as a school, college, or university

.gov = government agency

.org = usually (but not always) a nonprofit organization or political organization

.mil = U.S. military

.com = commercial site, including company websites and personal Web pages

Who's the author? (especially important if it's a .com site)

- What qualifications does he or she have?
- Does the website include biographical information? contact information?
- It may be necessary to use other sources to check the author's credentials.

What is its purpose?

- Is it biased, or does it promote a particular viewpoint? *If so, make sure you balance it with opposing information.*
- Is it selling or promoting a product or service?

Is the information accurate?

- Does the website document or cite its sources?
- Is it someone's personal opinion and not backed up by facts?
- Are there grammatical errors or typos?

Is the information current?

- When was the site created or last updated?
- Are there broken links? If so, the website may not be up-to-date.

See also ***Evaluating Web Pages: Techniques to Apply & Questions to Ask*** available at: http://www.lib.berkeley.edu/TeachingLib/Guides/Internet/Evaluate.html

4. WHEN AND HOW TO CITE WEB SOURCES   Plagiarism is using someone else's information, not giving that person the credit, and passing it off as your own work. This is illegal, and most colleges have a policy forbidding it. Students should cite a source if using any of the following:

- A direct quote from a writer or speaker
- A paraphrase from a writer or speaker
- The same sequence of ideas as a specific source

Since so much of the information in today's world comes from the Internet, below is a guide for citing from a website.

How to cite *an article* from a website in MLA style:

Author(s) of Internet article. "Name of Internet article." Name of website. Editor(s) of website. Date of electronic publication. Associated institution. Date of access.

How to *cite a general website* in MLA style:

Name of website. Editor(s) of website. Date of electronic publication. Associated institution. Date of access.

Source: http://www.easybib.com/reference/guide/mla/website which cites from the 7th edition of MLA Handbook.

Your instructor may require MLA or APA format. An easy way to cite your sources using these and other formats is by using a site such as www.makecitation.com or www.interaction-design.org/citation-maker/index.html.

Writing Like a Reader

Remember that paraphrases, or restatements of someone's thoughts and ideas in your own words, require giving proper credit, just as direct quotations do. Since plagiarism can result in a failing grade or even expulsion from school, it's important to understand how a proper paraphrase might appear. Simply changing a few words or changing the sequence of information does not result in a proper paraphrase. Consider the paragraph below and the example paraphrases that follow:

> When I was a young boy in Omaha, we never had a key to our house. The door was never locked. If our mother ever went to the hospital, the neighbor women would cook, clean, wash, and take care of everything. Now we don't even know many of our neighbors, and our doors are deadbolted. Some leave their outside lights on all night and have security systems for protection.
> —FROM MEMOIRS OF JOSEPH (CHIC) MANCUSO

Example of an **improper paraphrase:**

In the past, some people in Omaha had no house keys because doors were never locked. When mothers went to the hospital, neighbor women would wash, clean, cook, and take care of things. Now neighbors aren't as friendly, doors are locked with deadbolts, and security systems are used.

Example of a **proper paraphrase:**

In his memoirs, Joseph (Chic) Mancuso describes how neighborhood safety and relationships have changed in his lifetime. Unlocked doors and close, helpful neighbors have been replaced with deadbolt locks and limited neighborly connections.

Strategy Area C: Word Processing Basics— A Reference Guide

Readiness Quiz C

Choose **T** for true or **F** for false after reading each statement below.

1. _____ I know how to use a word processing standard toolbar.

2. _____ I know how to create a new document.

3. _____ I know how to edit a document.

4. _____ I know how to save a document.

5. _____ I know how to reopen a saved document.

6. _____ I know how to format a document.

If you answered **F** to any of the above statements, please refer to the appropriate section of the reference guide on the pages that follow.

C. Word Processing Basics—A Reference Guide

The purpose of this section is to give you a quick reference guide to creating documents. Most of the work you do in a college classroom will require completed computer documents (typed). Often, students have not received computer training, but have assumed skills by watching others. Some students have not had any computer experience in creating a document, but can surf the Web. Some students have no computer experience at all. This is a straightforward guide to working with Microsoft Word, a software program available on most computers in colleges across the country.

BASIC WORD PROCESSING REFERENCE GUIDE FOR MICROSOFT WORD
The Standard Toolbar

Function of Commonly Used Keys

Creates a new blank document based on the default template	Opens or finds a file
Saves the active file with its current file name, location and file format	Prints the active file - for more print options go to the File menu and select Print
Print preview - Shows how the document will look when you print it.	Spelling, grammar and writing style checker
Cut - Removes the selection from the document and places it on the clipboard	Copy - Copies the selected item(s) to the clipboard
Paste - Places the content of the clipboard at the insertion point	Format painter - Copies the format from a selected object or text and applies to other objects or text
Undo - Reverses the last command, use pull-down menu to undo several steps	Redo - Reverses the action of the Undo button, use the pull-down menu to redo several steps
Displays the Tables and Borders toolbar	Insert a table into the document, or make a table of selected text
Insert an Excel spreadsheet into the Word document	Columns - Changes the number of columns in a document
Displays or hides the Drawing toolbar	Zoom - Enlarge or reduce the display of the active document

CREATING A DOCUMENT

1. Open Microsoft Word by clicking on the icon or locating it by pressing the Start key.
2. Begin to type your document.
   - Press the Enter key only to start a new paragraph.
   - Use the Backspace key or the Delete key to remove unwanted letters, words, or sentences.
3. As you type, save what you have done every 10 to 15 minutes.
4. If a word is underlined with a red or green wavy line, right-click on the word, and select from the list of suggested spellings or grammar corrections.
5. Use the Print Preview key to see what your document will look like once you have printed it.
6. If it looks the way you would like for it to look, save it before printing.
7. To print, click the Print key on the standard tool bar.
8. To close your document, click the File menu, and select the Close option, or click the X in top right corner of page.

EDITING A DOCUMENT

1. Highlight the text to be moved or copied.
2. Click the Cut key if you want to move the text to a different location *or*
3. Click the Copy key if you want to copy the text.
4. Click where you want to paste the text, and then click the Paste key.

SAVING A DOCUMENT

1. Click the Save button on the standard tool bar.
2. Select Local Disk (C:) to save on the hard drive.
3. To save to a flash drive:
   - Click the Save button.
   - Click the down arrow in the list box.
   - Click F drive to save to the flash drive.
   - Type the file name in the File Name list box.
   - Click Save at the lower right corner of the dialog box.

REOPENING A DOCUMENT

1. Open Microsoft Word.

2. Click the Open 🗁 key on the standard tool bar.
3. Click the drop-down arrow to specify the drive [Local Disk (C) or Flash Drive (F)].
4. Double-click the file name from the list of files available.

FORMATTING A DOCUMENT

The Formatting Toolbar

| Normal ▼ | Arial ▼ | 12 ▼ | **B** | *I* | <u>U</u> | ≡ ≡ ≡ ≡ | ⊟ ⊟ ⊈ ⊈ | □ ▼ ⫰ ▼ △ ▼ |

Function of Commonly Used Buttons

Normal ▼	Select the style to apply to paragraphs	Arial ▼	Changes the font of the selected text
12 ▼	Changes the size of selected text and numbers	**B**	Makes selected text and numbers bold
I	Makes selected text and numbers italic	<u>U</u>	Underlines selected text and numbers
≡	Aligns to the left with a ragged right margin	≡	Centers the selected text
≡	Aligns to the right with a ragged left margin	≡	Aligns the selected text to both the left and right margins
⊟	Makes a numbered list or reverts back to normal	⊟	Add, or remove, bullets in a selected paragraph
⊈	Decreases the indent to the previous tab stop	⊈	Indents the selected paragraph to the next tab stop
□ ▼	Adds or removes a border around selected text or objects	⫰ ▼	Marks text so that it is highlighted and stands out
△ ▼	Formats the selected text with the color you click		

1. Highlight the text to be formatted.

2. Change the style of the text by clicking the Bold **B** , Italic *I* , or Underline **U** key from the Formatting Toolbar.

3. Change the font type by selecting a font from the Font List Arial on the Formatting Toolbar.

4. Change the font size by selecting the size from the Font Size 12 list on the Formatting Toolbar.

5. Create a bulleted or numbered list by clicking the Bullets key or the Numbering key.

6. Create a border around the page by clicking the Format menu, borders and shading, page border, and then select the border you like.

7. Change the document's margins by clicking the File menu, page set-up, margin tab, and then adjust the margins.

8. Add a header or footer by clicking the View menu, header and footer, then type what will be shown in the area.

9. Double-space the document by clicking the Format menu, paragraph, line spacing, and then select Double from the drop-down list.

QUICK TIP

Remember . . . You can also use keyboard shortcuts such as:

- Ctrl + A (select All)
- Ctrl + C (Copy)
- Ctrl + V (Paste)
- Ctrl + P (Print)
- Ctrl + Z (Undo)
- Ctrl + S (Save file)
- Ctrl + X (Cut)

┌─MyReadingLab───

For more help with **Information Literacy Strategies,** go to your
learning path in MyReadingLab at www.myreadinglab.com. Click on
"MySearchLab" in the left-hand navigation menu. This section will
help you research online. It contains a wealth of research tools,
including EBSCO's ContentSelect and Autocite.

└──

Chapter Summary

Searching the Internet: In order to search effectively on the
Internet, it's important to be familiar with the term and concept
of the World Wide Web, to understand four key factors involved
in a search, and to know the basics of beginning a search.

- *World Wide Web (WWW, OR W3):* An interconnected, hypertext-based network that allows you to browse a variety of
  Internet resources organized by home pages.

- *Four Key Components:* Include use of a browser, a search
  engine, Web pages, and links.

- *Beginning a Search:* Begin by opening a search engine,
  determining the topic of the search, identifying key words for
  the search, typing the key words into the search box, and
  finally, analyzing the search results.

Evaluating Websites: Entails determining the purpose of the
search and then analyzing sites for ease of use and validity of
information.

- *Purpose of Search:* To save time and effort, set a research
  goal before beginning the search for information. Determine
  what type of site will best meet your goal.

- *Ease of Use:* Major factors include a site's design and its navigability. Skim the home page (and other pages) for eye
  appeal and ease of use. Determine if it's organized in a sen-
  sible way.

- *Validity of Information:* Determining the validity of the information on a website is the most important part of the evaluation
  process. Things to consider include the sponsor and author of
  the site, the dates of the information on the site and when it was
  last updated, the content itself, copyright issues, and whether or
  not other sites or sources corroborate the content of the site.

- *Citing Web Sources:* Cite sources if using direct quotes or
  paraphrasing, and when following the same sequence of ideas
  as the original source. Use the citation format required by your
  instructor.

Word Processing Basics: Consult the brief guide at the end of this chapter for basic information on using a standard toolbar, and for creating, editing, saving, reopening, and formatting documents.

Check Your Learning (Learning Outcomes)

Have you mastered the Learning Objectives (LOs) for Chapter 8? Place a check mark next to each LO that you're able to do.

PART A

_____ LO1—Conduct an Internet search using the World Wide Web

_____ LO2—Differentiate between the four key components of an Internet search

_____ LO3—Begin a purposeful Internet search

PART B

_____ LO1—Determine if a site meets the purpose of your search

_____ LO2—Evaluate a site's design and navigability (ease of use)

_____ LO3—Assess the validity of website information

_____ LO4—Correctly cite Web sources

PART C

_____ LO1—Review, as needed, some of the basic concepts of word processing using the reference guide in this section.

Go back and review the sections that cover any LO you didn't check.

Quick Connections—Chapter Eight

NEWS SOURCE CONNECTION

Using the Internet, find and skim three different news websites to compare and contrast the reports on a current event topic of your choice. Be sure to identify the websites used. You may report your results in paragraph format, or you may use a graphic organizer such as a comparison/contrast chart.

TEXTBOOK CONNECTION

Use a textbook from one of your other classes (or a sample chapter provided by your instructor). Select an interesting topic that is addressed in the text or sample chapter. Then use the Internet to search for, and list, websites that address the same topic. Check for corroboration of specific ideas between the sites and the text. Write a brief report on your findings, and be sure to include your list of sites.

NOVEL CONNECTION

Use the Internet to locate additional information on the author of a novel you're reading in your current reading class. Create a list of sites you found, and write a one-page summary of your findings.

WEB CONNECTION ⚙️—[Complete this Exercise at MyReadingLab.com

Choose a topic from this course (or one of your other courses this term) to research on the Internet. Find at least five sites, and list them. Evaluate two of the five sites, using the evaluation checklist included in this chapter. Use a word processor to type a brief report on your findings.

Below are some other sites you could use instead of, or in addition to, the site listed earlier in this chapter:

http://www.lib.berkeley.edu/TeachingLib/Guides/Internet/Evaluate.html

http://www.library.cornell.edu/olinuris/ref/research/webeval.html

http://www.virtualchase.com/quality/

MyReadingLab™ CONNECTION ⚙️—[Complete this Exercise at MyReadingLab.com

Visit MyReadingLab.com to take a review quiz testing your mastery of this chapter's topics.

Credits

p. 26, William M. Oliver. *Community Oriented Policing 2e*. Upper Saddle River: Prentice Hall, 2001; p. 31, Johnson, McNally, & Essay, *Essentials of Dental Radiography for Dental Assistants and Hygienists 7e*. Pearson Education Inc., 2003; p. 32, "Keeping Her Promise to Our Kids" by *Newsweek*, October 3, 2005; p. 66, Nijole V. Benokraitis, *Marriages and Families*. Pearson Education Inc., 2005; p. 74, Yann Martel. *Life of Pi*. New York: Harcourt Inc., 2001. p. 75, Martha Doran. *Keys to Business Success*. Upper Saddle River: Prentice Hall, 2000; p. 77, Dave Pelzer. A Child Called "IT." Deerfield Beach: Health Communications Inc., 1995; p. 78, "This Could Be Your Kid," *Newsweek*, August 2003; p. 79, Bright Web site, www.bright.net; p. 80, Ann Rand Web site, www.aynrand.org; p. 83, "Free Tests for HIV Available," *Omaha World Herald*, June 23, 2005; p. 85, "Straight Talk on Jobs," *Omaha World Herald*, January 8, 2004; p. 90, Elie Wiesel. *Night*. New York: Random House, Inc., 1960; p. 116, Chapter 6, from *Cannery Row* by John Steinbeck. Copyright © 1945 by John Steinbeck. Renewed © 1973 by Elaine Steinbeck, John Steinbeck IV and Thom Steinbeck. Used by permission of Viking Penguin, a division of Penguin Group (USA) Inc; p. 119, "Family Violence: Why We Hurt the Ones We Love" by Sandra Arbetter, Published in *Current Health*, November 1995. Copyright © 1995 by Weekly Reader Corporation. Reprinted by permission of Scholastic Inc; p. 125, "Why I Want a Wife" by Judy Brady, Ms. Magazine, 1971. Copyright © 1970 by Judy Brady. Reprinted by permission of the author. p. 134, Dennis Ferraro. "Asian Lady Beetles Can Be Serious Household Pests," NU Cooperative Extension; p. 140, John J. Macionis. *Sociology* 3e. Upper Saddle River: Pearson Education, Inc., 1991; p. 159, Microsoft product screen shot reprinted with permission from Microsoft Corporation; p. 161, Microsoft product screen shot reprinted with permission from Microsoft Corporation.

Index